I0819930

THE MIDNIGHT WOLF

SILVER MOON

Noelle January

THE MIDNIGHT WOLF

SILVER MOON

The Midnight Wolf: Silver Moon

First Edition

Cover design by Noelle January

ISBN: 979-8-9935726-0-4 (Hardback)
ISBN: 979-8-9935726-1-1 (Paperback)
ISBN: 979-8-9935726-2-8 (eBook)

Content Warning

The Midnight Wolf: Silver Moon contains profane language, explicit sexual content, graphic violence, and death. Reader discretion is advised.

Dedication

For my pack: thank you for loving me through my crazy, supporting my hopes and dreams, and allowing me to always be a little wild.

CHAPTER ONE

Xander

"Last one in's a rotten egg!" Wiley called back over his shoulder, already racing towards Rock Lake. I chuckled as I glanced at Donovan, who laughed and shook his head. Heath just shrugged his shoulders before taking off after Wiley.

Donovan groaned a little but nudged me on my shoulder. "Come on," he said as we ran after them. We were all tired from our early morning training and perimeter run, but we couldn't resist cooling down in the crystal waters of Rock Lake.

As my Delta, Wiley, was lean and incredibly fast, he didn't need the head start he already had on us. He's the youngest and most lively of my unit, always keeping us on our toes. Wiley was also the only one of us to have found his mate, Jasmine. They have been together since they were 14 years old.

Wiley may be faster than the others, but no one's faster than me. I started out slow, letting him think he had the advantage, but as I smelled the blossoms that grew near the lake, Donovan and I kicked it up a notch.

We passed Heath and he let out a hearty laugh, "Show him who's boss!" I ran even faster, leaving Donovan and Heath behind chuckling.

I could see Wiley approaching the lake shore, thinking he might finally beat me. He glanced around with a wide grin on his face as he was just about to hit the sandy beach. I darted past him and dove into the water.

As I resurfaced, I turned to him and asked, "What took you so long?"

"Ah man, I almost had you this time!" Wiley exclaimed.

"Yeah right!" scoffed Heath as he sloshed into the water behind Donovan. "You think he was really going full out? The man could smoke you any day."

"Maybe so," shrugged Wiley, "but you definitely can't, slowpoke!" He smacked his hand along the top of the water, creating a wave that washed over Heath.

"I may be slow, but I'll still kick your scrawny ass!" Heath growled playfully as he tackled Wiley underwater. Heath's my Gamma, so he's naturally very muscular, bulkier than even myself. As an Alpha though, I still have a strength that is unmatched.

"Now, now children..." Donovan scolded. "Can't we all just get along?" He added playfully. Donovan is my best friend and also happens to be the best Beta anyone could ask for. He is just about as strong as me, incredibly smart, and the level-headed one out of the group.

"Yes, father!" Wiley and Heath replied in unison. I love my Alpha unit. We have all been best friends since birth.

It was the beginning of summer, and the weather was perfect, just starting to really warm up. This meant the Academy was letting out and the graduate students would be returning home soon. This made my wolf, Zeus, stir and wag his tail in my head.

"Hey, Xander, why you so quiet, man?" Wiley pulled me out of my thoughts.

"When do the new recruits get back from the Academy?" I asked.

"Any day now." Donovan replied, floating around, lazily doing the backstroke. "Dad said the girls left a few days ago. I guess they are taking a bit of a road trip on their way back."

"Yeah, my mom has been running around like crazy, preparing for Ari to get back. She's so excited." Heath laughed.

I was feeling excited as well. And anxious for some reason. My wolf was pacing in my head. My brother, Wesley, was coming home after being away at the Academy for two years. The program was tough, and their schedules were tight, so I really hadn't been able to talk to him much since he left. Or the others.

"Alright, you hooligans, it's about time to head back for class." Donovan reminded us. We all teach warrior training classes throughout the week. Donovan and I teach our top warriors, the Epsilons, while Heath and Wiley teach the younger warriors, the Zetas.

We all slowly waded out of the water. We were going to jog back to the pack house, by the time we got there, our shorts would be dry. We had left our shirts at the training grounds before doing our perimeter run.

As we were jogging, Wiley started in on me. "So, Xander, how's Princess Valerie?"

I just rolled my eyes.

"Come on, man, what do you see in her anyway?" Heath chimed in. "She's just so... she's such a..."

"Princess." Wiley finished for him with a grimace.

I really couldn't argue with them. When I had started dating Valerie, she was fun and adventurous. But I quickly figured out that it was all an act. She really just wanted me to take her as a chosen mate, so she could be Luna. But that wasn't going to happen. She was actually quite snooty and boring. She's the daughter of Alpha Phillip, from a pack a couple of hours away from here, Dark Moon. I met her at an Alpha Summit.

"Actually..." I cleared my throat. "I ended it with her."

Everyone stopped dramatically. "Seriously?" Donovan scrutinized me with a raised brow.

"Yeah, last week, actually. I was going to tell you, but I forgot." I shrugged nonchalantly.

"You forgot?" Disbelief was written all over Donovan's face.

"Dude! That is important information. Oh man, this is great news!" Wiley responded a little too excitedly, if you ask me.

"Honestly, Xander, you deserve so much better, but what made you change your mind about her?" Donovan asked.

I sighed and ran a hand through my dark auburn hair. "I don't know. It just didn't feel right anymore. I mean, I know she's not my mate and I don't love her. And... she was really irritating Zeus." My wolf, Zeus, had taken to growling in my head anytime Valerie was near.

"Well, thank you, Zeus! If you're the reason we don't have to walk on eggshells around Princess Valerie anymore, I will buy you a juicy steak!" Heath joked, putting his hand on my shoulder as we continued.

We all laughed. "I don't know why I stayed with her as long as I did. I guess it was just easier."

"I doubt that." Scoffed Wiley, "Nothing was easy with her." The guys all agreed.

We were getting close to the pack house now, just a little further through the woods. Suddenly, Zeus was fully alert in my mind. I froze and inhaled deeply.

The guys paused beside me and stared at me questioningly. They sniffed the air too.

"What is that amazing smell?" I asked.

"I don't know but it's incredible." Donovan said, taking a deep inhale. "It smells like honeysuckle and strawberries."

"No way, man. It's like... it's like cherry and vanilla." Heath said with his eyes closed.

"You're both crazy, it's cinnamon and orange blossoms." I took another lung full. It smells so familiar, but more decadent and delicious than anything I have ever smelled before.

Wiley stood there looking between us all like we were crazy. Then a wide grin spread across his face. "Oh my Goddess, it's your mates!"

We all glanced at each other before we took off running through the forest. We hit the clearing at the pack house and ran around to the front. I was the first one there. I froze in my tracks. Donovan ran up beside me, followed by Heath.

"MATE." Donovan and Heath growled out at the same time. All three girls turned and stared in shock.

CHAPTER TWO

Maxine

"Oh, I'm so excited, I can't wait to get home! I just know he's my mate. I can feel it!" Exclaimed Arielle from the passenger seat.

"You two would make an interesting couple." Ivy pointed out.

"Maybe you could get him to loosen up," I suggested as I rolled my eyes.

We all giggled at the thought of the serious future Beta, Donovan, and Arielle, the most bubbly, carefree girl in the world, being a perfect match. Donovan's my older brother, a really great guy, and Ari's my best friend. She also happened to be our future Gamma Heath's little sister.

Arielle turned 18 about a month ago while we were still at the Academy. She said she always wanted it to be Donovan, but now she was sure he's her mate. She said her wolf just knew.

When we were younger, we were always tagging along with the future Alpha team. Wesley, Ari, Ivy, and I were the younger siblings, the Junior Alpha crew, as everyone used to call us. It started out because our parents were always hanging out together, but then we all just became really close.

School has kept us apart in more recent years. The future Alpha unit had to leave for the Academy for two years when they were 16. When they came back two years ago, we spent the summer together before it was our turn to head off to the Academy.

The Academy was a grueling program. The training was relentless and demanding, but they always produced the top warriors. Our pack was stronger because we sent so many of our top recruits to the Academy before they joined the ranks.

I had a surprise for my dad. I couldn't wait to tell him that I was ranked top of my class. Not too shabby for a Beta wolf.

"Earth to Max! Where's your head at, space cadet?" Ari was waving her hand in front of my face. I had been staring blankly out the car window for the last 30 minutes.

"Oh, uh, I was just thinking about Luke." I knew this topic would give me a good excuse to be just sitting in silence.

"Oh, Max, you did the right thing!" Ivy reassured me.

"I know. It just really sucked to hurt him." I replied with a frown.

"Girl, he's an Alpha. I'm sure he'll be just fine." Ari said dismissively before turning serious. "You really don't think he's your mate?"

"I don't know. Onyx doesn't seem to think so, but I guess only time will tell." With that, I went back to staring out the window.

Luke and I met on our first day at the Academy. He was so funny and sweet, we became fast friends. He would spar with me after class for some extra practice. He asked me out for almost a year before I finally said yes. I always made it clear to him that I was waiting for my mate, and he never pressured me.

My birthday's just two weeks away and the closer we get to that date, the more sure Onyx feels that Luke is not our mate. I didn't want to take the chance of finding my mate while I was still involved with Luke, so I decided to end it. He promised to visit me for my party. He still thinks there is a chance that we could be mates.

In my heart, I know it's not him. I don't know who my mate is, but I know who I wish it could be. I have always had the biggest crush on Xander, our future Alpha. Not that he would ever see me that way. He's always been protective of me, but I think it was more like an older brother. After all, he was my brother's best friend.

Xander was obviously gorgeous. Alphas hit the gene pool jackpot when it comes to good looks. I mean, all werewolves are good-looking, but Alphas are the cream of the crop. Xander had the most unique auburn colored hair, piercing green eyes, and such handsome, masculine features. But it was more than that.

He was strong and kind, a truly fearless leader, and a really great listener. We had grown really close during my last summer home. He always seemed to be around, and I was just naturally drawn to him. The two of us would linger long after the rest of the group had left and had deep conversations. I missed him.

I heard he hadn't found his mate yet. But I'm sure he has a girlfriend. I mean he was just too handsome to be single. I sighed.

"Okay, mopey, that's enough!" Ari scolded, "We are going to have to cheer you up with some tunes!" She grabbed her iPod and scrolled through her playlists. "Yes! Here we go..."

She connected her iPod, blasted 'Girls Just Wanna Have Fun,' and sang along loudly with Cyndi Lauper. She was so animated in her singing that I couldn't help but crack up. Ivy joined in. Before I knew it, I couldn't resist belting out the lyrics with them.

When the song ended, we were all giggling, and I was in a much better mood.

"Alright, chicas, we are here!" Ivy exclaimed as we pulled up to the large, iron gates of Silver Moon. As we passed through, it felt like home. It was a long drive to the packhouse. We wound through the roads of the packlands, everything was the same as I remembered.

Our pack was beautiful, and I hadn't realized how much I missed it. My excitement continued to grow as we got closer to the packhouse. I noticed Ivy and Ari had gotten really quiet. They both appeared to be equally excited and anxious.

We pulled up to the packhouse and Ivy parked right in front, on the round driveway.

"Home, sweet, home." I sighed.

We climbed out of the car and stretched. I couldn't shake this jittery feeling.

We were just opening the trunk when we heard two distinct growls and the word "Mate."

The three of us turned around together, shocked to see three glistening men, breathing heavy with glowing eyes.

Donovan, Heath, and Xander.

The rest of the world melted away and there was only Xander.

CHAPTER THREE

Xander

"Mate!" Arielle shrieked and ran into Donovan's arms. He caught her as she wrapped her legs around his waist.

"I knew it was you." He said to her softly. "My beautiful, little mate." He tucked a strand of her strawberry blonde hair behind her ear and nuzzled her nose.

I heard Ivy whisper, "Mate." Just as Heath was wrapping her up in a bear hug and burying his nose in her neck.

None of it was really registering with me though. I was lost in the most electric blue eyes I had ever seen. Maxine was just staring at me as if in a trance. I felt like I was being pulled to her as my feet slowly closed the distance between us.

I stood right in front of her, peering down into her brilliant eyes staring back at me. She was so beautiful. I slowly lifted my hand to touch her cheek. A warm hum that started where I touched her and spread throughout my body. She closed her eyes and leaned into my hand.

I didn't have a chance to speak before Maxine was knocked back out of my grasp by a squealing Sabrina.

"You're home! You're home! Oh my Goddess, I missed you so much! I can't believe it's been two years!" Maxine's little sister was squeezing her tightly as she jumped up and down.

The distraction broke Maxine out of her daze. "Wait! You're mates?! Oh my Goddess, this is amazing!"

Donovan set Arielle down gently and cleared his throat, he was slightly pink with a goofy grin on his face. "Max, it's so good to see you. Happy to have you home." He gave Maxine a side hug, but didn't let go of Arielle, who was glued to his other side. "But if you'll excuse me, I'd like to spend some time with my mate." Arielle practically purred when he said 'mate.'

"Uh, yeah, us too!" Ivy added while still clutched in Heath's muscular arms. Heath finally lifted his head from Ivy's neck and growled. "Donovan, you better take it easy, that's my little sister."

"And that's my little sister that you have your paws all over." Growled Wiley playfully, whom I hadn't noticed until now. "Trust me, man, the mate bond is no joke. Donovan won't do anything to hurt her, you know that, bro." Wiley glanced around, "Speaking of mates, where is my beautiful goddess? Jazzy!" He paused, "Oh, yeah, welcome home, Ivy!" Wiley added before he wandered off inside the packhouse calling out for Jasmine.

As everyone dispersed in different directions, I was left just mesmerized by Maxine. I couldn't stop thinking about how incredible she was, I had missed her so much. She was talking with Sabrina and laughing at something she said. I watched her full lips, wondering what they tasted like when my thoughts were interrupted by someone tackling me to the ground.

I rolled over to see my brother Wesley looking awfully smug. "Wow!" he teased, "Where are those Alpha reflexes? You're slacking, bro! Guess I'll have to keep you on your toes now that I'm back."

"I guess they taught you something at the Academy after all." I replied as I shoved him off me and stood up. I offered him my hand to help him up when someone plowed into him.

"Wes! You're home!" Blake exclaimed as Wesley laughed and rolled him to the side.

I scoffed. "Nice Alpha reflexes." I teased Wesley.

"Woah! Who is this dude? It can't possibly be the same little runt that used to steal my favorite baseball hat." Wesley chuckled as he scanned Blake up and down.

Our little brother had grown so much in the last two years, Blake shot up like a weed. I guess I didn't notice it as much because I had seen him every day since Wesley left. But now that he was side by side with him, I could see it. Both my brothers were grown.

"You should see my wolf, Steel! He's massive." Blake boasted as he stood up.

"I bet." Wesley remarked and gave me an incredulous look. "It's a shame though, I think you're too big now to sneak through the vent into Dad's office."

"No way, I can still get into Dad's office!" Blake argued before he confessed, "I know the code."

"Oh Goddess." I laughed as I shook my head. "I'm going to pretend I didn't hear that." I said pointedly to Blake. Now that Thing 1 and Thing 2 were back together, we were all in for it. They were notorious for pulling pranks, especially on Dad.

I pulled Wesley up and dusted him off before tugging him in for a hug. "It's good to see you, little brother."

"You too, man." He clapped me on the back, "And you, you little rascal." He tousled Blake's hair much to his dismay. "Come on, I'm dying to see what baked goods Mom has made for me!"

He put an arm around me and one around Blake's shoulder, steering us away. I peeked back over my shoulder for Maxine, but Sabrina was pulling her excitedly off somewhere else. My wolf whined in my head.

What does this mean? I thought as I paced my room later.

With Donovan and Heath both finding their mates, I canceled the warrior training classes for the day. They needed time to bond with their new mates.

I had somehow managed to make it through our family welcoming Wesley back home, even though I felt as if I was in a fog the whole time. At the first opportunity, I made some excuse and slipped away.

Now, I was left alone with my thoughts. And my thoughts were solely on one little wolf. Goddess, she was all I could think about, and I ached to be near her. Just to see her.

Is this what I think it is? Zeus wagged his tail excitedly and let out a howl.

I'll take that as a yes. Of course, we won't know for sure until she turns 18, but this has to be the mate bond. She must have been feeling it too, she was drawn to me. I wonder if she felt that electric buzz when we touched. Did her wolf know?

What do I do? Should I tell her or wait for her to feel it? Goddess, her birthday isn't for another two weeks! How am I going to control myself until then? I groaned and flopped down on my bed, staring up at the ceiling.

Maxine.

Goddess, I think I have loved her since we were kids. I've always wanted to be around her and hated anyone else getting near her. I could never shake that overwhelming need to protect her. I missed her so much these past two years.

It was just about time to get ready for tonight. Mom, as Luna, is throwing together a welcome home party for all the returning recruits. This party will be extra special, as the newly found mates will be announced as well.

Maxine would definitely be there, I couldn't wait. I took a shower and got dressed in a black muscle shirt and some grey jeans. I was dying to get this party started.

CHAPTER FOUR

Maxine

What just happened?

I was in a state of shock from all that had just taken place. What a welcome home!

I'm thrilled for Ari, I knew she has been in love with my brother for a long time now. And by the looks of it, Donovan was quite smitten with her, too. I truly believed they would be the perfect balance for each other.

I was initially surprised about Ivy and Heath being mates, but the more I thought back to our last summer together, the more I remembered. There was always an energy between them and a sort of shyness that was adorable.

I was so happy for all of my friends, they deserve the most incredible mates. Funny how the group was pairing off...

Was I dreaming, or was Xander even more gorgeous? Goddess, the way he was standing there shirtless had me frozen in time. I couldn't help but stare into his intense eyes. And weren't they glowing at one point?

No, I must have been mistaken. It was definitely just Donovan and Heath who had the glowing eyes. Which makes sense, because their wolves came forward to claim their mates.

I wish I had a chance to talk with him more before Sabrina whisked me away. She's so excited, dragging me behind the packhouse to the treeline just beyond the clearing.

"Okay. Are you ready?!" She squealed again. She was about to show me her wolf. She turned 16 a couple of months ago, while I was away. She called me at the Academy bursting with excitement as she told me all about her first shift.

"Yes! Let's see her!" I replied with enthusiasm.

She scanned the area for others before quickly undressing. It was normal to still be shy about shifting at her age. But as werewolves, we were always shifting, so we got used to being naked around others pretty fast.

It didn't take her long to shift into her wolf, which impressed me. Usually, the shift is slow and painful when you're still new to it. It takes time for the bond to grow between you and your wolf. A quick shift early on means a strong bond with your wolf. My wolf and I bonded immediately. Onyx lifted her head and wagged her tail in agreement.

Sabrina's wolf was stunning; she reminded me so much of Onyx. Except, she had one white paw in the front, whereas Onyx was entirely pitch black.

"My, my, Miss Shadow, you sure are breathtaking!" I told her as I walked around her, running my hand through her soft, majestic fur. She snuffed in response and stood up straighter with her head held high and proud.

"But... Are you as fast as you are beautiful?" I teased. Shadow crouched down in a playful stance. "Let's see it then!" I urged. And like a shot, she dashed through the woods. I quickly stripped down and took off running. As I jumped over a log, I shifted into Onyx.

It wasn't long before I caught up to her and nipped her hind leg playfully. She darted in front of me, cutting me off, I had to slow down to keep from crashing into her. I decided to teach her a little lesson and tackled her. We rolled across the ground. We got to our feet and circled around one another, taking little lunges at each other.

When she was expecting me to lunge at her again, I bolted through the woods. She was quick to follow me. We ran for a while before arriving at Rock Lake, a favorite hangout spot. Our wolves lapped up the cool water and then flopped down on the shore.

I'm really happy you're home, Max. Sabby mindlinked me.

Me too. I sighed.

We stayed there for a bit before trotting back to our clothes. We shifted and redressed before heading towards the packhouse.

"Any idea where Dad might be right now?" I couldn't wait to see him. We entered the packhouse through the back patio. There were a few people around, but it was relatively quiet.

"He is probably either in his study or the suite by now." Sabby informed me. "He's been working late recently."

"I'm going to see if I can find him. Thanks!" I started to walk towards the grand staircase, when I turned back. "Sabrina. I'm really proud of you." She ran over and hugged me tightly.

"I love you, Max." I squeezed her tight.

"I love you, too." I pulled back and held her face in my hands, peering into her eyes. "You've grown into a beautiful woman." I told her and her blue eyes glistened, as she teared up a little. I kissed her forehead. Then, I took her hand in mine and gave it a little squeeze before heading up the stairs.

It had been so hard on us all when mom died, but I think it may have been hardest on Sabrina. She was just so young, she hardly had any time with her. I think we all tried our best to fill that void for her.

Dad was strong and carried us all through the loss. But I know he was broken inside. Marking your mate binds your souls together. When a mate dies, it's like that part of your soul is ripped away. Losing your mate is excruciating and most wolves don't survive it. I think Dad willed himself to live for us kids. Going through a pain like that can often turn a man cold or cruel even, but not Dad. He was the most loving father. We were truly blessed by the Moon Goddess to have him.

As I approached his study, I could smell his bergamot scent and knew he was in there. I knocked on the door.

"Come on in." He called out.

I opened the door. His office was the same as when I left. Mahogany bookshelves lined the walls, full of ancient texts about werewolves and pack histories. He had pictures of each of his kids on the desk, along with a family picture from when Sabby was a baby, and a group photo of all the Alpha team's families together at a barbeque. A grand painting of Mom hung on his wall.

He was still so focused on what he was writing, he didn't look up until I said, "Cadet Cooper reporting for duty, sir."

"Max!" He shouted as he sprang up from his chair. "I didn't know you were getting back today! Come here, sweetheart!" He pulled me into a massive hug. "Oh, I missed you so much. How was the drive?"

"It was a lot of fun, Dad, but I just wanted to get home. I missed you!" We stayed hugging for a little longer before I pulled back.

"Oh! I have a surprise, Dad..." I pulled my phone out of my back pocket and pulled up the email I had received. "Check this out." I said as I handed him my phone.

He leaned back against his desk as he read the screen quietly. Then, he looked up at me with an ecstatic smile on his face. "Top of your class?! Is there anything you can't do?" He wrapped me in another bear hug. "I am so proud of you, honey. Congratulations!" He kissed the top of my head. "This calls for a celebration!"

He went around to his desk drawer and pulled out a small box. "I was saving this for your 18th birthday, but I think now is the perfect occasion." He beamed as he handed me the box.

I took the box and studied him. "'Go on, open it." He urged.

I lifted the lid. There was a silver, silk scarf folded neatly. I gently unfolded the scarf. Inside was a white gold hair comb encrusted with diamonds across the top and a black diamond, crescent moon in the center. "It was your mother's. She wore it for our mating ceremony. She always wanted you to have it."

I peered up at my dad, and he had tears in his eyes. He looked lost in a fond memory.

"It's beautiful, Dad. Absolutely beautiful. Thank you." I pulled him in for a comforting hug.

After a moment, he pulled back, wiped his eyes, and cleared his throat. "She would be so proud of you, you know?" He gave me another overjoyed smile. "Alright, I suspect with you all arriving home, that Luna Clarissa is already preparing a party for tonight. So... we better get cleaned up! Have you seen your brother and sister yet?"

"Actually, I have. Sabby showed me her wolf. Dad, she's so grown up now!"

He chuckled, "I know, I know! You two are killing me. Before you know it, you will all have mates and pups of your own!"

I squealed, which surprised him. "Oh my Goddess, Dad, speaking of mates! Donovan found his mate! You'll never guess who it is..."

"Arielle."

"How did you know?" My jaw dropped open, shocked by how matter-of-factly he said it.

He gave a hearty laugh. "I have known it since Donovan was 10 years old. He always has his eyes on her. So protective."

I laughed a little surprised. "Okay, well, would it surprise you if I told you Ivy also found her mate today?"

"Let me guess... Heath, right?" He said, like it was obvious.

"Seriously? Come on, that one was a bit unexpected..." I was blown away. How did he know? I guess he had been observing us all closer than I thought.

"Oh, Maxine, my sweet girl. Nothing gets past your old man. Especially a mate bond. I can spot them a mile away."

"Wait, okay, so have I met my mate yet?" I prodded eagerly.

He took a deep breath and changed his demeanor. "Oh, that is not how this works, kiddo. Whether you have or have not, you'll get no spoilers out of me. Finding your mate is one of the most beautiful moments of your life. And it's best if it comes to you naturally."

I could tell he was serious about it, so I didn't push further. But it definitely had my head swirling with possibility.

"Come on, I've got to congratulate my son! This is turning out to be a wonderful day!" He boomed with a broad smile on his face.

CHAPTER FIVE

Xander

Mom had turned the dining hall into a vibrant party. It's amazing what she was able to do in just a few hours. There were streamers in our pack colors, navy and silver, hanging from the entire ceiling. Twinkle lights were sprinkled throughout. Long tables filled with delicious foods lined the back wall. A drink bar was in one corner, and a DJ booth was set up in another corner next to the stage, which was adorned with similar streamers and lights. Of course, there was a large open floor in the middle for mingling and dancing.

I was supposed to announce the return of our recruits and the newfound mate pairs. Technically, Dad was still Alpha, the title won't officially pass to me until I am fully mated as it will make me a stronger Alpha. An Alpha isn't complete without his Luna. Ever since I came back from the Academy two years ago, he has been giving me more and more Alpha duties. It's good for the pack to see me in that leadership role, it makes the transition easier when the time comes.

"Xander, sweetie," Mom called to me. She had been going non-stop, making everything perfect. "Have you seen your brothers? I want all three of you up on stage tonight. It's been so long since we've had the whole family together." She was beaming, so happy to have all her boys home.

I couldn't help but smile at her. "I just saw Blake. He was with Calvin, by the stairs. If I had to guess, I'd say Wesley is probably flirting with some poor girl."

Just as I finished saying that, Wesley strolled in with his arm around Maxine. A low growl escaped from my throat. My mother stared at me in shock.

"Alexander Black! What in the world has gotten into you?" I quickly composed myself.

"I'm sorry, Mom, I've just got a lot on my mind. Please excuse me." I briskly walked over to the bar and took a deep, calming breath. Get it together, I thought to myself.

"Whiskey, neat." I told the bartender. He nodded and quickly poured me a glass. I took it and downed the whole glass. "Thanks, Joe." I said as I set the glass down. I need to keep my emotions in check, or this is going to be a really long and difficult two weeks.

I know Wesley and Maxine are close. They've always been, since we were kids. But what if their friendship had changed while they were at the Academy together? Did she like him more than just a friend? My wolf growled in my head. This is not helping me stay calm. I need to get some air.

Just as I turned to head out back, I was met with dazzling blue eyes.

"Hey." The sweetest voice called to me.

"Hi." I replied softly.

"I didn't really get a chance to talk to you earlier. Sabby was super excited to show me her wolf." Her eyes were locked on mine and I couldn't think. "It was pretty crazy earlier, huh? I can't believe Ivy and Heath are mates. Well, I can and I can't, you know. Ari just KNEW that Donovan was her mate, so no big surprise there, right? Anyway, it's so good to see you, Xander. How have you been?"

Goddess, she is breathtaking. Her long dark hair cascaded down her bare shoulders. She was wearing a white tank top and blue jeans. So simple, but she looked incredible. She spoke with such an ease, like nothing has changed between us. Maybe she doesn't feel it.

"Good, I've been really good." I managed to find my words. "Happy to have you all back. It's been a long time. I missed you, kid." Kid? Why the hell did I call her kid? Ugh, I'm blowing this!

She looked down at the floor and then nodded her head. "Yeah. Yeah, it's been a long time. I guess a lot has probably changed for you. Last I heard, you were dating an Alpha's daughter. How's that going? I can't wait to meet her." She smiled but is that a bit of sadness I see in her eyes?

"Actually..."

"Max!" Squealed Arielle as she barreled in between us, grabbing Maxine and spinning her around. "Oh my Goddess, I have so much to tell you!" She pulled her away with a quick, "Sorry, Xander," over her shoulder.

Ugh! That did not go at all the way I wanted it to. She thinks I'm seeing someone, and I called her kid... I need to talk to her. My eyes followed her across the room while she talked excitedly with Arielle.

Donovan clapped me on the shoulder, successfully distracting me from staring like a creep. "Hey, man. You okay?"

"Yeah, yeah. Hey, congrats, brother! I'm happy for you." I said genuinely, as I gave him a hug.

"Thanks. I just want to get through this party so I can spend more time with her." Donovan was gazing dreamily at Arielle. She was watching him too as she talked and giggled with her friends.

"Well, I will try to make it short and sweet for you then." I patted his back and squeezed his shoulder. That's when I noticed a fresh mate mark on his neck. "Woah! You didn't waste any time, did you?"

Donovan reached up and lightly touched his new mark and blushed. He actually blushed. "It was Ari, man. She didn't want to wait. She's like a firecracker. As soon as we were alone, she jumped in my arms and marked me. It was... amazing. She's amazing." He resembled a lovesick puppy.

It was like their marks were connected, because as he was touching his mark, she was touching hers. They caught each other's eyes and just drifted towards each other, completely abandoning their conversations. They met in the middle of the room, lost in each other and kissed tenderly.

I averted my eyes and immediately found Maxine. She was watching them with a look of longing. Her eyes broke from them and locked in with mine. She smiled and her cheeks turned the cutest shade of pink.

"Let's get this show on the road!" My Dad thundered next to me. I honestly didn't even see him come in. But now that I was surveying the hall, I noticed it was full of pack members.

Dad and I made our way up to the stage where my mom had managed to wrangle both of my brothers. I stood center stage and raised my hand. It was like magic as the room fell silent and all eyes were on me.

"Good evening, Silver Moon. It is a momentous day for our pack. Today we welcome home this year's graduates from the Academy. Those students who spent two years training and working hard to better our pack. The Academy's program is difficult and requires determination and sacrifice. This class has grown and come back stronger, faster, and smarter than ever. They honor Silver Moon with their dedication. I am proud to welcome home our recruits!"

Everyone cheered and applauded our graduates.

"Now..." I added and the room settled again, "I am thrilled to inform you that not only do we have the strongest graduates, but one of our very own finished top of the class." I paused as my eyes found Maxine, who looked surprised and blushed again. "Silver Moon, join me in congratulating Maxine Cooper for graduating top of the class!"

The applause was thunderous and there were whistles and howls that rang out for Maxine. She waved and blushed profusely as she laughed and smiled.

I let her soak in the moment. When the cheering began to settle, I raised my hand again and the crowd fell silent once more. "The good news doesn't stop there. Today, the Moon

Goddess truly blessed the Silver Moon pack, because not just one, not just two, but four new mate bonds formed today!"

The pack roared to life again with cheers. "We must honor these sacred bonds and pray for the Moon Goddess, Selene, to bless their lives. Please celebrate with me these new mates: Daniel Jones and Natalie Freedman." The pack applauded each couple as they walked up on stage.

"Timothy Green and Hunter Marsh."

"My very own Gamma, Heath Anderson and Ivy Summers."

"And last but certainly, not least, Silver Moon's future Beta, Donovan Cooper and Arielle Anderson."
The room was so loud, you couldn't even hear yourself think. Once again, I gathered everyone's attention.

"Elder Mitchell will now bless these new mate bonds."

Elder Mitchell strolled over to the middle of the stage. When you hear the word 'elder' you probably think of an old, aging man. Werewolves aged gracefully though. Elder Mitchell was still healthy as a horse, with a thinner but muscular build, and silver hair with streaks of white. He could still pass for a human man around the age of 65. No one would know that he was over 150 years old.

"Mate bonds are sacred gifts from Selene herself.
Honor her gift and she will bless your bond for life.
May your bond bring joy to one another and blessings to your family for many generations to come.
May love and laughter fill your hearts and home for all the days of your lives.

May you face every challenge hand-in-hand and side-by-side, conquering all obstacles together.
May your bond always bring glory to the Moon Goddess.
And may the world be forever a better place because you found each other."

The entire pack let out a long howl as the elder finished his blessing. We cheered for them again as they descended the stage, rejoining the crowd. There were lots of congratulatory handshakes, hugs, and pats on the back.

"Thank you, Elder Mitchell, for that beautiful blessing. And a special thanks to my mother, Luna Clarissa, for arranging this wonderful party." Everyone clapped. My mom is a truly loved Luna. "Alright, Silver Moon, let the celebration begin!"

On that note, the DJ started playing upbeat music, while the pack began mingling.

I made my way over to the boys, who already had a drink in hand for me. As Wiley passed it to me, he quietly asked, "Hey, what happened earlier? I thought for sure you scented your mate, too."

I took a sip of my drink and shrugged. "Guess it was just Mom's baking I smelled. You know I have a super sensitive nose."

"Riiight." Wiley replied with a face that said he wasn't buying it. Luckily, he dropped it though.

I stood with the guys, watching our group of girls who were talking excitedly and laughing. They all looked happier than I had ever seen them. My gaze was drawn to Maxine. She was laughing with abandon and tossed her silky, dark hair over her shoulder, exposing her irresistible neck. Goddess she is sexy. I let out an appreciative growl.

"Did you say something, man?" Heath leaned over toward me. Thank Goddess it was loud in here. I quickly dismissed it and changed the subject.

"Congratulations, Heath. I'm really happy for you, man." I embraced him in a hug and gave him a pat on the back.

"Thanks. I can't believe it, Ivy is unbelievable. I just keep thanking Selene for blessing me with her as my mate." He was staring at Ivy with that goofy grin plastered on his face.

"You boys have got it bad!" I teased, as all three of them were just locked in a trance watching their women.

"Oh, just you wait, my friend." Wiley warned with a knowing gleam in his eyes, "Your time is coming, and you'll be a lost puppy just like the rest of us." He gave my shoulder a little nudge while he laughed.

"I can't wait." I truly meant it too.

CHAPTER SIX

Maxine

"What did it feel like?" Ivy asked excitedly as we all admired Ari's fresh mark.

"Like... Like fireworks, pure love, and the most amazing orgasm all at once." Ari gushed. "Utterly spectacular." She sighed. "Oh, and when he touches his mark, it makes me tingle, you know what I mean?"

"Girl, you will be happy to know that doesn't change!" Jasmine informed us.

"Oo, that will be fun while he's in an Alpha team meeting or warrior training!" Ari was already plotting ways to torture Donovan.

"Ugh, okay, that is my brother you're talking about, you know." I scrunched up my nose at the thought of him... tingling.

"Oh, Max, you are going to have to disassociate or something, because as your best friend, I have to tell you that my man has moves!"

I grimaced and the girls all erupted in laughter at my misery. I would definitely have to get used to this and just imagine she is talking about someone else, so I don't vomit.

"Ivy, why aren't you marked yet?" I asked, trying to change the topic.

"Heath is so sweet and gentle. We just spent the day talking and getting lost in each other. I think he wants to wait until we move in together and have our mating ceremony. It's a bit old fashioned but really romantic." She was practically cooing.

"Good luck holding out that long. The mate bond makes you super frisky!" Jazzy teased.

"Oh, no, we're still going to have sex! Goddess, could you imagine how possessive Heath would be? We're just going to hold off on the marking for now." Ivy clarified. We all laughed.

Everyone was so incredibly happy. I glanced over at the group of guys hanging out on the side of the room. Xander flashed me his killer smile and I melted a little. Good Goddess, that man was sexy.

The party had wound down, and the crowd dispersed. There were just a few of us left, helping to clean up. Of course, the mated pairs had taken off a while ago, probably because they couldn't keep their paws off of each other.

I was packing the leftover food away into containers to be sent to the kitchen, when Xander appeared beside me.

"Need a hand?" He offered with his kilowatt smile.

"Sure." I replied. "Thank you for what you said earlier. I didn't even know that you knew about my class ranking."

"Oh, yeah. The Academy called my dad directly to let him know we had the finest recruit in the entire Academy." Xander bragged.

I gazed up at him, and he winked at me. Oh, I think my heart just skipped a beat. I quickly looked away.

"Maybe we could spar together, and you can show me what you learned while you were away." He suggested. The idea really excited me, sparring with Xander.

"Absolutely! I'd love that!"

"Me too." The way he said that was so sexy, there was a little huskiness to his voice that made my spine tingle.

I cleared my throat. "I was thinking we should have a day at the lake, with the whole crew. We can barbecue, swim, and play football like we used to. What do you think?"

"I think that sounds like a genius idea. We can discuss it with everyone at breakfast." I was thrilled at the idea of spending a whole day with Xander. Goddess, he smelled so good. Like his familiar scent of cedarwood, but there was something new that I couldn't quite pick up. Maybe a new soap or something. It was enticing.

"Will your girlfriend be coming?" I queried and held my breath.

"I actually don't have a girlfriend. I've decided to wait for my mate." He replied. I silently let out my breath, relieved. "What about you? Seeing anyone from the Academy?"

"Actually, yeah." His brows shot up, and his eyes looked almost... pained? "I was, but I ended it before we left. It just didn't feel right, knowing that I'm turning 18 soon. I mean, I don't want to have a boyfriend and find out someone else is my mate. That wouldn't be fair to either of them."

"Yeah, that makes sense." He replied with a bit of a twinkle in his eyes.

We talked and laughed together just like old times. Before I knew it, it was getting really late.

"We should get to bed." I pointed out. And I swear his eyes darkened in the sexiest way.

He quickly looked away and cleared his throat, "Yes, it's late."

We walked together through the packhouse and up the stairs. Our packhouse was grand, six stories high. The first floor held the common areas like the kitchen, dining hall, living room, lounge, a theater room, and rec room. The second floor was for pack business, all the offices were located here, along with conference rooms, and suites for guests visiting from other packs. Our top unmated warriors lived on the third floor, the little apartments were too small for a family, so typically, a warrior would move out of the packhouse once they found their mate. The Delta and Gamma families lived on the fourth floor in luxury suites. We had the entire 5th floor to ourselves as the Beta family and of course, the Alpha family had the penthouse.

My dad and Alpha Jackson had been working on building their retirement homes for when they passed their titles along. I guess Dad, Sabby, and I will be moving into the new house soon, since Donovan is mated now. He would be moving Ari in with him as soon as possible and heaven knows they need their privacy!

We reached my floor, and I faced Xander. "Thanks for keeping me company this evening. I've really missed talking with you."

"I have too." He replied quietly.

"Well, I'll see you in the morning. Good night!" I turned toward my door, but Xander grabbed my hand and pulled me back into his muscular body. I just melted in his embrace.

"I really missed you, Maxine. It's good to have you home." He sounded so sincere. And then I swear, he smelled my hair.

He pulled away and said good night before he dashed up the stairs.

I stood there wondering if that really just happened.

I was lost in my thoughts as I walked through our suite. My dad was still up, so I wandered over to him and kissed him on the cheek. I think I mumbled out a 'good night' and I made my way to my room.

As I was getting ready for bed, my mind was swirling. Did Xander smell me? Was he attracted to me? But earlier today, he called me 'kid', so clearly he doesn't see me that way. But I could feel his eyes on me all night. Maybe I was mistaken, obviously it was the boys just watching our group since so many of them were mated. I'm just his Beta's little sister.

Ugh, but he was so gorgeous! And charming. And funny. And kind. Did I mention gorgeous? And we talked for hours just like old times. I was so comfortable around him, like I could really just be myself. I wish he could think of me the way I think of him. Oh, but at least he doesn't have a girlfriend. Not that it matters...

I groaned in frustration as I flopped down on my bed. I have to stop torturing myself.

I turned off the light to go to sleep, but when I closed my eyes, all I could see was his piercing green ones.

CHAPTER SEVEN

Xander

I woke up this morning with a spring in my step, eager to start the day.

Breakfast would be great; we were going to tell everyone about our plans to go to the lake. Then after breakfast, I was going to see if Maxine wanted to spar with me during our morning training session.

I dressed in a fitted grey shirt and some black athletic shorts and went down to the dining hall.

When I arrived, Wiley, Jasmine, Heath, and Ivy were already at our table looking cozy. I greeted them and then grabbed a plate of food. I sat down next to Heath. By the time I started eating, Donovan and Arielle were here. Donovan grabbed the seat next to me. As soon as Arielle sat down, he pulled her chair closer to him and wrapped his arm around her. I chuckled and shook my head at him. He just smiled and shrugged. He had it bad.

Then she walked in. Maxine was talking excitedly with Sabrina. She always lit up the room. She was wearing a black sports bra and matching workout leggings, with her hair pulled back in a ponytail. Her neck and midriff were exposed. I felt a small rumble in my chest and quickly looked away, hoping no one noticed. I could feel eyes on me at the table, but I just focused on my food.

Once Maxine and Sabrina had their food, they made their way over to our table. Maxine sat down right across from me, and before Sabrina got a chance to sit down, Wesley swooped into the seat next to Maxine.

"Hey Max, did you get that picture I sent you?" He was sitting way too close to her for my liking. I just glared at him. He glanced my way, but it didn't seem to faze him at all. He just focused on Maxine.

Maxine giggled. "Yes, you're so bad!" She gave him a playful nudge.

"Oh, you have to try these sticky buns!" Wesley enthused.

"I didn't see any sticky buns up there." Maxine scanned the buffet.

"No, they aren't from the kitchen. Mom made them for me. She's been baking all my favorites since I've been home." He stabbed a bite with his fork and raised it to her lips. She took the bite and immediately let out a little moan of delight.

"Mmm, oh Goddess, that's good!" She moaned again. She sounded so sexy, a growl escaped my throat.

Everyone at the table gawked at me in surprise.

I immediately started coughing and clearing my throat in an attempt to cover it up. "Uh, excuse me, uh, something in my throat, uh uh." I took a drink of my water.

I don't think I fooled anyone. Most of the girls were either giggling or smiling. Heath and Wiley both shook their heads, Wesley completely dismissed me, and Donovan was surveying me with his brows raised.

What was that? Donovan mindlinked me.

Nothing, just something in my throat. I lied.

Yeah, right. Wiley snorted. Heath was chuckling through the mindlink.

Ugh, I didn't realize Donovan had mindlinked the whole Alpha team.

I cleared my throat once more for good measure. "So, Maxine had a brilliant idea last night. Right?" I was eager to change the focus to anything but my growl.

Her face lit up immediately. "Yes! We need to have a lake day with the whole crew. We can barbecue, swim, and play games. It'll be so much fun! It's been so long since we've all been together." Her excitement was contagious. Everyone loved the idea.

"Let's do it tomorrow." Wiley suggested. "We don't have warrior training on Wednesdays, and the schedule is pretty light. We can easily move things around."

Everyone chimed in with their approval. "Alright, tomorrow it is then." I confirmed.

Wiley was leading the training group through stretches and warmups. My focus was on the upcoming sparring match.

Typically, the Alpha unit has our own training session in the mornings before we get on with the rest of the day. But today, our whole group was training together. It seemed none of us could bear to be apart at the moment.

I followed Wiley's lead absentmindedly. Stretching and glancing occasionally at Maxine. I couldn't help but admire her body. She had the perfect build for her frame. She was slender but physically fit. Her muscles were well-defined but not bulky. She had an athletic body with curves in all the right places. And that ass. I groaned to myself.

Once we finished warming up, people broke off in sparring pairs. The Alpha unit typically rotates through sparring partners because we all have different fighting styles that we can benefit from. Heath approached me as it was his turn to spar with me.

"Actually, do you mind sparring with Wesley today? I'm going to spar with the top recruit from the Academy." I declared.

His initial look of surprise quickly morphed into one of amusement. "Oh, this will be good!" Heath laughed.

I took my shirt off and peeked over towards Maxine. But instead of her normal, happy self, she looked serious and intense. She was focused and in the zone. She bounced on her toes, swinging her arms across her body, and rolling her neck. She was making sure she was nice and loose, ready for our match.

"Alright, little Beta. Let's see what you got." I teased her.

"Let's do this, *Alpha*." She replied while squaring off with me.

We circled each other, waiting to see who would make the first move. Just as I was about to make a lunge for her, she threw a roundhouse kick that landed squarely on the side of my face. I took a step back and touched my jaw while stretching it out.

I narrowed my eyes at her and slid for her legs. She was quick to jump over me into a forward roll and was back on her feet in a split second. She came at me with incredible speed, landing three blows on my torso before she swung herself around and climbed on my back, locking me in a choke hold.

I reached back and grabbed her while bending forward, flipping her over onto the ground. Maxine swiftly used this position to her advantage. She locked her legs around my neck in a scissor hold; she twisted and took me to the ground with her. Her delicious scent filled my senses and the precarious position we were in brought explicit thoughts to my mind. I let out a low growl.

Her eyes widened in shock. It was just the distraction I needed to roll her over and break loose from her grip. She was nimble and scrambled back to her feet in a ready stance. I threw a couple blows her way, but with her lightning-fast reflexes, she parried them, so they only glanced off.

I abruptly lunged forward and grabbed her in a body lock. But she was agile and twisted free. In one fell swoop, she spun to the ground and knocked my legs out from underneath me. I hit the ground with a thud. Before I knew it, she was on my chest, pinning me.

I gazed up into her gorgeous face. She was glistening with little beads of sweat and her chest was heaving as she caught her breath. Neither one of us made a move, we were locked in a heated stare as she held me to the ground.

"And that's why she's top of the class!" Arielle boasted.

I hadn't even noticed that everyone was watching us. Maxine scrambled off of me and held her hand out to help me up.

"Mighty impressive, little Beta," I winked at her. Her cheeks flushed.

"Looks like we've finally found someone to give you a run for your money, Alpha." Wesley called out with an extremely pleased grin on his face.

"Yeah, *Alpha*, just let me know if you want to spar again. I'd be happy to kick your ass anytime." Maxine teased as she stood there with her arms crossed, exuding a confidence that was sexy as hell.

"You should definitely train with us more often." Wiley chimed in, "We could all benefit from Xander getting his ass whooped every now and then."

"Hey, it would be a welcomed change, instead of wiping the floor with the three of you every day." I jabbed.

"Alright, get back to work everyone." Donovan chastised us all.

Maxine and I grabbed our waters and watched silently as the others sparred. There was an electric charge between us. I couldn't help but steal little glances at her, but she seemed to be avoiding my gaze.

"It's time for our perimeter run." Donovan informed us all. There was a collective groan that came from the mated pairs.

They took their sweet time saying their goodbyes while I stood around waiting for them.

Maxine was talking to Wesley who complimented her on her skills and technique. She was beaming. I couldn't help but feel irritated every time she talked to him.

By the time my team was ready, I desperately needed to run to get rid of this pent-up frustration.

CHAPTER EIGHT

Maxine

"Wow, Max, I can't believe you kicked the Alpha's ass!" Ari remarked excitedly.

"Well, I didn't really kick his ass." I replied modestly. "I was just able to evade his moves, and I got in a few lucky hits."

"Girl, don't be so modest! That was amazing!" Ari chided.

"Not to mention HOT!" Ivy exclaimed. I looked at her in surprise. "Oh, don't tell me I'm the only one who noticed," she retorted.

"Oh no, it was definitely steamy!" Jazzy added.

"As if! I wish you were right, but unfortunately, I think Xander just sees me as a kid." I countered.

"I wouldn't be so sure about that." Jazzy replied with her eyebrows raised.

We made it back to the packhouse and we're about to go our separate ways to clean up.

"Okay, let's meet back in an hour and then we'll go shopping!" Ari sang out.

As I took a shower, I played back the match in my head. My wolf was practically purring at the images that flashed through my mind. Xander had been shirtless the entire match, and it took all my strength to stay focused. His physique was absolute perfection. He had broad shoulders and a tapered waist with a 6-pack that you could drool over. His skin was a beautiful, golden tan with freckles sprinkled across his shoulders. There were times when his body was pressed up against me that I could hardly breathe. I was turned on just thinking about him.

I shook my head clearing my thoughts. There's no time for that. The girls are expecting me.

I hopped out of the shower and threw on a summer dress with some cute sandals. I tussled my hair dry, braided it and pulled it over my shoulder. I grabbed a small strappy purse, tossed a couple of things that I would need in there and went to meet the girls downstairs.

"Finally!" Ari exclaimed as she saw me descending the stairs. "Let's hit the road."

It was an hour and a half drive north outside of the packlands to the nearest human city. We shopped for hours as the girls wanted new lingerie for their mates. They insisted that I buy some too, not that I had any use for it. And of course, we all needed new bathing suits for the summer.

We were just walking out of the last store, when I literally bumped into Luke.

"Oh my Goddess, Luke! Hi! What are you doing here?" I asked, he was the last person I thought I would bump into.

"Hey, Max! It's so good to see you." He pulled me in for a hug. He didn't let go but instead kept his arm around my shoulder. "Hey ladies, long time, no see." He said to Ari and Ivy. The girls greeted him and introduced the others.

"This is Jasmine, poor thing is mated to my brother." Ivy teased and Jazzy rolled her eyes. "And this is..."

"You must be Sabrina!" Luke cut in. "You are just as beautiful as your sister." Sabby blushed.

"I can't believe we ran into you. How is it that you are here?" I said in disbelief.

"My pack is about an hour north of here. This is the closest human city with decent shopping. My mom sent my sister and I out to buy some 'summer evening attire.' Apparently, there are quite a few balls lined up for us this summer." He rolled his eyes and pushed his blonde hair back. He was always so handsome. Part of me wanted to kiss him like it was second nature and my heart ached at the thought that I couldn't. "I just finished up and was looking for my sister."

"We were about to leave, too." I said as I slipped out from under his arm. His hand caught mine and he pulled me a little closer.

"I've missed you so much, Max." He quietly told me as he gazed into my eyes with his golden ones.

"Hey! Dad told me that we are having a pool party at the packhouse this Saturday. You should totally come!" Sabrina burst out.

My eyes widened. Ari quickly nudged Sabrina. "Sabby!"

"I'd love to come." Luke quickly replied before we could rescind the invitation. His phone vibrated. "That's my sister. I gotta go, I'll see you Saturday!" He kissed my cheek and then darted away.

"Sabby! I can't believe you did that!" I hissed at her.

"What? It's just a pool party!" She said innocently.

I exchanged worried glances with Ari and Ivy. Having Luke at Silver Moon before I turned 18 was going to be difficult, for sure.

CHAPTER NINE

Xander

The guys continued to rag on me the rest of the day about the sparring match. But it didn't bother me at all. Maxine was an incredible fighter. She was so powerful and agile. It was hard to believe she was a Beta wolf. Her strength and skills were more like that of an Alpha. Donovan too. Their entire family is stronger than any other Beta I've ever met.

We had three of the pack's SUVs loaded up with picnic gear, towels, some sports balls, coolers, and a speaker for playing music. It wasn't a far drive to Rock Lake, so we piled into the three vehicles.

Heath was driving one vehicle, which meant obviously Ivy was riding with him. Sabrina and Heath's younger brother, Calvin, climbed in the back.

Donovan was driving the second SUV. I climbed in the passenger seat as Arielle and Maxine were getting into the backseat. "Oh, I forgot something!" Maxine declared before jumping out and running back into the packhouse.

Wiley and Jasmine were in the front of the 3rd SUV. Wesley and Blake had finished loading the coolers and closed the back of the SUVs. Wesley climbed in with Wiley and Blake took the seat that Maxine had just abandoned in our vehicle.

As she came bounding down the steps of the packhouse with her iPod in her hand, Wesley was hanging out the car door. "Max! Ride with us!"

She beamed at him and hurried over to the door he held open for her. Before she got in, she glanced at me with hesitation. I gave her a crooked smile and nodded my head.

I faced forward and let out a little sigh.

"What is up with you?" Donovan questioned. "You've been so... different lately."

"I don't know what you mean." I replied coolly.

"I know what's wrong," Arielle stated matter-of-factly. I turned to her with a raised brow. "All your buddies have found their mates. That's gotta be tough on an Alpha, to be the only one still waiting to find their soulmate."

Or maybe I've already found her, but I can't have her yet, I thought to myself.

"Oh, that's gotta be it." Blake piped up. "Xander is used to being the first one to do everything. He's probably going crazy because he's last at something for once in his life."

I chuckled a little. "You got me, Blake. I just wanted to be first. As usual." I said in a mocking tone.

I reached over and gave him a playful jab on the leg. As I was turning around, I noticed the look Arielle gave me. It was like she could see right through me. I cleared my throat and focused on the scenery out the window.

We decided to utilize the pack's lake house for the day, just for the amenities and a little convenience. We would still be outside all day.

Once the car was mostly unloaded, Wiley yelled, "Last one in's a rotten egg!" As he peeled his shirt off, tossed it to the side, and dove into the water.

We all laughed. "Some things never change." Jasmine said with a shake of her head and a smile.

The rest of the guys gave each other a quick glance before throwing our shirts off and shoving each other out of the way. We clambered into the water, splashing and making a ruckus. Even once we were all in the water, the rough housing didn't stop. We were dunking and splashing each other.

After a while, the commotion died down and Wiley called out, "Come on in, ladies, the water is nice!"

"Someone has to set all this stuff up." Ivy called back as she rolled her eyes at her brother.

Ivy and Jasmine were taking out the towels and making neat stacks in the back of one of the SUVs, so they were easy to grab. Sabrina was uncovering the grill on the patio of the lake house, making sure it was ready for use. Arielle set up the speakers, while Maxine chose a playlist.

"Hey, Jazz, can you toss me the football?" Wiley requested from the water.

"Sure, babe." She threw a perfect spiral from where she was standing at the back of the SUVs, right into Wiley's open hands. An impressive throw, to say the least.

"That's my baby!" Wiley whooped. Before tossing the ball to me. I lobbed it over to Blake. And we just kept on passing the ball around in the water.

"Ok, all set." Arielle told Maxine. She hit play and Maroon 5 blasted over the speakers.

"Yes!" Ivy cheered and all the girls bopped to the music. Maxine was swaying her hips back and forth with her arms above her head. I was mesmerized.

Maxine and Arielle sang along and pointed to each other while they sang "Girls Like You." They held each other's hands and bent over a little with laughter. They continued dancing holding each other's hands as they lifted their arms in the air and shook their hips.

"Oh do you remember this move?" Maxine quizzed. She kept both hands connected with Arielle's but pulled one down behind her head and Arielle did the same with her other arm. Then they danced away from each other by shimming their hips. They burst out laughing and high-fived each other.

"We still got it!" Arielle exclaimed.

"Yeah, you do, baby!" Donovan called out from the water. I hadn't noticed that all the guys stopped playing ball to gawk at the beautiful show that was taking place on the shore.

Thankfully, it made it less noticeable that I was entranced by Maxine.

"Enough already! Get in the water!" Blake demanded, clearly not interested in our gawking.

The girls started to remove their coverups and my heart thumped faster. Maxine was already looking sinful in her cutoff jeans and orange tank top, with her hair pulled up in a messy bun. I didn't know if my wolf could handle her in a bikini. Zeus was panting in my head at the idea.

Maxine grabbed the bottom of her shirt and lifted it over her head. Her back was practically bare, aside from the thin, blue bikini string that tied in the back. I was practically drooling over her delectable bare skin. She kicked off her shoes and unbuttoned her jeans. My heart literally skipped a beat as she stepped out of her cutoffs. Oh Goddess, that ass was to die for! And her toned legs went on for days. I groaned. I could feel my wolf fighting for control, so I sunk myself under the water. Get it together, Xander!

I held my breath and stayed under the water for as long as I could, trying to calm myself and Zeus down. When I came up for air, I met those electric blue eyes that were now right in front of me.

"Hi!" She greeted me softly.

"Hey." I pushed my wet hair back as I replied a little huskier than I should have.

"The girls want to play Double Decker Football, like we used to." She informed me.

"Oh, okay. That sounds like fun." I said.

"The thing is… everyone is all paired up already. So, I was wondering if you wouldn't mind being my partner?" Oh, hell yes! I thought. Maxine sitting on my shoulders, with those divine legs wrapped around me… Sounds like heaven.

I cleared my throat and responded coolly, "Yeah, if you want."

A glorious smile spread across her lips. "Perfect."

The other pairs were already stacking the girls on the guy's shoulders. Donovan wrapped his hands around Arielle's waist and lifted her up and over his head with ease. She giggled and leaned over to give him an upside-down kiss.

Once Jasmine was on Wiley's shoulder, he gave her bottom a good smack and she jabbed him in the ribs with her heel.

I turned my back to Maxine and lowered myself in the water so she could easily climb onto my shoulders. Her hands gently slid up my shoulders, and my skin sang in pleasure. Then, she lifted one leg over, followed by the other. My hand glided up her smooth legs and rested on her thighs to hold her in place. I swear I heard her inhale a quick gasp. She tucked her legs back under my arms to further secure herself before I stood fully. Everywhere our bodies connected, I could feel the slightest hum of electricity spreading across my skin.

"Alright ladies and gentlemen, I want a clean game." Blake announced. He was to be our referee today with Calvin. "No hair pulling, no kicking, no taking the Goddess' name in vain, and no crying to your mamas! Got it?"

"Got it!" "Sir, yes, sir!" "Yeah, yeah."

"Alright, the teams are Xander and Max, Donovan, and Ari versus Heath and Ivy, Wiley and Jazzy, and Wes and Sabby." Blake clarified.

"Wait, we're outnumbered! How is that fair?" Arielle whined.

"You've got an Alpha and two Betas on your team. You'll be fine!" Wiley countered.

"You've got an Alpha and a Beta, too!" Arielle pointed at Wesley and Sabrina, who just shrugged.

Blake barely glanced at Calvin before stating, "We have determined that it is fair."

"And Jazzy will get the ball first, because she bribed me." Calvin added quickly.

"Woah! Hey, come on now! Call a fair game, ref!" I shouted.

Blake ignored me, tossed the football to Jasmine and yelled, "Play ball!"

Jasmine tucked the ball under her arm and Wiley moved them forward. I immediately got in their way and Maxine put her hands up. But Jasmine threw a lateral to Ivy. Heath made a run for it through the water. Donovan moved quickly to block and Arielle dove forward, effectively tackling Ivy and taking all four of them crashing down into the water.

Arielle resurfaced with her arms in the air, "Woo! Not today, baby!"

The four of them reset and Blake hiked the ball to Ivy. Donovan moved in front of them. Instead of trying to go forward, Heath took a few steps back and Ivy threw one deep to Jasmine. I maneuvered us into the perfect position and Maxine intercepted the ball. I ran forward as Jasmine reached for Maxine. She missed and they went tumbling into the water. Wesley and Sabrina dove to tackle us, but I dodged out of the way just in time. Heath and Ivy stood in our way ready to defend, but out of nowhere Donovan and Arielle blocked their path. I ran us in for a touchdown and Maxine spiked the ball on the water.

"Yes! That's how it's done, people!" Maxine exclaimed. Donovan faced us and the girls attempted to chest-bump each other. It threw us off balance and we all wobbled back and forth until we could steady ourselves.

The game went on for a while, with some totally biased officiating from both Blake and Calvin. It was like they were rooting for us to lose. The other team managed to score on us as well, but in the end, we beat them because we're just that awesome.

"I'm famished!" Heath said and then nibbled at Ivy's ear. He was standing behind her with his arms wrapped around her body. She giggled and then pushed off of him.

"Then start barbecuing, mister." She teased. He pulled her back and nuzzled her neck some more.

"I'll get the grill going." Wesley declared, wading out of the water, followed by Blake and Calvin.

"Oh, no. I remember the last time you grilled something. You can watch." Wiley teased as he rushed out after him.

Heath lumbered out of the water, dragging Ivy with him. It seems he was not about to let go of her any time soon.

"I'll grab the plates and utensils from the lake house." Jasmine volunteered.

"I'll help!" Sabrina offered and ran after her.

"Oh, Donovan, I have to show you something..." Arielle glanced around. "Over there, by that rock." She lifted her eyebrows quickly a couple of times.

"Oh, interesting." He replied with lustful eyes. "Lead the way, baby." They swam off behind a large boulder, out of sight.

"Nice. Real subtle guys." Maxine called after them. And shook her head and wrinkled her nose. She started to wade out of the water. Her body slowly rose up out of the water and droplets cascaded down her curves. The water was just below her thighs, and I could see that scrumptious bottom swaying from side to side. She turned to me and said, "I'm going to help them set up. Are you coming?"

There was no way I could get out of the water without everyone's eyes being drawn to the bulge that had formed in the front of my shorts. "I think I'm going to go for a quick swim. I'll be out in a few." I explained.

"Okay." I watched her saunter back up to the SUV to grab a towel before heading to the patio. I slowly sank under the water. Oh Goddess, this girl is going to be the death of me. I rose back to the surface and took off toward the middle of the lake, hoping that the swim would help my problem.

CHAPTER TEN

Maxine

We had the best time at the lake. One of my favorite days ever. The weather was perfect. Everyone was together. We had a great time. I hope we can have many more days like that in the future.

I spent the past few days getting into a new routine. We'd all have breakfast together, then we would train. Sometimes we trained with the guys, but sometimes they trained separately. Then, I would clean up and head to either the hospital or the youth center to help out with whatever I could. I'd have lunch with Dad and Sabby. Afterwards, I'd either follow Dad back to his study to help with filing and other clerical things, or I would go for a run with Sabby in wolf form. I spent the evenings packing up with Ari, if she wasn't glued to Donovan's face; or shoot some pool with Wesley in the rec room before having dinner. Some nights, we kept it lowkey and just had a Beta family dinner. Other nights, we joined all of the Alpha unit families for a lively meal.

We were in the process of packing up our suite and moving into Dad's retirement home, and I was also helping Ari pack up her things to move in with Donovan. It was totally weird for me to be moving myself out and my best friend in. But I was really excited for both Ari and Donovan. I could see their love blossoming more every day. Two of my favorite people were completely head over heels for each other. What could be better than that?

Tonight was the pool party that Dad and Alpha Jackson had planned for us. Of course, they left all the actual party planning to Luna Clarissa because no one throws a party like her. Dad told me that they were having their own party over at the lake house tonight. He said it was to give us room for our own celebration, while enjoying the fact that they would all be retiring soon. I thought that was weird, because the only thing standing between them and retirement is Xander finding his mate. Once he is mated, then he can take over the pack with his Alpha team.

They say an Alpha without a Luna can turn vicious and power hungry. His soul needs to be complete, and his Luna will round him out with compassion. But there was no way of knowing when Xander would actually find his mate. The thought of him finding some beautiful, Alpha shewolf made me feel sick inside.

I was actually really excited for the party, but also kind of dreading it.

Luke is going to be here. My heart didn't know how to feel about it. I missed Luke. He was an amazing friend. He was also a great boyfriend. But I think I missed the idea of him being with me more than I actually missed *him* being with me. I mean, don't get me wrong, he's very handsome and charming. I just don't think he's my mate. It doesn't feel right.

Things were also a little strange with Xander. I was getting real hot and cold vibes from him. We would be hanging out like always and things would just feel so right. Then he would get real tense and leave suddenly. Other times, I would catch the way he was staring at me, or he'd touch me in a way that sent a shiver down my spine. Maybe it was all in my head, just wishful thinking.

The girls decided to get ready for the party at Jazzy and Wiley's place. It was a pool party, so it wasn't like we were getting fancified or anything. We just loved an excuse to get together.

I was stretched out across Jazzy's bed, waiting on everyone else. I had my new, white bikini on with a silver kimono-style cover up. Jazzy was doing Ivy's hair in the bathroom. Ari was putting a little makeup on in the vanity mirror. Sabby was dancing around the room, singing with the radio.

I checked the time on my phone again. "Ugh, hurry up! We're already late." I groaned at them.

"Done!" Ari answered and she stood back from the mirror. She wore a teal bikini and sarong that matched her eyes.

"Almost finished, just one more curl." Jazzy replied. She was adding soft waves to Ivy's golden blonde hair.

When we finally got down to the party, it was in full swing. There was a DJ blasting music, a couple of cute little tiki bars set up here and there. People were already in the pool, while others mingled or danced on the pool deck. There were also tables and chairs set up on the lawn with tiki torches lit all around.

My eyes scanned the party and immediately landed on the most exquisite man, who was staring at me with devilish eyes. The Alpha unit was gathered at one of the tiki bars. Xander was leaning back with his elbows on the bar behind him. He was wearing navy blue swim trunks with a white-linen, collared shirt that was left completely unbuttoned, exposing his flawless body.

"Mm, those boys look good tonight!" Jazzy announced. The girls all agreed. I was caught in a trance-like state, eyes locked with Xander's from across the pool.

Wes swooped in and grabbed me by the waist, lifted me up, and spun me around before setting me down again to pull me in for a hug.

"Hey, Max! You ready to party?" He asked. Then he pulled back and scanned me over. "Damn, Max, you look hot!" He gave me a wink. I thought I heard someone growl nearby, but when I glanced around, I didn't see anything unusual. I just caught a glimpse of Xander and Donovan heading inside as Heath and Wiley sauntered towards us. Sabby dashed off with Blake and Calvin.

"You don't look too bad yourself, young Alpha." I complimented Wes with a grin. Wes and I were extremely close, but in a best friend or brother/sister sort of way. Like, don't get me wrong, he is totally handsome, but we just weren't into each other like that. Sometimes I felt like I could talk to him more than I could with my own brother or even Ari.

"Who do you have your eyes set on tonight?" I jabbed him. He was quite the flirt.

"Don't know yet. We'll see how the night plays out." He gave me a cheeky grin.

"Hey, Jazz, you are smokin!" Wiley said as he pulled her into his arms, admiring her peach bikini that was gorgeous on her rich, brown skin.

"Baby, I don't know if my wolf can handle you wearing that little bikini around all these other wolves." Heath grumbled.

"Oh, don't be like that! You know I only have eyes for you, handsome." Ivy said reassuringly as she teased her finger over his marking spot. Heath let out a playful growl and kissed her.

"On that note... I'm going to get a drink!" I laughed and steered towards one of the tiki bars with Ari and Wes. The drinking age for werewolves was 18, due to our high metabolism, the alcohol burns off quickly. I wasn't quite 18 yet, but we were at our own packhouse, so no one here would mind.

We were sipping our drinks and dancing when I noticed Donovan and Xander come back outside. They both dove into the pool and swam across to the edge where we were standing. Donovan pulled himself out of the water. He shook his head, flinging water all over us and caused us to squeal.

"Hey, baby, you look gorgeous." He told Ari before planting a wet kiss on her neck.

I was getting warm from dancing, so I slid my kimono off my shoulders and tossed it on a nearby lounge chair. Xander groaned and disappeared under the water before swimming away. He must find my brother's romance sickening also.

I teased them, "Get a room, you two!"

"Don't tempt me." Donovan countered. Ugh. Disassociate. Disassociate. I chanted in my head. The two of them swayed in a slow dance, even though the music was upbeat. I shook my head. I did not need to be around for this.

I spotted some friends I hadn't seen in a while and made a beeline towards them.

"There you are!" I heard a familiar voice from behind me before I reached my destination. "I've been searching everywhere for you." I turned around to see Luke, looking handsome in just a pair of red swim trunks. My heart rate picked up. I wasn't sure what to say to him.

He gave me a sly grin and pulled me in for a hug. He buried his face in my hair, "Your scent drives me crazy." His hands rested on my lower back as he pulled back to gaze at me. He had his hips pressed against mine.

"And you look amazing too, baby girl." Luke's eyes roamed down my body. I heard a growl from off in the distance. I put my hands on Luke's chest and pushed back a little creating some distance, but he didn't let go of me. His fresh birch scent was almost suffocating me and not in a good way. Suddenly, everything about this made me desperate to get away from him, his scent, his touch, and the way he called me 'baby girl'.

"It's nice to see you, Luke. How have you been?" My heart was pounding; this didn't feel right. I tried to subtly wiggle away a little further, but Luke kept an arm wrapped around my waist. His other hand came up and swept a strand of hair away from my face as he gazed at me.

"I'm better now, gorgeous. I've missed you so much." Glass shattered behind me. I tried to turn and look, but Luke's hand held the side of my face.

"Luke. I can't do this." I pleaded with him and stared down at my hands that were still attempting to hold him off. As a warrior, I knew I could get out of his grasp, but I didn't want to hurt him if I didn't have to. He moved his fingers under my chin and lifted my face towards his. He was leaning in as if he was about to kiss me. Oh Goddess, no. "Luke–" I was cut off by a vicious growl.

Surprised, I turned just in time to see Xander's fist collide with Luke's jaw.

CHAPTER ELEVEN

Xander

I was really stressed about the pool party. On the one hand, it was always great hanging out with my friends and I couldn't wait to see Maxine in a bikini again. On the other hand, I couldn't wait to see Maxine in a bikini again. My wolf was getting more anxious each day. When I was with her I wanted to take her in my arms and when I was apart from her, I just wanted to be near her again. I don't know how much longer I can keep Zeus in check.

I made my way down to the pool early, just to make sure everything was good to go. The guys came to help me out. Slowly, pack members started showing up. We greeted people and grabbed some drinks.

We were chilling at one of the tiki bars when the most stunning woman walked out of the packhouse. Good Goddess, it was like time stopped, she was so breathtaking. She wore the tiniest, white bikini that made her golden, tan skin look irresistible. Draped in a see-through, silver cover up that wasn't hiding much, she had her wavy, dark hair loose around her shoulders. I was hypnotized.

Those captivating blue eyes found me. I watched as her eyes slowly roamed down my body and back up again. I couldn't tear my eyes away from her as she gazed back at me.

Out of nowhere, Wesley came barreling in and scooped Maxine up, then held her in his arms. My wolf let out a deep growl.

All of the guys turned to me. "What was that about?" Heath questioned. But I couldn't answer him, I was fighting my wolf hard.

"Woah, woah, let's go." Donovan pulled me by my arm towards the packhouse. "I've got this, you guys just chill." He told Heath and Wiley.

Donovan ushered me past everyone that was still in the house, through the kitchen and into the empty pantry.

"Xander, you have to calm down, man." He said with his hands on my shoulders. I shrugged him off and paced the tiny area. "What is going on?"

I took a deep breath and ran my hand through my hair. "It's Maxine."

"Max?" Donovan looked confused. "What about Max?"

"I can't..." I let out a heavy sigh and stopped to meet his eyes. I had to tell him. "She's my mate."

Donovan didn't say anything at first. He just stared at me with measuring eyes. "You're sure?"

"Yes. I scented her the day she came home. The same time you and Heath scented your mates. But she's not 18 yet, so she doesn't know." I groaned in frustration.

Donovan slowly nodded his head, processing everything I was telling him.

"Okay. First of all, congratulations! You're one lucky bastard; Maxine is literally the most incredible person I know. Second of all, I don't think I need to say this, but if you hurt her, I will rip your throat out." He was joking but also giving me the most intense stare. I nodded to him, acknowledging the weight of the situation. "And third, you've got to get Zeus under control, man. Things are going to get messy if you don't keep him calm."

"I'm trying. But I just go nuts when anyone touches her." I growled out.

"Easy, bud, easy." Donovan grabbed both of my shoulders, locking eyes with me. "Okay, let's just go for a quick swim to cool you off and calm you down. We'll work on the rest as we go, one thing at a time."

"Alright. Let's get out of this pantry." I chuckled. Donovan's eyes swept around the tiny room as if just realizing where we were and he started laughing too.

We exited the packhouse, back into the party. Maxine was dancing with Arielle. I groaned and threw my head back.

"You got this, man. Come on." Donovan encouraged me. We slid off our shirts. Then, we took a couple of quick steps and dove into the pool. The water did help me relax a bit. We swam to the other side, near the girls. Donovan climbed out and was instantly wrapped up in Arielle. When Maxine slid her cover up off her shoulders, I couldn't take it. Her body was divine in that white bikini. I groaned again and sank back under the water to swim away. I had to get some space before I made a wrong move.

I climbed out of the water on the opposite side of the pool and went to the tiki bar to order a drink. I downed it as soon as the bartender gave it to me. "Thanks, another, please."

Heath and Wiley approached me. "Why the long face, bro?" Wiley asked as he gave my shoulder a pat.

Before I could answer, I glanced up and saw some guy I didn't recognize holding Maxine incredibly close. His hands were on her lower back, touching what was *mine*. I let out a deep growl.

"Woah, what the hell, man?" Wiley looked confused.

"You okay, Xander?" Heath asked.

This asshole was touching her face in such a tender way. An uncontrollable fury built inside of me, and I crushed the drinking glass in my hand.

"Fuck, Xander." Wiley's words barely registered at all.

Maxine was so distraught. She was clearly trying to get away from this creep. I move angrily towards them.

Donovan stepped into my path and placed his hand on my chest to stop me. I glanced down at his hand and up at his face. "Don't." I snarled out. He pulled back and put his hands up in the air in surrender.

I focused my attention back on Maxine's distressed face as that fucker tried to lean in for a kiss. I sprinted over to them in a flash as I let out a vicious growl. Before he even saw me, I punched the jerk in his face. He stumbled backwards and growled at me. I took a fighting stance, my claws elongated as I let out an earth rumbling growl.

The entire party had stopped at this point. The guys jumped into action. Wiley and Malik, my top warrior, grabbed the other guy's arms. Donovan and Heath were struggling to hold me back. Wesley rushed to their aid, placing himself in front of me, blocking me from this asshole.

"Get him out of here!" Arielle yelled as she rushed to Maxine.

They tried to pull me away, but I wouldn't budge. Some more of my warriors raced in to keep the other guy back, so Malik and Wiley could help Wesley, Donovan, and Heath haul me away.

Maxine was just standing to the side in complete shock.

My men dragged me through the packhouse, into the kitchen but I was enraged.

"I'm gonna fucking kill him!" I yelled out.

"Xander, you have to calm down," said Heath. I let out another mighty roar. I threw whoever was holding me to the side.

"Careful, Zeus is in control!" Wesley shouted, "Block the door. Malik, make sure the warriors get that guy out of here." Malik nodded his head and rushed out of the room.

"Wiley, go get Max." Donovan ordered. I growled again when he said her name and knocked a kitchen appliance off the counter as I swung around trying to break free from their holds.

"Max?" Wiley looked puzzled.

"Just do it!" Donovan yelled. "Hurry!"

Wiley ran out of the room. I broke free from their grasps and threw a bar stool across the room. It shattered in a million splinters.

"Easy, Xander. Max is fine. Everything is alright." Donovan attempted to calm me down.

"He had his fucking hands on her!" I roared. I punched a hole in the wall with my fist.

"Shit." Wesley breathed out. "Xander you gotta chill, man. You know Max can take care of herself." He said and laid a hand on my arm.

I tore my arm away from him and bellowed, "You! Get the hell away from me!"

Donovan jumped in and pushed me back. "Wes, I think you should leave."

"What the hell did I do?" Wesley asked, bewildered and hurt.

"Not now, man. Just go!" Donovan pleaded as he struggled to keep me from tearing into Wesley.

Wesley reluctantly slipped out the door. Seconds later, the door opened again, and Wiley entered followed by a very concerned Maxine.

I growled when I saw her. Her eyes darted to Donovan. "What's happening?"

"He needs you, Max." Donovan explained.

"Me?" She was so confused as she glanced around the room at the destruction. I pushed Heath off me, I hadn't even realized he'd been holding me back as well.

"You gotta calm him down, Max. Now!" Donovan pleaded.

CHAPTER TWELVE

Maxine

I rushed over to Xander and touched his arm gently. "Xander?"

His attention snapped to me. His eyes were glowing, letting me know that Zeus was in control.

"What's wrong?" I asked, placing both hands on his arm.

Xander turned his head away, his chest was heaving and he growled out, "He had his hands on you!"

"Go." I heard Donovan whisper to the others, and they silently left the room.

"Hey, I'm fine." I reassured him. "Xander, look at me." I reached up and put my hands on either side of his face, forcing him to meet my eyes. "I'm fine. Everything is okay." I gently stroked his cheek with my thumb.

Xander sighed and his arms slipped around my waist.

He pulled me closer to his body, and I felt a warmth spread throughout me as I wrapped my arms around his neck and hugged him. He buried his face in my hair and let out a soft growl. "Xander?" I called out delicately to him. He made no attempt to move. We stayed like that for a while, and he seemed to be relaxing a bit.

He moved his head back slightly. "Xander, are you--"

Before I could finish my question, his lips were on mine. It surprised me, but I definitely didn't fight it. My lips tingled as they moved with his. His hand slipped up my back and into my hair, holding my head in place. He kept his other arm wrapped around me, pressing my body into his. I slid one hand down to his chest and the other stayed holding onto his neck.

His chest rumbled and he squeezed me tighter causing me to let out a little gasp. He took the opportunity to slip his tongue into my mouth. I welcomed his tongue with my own. It was a slow, tender kiss. It was everything I ever imagined and more. I was lost in the moment. Xander's fingertips gripped into my skin. He deepened the kiss, and it became heated. I was dizzy from the passion. So much of our bare skin was touching, I was tingling throughout my body. I let out a soft moan.

Xander broke the kiss and backed away quickly with a growl as he squeezed his eyes closed.

I was disappointed in the sudden loss of his body. "Xander?"

He turned away from me. "You have to go." He gritted out. His words made my heart ache. What did I do?

"Xander, I don't under–" I began, but he cut in.

"I can smell your arousal, Maxine." He faced me with heated eyes. "I won't be able to stop myself if you don't leave."

I took a step towards him; I didn't want him to stop. "Please go." He pleaded with me in a strained voice as he moved further away.

I didn't want to leave him. I wanted to comfort him. I wanted to hold him. But if I stayed, what would happen? "Please." He begged.

I started to walk out but stopped when I reached the door. I peered around the room at the mess and wondered what had happened. "It's ok, I'll clean it up." Xander said, sounding a little more like himself. "I'm fine. Go."

After closing the door, I leaned my forehead against it and sighed.

"Is everything alright?" Ari asked from behind me, startling me. I spun around quickly to see everyone staring at me with worried faces.

"Um… He's calm now. I think he needs you, Donovan." I said in a quiet voice. "He asked me to leave."

Donovan looked at Heath and Wiley, tilting his head for them to follow him. Quietly, they made their way back into the kitchen.

Ari, Ivy, and Jazzy rushed over to me. "Are you okay?" "What happened?" "Do you need anything?"

I know they were just being caring and sweet, but their questions were overwhelming me. I was still reeling from what had just happened.

"I'm fine. I'm fine." I insisted. "But I think I'm going to turn in for the night. I'll talk to you tomorrow."

I headed towards the stairs when Ari called after me, "Max, do you–"

"I'm really okay, you guys. Don't worry. I just need to be alone." I reassured them. Then, I darted up the stairs to my room.

Holy shit, what a crazy night.

I couldn't even begin to process what had happened or why it happened.

I decided to take a bath to try to decompress. I turned on the water and let it get warm as it filled up. I took off my bikini and tossed it in the laundry bin before stepping into the tub. I sank down into the warm water and my body relaxed.

Sweet Moon Goddess, what just happened? I kissed Xander. Actually, Xander kissed *me*. And it was unbelievable. It was so intense and tender at the same time. And the way his skin felt against mine was like nothing I had ever experienced before. I got goosebumps just thinking about it. My body was getting warm again and there was an aching need within me. I was so turned on, just thinking about that kiss.

I touched my lips, remembering how soft Xander's were as they pressed into mine. I slid my hand down my neck as I thought about his warm breath on my skin. My hand moved further down, caressed lightly over my breasts and hardened nipples. My fingers glided over my stomach and below my abdomen. My fingers ran over my lower lips as I parted my legs wider. I skimmed one finger up my slit and circled my clit. I imagined what it would feel like if it were Xander instead of me. I slipped my finger inside and slowly slid it back out. As I played with myself, I tease my nipples with my other hand. I pictured Xander's shirtless body pressing against mine as I increased my pace. I was building myself up quickly. As I climaxed, I moaned out, "Oh, Xander!"

Yes, Maxine? Xander's husky voice growled in my mind.

My eyes shot open wide. Oh my Goddess! In my pleasured stupor, I must have reached out and mindlinked him. I quickly closed my mind to any links.

I covered my face with my hands. What was I thinking? How could this happen? I've never unintentionally mindlinked someone before. Ugh! And it just had to be mid orgasm! I was so embarrassed. How will I be able to face him now?

I quickly washed my body and climbed out of the tub. I dried off, while I silently cursed myself over and over. I wrapped the towel around my body and walked back into my room. I sat down on my bed and sighed loudly as I facepalmed myself.

There was a knock at my door.

CHAPTER THIRTEEN

Xander

Maxine left the kitchen, and I immediately missed her presence. But I could still smell her delicious scent that had my wolf going absolutely nuts. I know if we had continued, I would have gone too far.

I paced the room and took some deep breaths to try to calm myself down now that her scent was fading.

I finally began to feel relaxed when Donovan, Heath, and Wiley cautiously walked in, closing the door behind them.

Guilt washed over me as my friends looked at me warily. "Fuck! Guys, I'm so sorry." I said, "I couldn't control myself. Are you alright?"

"It's fine, Xander. We're all good. But what the hell happened, dude?" Wiley asked.

I took a deep breath and tried to keep calm. "Some guy was all over Maxine." I said through a clenched jaw.

"Yeah, that guy is a future Alpha of some pack a few hours north of here." Heath noted.

"He had his hands on her." I growled. "And he tried to kiss her." I fumed.

Heath and Wiley stared at me with raised brows, waiting for more. Obviously, Maxine could handle herself, they weren't understanding why I flipped out.

I rubbed the back of my neck and told them, "She's my mate."

"Oh, shit." Wiley whispered. Heath just nodded his head as he mulled it over. "That's why she was able to calm you down."

"Does she know?" Heath wondered.

"No. Well, she might know now? I don't know." I shook my head with a shrug. "I kissed her."

"You kissed her and then asked her to leave?" Donovan asked in a stern tone.

"I didn't trust myself. I wasn't in the right state to explain things to her, and I didn't want to fuck everything up by pushing her too far." I clarified the best I could.

"Ok. Let her take some time. Her birthday is like a week away; she might be feeling the bond already." Heath reasoned.

"Dude, you punched another Alpha in the face." Wiley pointed out. "Shit might get messy."

"I'll talk to Dad in the morning. We'll have to explain everything to the guy's father. But it'll be fine. She's *my* mate." I stated firmly.

The guys were really understanding and even helped me clean up the mess that I made in the kitchen. It was getting late, and the party had apparently ended after the big commotion, so we were calling it a night.

"Oh, Xander, you'll need to talk to Wes in the morning, too." Donovan added, "You took some of your anger out on him and I think he's beating himself up over it."

"Damn, okay. Thanks, man." I didn't mean to hurt my brother's feelings. "Seriously, you guys, I really appreciate what you did for me tonight."

"Of course, bro." "Anything for our Alpha." "We've always got your back."

I nodded and hugged each of them as they left the kitchen.

I took one more look around, turned off the lights and closed the door behind me. I was about to head upstairs when Maxine's sexy voice filled my head.

Oh, Xander!

Fuck, that was hot. I mindlinked her back with a husky growl. *Yes, Maxine?*

I got no reply. In fact, the mindlink was closed. My mind flooded with images of what she was doing to herself to sound so sexy. And she was thinking about me.

I groaned out loud and dashed up the stairs. I found myself standing outside of the Beta suite in no time. I knew the key code to get in. Quickly, I reminded myself that Beta Charlie was at the lake house and Donovan was staying with Arielle. I punched the code and slipped through the door.

The lights were off, but there was a slight glow coming from Maxine's room. I stood at her door and could smell her fresh orange blossom and cinnamon scent. I took a deep breath and knocked.

It was silent inside for a minute. Then I heard her soft footsteps approach the door.

When she opened it, my eyes darkened at the sight in front of me. She stood there barely covered in a small, white towel.

I growled and took a step into her room. I was standing so close to her, her breath fanned across my neck as she peered up at me with wide eyes.

I slowly closed the door behind me without tearing my eyes away from her gorgeous face. "Xander." She whispered.

"Maxine." I replied in a gravelly voice.

I slid my hand behind her neck as I lowered my head. I inhaled deeply and hummed in delight. I lightly kissed the exact spot where I planned to mark her one day. She shivered against me and let out a soft moan. I slowly licked her neck and sucked on her marking spot. This time she moaned louder. "Xander." She cooed breathlessly.

I left a trail of kisses up her neck and jaw, working my way to her mouth. When our lips crashed together, everything became heated. She wrapped her arms around my neck, and I pulled her body flush against mine. Our tongues danced together until we were panting for air.

I groaned. "Maxine, you don't know what your scent is doing to me right now." My chest rumbled in delight. "Tell me to stop."

"Don't stop, Xander." Maxine pleaded. My eyes darkened as I stared at her with desire.

I walked forward and she moved backwards with me until she was just in front of her bed. I stroked her face and took a slight step back. I reached out and untucked her towel, letting it fall to the floor.

Maxine stood in front of me completely naked. My breath hitched in my throat. She was utter perfection. I took my time letting my eyes roam her impeccable body. I was memorizing every curve and valley. She stood there breathing heavily, waiting for me to make a move.

I closed the distance between us and slid my hands over her body. I trailed one hand up to her breast and let my thumb just barely graze her erect peak. I held her gaze while I traced circles over her pink nipple. She let out a soft whimper.

I scooped her up by her thighs, wrapping her legs around my waist. I could feel the warmth of her center on my bare abdomen. I pulled her in for a passionate kiss as I stepped closer to her bed.

Gently, I laid her down, pressing my body into hers. As my tongue swirled with hers, my hand caressed her breasts and then slid further down her abdomen. I ran my finger up her slit, and she gasped into my mouth. I pressed on her sensitive bud and circled my finger over it.

"Mm." She moaned as I dipped my finger inside of her. I pulled my finger out and brought it to my lips. I licked her wetness off my finger.

"Mm indeed." Maxine watched me with lust-filled eyes. "I think I need a better taste." I whispered into her ear. I felt her body shiver underneath me.

I kissed her neck just below her ear, then that beautiful marking spot right at the base of her neck. I continued to kiss my way down her body, stopping first at her collar bone. Next, I kissed her perfect nipple, which I gave a quick swirl with my tongue, eliciting another sexy moan. I kissed the valley between her breasts and then under her navel. I trailed my lips down to her inner thigh, until I was positioned right in front of her glistening core.

I looked up at her. She was practically panting as she watched me slide my tongue up her slit. I growled in appreciation, she tasted divine. I flicked my tongue around her clit and sucked on it. Maxine gasped. I brought one hand up to play with her nipples and held her hips down with my other arm wrapped around her delicious thigh.

I plunged my tongue inside her warmth. I swirled it around and licked up to her clit and back down again. I quickened my pace as she squirmed and moaned.

I continued to hold her thigh with one arm and inserted a finger into her core with my other, while I sucked on her clit. "Oh, Xander!" She cried out.

"Yes, Maxine." I growled against her clit as I continued to pump, inserting another finger. She moaned louder. "Xander!"

"That's it, Beautiful." I coaxed her in between licking and sucking on her clit. "Come for me." I demanded.

As if my words pushed her over the edge, Maxine climaxed. The sounds of her orgasm filled the room and her body shuddered as I continued to hold her while she rode out the waves of pleasure.

I planted one more kiss on her lower lips before wandering my way back up her body. The look on her stunning face was euphoric.

I kissed her lips slowly and then nuzzled her nose gently with mine. I laid my body next to hers and pulled her into me. She laid her hand on my chest and looked at me sleepily.

"Xander?" She mumbled.

"Yes, Maxine?" She was so beautiful, and she was trying hard to fight the exhaustion that was taking over.

"What is this?" Maxine questioned.

"Shh... I'll explain everything tomorrow." I reassured her. "Just close your eyes."

She didn't fight it and happily dozed off in my arms.

CHAPTER FOURTEEN

Maxine

I woke feeling extremely well rested. I stretched and realized I was naked. Flashes of last night came flooding through my mind. Xander. I rolled over and found the bed empty. I looked around towards the bathroom, but he was gone. Disappointment and worry began to creep in.

I started to get up and noticed a note on my nightstand. I picked it up and read:

Maxine,

You looked so peaceful, I didn't want to wake you. I'm sorry I couldn't stay. I have some urgent business I need to take care of this morning. I don't know if I'll have time to make it back before my training duties, though. I promise I will find you when I'm done and we can talk.

Xander

I sighed. I just wanted to know what was going on.

I couldn't believe what happened. Last night was unbelievable, to say the least. I've never felt like that ever.

That kiss was cosmic and the rest of it was... mind blowing. I've never experienced anything like it before.

I mean, don't get me wrong, Luke and I had fooled around, I'm not that inexperienced. But I have been saving the most intimate moments for my mate. Still nothing ever felt as good with Luke as it did with Xander. There was no comparison.

Xander was probably very experienced. He certainly knew what he was doing last night. Girls always throw themselves at Alphas and I know he's had girlfriends before. I got irritated at the thought, but then my nerves took over. What if I don't measure up? What if I disappointed him somehow?

Goddess, I hope it won't be too long before we can talk. I glanced at the clock and couldn't believe it was 11:47! I never sleep this late!

I jumped up and dashed to the bathroom. I took a quick shower, brushed my teeth, and threw on some red athletic leggings, a black sports bra and a grey loose fitted, cropped tank top. I quickly slipped on some running shoes and rushed out of my room while I twisted my hair up into a messy bun.

I was greeted with the smell of bacon cooking. I perked up, thinking maybe Xander had come back already. I quickly rounded the corner and saw the girls in the kitchen, talking in hushed voices.

Jazzy saw me and nudged Ari in the ribs with her elbow.

"Hey! Lazy Bones!" Ari chirped. "We heard you in the shower, so we made lunch! Grilled cheese and bacon sandwiches." She held up a plate with a smile.

Ivy and Jazzy quickly set places at the table in the kitchen nook and poured juice into glasses. My stomach grumbled a little, right on cue.

"Thanks." I took my seat and the rest of them sat down too. "It smells delicious."

We started eating quietly and I could feel their eyes on me. I knew they wanted to ask me a million questions.

I took a drink of my orange juice and sighed, "Just say something already!"

"What the hell happened last night, Max?" Ivy asked.

"Donovan said some guy was all over you and Xander totally flipped out. Are you okay?" Jazzy was watching me with concern in her eyes.

"I'm fine. Really." I assured them. Then, I took a deep breath. "It was Luke." Ivy and Ari's eyes were the size of saucers.

Jazzy raised her eyebrows. "Luke was all over you? I thought you told him you needed time to see if you find your mate when you turn 18?"

"I did. But..." I fiddled with my napkin and sighed before looking back up at them. "He was different. He said my scent was driving him crazy and he couldn't keep his hands off of me. I tried to push him back, but he was so persistent. It was like his wolf was taking over, but his eyes weren't glowing." I explained, still not understanding why he had acted that way. It was so out of character for him.

"Do you think he's your mate?" Ivy asked incredulously, like she couldn't imagine Luke being my mate.

"No. He can't be. It all felt so wrong." I stated firmly.

"So... That's why Xander went all beast mode?" Ari questioned with one brow cocked.

"I don't know. Xander just flew in and punched Luke in the face." I recalled, "They looked like they wanted to kill each other."

"It took the whole Alpha unit *and* Wes and Malik to drag Xander inside." Ari reminded us. "I've never seen him so enraged."

"It's not like him to lose control like that." Ivy remarked.

"The warriors that stepped in basically threw Luke out of the party." I had just stood there watching everything moving around me in a stunned state. "Then, Wiley came running out saying that Xander needed me. When I got to the kitchen, it was absolute chaos."

I remembered how Xander was being held back by his friends and broken bits of a stool laid scattered across the room. "Zeus was in control and he was raging out. He seemed to calm down when I got him to focus on my voice though." I stopped there, remembering everything that happened after.

"Wait, so he was completely out of control, Hulking out, destroying everything, and you were able to calm him down by talking to him?" Ari recapped in disbelief.

"Yeah, I put my hands on his face and made him focus on me." I replied.

"Is Xander your mate?" Jazzy asked, completely serious. "When Wiley is pissed off, which rarely ever happens, my touch calms him down. It sounds like that's what you did with Xander."

"I don't know." I said, my heart pounding. "We didn't get to talk much since everything happened."

"What happened when he calmed down?" Ivy prodded.

"Well, actually, he held me in his arms and then... he kissed me." I was staring at the table, but I could feel their shock and excitement.

"Oh my Goddess, he kissed you?!" Ari squealed.

I nodded my head with a smile on my face. I wasn't about to share my embarrassing mind link incident or the incredible encounter that took place as a result. I was keeping those memories to myself. "It was amazing and *really* intense." I said with a flush rising to my cheeks.

"Do you feel a pull towards him?" Jazzy inquired.

"Yes? I mean, I'm really drawn to him, but... it's Xander. He's absolutely incredible, it's hard not to be drawn to him." I reasoned. I still didn't want to get my hopes up. "He is an Alpha wolf, you know."

"Well, he's my Alpha, too, and I've never been drawn to him to the point of wanting to kiss him." Ivy countered.

We laughed and I rolled my eyes. "He told me we could talk later today. He had some stuff he had to take care of."

I stood to clear the table. The girls all helped, and we had everything cleaned up in no time. "I was going to go for a run and a workout. Do you want to join me?"

"Sure. We'll get changed and meet you downstairs in 20 minutes." Ari declared and the girls left.

I wandered back to my room, in less of a rush. I made my bed and brushed my teeth again before moseying down to the main floor of the packhouse to wait for my friends.

I was standing in the entryway, leaning against the wall with my arms crossed and one leg bent, completely lost in thought. The room filled with a burst of laughter as the Alpha unit entered through the front doors of the packhouse.

They were all shirtless and slightly glistening in sweat. They had probably just finished their perimeter run. Right on time, Ivy, Ari, and Jazzy bounded down the stairs, their mates' faces lit up when they saw them

They all coupled up instantly. Ari leapt into Donovan's arms, who caught her eagerly. Wiley wrapped Jazzy up in a bear hug, she squealed and squirmed because he was all sweaty. Ivy and Heath just started making out in the middle of the entryway.

My eyes were immediately glued to Xander. My heart was thumping so hard I swear he could probably hear it. He looked like a Greek God as he sauntered over to me.

"Hey, Maxine." He said with a crooked grin that gave me butterflies.

"Hi." That was all I could muster up. He leaned with one arm resting on the wall above his head next to me. He was so close. His cedarwood scent filled my senses. What is that other scent? I can't quite make it out. It was driving me wild.

"Sorry about this morning." He whispered. "How are you feeling?"

"Honestly, a little confused." I replied. He frowned a little and nodded his head as if he understood. "We really need to talk." I reminded him.

"I know. I really want to talk to you about everything." He said in a sincere voice. "But we have a warrior training class in ten minutes that we have to get ready for. Can I find you after?"

"Yeah, that's fine. I was about to have my own workout with the girls."

"Mm." Xander's eyes traveled down my body and back up again. "Whip 'em into shape." He gave me a sexy wink that totally turned me on. He inhaled, probably smelling just how turned on I was, and he let out a little growl. My cheeks blushed.

"Yo! We gotta get moving or we're gonna be late." Donovan called out to everyone.

"Can't wait to see you later, Maxine." Xander leaned in and kissed the top of my head before jogging off with his friends.

Ari caught my gaze and bounced her eyebrows up and down at me. I rolled my eyes as I fought the smile tugging at my lips. "Okay, let's go." I called as I pushed off the wall towards the doors.

CHAPTER FIFTEEN

Xander

I watched Maxine sleeping in my arms for hours before I dozed off. I didn't sleep long, but it was the most peaceful sleep I have ever had.

I forced myself to get up early, even though it killed me to leave Maxine alone. I knew when she woke up alone, she would be confused, and I didn't want to hurt her. But I had a lot of things to straighten out before I started my normal, daily responsibilities.

First, I needed to tell Dad everything that happened. Then, we would need to make a call or two. I also really needed to explain everything to Wesley. I never wanted to hurt my brother, and I needed to clear everything up with him as soon as possible.

Even though it was early, I mindlinked my dad, asking him to meet me in his office. I also mindlinked Donovan. I would probably need his help sorting everything out.

Donovan was already waiting for me when I walked into my dad's office. "Hey man, thanks again for everything last night. Sorry shit got so crazy." I said to him as I gave him a hug and patted his back.

"No worries, Xander. You know I've always got your back." He placed his hand on my shoulder and gave it a squeeze.

My dad strolled in, looking chipper. I hated that I was about to rain on his day. "What can I do for you, gentlemen?" He asked as he sat in his desk chair.

"Dad, there was an incident at the pool party last night that resulted in me attacking another Alpha." I came right to the point.

My dad's face changed into a look of shock and anger. "You did what?" He asked in disbelief. "What on earth would possess you to do such a thing, Alexander?"

"Sir, he was attempting to be forcefully intimate with Maxine." I gritted out. Dad raised his brows in disbelief and anger, as he turned to Donovan, since she is his sister. "Dad, she's my mate."

Dad's attention whipped back to me. "She's not 18 yet. You're sure?"

"Yes. Maxine is my mate." I stated confidently. "And that '*Alpha*'," I scoffed at the word 'Alpha,' "had his hands all over her. She was trying to get away from him."

"Okay, well, you were within your rights, son." Dad nodded as he thought this through. "Who is this other Alpha?"

Donovan jumped in with information that I didn't have. "Alpha, his name is Luke Vance of the Dark Moon pack." My head snapped to Donovan. "He was Maxine's boyfriend at the Academy. They had recently broken up." Donovan informed us both. I had no idea that he was her ex.

"Dark Moon? As in Alpha Phillip's Dark Moon pack? He's Valerie's brother?" I asked in complete shock.

"Yes." Donovan confirmed.

"Shit." I breathed out.

"Ok, we will need to call Alpha Phillip." My dad decided. "We need to get this whole thing straightened out before it becomes a bigger deal than it is. He's a reasonable man and our packs have been allies for years."

Donovan pulled out the file on Dark Moon, dialed the number for Alpha Phillip, and placed the call on speaker phone.

"This is Alpha Phillip." He picked up after a few rings.

"Good morning, Alpha Phillip. This is Alpha Jackson over at Silver Moon. How are you?" My dad addressed him in a pleasant tone.

"Ah, Alpha Jackson. To be honest, I'm not doing too well. It seems *my* son was invited to a party in your pack and then attacked by *your* son." He was clearly pissed.

"Yes, Alpha Phillip, it was an unfortunate situation, and I would like to apologize for the way it was handled." Dad began, "However, it seems it's a bit more complicated than that." Dad nodded to me.

"Alpha Phillip, I'd like to apologize for any strain that I may have put on our relationship with Dark Moon. I was quick to react in such a way because your son was attempting to be intimate with Maxine Cooper. She is my mate." I explained.

"What?!" I could hear Luke growl out in the background. "She can't be! She's not even 18 yet!"

My anger spiked when I heard Luke's claim. "I assure you, Alphas, she is *my* mate, and I cannot tolerate another wolf touching what is *mine*." I gritted through a clenched jaw. Donovan placed his hand on my shoulder, reminding me to keep my cool. Dad put his hand up and gave me a slight nod.

"Alpha Phillip, again, we would like to apologize for the way the situation was handled, but as you can see, my son was in a difficult position. As an Alpha with a mate of your own, I'm sure you can understand where he is coming from."

"Yes, Alpha Jackson, I do understand." Alpha Phillip replied calmly. Luke scoffed loudly in the background. "I'd like to apologize on behalf of my son. Mate bonds are sacred and are to be respected. Please accept my sincere congratulations on finding your mate, Alpha Xander. I hope we can put this whole incident behind us."

"Thank you, Alpha Phillip. I would like that. We have always had a good relationship with Dark Moon, and I would like that to continue." I replied, though I wasn't sure how the relationship would be once Luke took over as Alpha.

"Very good." Alpha Phillip replied. "Have a good day." The line disconnected.

"That went well." Dad said in an upbeat tone. "Thank you for handling this efficiently and calmly, Xander. You're going to be an excellent Alpha." He patted me on the back.

"Thanks, Dad." I smiled. "I've got to go find Wesley before we begin training."

Wesley was lounging out back by the pool.

"Working on your tan?" I teased.

"Hey, man. How are you?" He sat up quickly, instantly concerned.

"I'm fine, I'm fine. Sorry about last night, man. Seriously, I didn't mean to take my anger out on you." I felt so bad. "I was completely out of control."

"What happened, bro? I've never seen you like that." Wesley leaned forward. I sat down next to him.

"Apparently, Maxine's ex from the Academy showed up to the party." I began.

"Oh, yeah, Luke. Shit, is that who you hit? I didn't even realize it was him in all the chaos." Wesley said in surprise.

"Yeah, well, he was pawing at Maxine and trying to kiss her, but she was pushing him away." I explained.

"Woah, not cool. That doesn't sound like Luke, though. He's usually a really cool guy." I was getting annoyed that Wesley was defending this guy.

I huffed. "Well, he was acting like a real creep last night."

"Okay, okay, I can understand why you would punch the guy. But what the hell happened afterwards? Why were you going psycho?" He asked, puzzled.

"Well, I've been really possessive lately because... Maxine is my mate."

"Woah." Wesley ran his hands through his hair as he processed the information. "That's awesome, man! You and Max are perfect for each other. Congratulations!" He leaned over and gave me a huge hug.

"Thank you. But she doesn't know we're mates, yet. Her birthday is not for a few more days, so I think she is pretty confused right now." I felt a pang in my chest.

"Oh, right." Wesley nodded. "Well, now it makes sense how weird you've been around her lately. But bro, you've got nothing to worry about from me, she's like the best sister I could ask for."

"I know. I'm sorry. It's just the mate bond; it's been making me a bit... crazy. Are we okay?" I asked.

"Of course! No worries, man." He gave me another hug.

CHAPTER SIXTEEN

Maxine

I finished working out and running with the girls. I took a shower and got dressed in some black jean shorts and a blue tank top. I slipped on a pair of low top chucks and left my hair down.

I was feeling really nervous and anxious. It had been hours since I saw Xander. I was beginning to miss him whenever he wasn't around. Was this the pull Jazzy was talking about? Is Xander my mate? Onyx howled in my head.

Goddess, I hoped that meant yes.

I was unsure of when we would be able to talk. But I was hoping to see him soon.

I wandered around the main floor of the packhouse and slowly made my way outside. Without thinking, I started down the path to Plum Creek. It was so peaceful there. I would often go there to think or study when I was younger. There was a beautiful gazebo right by the water that had a gorgeous view.

I sat in the gazebo, soaking in the sounds of the creek. I inhaled deeply and sighed. I missed this place.

I decided it was time. I had been putting it off all day, but I needed to call Luke. I was upset with him, and we may not be dating anymore, but he was still my friend.

I took out my phone, found his number in my contacts and pressed the call button. It rang a few times before the line picked up.

"Yeah, whatever." I could hear him say to someone in the background before he spoke into the receiver.

"Hello?" He sounded angry.

"Hey, Luke." I answered quietly.

"Max?" His tone changed immediately. "Are you alright?"

"Yeah, I'm good." I replied. "How's your jaw?" I asked carefully.

"It's fine. I think my ego was hurt more than anything." He joked. There was a pause and then he huffed. "Listen, Max, I'm really sorry about last night. I know you said you needed time, and I wasn't respectful of that. I honestly don't know what came over me. I just needed to be close to you. I miss you, Max."

He sounded so sincere and remorseful.

"I miss you too, Luke." I really did miss my friend. "But… not in the same way." I added hesitantly.

"Max, who is that guy to you?" There was something weird in his voice.

"Xander is one of my closest friends and my Alpha." I replied simply.

"Do you have feelings for him?" He asked me flat out. There was an edge to his voice. He sounded a little angry and hurt at the same time.

"It's really complicated…" I started.

"It's an easy question, Max." He responded quickly, sounding irritated. Then he sighed. "I'm sorry, it's not my business anymore." He sounded defeated. "I just want you to be happy."

My heart ached. "I know. I want you to be happy too, Luke."

"I gotta go, Max." There wasn't much left to say. "Just promise me you'll take care of yourself. I mean, I know you can kick anyone's ass, but protect your heart too."

"You don't have to worry about me, Luke." I reassured him.

"I know." He replied quickly. "But I will. Bye, Max."

"Bye, Luke." I replied before he disconnected the call.

I let out a big sigh and placed my head in my hands with my elbows resting on my knees.

That's when I felt his presence behind me. I just knew it was Xander without even looking. I stood up and spun around to face him.

He was leaning against a tree looking like utter perfection. Goddess, did he have to be so gorgeous? I wondered how long he had been standing there.

He pushed off of the tree and strolled this way. When he reached the gazebo, instead of walking around to the opening, he easily hopped the railing.

"Hey, Maxine." He greeted me with an alluring smile.

"Hi." I replied as I leaned back against the railing. "How's your day?" I asked, not really knowing what to say.

"Pretty busy." He responded, leaning against the railing opposite from me. Even from this distance, his scent was driving me wild. "I'm sorry it took me so long, I know you must be confused about last night." He was studying me, like he was trying to read my thoughts.

"It was definitely a very... *intense* night." I replied. His eyes darkened hungrily, and I could feel my face flush.

"Indeed, it was." His voice was smooth like silk.

I stared down at my hands. "Xander, what happened to you?" I brought my eyes back up to his face, searching for answers. "Why did you lose control like that?"

Xander held my gaze and answered directly. "I feel very protective over you, Maxine. I didn't like the way that wolf was touching you."

"Why?" I whispered.

"I don't think you liked it either, judging by the way you were pushing him." He stated.

"No, why do you feel protective of me?" I clarified.

"Before I answer that, let me ask you something." He countered thoughtfully. "How do you feel about me?"

My face grew warm and my heart hammered in my chest. "I care about you a lot, Xander. You're one of my best friends."

"And?" He pressed. "How do you feel when you're near me?"

"Nervous." I let out a small laugh. "And excited."

"Is that all?" He asked with a gleam in his eye. He slowly stood upright and strode towards me. "Because when I'm near you, I feel like I can hardly breathe. All of my senses are dialed in to you; the intoxicating way you smell, your angelic voice, I can't tear my eyes away from you." He explained. He was standing so close to me now, my heart was racing.

"Maxine, do you feel it too?" He whispered. His lips were so close to mine I could almost taste them. I couldn't speak. I silently nodded my head, staring into his extraordinary green eyes.

He slipped his hand up my neck, behind my head. I closed my eyes and whispered, "Xander, are you my ma–"

Howling broke out near the north border. Xander and I both snapped our heads in that direction.

"It's the Sentinels." I recognized their warning call. The Sentinels are our pack's border patrol warriors.

"Rogues." Xander growled and we both took off running towards the northern border.

CHAPTER SEVENTEEN

Xander

As soon as I heard the howling, I received a mindlink from the Sentinel leader. *Alpha, rogues are attacking the north border. There appears to be about 30 of them.*

I'm on my way. I replied. "Rogues." I growled out to Maxine.

Without hesitation we sprinted towards the border. I quickly mindlinked my men and they confirmed that they were on their way too.

"Maxine, you should go to the packhouse." I pleaded. I didn't want anything to happen to her.

"No. I can fight." She stated firmly. Of course she can, but I don't want her to be in danger.

"It's safer–" I argued.

"Don't. You know I can take care of myself." She countered. Ugh! She was right, she was top of her class, and she practically kicked my ass. We didn't have time to argue. I nodded my head, and we shifted into our wolves, tearing through our clothes.

Maxine's wolf was amazing. Her pure black coat shimmered in the sunlight. I had seen Onyx before, but what was truly astonishing was her size. She was much larger than she had been two years ago. Her wolf was too big for a shewolf, even one of Beta blood. Her stature was that of an Alpha, almost as large as Zeus. I had to push the thought aside, my focus needed to be on protecting our borders.

We ran full out, I was impressed that Onyx easily kept up with Zeus' speed. We made it to the border before reinforcements arrived.

My Sentinels were doing their best to hold them off, but they were outnumbered. I threw my head back and howled, letting the rogues know the Alpha had arrived.

Their focus shifted and they charged toward me. The first rogue to make it to me snarled as he leapt through the air. I caught his neck in my jaws and shook hard. I felt him go limp and slung him to the side.

I heard more howls as my unit joined the fight, springing into action.

Two wolves lunged toward me, and I rolled out of the way, vaulting back to my feet. One of them circled me, so I couldn't see them both at the same time. They both jumped forward, I turned to my right and latched my teeth around the rogue's front leg and hurled him into the other rogue on my left. His leg snapped. Good, now I could focus on the second rogue who stumbled back to his feet.

The rogue bared his teeth and dove towards me, but I swatted his snout with my claws. He yiped and before he could regain his stance, I pounced on his back. He twisted and bucked but couldn't shake me. I ripped a chunk from his neck, and he fell, lifeless to the ground.

I didn't bother finishing off the rogue with the broken leg. He just laid there helplessly.

I surveyed the scene, we were still outnumbered but my men appeared to be fighting them off. Where's Maxine? Panic ran throughout my body as I searched frantically. I spotted her wolf about 30 yards away. She was surrounded by three rogues, and two more were running straight for her.

They're targeting Maxine! I mindlinked my men. I dashed towards her.

She grabbed the nearest rogue by the neck and tossed him to the side. Another rogue launched himself onto her back. She shook violently and snapped her teeth into his flesh as she flung him forward.

Donovan's wolf, Eclipse, bulldozed through two of the wolves that were about to attack. He snarled viciously, before tearing through a rogue's side with his claws. He grabbed the other rogue with his jaws and snapped his neck.

Timber and Blitz, Heath and Wiley's wolves, were fighting side by side, protecting Onyx on her left flank.

I caught a rogue midair as he leapt towards Maxine. He was dead in an instant.

Onyx let out a painful howl as a rogue sunk his teeth into her shoulder. She clamped her jaws around his leg and forced him into a roll, pinning him to the ground. She bit down viciously and tore out his throat; his body fell limp.

The surviving, uninjured rogues retreated and took off beyond our borders. I glanced around to make sure no rogues remained.

I looked back towards Onyx. She stood up from her last kill and took a step before stumbling to the ground. I rushed to her side. *Xander*, she called weakly in my mind before she lost consciousness.

Her body shifted back into her human form, indicating she was seriously injured. I shifted back and checked her pulse. It was low. She was covered in blood, so I couldn't see the extent of her wound.

"Donovan!" I yelled out. "Link the hospital. Let them know we have a serious injury coming in." I ordered as I scooped Maxine into my arms. Donovan nodded and his eyes glossed over. Everyone had shifted back.

"Heath, take any surviving rogues to the prison." I demanded as I rushed towards the pack hospital. "Wiley, see that our men get medical treatment." I called over my shoulder.

I ran as fast as I could. Donovan was right behind me.

We made it to the hospital as doctors rushed to meet us with a gurney. I gently laid Maxine's body down. "I don't know what's wrong." I explained. "She was bit on the shoulder, but I think it's more than that. She should be healing by now." I explained. There was so much blood. Her wounds weren't closing; werewolves have the ability to heal from bites like this almost instantly.

There were several doctors and nurses working on her at once. Two were checking her vitals, another inspecting her wounds, and one drawing blood. "Get this tested for poisons immediately," the doctor demanded as she handed the vials to a nurse.

"We need to get her to an OR right now." Called out the doctor that was inspecting her wounds.

They began to wheel her away and I growled, unable to let go of her hand that I had been grasping.

"Alpha, we have to take her now." The doctor said firmly.

"Xander." Donovan placed his hand on my shoulder. "They'll take care of her. Trust them." He gently pulled me away from Maxine.

I reluctantly let go and they raced her away.

"By the looks of it, I suspected the bite was laced with wolfsbane." A doctor informed us. "We will inject her with an antidote and close up her wounds until she is able to heal on her own." I nodded my head at her, unable to speak. She quickly disappeared behind the doors they had taken Maxine through.

"Fuck!" I yelled as I paced the lobby. I ran my hands through my hair. "I should have protected her." I gritted out.

"Maxine is tough. She's a fighter." Donovan reminded me. He sounded scared though as he stared at the door she had gone through. He stared at me, "She's gonna be ok." He choked out.

A nurse came over with two pairs of folded sweatpants. "Alpha. Beta." She bowed, averting her gaze away from me and Donovan. That is when I realized we were still naked from the shift.

"Thank you." I grabbed the pants and tossed a pair to Donovan. We pulled them on and I continued pacing. Donovan stood like a statue with his arms crossed, staring at the door.

It seemed like they had been working on Maxine forever, the wait was agonizing.

"Donovan!" Arielle shrieked as the doors to the hospital slid open. She ran to him, inspecting his body. "Oh Goddess, are you okay?"

"I'm fine." He huffed out, pulling her into his arms tenderly.

Ivy and Jasmine entered the hospital behind Arielle.

"We came as soon as we heard. Is Max alright?" Ivy asked.

I shook my head. "I don't know." I replied helplessly.

"Oh my Goddess, is that her blood?" Jasmine gasped, horrified.

I peered down and realized that my chest and arms were smeared in Maxine's blood. My insides twisted as I gave a small nod.

"Oh, shit." Ivy breathed out.

Wiley and Heath came running through the doors. They were covered in dirt and specks of blood too but had managed to throw on some gym shorts.

"How is she?" Heath asked as he surveyed the state of the room.

"They don't know." Ivy answered as she leaned into his chest.

Wiley was staring at my bloody chest as he gave me an update. "The medics arrived to check on the wounded warriors. There were no casualties on our side, with minor injuries." He paused. "Aside from..." He trailed off, not wanting to say it. Jasmine wrapped her arms around Wiley and buried her face in his neck.

I began pacing again, unable to bear this wait.

"Xander, we captured three injured rogues." Heath reported. "They are being guarded in the prison, ready for interrogation." He hesitated before continuing. "We found capsules hidden in their mouths. I sent them off to be analyzed at the north lab. I told them to put a rush on it and send their findings to the hospital ASAP." I nodded in acknowledgement. "It appears as though they are lacing their bites with poison. Possibly wolfsbane." Heath added grimly.

I growled out of frustration.

How the fuck do rogues have access to wolfsbane capsules?

A different doctor came out and addressed me. "Alpha, she is stable." I let out a sigh of relief. "She's still unconscious and likely will be for a few days." He informed me. "She lost quite a bit of blood, and her healing has been stopped with what appears to be wolfsbane. We'll know more once the tests come back, but we've already started her on an antidote drip."

"Can I see her?" My voice wavered.

"Yes. Follow me." He led me through the doors and down a corridor to a private room.

Machines beeped and whirred as I approached her bed. She looked so small lying there. I tucked a strand of her hair behind her ear and kissed her forehead.

Just then, Beta Charlie burst into the room. He glanced at Donovan, who apparently had followed me and was standing just inside the room the whole time. "Is she alright?" He croaked out.

"She's going to be." Donovan stated firmly, but I haven't seen him so worried before. Beta Charlie approached the other side of her bed. "They think she was poisoned with wolfsbane." Donovan added and I heard his voice crack.

"Oh Goddess, Maxine." Her father breathed out, and he collapsed to his knees. He grabbed her hand and kissed it. "Come on, baby girl. Be strong." He had tears in his eyes as he pleaded with her.

"Daddy!" Sabrina cried out as she ran into the room. She threw her arms around him and cried into his shoulder. Everyone from the lobby, along with Wesley, had followed Sabrina into the room.

No one said a word. We all just watched Maxine, hoping that she would miraculously open her beautiful, blue eyes.

The doctor returned with a file in his hands, surprised to see the room was crowded with people.

"I'm sorry, you can't all be in here." He stated.

"Any update, Doctor?" Donovan urged.

"Yes, the test results came back and there were high levels of wolfsbane in her bloodstream." Some of the girls gasped, while a few of the guys cursed under their breath. "We're doing everything we can for her at the moment. She just needs time to heal." He peered around sternly. "And I must insist that everyone who isn't family wait in the lobby."

The others filed out of the room, but I didn't move a muscle. "I'm sorry, Alpha. That means you, too." The doctor gave me a firm stare.

"It's alright." Beta Charlie told the doctor and looked me in the eyes. "He's her mate."

CHAPTER EIGHTEEN

Maxine

There was a throbbing in my head that was excruciating, and it felt like there was fire in my veins. I couldn't seem to open my eyes or move my body, no matter how hard I tried. But I felt a stabbing pain in my left shoulder. I heard beeping and buzzing sounds. Then I noticed hushed voices that were slowly becoming clearer.

I focused my concentration on the voices.

"--tests look good. It appears to be completely out of her bloodstream." An unfamiliar voice was talking. "Now, we just have to wait for her body to heal itself." Is he talking about me?

"How long do you think that will be?" I recognized Donovan's calm voice.

"Hard to say. It could be hours, but more likely a few days. It really depends on her wolf." The voice replied.

My wolf. Onyx. I could feel Onyx, but she whimpered in my head as another pain shot through my shoulder blade.

"Thank you, Doctor." My dad's voice sounded full of worry. I wanted to comfort him. He's been through enough stress in his lifetime.

Ugh! Why can't I move my body? Then, I remembered the rogue attack. There were so many of them, they kept coming at me two and three at a time. I had managed to hold them off, but then I felt a searing pain in my shoulder. I had killed that rogue too. But this burning fire spread throughout my body. I tried to get up but my legs were weak. The last thing I remember was a pair of dismayed, green eyes.

Xander.

His eyes were terrified and helpless as my vision faded to black.

The voices continued talking quietly. "You really should go get some sleep at home." Donovan urged.

"I'm fine." Replied the most melodic voice I have ever heard. "I can't leave her." Someone took my hand in theirs. Warm tingles instantly spread from my hand. "I need to be by her side." He added and I felt a kiss on my hand. There was another wave of tingles that spread throughout my body.

"Xander." I managed to murmur as I fluttered my eyes open.

"Maxine?" Xander replied, his voice full of hope.

"Xander." I mumbled again. My vision focused in and out, as I peered into his emerald eyes before the darkness took over again.

I don't know how long I was lost in the darkness before a warm light filled my senses. The light faded to reveal a moonlit beach. I could feel the sand underneath my toes. Waves were crashing and breaking on the shore. The salt air mixed with a summer breeze. It was so peaceful.

I gazed out at the horizon and a small glowing light drifted down from the moon. It appeared to be growing larger as if it were approaching me. I wasn't scared. This light felt like home and caused a warmth to fill my chest.

The glowing orb paused just in front of me and gradually revealed the figure of a woman. The light faded as if it was slowly seeping back into the woman.

She was stunning. With long, flowing, white hair and luminescent, silver eyes, she stepped down from the sky onto the soft sand with her bare feet. She wore a white silk dress that cascaded to the ground and was iridescent as she moved.

I knew who she was in my heart.

"Selene" I whispered and bowed my head to the Moon Goddess.

"Come, my child, there is no need for that." Her voice was like music.

"I don't understand." I was puzzled. "Am I dead?"

"No, Maxine. It is my hope that you still have a lot of life to live." She smiled sweetly and a sense of calm washed over me.

"But I must warn you, Maxine, you are not an ordinary wolf. Others will continue to come for you; they seek to destroy you. You must be very careful." She added solemnly.

"What do you mean?" I didn't understand.

"You are no Beta wolf, Alpha blood runs through your veins." I gasped. "You are also a Midnight Wolf."

"A Midnight Wolf?" I'd never heard of such a wolf before.

"Midnight Wolves are my direct descendants. Your mother was a Midnight Wolf." She explained.

"My mother?" I felt overwhelmed.

"You have much to learn about your lineage but now is not the time. You are not ready yet. Soon though, you will have answers. You must stay vigilant; I cannot bear to lose another one of my children at the hands of those foul creatures. Losing your mother was devastating." She was calm but there was anger in her voice.

"Are you saying my mother was murdered? By who?" Tears stung my eyes.

"Demons of the Night. Vampires." Selene stated. "They want to end the Midnight Wolves, but it is imperative that they do not succeed." Selene urged.

"But–"

"That is all I can tell you now, my child." Selene began to glow again. "Take care of yourself, Maxine." Her voice rang out as the light grew brighter until she vanished.

I gasped and opened my eyes.

CHAPTER NINETEEN

Xander

It had been two days since the rogue attack. Maxine woke up yesterday for a brief moment. The doctors were still confused as to what happened. They don't understand how she had awakened and was able to speak.

But it was my name she had called out. My heart ached to hear her voice again, to see those stunning blue eyes open once more.

I had barely left her side since we arrived at the hospital. Donovan had forced me to clean up at some point. He said Maxine didn't need to wake up to see me covered in her own blood.

Before I cleaned up, I decided to pay a visit to the pack prison. I left Wesley with Beta Charlie to watch over Maxine. I told him to mindlink me immediately if anything changed.

I walked into the prison with Donovan by my side, followed by Heath and Wiley. I channeled all of my worry for Maxine into anger, and I was seething. My men had captured three rogues and placed them in adjacent cells. Two on one side and one on the other side of the corridor. Each rogue was chained to a chair in the center of their cell.

Our prison was clean and bright. Not like those dark, dank dungeons other packs used. We kept it well lit, to prevent our prisoners from getting enough rest. The walls and floor were sealed concrete, and every other surface was stainless steel. It made each cell easy to hose down and disinfect.

"Talk." I demanded outside their cells. No one said a word.

I slammed my hand against the bars of the closest cell, one of the rogues jumped in fear. "You see this?" I referenced the blood smeared across my chest and arms. "I'm covered in my *mate's* blood because of you." I snarled. "Unless you want me to be covered in *your* blood, I suggest you talk."

One of the rogues spat on the floor and glared at me. "You'll do." I said in a sinister voice. Heath opened the cell without a word. I stepped in, eyes locked on the scum before me. I held out my hand and Wiley placed a knife with a silver blade in my palm. The rogue's eyes jumped to the knife and then back to my face.

"Go to hell." He sneered. I dragged the blade deep across his chest and he let out a guttural yell. Silver burns a werewolf's skin and interferes with their ability to heal.

"Why did you cross into my territory?" I drilled.

"Fuck you." He said between clenched teeth.

I growled, then flipped the knife in my hand before I jabbed the blade straight into his thigh and left it there. He roared in pain. I silently held out my hand again, never taking my eyes off of the garbage in front of me. Wiley placed another silver-bladed knife in my hand. I stabbed it into his other thigh. He screamed in agony.

"I'll come back to you." I said and turned to exit his cell as he panted heavily, trying to breathe through his pain.

I faced the other two rogues. "Why did the rogues cross into my territory?" I repeated in a chilling voice.

"We were paid to." One of the rogues answered right away.

"Shut the fuck up, you coward." The other rogue hissed out. I snapped my head in his direction. I had more anger raging inside of me.

"Why were the rogues only targeting one wolf?" I asked as I entered his cell. I could see fear in his eyes, but he held a false bravado.

The other rogue called out, "We were paid to attack the large, black shewolf. They want her dead." I locked eyes with Donovan, who appeared about as pissed as I felt. They were paid to kill Maxine?

"I hope she's dead." The rogue in front of me spat out. Fury rose within me and I lost it. I punched him over and over. I hit him in the face and torso. Blood burst from his nose and lip. I heard his ribs crack as he gasped and wheezed in pain. I stopped and stepped back. He spat out blood and a tooth.

"Is that all you've got, Alpha?" The rogue slurred out through a swollen, bloody face.

"No, but my Beta would like a turn, seeing how that wolf is also his sister." The rogue's eyes darted to Donovan. Donovan moved in and cracked his knuckles before he slammed his fist into the rogue's face over and over. The rogue's head snapped back until Donovan was finished and it flopped down on his chest.

I focused on the rogue who was actually giving up information.

"Who paid you?" I snarled, losing any patience I had.

"Please, they'll kill me if they find out I talked." He begged.

"I'll kill you if you don't talk." I threatened.

"It doesn't matter; they're going to kill you all anyway." The wolf with the knives in his legs mumbled and then choked out a laugh.

I spun to face him. He continued to laugh maniacally. I reentered his cell and snatched a knife from his leg. The wound started pouring blood and he yelled out in agony. "I hope this is slow and painful for you." I hissed. He growled at me as I thrust the knife into his ribs. He couched and sputtered out blood.

I took a step back and watched the panic in his eyes as he realized his wolf wouldn't be able to heal him. He gasped and gurgled, choking up blood as it filled his lungs.

I turned back to the last rogue. "Who paid you?" I roared.

"Vampires." He cried out. "It was vampires. They want the large, black shewolf dead."

"Why?" I asked through clenched teeth.

"I don't know. I swear, I don't know." He insisted. "But their leader's name... Their leader's name is Massimo. Massimo Zanzara."

I let out a loud growl and left the prison. I took a hot shower and rushed back to the hospital.

I hadn't left her room since. My dad came and told me not to worry about pack business; everything would be covered. He said to just focus on my mate. When my mom came by, she didn't ask questions, she just forced me to eat every now and then.

I slept on the small couch when I absolutely needed to. Otherwise, I was planted in the chair beside Maxine's bed.

Her dad never tried to push me to leave. He just watched me with knowing eyes. He understands what I'm going through better than anyone else could. But I knew that Maxine would pull through.

It had surprised me that Beta Charlie knew I was Maxine's mate. When Dad came by, I asked him if he told him. He said that he didn't tell anyone, not even Mom.

Beta Charlie silently observed as I cared for Maxine. He prayed to the Moon Goddess regularly, pleading with her to let Maxine come back to us.

Donovan was really quiet. He'd stand like a guard and watch Maxine like a hawk, searching for any sign that she might wake up. He would stay for several hours before he had to leave, he needed Arielle to keep him sane.

Sabrina couldn't keep from crying whenever she was here. It was clear that she was terrified of losing Maxine, too.

Jasmine and Ivy were doing their best to take care of her while Charlie was at the hospital most of the time.

Maxine’s vitals were strong, and her wound was almost completely healed. The doctors said it was a really good sign. It meant her wolf was healthy and strong. We just had to give it time. She would wake up when she was ready.

As I sat and watched Maxine’s motionless body, I was so disappointed in myself for not protecting her.

I sighed out loud, "I should have gotten to her sooner.” I relived the attack for the millionth time.

"There’s nothing you could have done, Xander.” Donovan stated again, "We were all right there, fighting off the rogues. Maxine was the top of her class for a reason. She’s a badass. It's not like this was something that anyone could have seen coming. Rogues with wolfsbane laced bites, it's unheard of.”

"I shouldn’t have let her fight.” I countered. "I should have demanded that she go back to the packhouse.”

"I wouldn’t have listened.” Her angelic voice rang out.

My head snapped to her face and those electric blue eyes were gleaming back at me.

CHAPTER TWENTY

Maxine

My eyes opened.

I heard voices around me as I adjusted to the harsh lights. It took a minute for my senses to snap back. I heard Xander and Donovan talking in hushed voices. I noticed my dad was sleeping on a small couch.

"I shouldn't have let her fight." Xander was beating himself up. "I should have demanded that she go back to the packhouse."

"I wouldn't have listened." I countered; my voice was raspy.

Xander and Donovan nearly got whiplash with how quickly their heads turned my way.

"Oh, thank the Goddess, you're awake." Xander kissed my hand, and I felt a warm hum on my skin that spread up my arm.

"Max! I've never been so scared in my life." Donovan said as he leaned forward and kissed my forehead. Then, he rushed over to wake up Dad.

"Please don't ever do that again." Xander pleaded with me, his eyes were full of fear and relief all at the same time.

"I don't really plan on it." I smiled. My throat was so dry, it was hard to swallow.

"Max?" My dad cried out as he scrambled off of the couch towards the bed. "Oh Goddess, baby girl, you scared the hell out of me!"

"I'm sorry, Dad." I croaked.

"Here, take a sip." Xander held up a cup of water with a straw for me. "I just mindlinked the doctor."

After lots of tests and exams, and arguing on my part, the doctor told me that I could go home tomorrow. I really wanted to get out of this bed now though. But no one was on my side this time. They all agreed with the doctors that I should stay for observations.

Apparently, I had been out for two whole days. Which meant, my birthday was the day after I was to be released.

They did let me get up and shower on my own. While I was in the bathroom, I heard my dad insist that Xander go home.

"Now that Maxine is awake, I think it is best if you went home. Get some rest, clean up. You can see her again tomorrow." My dad was kind but firm in his tone. Had Xander been here the entire time?

I inspected my shoulder in the mirror. The wound from the bite was mostly healed. It was slightly pink, like a fading scar.

When I finished with my shower, Xander was gone, and Sabby was waiting in my room. She practically tackled me with a massive hug when she saw me. "Hey, hey, it's alright. I'm fine." I soothed her as she sobbed into my shoulder.

"I was so scared, Max." She gripped me tightly. "Please don't leave me. Please." She begged.

"Hey, nothing's going to happen to me, kid." I replied lightheartedly.

The rest of the day was just us Coopers; my dad, Donovan, Sabrina, and I. We talked and laughed, played cards, and Sabby passed out snuggled next to me in my bed as we watched some movies.

I kicked Donovan out to go be with his mate. I began dozing off, so Dad covered me and Sabby with a blanket and kissed my forehead. "Good night, honey." He whispered before squeezing himself onto the little couch to sleep.

The next morning, I was eager to get going. I felt great and ready to get out of this room. I waited impatiently for the doctors to come check me out and sign off on my discharge.

Onyx was back to her normal self and very anxious to get outside.

The doctors told me that there wasn't really any reason why I couldn't resume my usual activities. But they cautioned me to take it easy and to come straight back if anything felt off. I thanked them profusely for saving my life.

As I walked out into the lobby with my dad and Sabby, Xander was standing there with his hands in his jean pockets. He looked so hunky, Onyx perked up and wagged her tail in my mind. Donovan and Ari were waiting with him.

"Max!" Ari squealed as she rushed forward to crush me in a hug. "You have no idea how badly you scared us all, girl!"

"Easy, Arielle, you don't want to send her back into the hospital." My dad chuckled.

"Right, sorry." Ari loosened her grip but didn't let go of me. She pulled back with a smile and watery eyes. "It's good to have you back."

"Thanks, it's good to be back." I agreed. "Now, can we please get the hell out of here?"

We laughed as we walked out of the hospital. Ari and I had our arms around each other's waists. "Goddess, I hope I don't have to come back here for a really long time." I expressed.

"That would be ideal." Donovan agreed.

"Sabby and I are going to drive back to the packhouse, I've got some things I need to take care of." Dad stated. "Do you want a lift?"

"No thanks, Dad. After being stuck in that bed, I really just want to walk. I need fresh air and sunshine." I replied.

"Ok, just don't overdo it." He kissed me on the forehead before heading to his car. "Keep an eye on her." He instructed Donovan.

Or, at least, I thought he was talking to Donovan, but Xander gave him a firm nod. "Yes, sir."

I sent a puzzled look to Ari, and she bounced her eyebrows at me. I just rolled my eyes.

"Okay, so, your party is on for tonight. I was thinking the girls could come get ready in your room around 7 or maybe 8." Ari talked excitedly.

"Wait, we're still having my party?" I asked.

"Dad cleared it with the doctors." Donovan informed me. "As long as you're up to it."

"Yeah, that sounds like fun and I think we all need some fun right now." I was a bit excited.

"Yes!" Ari cheered. "Let's just hope this party turns out better than the last one."

I gave her a little nudge. "Ari!"

"What? I'm just saying." She shrugged.

I stole a glance at Xander who was being really quiet. He was staring at the ground with a grin on his face. Donovan nudged him and they smiled at each other. Hmm... I wonder what that was about.

"Okay, anyway..." Ari continued, "We don't need to come over until late, because the party won't start until 10, since you don't turn 18 until midnight. But I think the girls will want to spend some time with you, so do you think 7 or 8 would be better?"

Midnight. All of a sudden, my encounter with the Moon Goddess came flooding back to me. I was a Midnight Wolf.

"Max? What's wrong?" Ari asked me.

I was so lost in thought, I had stopped walking and listening.

"Max? Are you hurt?" Donovan asked, but it didn't register. I was trying to recall every detail Selene had told me.

"Maxine." Xander called me as he gently placed a hand on the side of my face. My eyes focused on his eyes, full of concern.

"Xander." I breathe out.

"Hey." He said tenderly with that gorgeous, crooked smile. "Where'd you go? You looked like you were a million miles away."

"Sorry, there's just a lot going on." I shook my head. "If you don't mind, I'd like to go down to Plum Creek." I said to everyone.

"Yeah, we can head that way." Donovan agreed.

"Actually, I'd like to go alone." I clarified.

Donovan and Xander stared at each other, clearly mindlinking.

"I don't think that's a good idea." Donovan stated firmly.

"Sorry, I wasn't asking for permission." I crossed my arms. They were mindlinking again. I rolled my eyes. "Look, I'll text you every 20 minutes to let you know I'm alright. Okay?"

Donovan glanced at Xander again. "I'll be fine. Promise."

"Fine. But I want you to text me every 10 minutes, and if I don't hear from you, I'm bringing a team to come get you and drag you home if need be." Donovan said.

I laughed and shook my head. "Jeez, overprotective much?" I stood on my tiptoes to kiss Donovan on the cheek. "I'll see you later. Ari, 7 sounds good." I peered up at Xander who had a strained look on his face. "See you tonight?"

"I wouldn't miss it for the world." He gave me a wink that made me melt.

I turned down the familiar path. I could feel their eyes watching me as I disappeared into the woods.

Sitting in my favorite gazebo, I was at peace surrounded by nature. It was a much-welcomed change from the walls of my hospital room. Every 10 minutes, I texted Donovan a thumbs up emoji.

My mind wandered back to what the Moon Goddess had told me. How did I not know about Midnight Wolves? And that I am one, apparently. And an Alpha? How could dad keep this from me? Does Donovan know?

The Moon Goddess had mentioned vampires, too. Vampires wanted to destroy the Midnight Wolves? They want to kill me?

I know there is more than she is telling me, but she said I wasn’t ready. When would I be ready? Soon I would have the answers, she said. Soon I will be 18, maybe it has something to do with my birthday.

I’m just hours away from turning 18. My heart fluttered at the thought. I hope I find my mate tonight.

My mind wandered to Xander. Is he my mate? The idea makes my heart skip a beat. I hope he is; he makes me feel things I've never felt before.

I thought back to the last time I was in this gazebo, with Xander. The things he said to me came rushing back. I got goosebumps thinking about it. He has to be my mate; everything just feels so right with him.

"Maxine?" Speaking of the handsome devil, Xander came sprinting down the path and leapt over the gazebo railing. He sounded panicked as he rushed towards me.

"Xander, what's wrong?" I asked, afraid there may have been another attack.

"Donovan said you stopped texting him and you weren't answering your phone. Are you okay?" He asked, full of worry as his eyes scanned me for signs of injury.

Shit. I had set my phone down on the bench as I was pacing the gazebo, lost in thought.

"Oh Goddess, sorry! Yeah, I'm fine. Just a bit distracted." I replied and pointed towards my phone on the bench. "I set it down and--"

Just then, the entire Alpha unit came running down the path scanning the area on high alert.

"She's fine." Xander called out.

"Ok, this is a bit much." I said with my hands on my hips. "Donovan, what is going on? This is extreme."

Xander and Donovan were mindlinking again.

"Stop it! Talk to me." I demanded. "Is something wrong?"

"She should know." Xander said out loud. Donovan nodded in agreement.

"Let's go back to the packhouse. We'll explain everything." Donovan replied.

CHAPTER TWENTY-ONE

Xander

Leaving Maxine had become increasingly difficult since she was brought to the hospital.

Beta Charlie had insisted that I go home after she woke up. I think he didn't want to overwhelm her; in case she was beginning to feel the mate bond.

I had a lot of things to take care of. The information the rogue had given me filled me with anger and fear. I couldn't let anyone hurt my mate. I had already failed her once.

I filled my dad in on all that the rogue told us. We disposed of the dead rogues, burning their bodies. I sent my best trackers out to find the rogues that retreated from our borders. The trail led to a river, where they lost the scent.

I had been researching vampires and digging for any records on Massimo Zanzara. So far, I haven't found much of anything that would be useful.

Vampires were vile creatures. We call them Demons of the Night. They aren't anything like the ones depicted in those love stories, more like those out of horror films. For centuries, werewolves and vampires had fought each other. Humans also hunted vampires, because vampires would feed on the humans and slaughter entire villages. This dwindled the vampire population to near extinction. Werewolves have remained relatively hidden from humans. It is a werewolf law that no harm shall come to humans, unless the situation is life or death.

I needed to do whatever it took to keep Maxine safe.

Letting her go to Plum Creek alone had my wolf going crazy. I didn't want to leave her side, but I had to respect her need for space.

We were having a meeting to discuss steps we could take in trying to find these vampires, but I couldn't focus.

Every time Donovan checked his phone, my heart leapt into my throat. He would give me a small nod, indicating everything was alright. Time ticked by at an agonizing pace. It felt like forever since Donovan had received a text. I checked the clock, and it had been nearly 25 minutes since her last message.

"Donovan, have you heard from Maxine?" I interrupted whoever had been speaking at the moment.

He checked his phone again. "No." He replied grimly as he quickly dialed her phone. It rang and rang. My heart pounded, I quickly stood from my chair.

"Try her again." I urged as I tried to reach out through the mindlink. I was getting a block, which could mean a number of things.

"She's not picking up." Donovan declared, rising from his seat as well.

"Let's move." I demanded and sprinted out of the room. My team followed closely behind. However, once we were outside, I took off at full speed. My mind was racing with all kinds of terrible situations. Please be okay. I prayed as I ran down the path.

The gazebo came into view, and my heart skipped a beat. Maxine was pacing back and forth, lost in thought. "Maxine?" I called out to her.

I startled her and my panicked state put her on edge. Once I confirmed she was okay, I could breathe again.

Maxine was not happy when my whole team arrived, ready for a fight. She demanded answers. I knew that we had to tell her what was going on.

Back at the packhouse, we all settled into a conference room with my dad and Beta Charlie, too.

"Okay, someone want to tell me why everyone is freaking out?" Maxine demanded.

"Max, the rogues that attacked our pack were targeting you." Donovan cut to the point. There was no sense in beating around the bush.

"Me?" Maxine asked. At first, she appeared shocked, but then something registered on her face. "Do you know why?"

"We managed to capture a few of the rogues and interrogated them." I explained. "It seems they were paid to attack our pack... with the goal of killing you." I could feel a fury building inside me at the thought.

"Who paid them?" Maxine asked calmly. Too calmly for someone who had just found out there was a hit out on her. I exchanged glances with Donovan. He noticed it too.

"Vampires." I studied her face for any indication of surprise. There was none. She nodded her head slightly, deep in thought.

"Max?" Donovan pulled her out her thoughts.

"Can we have the room, please?" She addressed Heath and Wiley in a collected tone. "I'd like to speak privately with the Alphas and Betas."

They nodded and left.

"What is it, Max?" Donovan urged as soon as the door was closed. I noticed that Beta Charlie was really quiet in all of this.

She looked thoughtful, as if trying to choose her words carefully. Then she turned to her father. "Do they know the truth?" She asked him with a hint of anger and hurt in her voice. "Does Donovan know what he is?"

All eyes snapped to Beta Charlie, who looked as though he was bracing himself for a fight. He gave a slight shake of his head. "No, he doesn't know. No one knows the full truth." He explained. Donovan and I exchanged worried glances.

"Alpha Jackson knows that we are not Beta wolves, he knows the reasons why we had to keep it hidden. But–" Donovan cut him off.

"What do you mean we're not Beta wolves?" Donovan sounded pissed and confused.

"We are Alpha blooded." He stated firmly. Donovan raised his brows as he slowly sank back against his chair and placed a hand over his mouth.

"I was born an Alpha. Your mother was a special wolf. We had to keep her identity hidden to protect her from those who were searching for her. I left my pack and abandoned my title to protect her." Charlie explained. "Alpha Jackson and I had been best friends at the Academy. He offered me his Beta position, further concealing our identity."

Charlie glanced at my dad and gave him an appreciative nod.

"We lived hidden for many years, happy with the life we had built here in Silver Moon. But we let our guard down. Your mom was traveling back to her home pack to visit her mother. I wasn't able to join her, but I sent her with a warrior escort. Somehow, they found her." He choked out. Pain and regret filled his eyes.

"She was murdered." Maxine's small voice cried. She had tears streaming down her face. I reached over and held her hand in mine, rubbing circles over the back of her hand with my thumb.

This was a lot to process. But Maxine and Donovan being Alpha blooded wasn't difficult to believe. They were incredibly strong wolves.

"Why didn't you tell us?" Donovan didn't bother trying to hide the hurt in his voice.

"I thought I was doing the right thing, keeping Maxine safe. The less who know the truth, the less likely that the vampires find her." His father replied sadly.

"Max, how did you know?" Donovan asked, confused.

Everyone shifted their gaze to Maxine as she spoke, "The Moon Goddess told me."

CHAPTER TWENTY-TWO

"The Moon Goddess spoke to you?" Xander was surprised. His eyes were full of concern but also, he seemed a little awestruck.

"Yes, while I was unconscious in the hospital." I replied.

"What else did she tell you?" Dad asked eagerly.

I replayed her words in my head. "She told me I am an Alpha, and something called a Midnight Wolf. She said the vampires want to eliminate the Midnight Wolves, but it is important that they don't succeed. They are going to keep coming for me."

Xander let out a growl and squeezed my hand. Donovan slammed his fist on the table in anger. I eyed Xander closely, he seemed to be warring with himself, holding himself back.

"What is a Midnight Wolf? I've never heard of one. Did she say anything else?" Donovan questioned.

I shook my head. "I don't know. She said that's all she could tell me for now. And that I'm not ready to hear everything yet, but that I will have the answers soon."

Dad ran a hand down his face in distress.

"You know more about it though, don't you, Dad?" I knew he was keeping things from me. "Why is all of this happening?"

My dad sighed and shook his head. "If the Moon Goddess said you're not ready, then you must wait." He was clearly upset.

"If you know something that could help protect Maxine, you need to tell us." Xander demanded.

"Who am I to go against the Moon Goddess?" My dad countered. "Sometimes, you have to let fate play out. There is more to all of this, things that cannot be revealed until the time is right. I'm sorry." His eyes were pleading with me to trust him. And I did. He would never do anything that wasn't in his children's best interest. He continued, "I trust in Selene. Also, you have one advantage that we never had."

"What's that?" I asked, confused.

"A name." Dad said thoughtfully to Xander.

"Massimo Zanzara." Xander gritted his teeth in anger.

"Maybe instead of focusing on trying to keep Maxine hidden, we should work on finding these damn vampires before they find her." Dad suggested. "And end them."

"I will destroy them all." Xander swore under his breath with so much intensity. Are his eyes glowing?

Alpha Jackson cleared his throat, pulling everyone's attention to him. "I've put in some calls to a couple of my most trusted allies who might know more about this vampire." He informed us. "They have connections and may be able to help us pinpoint a location or give us any information that could help."

"In the meantime, Max should avoid shifting." Donovan added. "It is clear they were searching for her unique wolf. They may not know what she looks like, just Onyx. We don't want to make it any easier on them."

Onyx whined in my head. I didn't like the idea of not being able to shift either. I hope this isn't a long-term solution.

"Maybe we shouldn't be having a party tonight." I replied pensively.

"No." Dad said firmly. "The Moon Goddess has a plan for you. She gave you this warning so we can be cautious, not for you to stop living your life." There was something cryptic in what he was saying.

"We will place more Sentinels on the borders, until we have some answers." Alpha Jackson declared.

My head was swirling with questions. Why was all of this happening? I was lost deep in thought until a gentle voice pulled me back.

"Maxine? Are you okay?" Xander was still holding my hand. He brushed a strand of hair away from my face with his other and gave me a small smile.

"Yeah, it's just a lot. I think I'm going to lie down for a bit." I said as I stood up. Xander continued to grip my hand. He stared down at our hands as if he didn't want to let me go.

"I think that is an excellent idea." My dad said gently, but he was staring at Xander, silently telling him to let me leave.

Xander nodded his head and kissed my hand. It was sweet and comforted me somehow. I was already beginning to feel less anxious. I smiled at him before leaving.

I went upstairs to my room and flopped down on my bed. Thinking about everything left me feeling overwhelmed, so I did my best to shut it all out. I finally drifted off.

My sleep was uneasy. I tossed and turned, dreaming of rogues and vampires. I ran through the woods in wolf form, when something crashed into me. I was pinned to the ground, but I couldn't see anything. Suddenly, I was facing a pair of blood-red eyes.

I sat straight up in bed, panting hard. The dream had felt so real, it was unlike any I'd had before.

I checked at the time and decided to take a shower before the girls showed up.

If you ever need to forget about your worries, you should hang out with Ari. That girl can always pull me out of a funk. We spent the next couple of hours talking and laughing until it hurt.

My room was transformed into a full-fledged salon. Makeup, hairbrushes, curlers, flat irons, jewelry, shoes, and dresses were strewn about the room.

There are a few momentous occasions in a werewolf's life; gaining your wolf on your 16th birthday, turning 18 is a sort of 'coming of age' milestone, finding your mate, your mating ceremony, and of course, having your own pups.

To celebrate this milestone birthday, we were having a semi-formal soiree, so tonight, we're getting fancified.

Ari just finished doing my makeup and said, "Ta da! Still gorgeous!" My dress was a deep, navy blue, silk V-neck dress with an open back. You couldn't even see a mark on my shoulder from the attack anymore, it was fully healed. The bodice was fitted, and it cascaded down from my hips with a high slit on one side. I wore a dainty chain with a single diamond pendant that rested in the center of my chest. My hair was pulled back in a low, loosely braided bun, with little wisps of curls framing my face.

"Damn, ladies, we look fine as hell!" Ivy announced and we all giggled.

"Okay, I cannot wait to see how smokin' hot the boys look!" Jazzy added.

"Well, what are we waiting for? Let's go!" Ari enthused.

We shuffled out of my room, towards the door to our suite. "You go ahead, I'll be right there." I told them, spotting my dad standing in the living room in his suit.

I gave him a hug as the girls left. "You look absolutely beautiful, Maxine." My dad said, his eyes were shining with love.

"Thanks, Dad. You look dashing." I replied.

"Max, I want you to promise me that you will cherish every moment tonight. I want you to forget about what's going on, this is a momentous occasion for you. Just enjoy your night and soak it all in, you deserve it." His eyes were so proud with a gleam as if he knew something that I didn't.

"Okay, Dad, I promise." I replied.

"I'll see you out there. And save a dance for me." He added as he left the suite.

I took a moment to center my thoughts and clear my head of all the negativity. Then, I began the descent down to the main floor of the packhouse.

As I came to the final flight of stairs, I saw all the guys gushing over their mates. All except one, breathtakingly gorgeous man, standing alone, staring up at me.

CHAPTER TWENTY-THREE

Xander

The conversation this afternoon had left me feeling a mix of emotions. I'm pissed that these vampires are trying to kill my mate, confused about her being a Midnight Wolf, worried about her safety, annoyed that Beta Charlie knew more than he was willing to tell us, amazed at how incredible my mate is, and anxious for tonight.

With everything I know now, I didn't want to let Maxine out of my sight. Every second apart was excruciating to me. I needed to know she was safe. When she left, I was dying to follow her. Just to be near her.

But tonight is going to be a night that we will never forget, and I need her to be rested and relaxed so she can fully enjoy it. Tonight, I am going to claim my mate. Finally.

After Maxine left to rest, I went to work out. I needed to blow off some steam and get rid of this pent-up aggression that the vampires were causing. I lifted weights, worked the punching bag, and ran a few miles.

I was just heading back to the packhouse when I got this eerie feeling like I was being watched. Pretending to just be taking a sip of my water, I stopped to survey the area. I heard a twig snap to my left, causing me to turn my head. I dialed in on a bush and took a deep breath to see if I could catch a scent, when I was pummeled from above.

A body jumped from the tree above me and tackled me to the ground. The wind was knocked out of me and a pain shot through my back from them landing on me, but I scrambled to my feet quickly. Growling, I spun around to face my attacker, ready for a fight.

Blake lay on the ground holding his stomach as he laughed hysterically. "Oh Goddess. You should. Totally. See your face." He croaked out in between fits of laughter.

"Oh my Goddess, dude, what the fuck!" I growled and clutched my chest. My heart was hammering, and my nerves were shot.

"Oh man, we got him so good!" Calvin exclaimed as he crawled out from the bush. He high-fived Blake. "Alright, I gotta go before Heath finds the surprise I left for him." He said with a wicked grin before running off towards the packhouse.

Wincing from the pain in my back, I lowered myself to sit on the ground next to Blake who was still reveling in his triumph.

"You're a shithead, you know that?" I said as I poked Blake in his ticklish ribs.

"Hey, hey!" He squirmed away from me. "You gotta be more aware of your surroundings, Alpha." He teased and finally stopped laughing.

"Yeah, I've just got a lot on my mind." I ran my hands through my hair and sighed.

"You wanna talk about it?" Blake asked seriously.

"I'm just worried about Maxine." I answered honestly.

"Because of the attack? You know she's a badass though, those mangy mutts had to cheat to hurt her. She could kick anyone's ass." Blake sounded very fond of Maxine, but that wasn't surprising, she was loved by everyone.

"Yeah, well..." I trailed off, not knowing how to explain it. "Can you keep a secret?" I raised my brow at him, letting him know I was serious.

"Of course. I would never betray my Alpha's trust." He said with a grin.

I rolled my eyes. "Right, you'd prefer to try to kill him by dropping out of a tree onto his head."

"Hey now, I specifically aimed for your back and not your head!" Blake scoffed as if I was completely off base.

"Right." I laughed. "Anyway, this is a big deal, you can't go telling Calvin or Sabrina, especially Sabrina." I said with a pointed look, knowing how close they were.

"Alright, alright. I promise I won't tell." He sat up more, leaning closer to me.

"Maxine is my mate." I loved saying those words. I couldn't wait until everyone knew the truth, but she needed to turn 18 first.

"For real? That's amazing! Congrats, bro!" Blake threw his arm around me. "Tonight is a big night for you then. We gotta get you out of these dirty, sweaty clothes and make you presentable!" He hopped up and pulled me to my feet. He hyped me up the entire walk back to the packhouse. He was a great little wingman.

I met my men in the entryway on the main floor of the packhouse. We decided to gather here as we waited for the ladies to come down.

The guys were all dressed sharp in suits for Maxine's party. They cleaned up nicely. I was wearing a dark, navy-blue suit with a white dress shirt that I left unbuttoned a third of the way down.

"Big night, Xander." Wiley said with a wink. "You nervous, man?"

"Anxious, for sure." I replied. "I just can't wait to see her."

"And you called us lovesick puppies." Heath scoffed, "You should see your face right now."

"Just relax, man." Donovan chimed in. "This is going to be a night to remember."

Time crawled while we waited for the girls to come down. Then, I heard laughter as they approached the stairs. We all perked up and turned towards the stairs.

First, I saw Ivy and Sabrina walking down the stairs. Heath nearly had a heart attack when he saw Ivy in her tight, red dress, I thought he might mark her right then and there.

Jasmine and Arielle followed closely behind. "Wow" was all Donovan managed to say.

"Wow yourself." Arielle replied with a wicked grin.

Wiley took Jasmine's hand and spun her in a slow circle, appreciating every angle. "Damn, baby, you look amazing!"

"Thanks! You look smokin' hot, as always." She smirked as he pulled her in for a kiss.

Where is she? My wolf was beginning to pace in my head. I couldn't stand this wait.

"She'll be down soon." Arielle told me with a knowing smile on her face. I guess I have made it pretty obvious lately.

When Beta Charlie came down the stairs alone, I felt like I was going to explode. Where is she?

"Xander." Beta Charlie approached me, put his hand on my shoulder and shook my hand. "Cherish and protect her, and love her with all your heart and soul." He stared me straight in the eyes. There was love and firmness in his words, as if giving me friendly advice but also a stern warning.

"Yes, sir." I replied. "I swear to you, on my life." Then he pulled me in for a hug.

"Have fun, kids." He said to the rest of the group before he walked to the dining hall that my mom had transformed into a ballroom.

I'm sure it wasn't long, but seconds felt like hours at this point. Everyone around me was talking, flirting, laughing, and having a great time. But I was frozen in place, fixated on the top of the stairs.

When she appeared, it was like magic, I could breathe again. Everyone else faded into the background, there was only her.

She slowly made her way down the stairs. I took this time to appreciate how divine she looked. With every other step I got a flash of her delicious leg. Her hair was done up, exposing her slender neck. My wolf was howling at the sight. The dark blue color of her dress made her electric blue eyes stand out even more, and they were locked in on me.

As she reached the bottom of the stairs, I walked toward her.

I leaned forward and said in a low, husky voice, "Maxine, you are absolutely stunning." I felt her shiver. I placed a light kiss on her cheek before straightening up. I gently caressed her beautiful face.

"You look very handsome, Xander." She replied smoothly. There was a twinkle in her eyes. I couldn't tear myself away from them.

"Would you like an escort?" I asked as I offered her my arm.

"I'd like that very much." She slipped her hand in the crook of my arm.

"Yes! Let's party!" Arielle exclaimed as we all moved toward the hall that already had music playing.

As we stepped into the room, we stopped to take in the scene. Black and silver silk fabric had been draped down from the center of the ceiling to the walls and then cascaded down to the floor. It gave the room a softer feel. There were mirrored, north star shaped lanterns hanging here and there, casting shimmering lights around the room. Cocktail tables covered in black linens were scattered along the far side of the room. The French doors were open to the back patio where small tables and chairs were spread out. There was a bar inside and on the back patio.

It looked like we were the last ones to arrive, the room was bustling with conversations and people already dancing.

I turned to Maxine and just as I was about to speak, the music changed to a Dua Lipa song. Arielle squealed and grabbed Maxine, dragging her to the dance floor along with the other girls. "I love this song!"

Donovan chuckled at his energetic mate. "She never stops."

We all stood watching our beautiful women dancing and enjoying themselves. They were singing to each other and laughing while they swayed their hips and spun each other around.

"Do you think she knows?" Heath asked me. He tilted his head towards Maxine.

"She knows." I replied. "I know she feels it. She was about to ask me right before... before the rogue attack." I said gravely as I recalled what followed. I pushed those thoughts from my head. "I can't wait until midnight."

Wiley gave me a sly grin, "Look who's got it bad now!" He laughed and I shrugged. "No, seriously, I've had to put up with it from all of you for years, and now you all have it coming."

"Go for it." Donovan shrugged. "I honestly don't care, as long as I get to have her." He said dreamily watching Arielle as she bounded toward him singing.

She threw her arms around Donovan's neck and planted a big kiss on him. Then she grabbed his arm, "Let's go, Sugarboo!"

We were all cracking up as this large, strong man was dragged away by his tiny mate.

"That's it! I can't take it anymore." Heath growled out before thundering over to Ivy. He pulled her in tight as he buried his face in her neck.

Wiley grinned at me. "Gotta seize the moment." He said with a wink before he joined Jasmine on the dance floor.

I watched Maxine as she was lost in the music. She had her eyes closed as her hips swayed to the music with her arms above her head. It was like she was a magnet, pulling me in, my feet carried me to her without even realizing it.

The song changed to a slow one. I stood behind Maxine and slid my hands across the silky material on her waist. She leaned back into me and placed her hands on top of mine. Without opening her eyes, she sighed and said, "Xander."

I lowered my head to her neck and growled softly in her ear. She shivered in my arms as our hips slowly swayed to the music.

I flattened my palm against her tight abs, pressing her body into mine. I couldn't get her close enough. The lyrics to the song caught my attention. *What am I waiting for?*

I lifted my other hand, gently tilting her face towards my own over her shoulder and kissed her delicate lips. She melted into me, returning the sensual kiss. It was like fireworks.

We were lost in the moment together, everything and everyone else disappeared. Until we heard Arielle gasp, "Oh my Goddess!"

Our eyes flew open as we broke the kiss to find all of our friends gawking at us. The girls looked surprised but thrilled. Jasmine poked Arielle in the ribs and shushed her. Maxine blushed profusely.

Just then, the music faded out, and Beta Charlie cleared his throat from the stage. He was standing with my father, the rest of his unit, and their mates. Maxine took a small step to compose herself, standing to my right. As she distanced herself, my hand slid from her waist to the small of her back, resting there. I just had to be touching her.

CHAPTER TWENTY-FOUR

Maxine

Once the night started, I actually found it easy to block out the crazy vampire/rogue situation. I was instantly lost in Xander the moment I saw him.

The pull to him was magnetic. My wolf was acting like an excited pup. I couldn't wait until midnight. I just knew it had to be him.

Luna Clarissa did an amazing job on the party. Everything was so elegant. I can't believe she did all this for me. I had to be sure to thank her.

Ari's energy was infectious. She led me out to the dance floor with Ivy and Jazzy. I've always loved dancing with the girls, I felt so carefree. I remembered my dad's words and reveled in this moment with them, laughing and dancing.

"Xander can't keep his eyes off of you." Ivy pointed out. I stole a glance at him and sure enough he was watching me with a fire in his eyes that gave me butterflies. He looked incredible in his fitted suit that just happened to match my dress. He had left those top buttons of his dress shirt undone and it was so tempting. His auburn hair was pushed back; it was slightly messy and very sexy.

"That's it!" Ari exclaimed, "I need my man!" She ran over to Donovan and dragged his ass back out to the dance floor. We all laughed, but I did not want to watch my brother grind on his mate, so I closed my eyes and got lost in the music.

The music changed to a slow Ellie Goulding song. Two hands slip around my waist, pulling me back against a strong body. A warmth spread throughout me and I sighed. "Xander." He growled in my ear. It sent a tingle down my spine that caused me to shiver.

We slowly danced to the music. He pressed my back closer into his firm chest. I felt his hand caress my face and slowly turn my chin towards him. My lips met his as he kissed me tenderly over my shoulder. The kiss was all consuming, nothing else existed outside of us in this moment. It was just me and Xander in a passionate haze.

Until Ari yanked us out of our fog with a loud gasp. All eyes were watching us and my cheeks flushed. Oh Goddess.

Luckily, at that moment, my dad signaled for everyone's attention. He cleared his throat, "Good evening, Silver Moon." He began. "I'd like to thank you all for joining us this evening to celebrate my daughter's 18th birthday. I would also like to thank our Alpha and Luna for hosting such an elegant event. It means the world to me." He smiled at them.

"Now, we are approaching midnight, and before the evening gets away from us, please join me in wishing Maxine Cooper the happiest of birthdays!" Dad requested.

The room collectively cheered, "Happy birthday!" Followed by a howl.

My dad continued, "Maxine, happy birthday, honey. I am so proud of you, and I know your mother is with Selene watching you with a full heart tonight. Enjoy your night, sweetheart."

I was misty-eyed as applause erupted throughout the room. I made my way up to the stage and gave my dad a warm hug. "I love you, Dad." I told him. "I love you too, baby girl." He replied. I kissed him on the cheek and turned to face the pack.

Once the crowd quieted down, I spoke, "Thank you, Dad. And thank you all so much for celebrating with me tonight. It means so much to me. Alpha Jackson, Luna Clarissa, thank you for this incredible party. I don't know how you do it, Luna, but this party is phenomenal. Thank you." I clapped for her, and the pack joined me.

I hugged her tightly; she has always done so much for my family since we lost my mom. Then, I hugged Alpha Jackson, thanking them both again for the celebration. I hugged Ari and Ivy's parents too as they wished me a happy birthday, they were like aunts and uncles to me.

The DJ began playing music again. After leaving the stage, I was greeted by many different pack members who sent their well wishes. I hugged and chatted briefly with each of them.

Nearby, I caught part of a conversation between Xander and Luna Clarissa. "You look so handsome, sweetie." She fussed over him, "Alexander, is that lipstick?" She wiped at his lips and he just stood there with a smirk on his face. His eyes caught mine and he gave me a quick wink before focusing back on his mother.

As the crowd of people around me dispersed, Ari darted over to me. "It's almost your birthday." She sang out. She was bouncing on the balls of her feet like a kid on Winter Solstice about to open presents. "Come on, let's go freshen up before midnight." She grabbed my hand and pulled me away, gathering Ivy and Jazzy along the way.

In the bathroom mirror, I steadied myself and took a deep breath. I needed to keep myself and my wolf calm. Goddess, I was so nervous!

"Relax and just enjoy the moment, girl." Jazzy said, eyeing me in the mirror. "It's going to be perfect."

I took another deep breath and nodded my head.

"Ok, check!" Ari demanded. I turned toward her, and she checked me over. She smoothed my dress and fussed with my hair, while Ivy and Jazzy did the same behind me. "Gorgeous as ever!" Ari declared.

Then she looked me in the eyes, "I'm so happy for you, Max." She said softly to me. I hugged her. "Now, go get 'em, tiger!" She exclaimed and smacked me on my bottom.

I was laughing as we exited the restroom. I glanced up at the clock, and it was 11:59. My heart thumped in my chest. I closed my eyes and took a deep breath before I stepped into the hall. When I entered, Ed Sheeran's 'Perfect' started playing. Everything became hazy as my eyes traveled through the crowd of people. Onyx was fully alert.

An incredible spearmint and cedarwood scent invaded my senses, everything was happening in slow motion. My eyes landed on Xander. It was as if fireworks were exploding in my mind. Those intense, green eyes were beckoning me. That magnetic pull guided me towards him; the room seemed to part for us as we met in the center. Onyx howled.

The world stood still. I could hardly breathe as Xander placed a hand on my waist and the other on my cheek, his eyes glowing. "Mate." He said triumphantly with a little growl, as if he had been dying to say that his entire life.

I slid my hands up his chest. "Mate." I answered back breathlessly before our lips met in the most ardent kiss. It was electric. An incredible tingling sensation spread throughout my body wherever he touched me.

We gently pulled back from the kiss, staring into each other's eyes. I felt like he was peering into my soul. The world around us gradually faded back into focus and I realized the entire pack was howling and cheering for us.

The biggest smile spread across Xander's face and I couldn't help but mirror it. "The Moon Goddess has truly blessed me." Xander proclaimed. "You're so incredible, Maxine. I've never met anyone like you, I can't believe you're mine." He gazed at me with so much affection.

"I've always wanted it to be you, Xander." I touched his cheek and those sparks tingled through me. "You're my best friend and now my mate." He growled playfully at the word 'mate.'

"Say it again." He requested.

"My mate." I happily obliged. His eyes twinkled as he beamed.

"Goddess, you're perfect." He whispered before dipping his head to me for another passionate kiss.

Xander held me close, and we danced. We swayed to the song that just happened to be perfect for us. I wanted to stay like this forever. It was heaven. He nuzzled his nose gently with mine.

Howls from the north border broke through our tender moment. Then, there was howling from the southern border, quickly followed by the eastern and western borders. Our entire pack was under attack.

The room erupted in gasps and panic. Xander's eyes quickly turned to fear as they darted to me, not wanting to leave. "Go." I told him.

He grabbed my hand, tugging me along as he met up with his team and his father's Alpha unit.

"There are rogues attacking on all borders. I've already commanded warriors to their stations." Alpha Jackson stated. "I will defend the eastern border with Delta Nick. Charlie, I need you and Gamma Dylan on the southern border. Xander and Wiley will take the western, Donovan and Heath defend the north."

They all acknowledged their orders. "My love, I need you to get the non-warriors and children to safety. Lock it down." He told Luna Clarrisa. She nodded her head, kissed him, and rushed off to guide the others.

"Maxine, I need you to go with her." Xander stated firmly.

"No, I can help. I'm a warrior." I shot back.

"Please, Maxine." He pleaded, holding my face in his hands. "I can't focus if you aren't safe."

"Stay and defend the packhouse." Alpha Jackson order. "All of you." He indicated to Ari, Jazzy and Ivy too. Frustration filled me, we are all capable warriors. We went through extensive training in the pack and at the Academy. Hell, I was top of my class.

"Yes, sir." I gritted out reluctantly; I can't go against my Alpha's orders.

"We have to go. Now!" Alpha Jackson commanded. Everyone bolted into action.

My heart was screaming for Xander to stay. "Xander!" I cried out.

He rushed back to me. "Stay safe." His eyes were begging me.

"Be careful." I implored. He kissed me quickly before taking off towards the fight.

Onyx howled.

CHAPTER TWENTY-FIVE

Xander

My world transformed as Maxine walked into the hall. There was only her. Nothing else even existed. When our eyes met, I felt my synapses burst to life.

I was consumed by her electric eyes as I drifted toward her. Her intoxicating scent was stronger than ever, permeating inside my soul. My body ignited wherever it met hers.

I had never been so happy to say one word in my life. "Mate." I have been dying to claim her since she came home. Her gorgeous eyes were glowing. It was like heavenly bliss hearing her claim me back. "Mate." Perfection.

When we kissed, I could feel it in every fiber of my being. There was an electricity between us that tingled all the way to my toes. It was intense, dizzying, and addictive. I wanted to kiss her forever.

The pack came to life howling and applauding for our new bond. An Alpha finding his mate is historic in a pack. I am thrilled that Maxine will be our Luna. She is the epitome of what a Luna should be. Loving and compassionate, but also fiercely protective. I'm so proud of her.

Hearing Maxine call me her mate was everything. It was like the air I needed to breathe. "Say it again." I teased her. But it was truly like music to my ears. "My mate." She purred to me.

I had waited my entire life for this one moment. I never wanted it to end. I pulled her close to me, gazing into her affectionate eyes as we swayed to the song that I had picked out for this very occasion. She is perfect.

My heart was so full that it might actually burst. This gorgeous creature in front of me was all mine. I couldn't thank the Moon Goddess enough for this blessing.

I gently ran my nose along her adorable nose. I closed my eyes and pressed my forehead to hers lovingly. This all felt like a dream, and I never wanted to wake up.

The blissful bubble came crashing down in an instant. The sentinels were howling out warnings across the entire packland.

Fear and panic were flooding my body. They're here for her. Staring at my beautiful mate, a furious need to protect her rose up. We joined the others, to determine the plan.

Dad doled out orders. I didn't want to follow them; I just wanted to stay with Maxine. I needed to keep her safe. But an Alpha has to protect his pack.

She was angry that she was being commanded to stay and guard the packhouse. I know what an incredible asset she and the other girls are to have in a fight, but she has to understand that she is the target of the attack. There's no way we're letting her waltz right up to them.

I kissed Maxine's sweet lips and had to tear myself away from her. As I sprang into action, I mindlinked my brothers and my dad to keep him informed.

I need Wesley and Blake with Maxine at the packhouse. Protect your future Luna. I ordered. *Don't let her shift.*

Yes, Alpha. They replied to me quickly.

I threw off my suit jacket as Wiley, and I ran full speed towards the western border. We were receiving updates through mindlink from around the pack. The number of rogues attacking on each side was relatively low. I was suspicious of their actions. I mindlinked the two Alpha teams. *This is either an incredibly stupid plan, or there's more to it. Stay alert.*

As we reached the fight, I let out a vicious roar. A rogue jumped at me; I caught it by its open jaws and pulled them apart. He fell to the ground motionless.

We received a mindlink from Luna Clarissa letting us know that all of the non-warriors and children were accounted for, the bunker under the packhouse was sealed and armed.

I didn't shift, but instead, grabbed a rogue by the fur as it jumped on a warrior's back and slung him into a tree with a sickening crack. He didn't get back up.

I was thankful Dad had increased border protection. Our warriors were well trained, dead rogues were already strewn about the border.

Another wolf leapt at me, I grabbed him, wrapping my arms around his neck. I squeezed until I felt it snap, then, I tossed him to the side.

There were only a few rogues left standing on the western border. Updates came pouring in that the rogues were dealt with, and the borders were secured.

Vampires! There are vampires attacking outside of the packhouse. We have four warriors with us. We are holding them off, but we need back up! Wesley called through mindlink.

I slammed the last disgusting rogue in my hands to the ground with a crunch.

"*Maxine!*" I roared. Before I could make a move, a gunshot rang out.

CHAPTER TWENTY-SIX

Maxine

Watching Xander run off towards danger was agonizing. Every fiber of my being was screaming to be with him. But the Alpha gave me orders.

We quickly helped Luna Clarissa usher everyone into the bunker. There is a secret passage under the main stairs in the packhouse that leads to a large, underground safe room.

Once everyone was in, we did a quick sweep to check for stragglers, while Luna Clarissa and her helpers counted pack members. We confirmed everyone was accounted for and locked the room down, setting a security alarm.

I turned to my friends, who were distressed but focused. "Let's secure the perimeter of the packhouse." I instructed. I kicked off my heels, suddenly feeling ridiculous in this dress.

We hurried outside and were met by Wesley and Blake.

"Is everything okay?" I asked, slightly panicked, afraid that something bad had happened.

"Xander ordered us to stay by your side." Blake informed me.

"I'm fine, I don't need you to watch over me." I stated firmly, feeling irritated.

Wesley gave me a look, "You're the future Luna, now. You must be protected."

His words struck me. In all this time I dreamed of being Xander's mate, I hadn't even really thought about the fact that I would be his Luna. I couldn't dwell on it now, though.

"Do you smell that?" Ari asked, with a grimace on her face.

I sniffed the air and cringed at the disgusting smell that could only mean one thing.

Vampires. I mindlinked those around me. *Stay alert.*

Xander said not to shift. Blake reminded me. That is fine. Fighting in wolf form definitely has its benefits, it gives you more strength and instincts, but fighting in human form gives you more speed and agility. Both are needed when fighting a vampire.

I heard a hiss and then red, glowing eyes appeared in front of us. There were about 20 of them. They moved forward out of the shadows. They were creepy, tall and thin with sharp fangs and long claws, pointy ears, and beady, red eyes.

Four more warriors rushed out from the packhouse and defensively stood in front of me and the girls. I took a fighting stance, ready for what was about to take place.

The vampires sprinted forward. They were so fast. Fighting broke out everywhere at once. Wesley and Blake both immediately ripped two vampires' heads off. The warriors were fighting multiple vampires at a time. The girls jumped into the fight too.

A vampire ran straight at me, I slammed my fist into his throat, crushing his larynx. While he stumbled around gasping, I tore off his head. As disgusting as it sounds, it's one of the only ways to kill a vampire in combat. Luckily, they are dead and don't have blood in their bodies or it would be a gruesome scene.

Another vampire rushed towards me, I maneuvered out of the way and flung him headfirst into the packhouse stairs. Before he could get up, I grabbed him from behind and beheaded him.

We had managed to kill most of the vampires, when more showed up. *I'm calling for backup.* Wesley mindlinked us.

I landed several blows on a vampire and turned, securing him in a headlock over my shoulder. I leaned forward, throwing him over and twisted, effectively removing his head.

"*Maxine!*" Xander roared out in my mind. My body went ice cold with fear. What's wrong?

An excruciating pain ripped through my chest. I screamed out and fell to my knees, clutching my chest. *Xander!*

Wesley, Blake, and Ari rushed to my side.

"What's wrong?" "Are you hurt?" "I can't find a wound."

I felt as if my heart was being ripped from my chest. Tears were pouring down my face as I struggled to find air. "Xander!" I yelled out. I knew the pain I was feeling was his and not my own.

I stumbled to my feet and threw the remaining vampires to the side, taking off towards the western border as fast as I could.

"Max! Wait!" Someone called after me, but I wouldn't stop for anything. The pain in my chest was growing stronger. I have to get to him.

I ran faster than ever before. I was barefoot, sticks and rocks cut into my feet, but I didn't feel it. I focused on the pain in my chest. I tried to reach out to Xander, but I couldn't link him. Fear spiked again and I pushed myself harder.

I arrived at the border and quickly scanned the area. "Xander!" I screamed. There were bodies everywhere and warriors rushing around.

"Max!" Wiley shouted at me. I darted over to him. He was covered in blood, crouched over a large body lying on the ground.

"No!" I yelled out, falling to the ground beside him. Xander was bleeding heavily from his chest. "Xander!" I pressed my hands over the wound, taking over for Wiley.

He opened his green eyes, "Maxine." He sounded so weak. His breath was shallow and his heartbeat was faint.

"What happened?" I demanded.

"There was a gunshot. Silver bullet." Wiley said in disbelief as he shook his head.

"Oh Goddess!" I cried out. "Xander, look at me!" I pleaded with him. His eyes were glossy and out of focus. "Stay with me, Xander!"

The pain in my chest was fading and so were the tingles.

"Maxine..." Xander breathed out before closing her eyes. He stopped breathing. I couldn't feel his heartbeat. He can't die!

"No! Xander! Don't you leave me!" I yelled as I clutched his chest. A surge of anger and energy flowed through me. There was a bright light as I screamed, "No!"

Xander gasped and his eyes opened. "Maxine." He croaked out, I felt incredibly weak. "You're glowing."

Then my vision faded to black.

CHAPTER TWENTY-SEVEN

Xander

A gunshot rang out, and searing pain ripped through my chest. I roared in agony.

I looked down and touched the small hole in my chest that was now pouring blood. My white shirt grew redder by the second.

I clutched my chest and fell to my knees. In an instant, Wiley was by my side, holding me up.

"Fuck! Xander." He shouted. He helped me gently lie down and pressed on my wound. He barked orders at everyone around him. "Get me a medic! Mindlink the hospital, we need an ambulance to the western border, now!"

I heard him mindlink the Alpha teams too. *I need immediate assistance! Xander's been shot! I think it's a silver bullet!*

There were responses and people shouting all around me, but I could no longer hear them. My head was pounding, and a fog took over.

All I could think about was Maxine. She was at the packhouse surrounded by vampires who wanted her dead and I couldn't protect her.

"Maxine." I choked out. The pain was intensifying and the silver bullet burned from within my flesh. I was getting weaker. I couldn't feel Zeus.

My body felt cold, and my eyes were heavy.

"Xander!" The most beautiful voice called to me. I forced my eyes open and saw my favorite blue ones full of terror and anguish.

"Maxine." I managed to say. There was a slow calm washing over me. I didn't feel the pain very much anymore. There were voices whirring around me, but I couldn't focus on them or anything. My vision was becoming darker.

"Xander! Look at me! Stay with me!" I could distantly hear my mate begging me, but I couldn't keep my eyes open any longer. Everything slowed to a stop as I closed my eyes. Blackness consumed me.

I was jarred out of the dark by a jolt of electricity through my chest. I gasped and opened my eyes.

My vision focused on my mate hovering over me. "Maxine." I rasped. Confusion filled me as I realized, "You're glowing." Maxine's eyes were glowing a bright blue, but also, her entire body had a white halo of light around it. It was astonishing.

The light faded. Maxine appeared drained as her eyes drooped closed, and she collapsed to the ground.

"Maxine!" I yelled as I tried to move but pain shot through my chest again. My eyes darted to Wiley who continued putting pressure on my wound in Maxine's absence. He looked bewildered as he shouted out, "We need help!"

Wesley came sliding in on his knees as he scooped Maxine into his arms. He quickly checked her pulse.

"Strong pulse, she's okay!" He reassured me. And then his eyes surveyed my wound and the blood that covered me, Wiley, and Maxine. "Fuck! Where the hell is the medic?!" He screamed out.

A medic ran over to me and started triaging my wound. "We need to get the bullet out, I can't do it out here," the medic informed.

An ambulance arrived at the same time as my father and Donovan. I couldn't focus, voices shouted around me. My brain could only think about Maxine. I needed her to be okay.

I watched as Donovan took Maxine from Wesley. There was anger and concern in his eyes. "What happened?" He demanded.

Wiley still had a baffled look on his face. "I don't know. Xander… he was… and then she was glowing… she saved him." Wiley was staring at Maxine in amazement and shock. "He was dying. She was glowing and she saved him… Then she passed out."

He peered, wide-eyed up at Donovan who was staring at him as if he were insane.

"Vampires?" I choked out as another wave of pain crashed over me. "The packhouse?" Last I knew they were under attack. What happened?

"We killed them all." Wesley updated me as they hoisted me onto a stretcher. I saw Blake to the side frozen in fear as he stared at my blood-soaked shirt.

"The pack lands are secure." My dad confirmed. "We have to get you to the hospital." Dad's face was ashen, and his eyes were wide with panic, I've never seen him scared before. "NOW!" He roared to the medics who were working on me.

I was loaded into the ambulance. "Maxine!" I cried out, not wanting to be away from her.

Donovan climbed into the back of the ambulance with Maxine's limp body still in his arms. With great effort, I reached out to hold her delicate hand in mine. The tingles instantly spread up my arm and helped calm me. I closed my eyes.

The next thing I knew, there were bright lights and lots of voices talking. I was disoriented and it took a moment to realize I was in the hospital.

"He needs surgery. We need to get the bullet out, immediately, before there is further damage to his wolf." Someone was saying.

"Maxine..." I said in barely a whisper. I couldn't see or feel her anymore. Where is she? "Maxine!" I yelled.

"It's alright, Xander. The doctors are checking her over now. She's okay. Donovan is with her." Dad's steady voice told me. It was all the information I needed to hear for my body to relax and slip back into the darkness.

I opened my eyes, and I was standing in a meadow of flowers. It was a beautiful, clear night and the moon was shining brightly. The smell of wildflowers filled the air.

I heard children giggling and I spun around to search for them. A little boy and two younger girls came galloping out of the woods that lined the meadow.

"Come on!" The boy called back to the girls as he laughed. The boy had the same auburn-colored hair as me, with bright green eyes.

He ran back and scooped up the smaller of the two girls in his arms and she squealed. Her dark hair fell in little ringlets around her face, framing her emerald-green eyes. The boy swung her around and carried her to the far end of the meadow. "Come on, let's pick some for Mom." The boy said to her.

The other little girl had beautiful, dark hair and the most electric blue eyes that pierced my soul. She looked right at me with the biggest smile on her face. "Come on, Daddy, let's pick flowers for Mommy!" She ran over to me and grabbed my hand, pulling me along behind her towards the other two.

We reached the others, and they beamed up at me. "Look, Daddy!" The littlest girl said, "I got flowers for Mommy!" She held up a bundle of lupines, purple coneflowers, bluebonnets, golden poppies, and evening primrose.

I knelt down next to her, and she jumped into my arms, hugging my neck. "Stay with us, Daddy!"

CHAPTER TWENTY-EIGHT

Maxine

I found myself on a familiar moonlit beach. The night air was warm and salty, with a gentle breeze that felt amazing. I closed my eyes and sighed. I love it here, it's so peaceful and serene. The waves were slow and calm, lazily lapping at the sandy shore.

I remember this place, I thought to myself, as I gazed towards the horizon, waiting for a visitor.

Sure enough, the small orb of light appeared in the distance and made its way to me. "Selene." I whispered as the Goddess gradually appeared from the ball of light.

She stood in front of me, more gorgeous than I remembered. "Hello, Maxine."

I bowed to her, still in awe of her presence.

"My child, we have much to discuss." She stated melodically, her voice was so tranquil as she lifted my chin to face her. "There are many questions you must have for me."

Oh yes, I thought, where to start? This ethereal place had my mind in a fog like calm, I had to think hard about the questions I wanted answered. Then, like a ton of bricks, everything hit me. "Xander!" I gasped. "Is Xander okay?" Fear seized my heart.

Selene gently reached out and touched my cheek, a wave of serenity spread over me. "Xander is alive. You saved him." She reassured me.

"I saved him?" I furrowed my brow, confused. "How?"

"You are a Midnight Wolf, Maxine. As one of my direct descendants, there is a power within you." She explained, "Most do not have the strength to access this power, but you are exceptional, Maxine."

"I don't understand." I was confused, "What do you mean?"

"You are a strong wolf, my child. And your love for your mate is fierce." She continued, "The fear of losing Xander allowed you to harness the power of the Midnight Wolf. Your bond is unlike any other. It is special." She said with a clever grin.

I thought about Xander and our bond, still so new to me. "Special. How?"

"The mate bond for a Midnight Wolf is unique. The most sacred and ancient bond." Selene explained, "It is imperative that a Midnight Wolf bonds with her one true mate. The strength of all werewolves relies on that true mate bond. Without it, the werewolf species will lose their connection to their wolves forever."

It was hard for me to process her words. "Our connection to our wolves depends on my mate bond with Xander?"

"Yes." She gave me a tender smile. "When I created werewolves, in order to give them the connection with their wolves, it required a special bond. I offered my daughter as a symbol of my love for the wolves. It was difficult to have my child leave me, so to ensure that she would always be loved and protected, I paired her with her perfect soulmate. Thus, creating the first mate bond."

Her eyes shined with love. "I have chosen the perfect mate for every werewolf throughout history. Some choose not to follow their hearts and reject their mates." She grimaced when she said this and turned her head. "But as a direct descendant of the Moon Goddess, you have a true mate bond." She looked back at me with a sweet smile.

"A true mate bond." I repeated, trying to absorb all this information. "But my mother..."

"Your mother and father shared a true mate bond. The Demons of the Night attempted to prevent it, but your parents were able to keep it hidden and lived a truly happy life. The vampires were not aware that they couldn't destroy the bond after your parents were fully mated and they tragically ended her life anyway." Selene explained with tears in her eyes.

Tears ran down my own cheeks as I thought about my mother and the pain my father must have felt.

"Now that you have found your mate, you must know the importance of your bond." Selene's voice invaded my thoughts. "You must not let anything come between you and your true mate." She urged.

"How do I..." I began to ask.

"I cannot give you all the answers, my child. You will know what to do when the time comes." She replied. She placed her hands on either side of my face and kissed my forehead. "You must go back now; your mate needs you. Take care, Maxine."

Then, her glow shined brighter until she vanished into the light.

I slowly opened my eyes, trying to adjust to the blinding lights above me. "Xander." I mumbled as I fluttered my eyes, trying to force them back into focus.

"Hey, Max!" A soft, familiar voice called me. I turned my head to see Donovan sitting beside me. He looked terrible. He was dirty, tired and stressed. "How are you feeling?"

I thought for a minute. I was in the hospital again. What had happened? Was I in pain? I surveyed the state of my body and there wasn't anything unusual other than exhaustion. "Tired." I replied weakly.

"You just need to rest. The doctors said everything looks fine." He informed me.

I glanced around the room. No one else was here. Where is he? My heart picked up pace. "Xander?" I asked Donovan, a little panicked.

"Shhh... It's okay. Xander came out of surgery about 10 minutes ago. They were able to get the bullet out quickly." Donovan stated calmly, trying to keep me pacified. But it didn't work.

Like a bus hitting me, the night came rushing back. Xander had been shot! My heart rate spiked on the monitor above me.

"Where is he?" I asked, trying to sit up. "I have to see him!" I couldn't manage to pull myself up, my body was so tired.

"Max, just wait!" Donovan pleaded with me. "You need to rest!"

A doctor and nurse rushed into the room and attempted to get me to lie back down. "Please, I have to see him!" I shouted. I struggled to get out of bed, and collapsed on the floor, that's when I realized I was still in my gown.

Donovan carefully picked me up off the floor and held me close to him. "It's alright, Max." My fighting had left my body feeling completely exhausted again. My eyes lids were drooping. "Just rest. Everything will be okay." I heard my brother say before my eyes drifted close.

A deep sleep took over. There weren't any dreams. Just darkness.

When I woke up again, I was in the same hospital room. Donovan was standing just outside of the room, talking to Alpha Jackson, Dad, and some doctors.

I felt better, rested. I glanced around quickly. I need to get to Xander. I reached over and turned the sound off on the monitor before I quickly detached the cords and wires that were hooked up to me.

I climbed out of bed and winced, the bottoms of my feet were sore, but I didn't care. They would heal. I could feel

Onyx, but she was asleep in my mind. I would have to find Xander without her excellent sense of smell.

I silently crept to the door. The doctors were pointing to something on a chart, so I quickly darted out of the room and rounded a corner. I closed my eyes and focused on Xander. There was a pull in my chest, and I started walking.

As if we were magnets, I could feel a pull to him, drawing me in. Instinctively, I knew each turn to take and came to a door that was guarded by a disheveled and distraught Wesley. He seemed shocked to see me. "Max?" He rushed towards me as if he was worried I might collapse. "Are you alright?"

"I need to see him." I pleaded. He stared into my eyes, then nodded his head. He stepped to the side, opening the door to Xander's room.

I walked in and fear clutched my heart. Xander was lying in bed with so many wires and tubes hooked up to him, including one in his mouth. The severity of his injury crippled me with anxiety.

"Xander?" I whispered as I crept towards him. He laid there shirtless with his chest wrapped in bandages and a blanket pulled up to his waist. They had cleaned off the dirt and blood from his body. I reached out and touched his arm. Those wonderful tingles spread and I sighed.

I pushed his messy, auburn hair back and kissed his forehead as tears rolled down my cheeks.

"Come back to me, Xander." I quietly cried as I climbed into the bed with him, being careful not to tug on anything or hurt his wound. I just needed to be touching him. Wes quietly closed the door as I curled up against Xander.

CHAPTER TWENTY-NINE

Xander

A sweet voice pulled me from the darkness. "...she brought me some orange, cranberry muffins. She said they're your favorites. Your mom is so sweet. She visits you multiple times every day. She likes to fuss over you until your dad makes her leave." Maxine. I just lay here with my eyes closed, listening to my mate's soothing voice.

"I'm a little worried about your dad. He's been working nonstop, I don't think he is sleeping much. He's been meeting with different Alphas, trying to find the vampires' location. Your dad loves you so much, Xander." Maxine sniffled a little. "I wish you could see the way he looks at you." I could feel her holding my hand and the warmth of tingles that came from it.

"And Wes..." She chuckled. "Oh Goddess, let me tell you. That boy has made it his mission to protect me. I don't know what you said to him that night, but he is never more than a mindlink away." She lowered her voice to a whisper, "He's just outside the door now. He follows me everywhere. You're going to have to reign him in." She sighed. "Blake is being tough, but I know he's really worried about you. It's hard for him to see you this way." She sounded so sad, I wish I could hold her.

"I need you to wake up now, baby." I wanted to comfort her, but I couldn't move. I focused all my energy on squeezing her hand. "Xander?!" She gasped. That's all I heard before I slipped back into the silent darkness.

I was lost in an abyss, the only thing that seemed to pull me from it was the sound of my mate's voice. I could hear her talking to me and praying to the Moon Goddess. Her voice would call to me, coaxing me to the surface before I was pulled back under.

Maxine talked and I listened. She told me how they had found some accounts that were in Massimo Zanzara's name and were attempting to use them to track his location. Maxine said the pack would pray together every morning for me to wake up. She informed me that Donovan has continued to keep up with our training duties, he didn't want the warriors getting soft while I'm laid up.

She explained my medical status to me; the doctors had taken the bullet out, it nearly missed my heart. The silver had gotten into my bloodstream and almost killed me. The doctors said I was strong and willful, because four days ago they were able to extubate me. My wound was healing nicely, but the silver had weakened my wolf. Even when I concentrated hard, I couldn't feel Zeus.

Maxine was updating me on our friends when I heard her voice break. "Xander, please. I need you." I could hear the tears in her voice. "It's not supposed to be like this. We're supposed to be in a hazy bliss where we can't keep our hands off each other." She let out a little sob. "Come back to me, Xander. Please."

My heart couldn't bear to hear her like this. I focused my mind and pried my eyes open, blinking several times in the harsh light. "Maxine." I could barely choke out, my throat felt like sandpaper.

"Oh my Goddess! Xander!" Maxine cried as she brought her face closer to mine. Finally, I could see those beautiful blue orbs I was so fond of staring back at me.

"Hi." I whispered to her.

She burst out in tears of joy and laughed. "Hi!" She proceeded to cover my face with kisses. She was so adorable, I started to laugh. But oh Goddess, did that hurt.

"Let me get the doctor." She mindlinked someone. "Here, have some water." She brought a straw to my lips, just as I had for her once.

"I'm so happy you're awake, Xander. You have no idea how scared I've been." Maxine said as she stroked my hand.

"I have a little bit of an idea." I rasped, remembering my time spent at her hospital beside.

"Xander, you've been out for eight days." She explained. Eight days? Had it really been that long?

The doctor entered the room with my father. "Xander? Thank the Goddess, you're finally awake!" Dad exclaimed.

The doctor checked me over. My wound was still healing slowly, but my vitals were strong. He asked me if I could feel my wolf yet. But Zeus was nowhere to be found. Everyone was really worried when they heard that. There have been documented cases of some werewolves losing their wolves to severe injuries. The wolf ultimately sacrificed themselves to save their human counterpart. I know everyone was scared that this was what Zeus had done.

"Give it some more time." The doctor said, "Your body went through something incredibly traumatic. If it weren't for your mate, we wouldn't even be having this conversation now." He said with a nod towards Maxine.

I stared at Maxine and an image of her with her entire body glowing flashed through my head. "You saved me." I was amazed by my mate. "How did you do that?"

"We'll give you two some time alone." Dad interrupted before ushering the doctor out of the room.

"Maxine, I remember you were glowing. What was that?" I asked, mystified.

"I don't know how I did it, but I was terrified of losing you. Your heart had stopped and you weren't breathing. I fought against it with every ounce of my being, and this energy just poured out and brought you back to me." She said, sounding unsure of herself. "Xander, I was so terrified." She cried.

"Hey, hey, it's okay. I'm here." I tried to soothe her. "It's going to be alright. Come here." I beckoned her and she carefully crawled into the bed and snuggled up to me. I wrapped my arms around her, feeling the tingles spread throughout my body. It helped ease the aching pain in my chest.

"Now this is heaven." I said, feeling her body against mine was all the comfort I needed. "Better than any medicine." I kissed the top of her head.

She sniffled. "I told you I didn't want to come back here for a long time."

"I know. Trust me, there were plenty of other things I wanted to be doing after finding my mate." I tried to lighten the mood.

"Xander, they got the rogue who shot you." Maxine explained.

"I know. I heard everything you said to me." She sat up, leaning on her elbow to face me.

"You did?" She asked in shock.

"Yes, your beautiful voice would pull me out of the darkness. I couldn't do anything but listen, but it was comforting to hear." I told her.

She gently leaned forward and kissed me. Goddess, the feeling of her lips on mine was euphoric. She pulled back and gazed into my eyes. "Thank you for coming back to me." She stroked my face tenderly.

"Always, Maxine." She nuzzled back down beside me. We talked a little more until we both fell asleep.

CHAPTER THIRTY

Maxine

Xander woke up three days ago, and they are finally letting him out of the hospital. His wound isn't fully healed, he still has stitches, but they said he could heal from the comfort of his own room now. It worried me that he still couldn't feel Zeus. He's still there somewhere, I just felt it in my soul.

Onyx had been utterly distraught, desperately worried for her mate.

I hadn't left Xander's room since the night I woke up in the hospital. The girls brought me clothes, and I showered here. Wes and Luna Clarrissa kept me fed regularly. I just couldn't leave his side.

I worked with Luna Clarissa to get everything ready for Xander's return home. I talked with the doctors extensively, finding out all of his limitations and anything that he might require. I relayed the things we needed for him to Luna Clarissa, and she made sure to take care of it.

The doctors insisted on Xander being carted out of his room in a wheelchair. He fought it tooth and nail, but eventually he caved for me. When the time had finally come, I pushed his wheelchair out into the lobby where our parents and friends were waiting for us.

"Ah, come on, guys. You don't need to see me like this." Xander groaned.

"Hey, man, we're just happy to see you awake again." Heath stated as he patted Xander on the back.

"I swear to the Goddess, Xander, if you ever do that to me again..." Wiley began but swallowed hard trying not to get emotional. Being the one who was there with Xander when he was shot had been traumatizing for him.

"Hey, Wiley, thank you for stepping up. I heard you were a true leader. I'm proud of you." Xander said as he shook his hand, then pulled him down for a hug. I think Wiley had tears in his eyes.

"Alright, I think it's time Xander got home so he can rest." Donovan declared, always the one to set everyone back on track.

Outside of the hospital, there was a crowd of pack members waiting to see their future Alpha. Xander refused to be wheeled out in front of the pack. "I can walk from here to the car. Just let me do this." He was firm. "I need the pack to see that I am alright." His eyes pleaded with me.

I peeked over at his dad who gave me a silent nod. "Okay, but I am right here if you need to lean on me." I told him.

With some effort, Xander stood on his own. I slipped my arm around his waist, and he draped an arm over my shoulders. "Ready?" I asked him. He smiled down at me with a nod.

We walked out the front doors, and the pack greeted him with loud cheers and howls. Xander waved to them. Before we got in the SUV, he turned to face his pack members.

"Thank you!" He called out to the pack. "Your future Luna tells me that you all have been praying daily for my recovery. Your love and support means the world to me. I cannot thank you enough." He was beaming with pride. "I hope to see you all back on the training grounds soon." He added before he waved to them goodbye.

Donovan stepped up and lent him some strength as Xander climbed into the backseat of the SUV. I made my way around to the other side and climbed in next to Xander.

Alpha Jackson slid into the driver's seat as Wes hopped into the front passenger seat. He quickly scanned the backseat to make sure everything was alright.

"Seriously, Xander, make him stop!" I whispered. Wes was so protective over me, it was seriously getting annoying.

"I told him to protect his future Luna." He said with a smile and a shrug. "It was an Alpha Order."

"Well, un-order it!" I demanded with a huff.

He just shook his head with a gorgeous grin on his face, as he pulled me closer to his side. "I need you safe, Maxine." He wrapped his arm around me and kissed the top of my head.

When we arrived at the packhouse, the fussing commenced. It was as if Luna Clarissa was ordering everyone to battle stations, she was so sweet but also fierce. She commanded the men to help Xander up the packhouse steps. She put in a request to have food delivered to Xander's room in an hour. She distributed things for people to carry and then shooed them all away.

There was a service elevator in the back of the packhouse that we would be using for Xander. There was no way in hell he was climbing five flights of stairs.

It was just the two of us in the elevator. Xander had insisted. I think he was beginning to get irritated with all the attention. He walked in and leaned against the back wall, completely exhausted. He tilted his head back and closed his eyes.

I gently touched the healthy side of his chest. Without opening his eyes, he reached out and pulled me in so that my body was pressed against his. I carefully laid my head on his shoulder. We just savored the quiet moment together.

The elevator dinged and the doors opened to the Alpha suite. I stayed by his side in case he needed to lean on me. We walked through the living room, where his dad was waiting. He told Xander how happy he was that he was finally home and encouraged him to get some rest.

We made our way to his room. His mother was waiting at the door. She explained some of the things that she had provided for him and said a nurse would be by to change his bandages tonight. Then, she left us alone.

I helped Xander remove his shirt, and he stepped out of his shoes. Then, I pulled back the comforter and Xander slipped into bed without resistance. I could tell he was completely exhausted. I turned to sit on the couch when Xander caught my arm.

"Where do you think you're going?" His eyes were closed, as he pulled my hand towards him.

"I was going to sit on the couch..." I explained.

"No." He said as he opened his emerald eyes. "I need my mate." There was no room for argument in the way he said it.

I went around to the other side of the bed, took off my shoes, and slid under the comforter. Xander pulled me to him and tucked me inside his arms. I placed my hand on his chest, careful not to hurt him.

"It's okay, I'm not made of glass." Xander said with his eyes closed again. "You're not going to hurt me, Maxine."

I relaxed a little and my body melted into his. It was only a matter of minutes before his breathing changed, and I knew he was asleep. I watched him resting so peacefully and silently thanked the Moon Goddess for giving me such a perfect mate.

My true mate. I had told Xander about my conversation with Selene when he was still in a coma, but we hadn't talked about it since he had been awake. I was afraid to bring it up.

Without Zeus, Xander couldn't mark me, and we couldn't complete the bond, yet. There wasn't much point in bringing it up now, it would only upset him. But it weighed heavy on my mind.

CHAPTER THIRTY-ONE

Xander

I had been back home for two days, and I was beginning to go stir crazy. Don't get me wrong, being cooped up in a room with Maxine for days was fantastic. However, I wasn't able to do the things I wanted to do with her.

I wanted to explore her naked body some more. I wanted to mate with her. I wanted to claim her and give her my mark. But I couldn't do any of those things. Obviously, without Zeus, I wouldn't be able to mark her yet. This frustrated me, the need to claim my mate was intense. As for the rest of it, the doctor had given me physical restrictions, and she was taking them seriously.

It wasn't for a lack of trying though. Every chance I got, I attempted to get Maxine naked. In the end, it only left me feeling more frustrated, wanting her even more as she put distance between us.

We were watching a movie last night and she was lying at the foot of the bed on her stomach with her legs crossed at the ankles. I was sitting up against the headboard and was extremely distracted by her perfectly round ass.

I reached out and placed my hand on her thigh and slowly slid it up towards her bottom. She peeked over her shoulder at me, and I could see the heat in her eyes. She groaned and rolled away from me. I leaned my head back, sighing in frustration.

The doctor was here, giving me a checkup. He had me up and walking around the room. I felt a lot better, less exhausted and weak. He checked my wound and was surprised to see it had healed a lot since we left the hospital.

"Is your wolf back?" He inquired optimistically. I sadly shook my head. "Hmm... Your increased healing would indicate that your wolf is getting stronger. Or perhaps, it is just the change of environment and time spent with your mate. It's hard to say at this point." He concluded.

"Speaking of time spent with my mate, Doc. Can you please give us the green light to be... physical with each other?" I was not too proud to ask this. I needed my mate. Maxine, on the other hand, blushed at my question. She's so adorable.

The doctor chuckled a little. "Yes, I suppose that would be alright." YES! I was thrilled! "However, you need to take it slow and if anything hurts, you need to cease physical activities immediately." He was very serious.

"Thank you, Doctor." I replied. Maxine asked him a few more medical questions, it seemed she knew a lot from her classes at the Academy and our extended stay in the hospital. She walked the doctor out of the suite, thanking him.

When she returned and closed the door, I had one thing on my mind. I eyed my mate hungrily and she blushed again.

She just stood there leaning against the door staring at me. She bit her lower lip nervously. I slowly stalked towards her, like the hungry predator I was. Her eyes drifted down my body and back up. I didn't have a shirt on, since the doctor had inspected my wound. I just wore a pair of black sweatpants.

When I reached Maxine, I caressed her bare arms, and she shivered. "Don't be nervous." I soothed her as I bent forward and kissed her lips. I could feel her relax as our lips melted together.

I pressed my body up against her and she gasped as she felt my excitement. I wanted her so badly. I needed her.

She gave me a devilish look as she slipped out from underneath me and turned me around, so my back was now against the door. Oh, I liked this side of her. She kissed me passionately, our tongues intertwining. I slid my hands around her body; one traveled up into her hair and the other slipped down and squeezed her fine ass.

Her arms were around my neck as we kissed. I pressed her body into mine again. She slowly slid one of her hands down my body, causing tingles and goosebumps to spread across my skin as she glided over my chest and abdomen.

Her hand slipped inside of my sweatpants. She lightly trailed her fingers over my shaft, and I moaned softly into her mouth.

She gently ran the palm of her hand back down my length before caressing her fingers back up again. Her hands were so soft and silky. She wrapped her hand around my hard cock and slowly pumped it.

She tenderly kissed my jaw, then my neck. She gave my sensitive mate spot a little nibble that made me moan and shiver. She continued to kiss her way lower down my body, my collarbone, my chest, and my abs. She knelt in front of me, peering up with a sexy glint in her eyes as she hooked her fingers in my waistband and pulled my pants down, freeing my hardness.

She maintained eye contact as she licked up my shaft from the base to the tip. She flicked her tongue and swirled it around the head of my cock. I groaned again; the sensation was incredible.

She licked her lips as she wrapped her hand around the base of my shaft. She closed her eyes as she took me into her mouth. I sucked in a breath, making a hissing sound. I could feel the mate tingles along with the pleasure of what she was doing to me.

She slowly pulled back and ran her tongue over my tip again and kissed it before taking me all the way inside her mouth. She bobbed her head back and forth slowly gliding me in and out of her mouth. Her hand pumped the base of my shaft while her divine mouth worked my cock.

She was building up speed, and I moaned. She used her other hand to gently rub on my balls. When I moaned again, her eyes locked on my own. She let out a little moan as well, what she was doing to me was turning her on.

"Fuck, baby." I sighed. I slipped my hands in her hair and eased her back off my cock. "I can't take much more." I warned her.

"Don't." She interrupted. "I want to taste you." She pulled me back to her delicious lips and sucked me back into her mouth. She was so fucking sexy.

She kept her eyes on mine and she resumed pleasuring me. The intensity was growing; I felt my dick harden before I moaned out and found my release down her throat. I swear there was a howl from somewhere deep inside my mind. She continued to bob on me until I was done spasming. She swallowed and pulled back, licking my shaft clean. Then, she placed one more kiss on the tip before she stood back up, gently slipping my pants back into place.

I tried to protest; there was so much more that I wanted to do to her. But she wouldn't let me. "I think that is enough excitement for you today." Maxine sounded so sultry but also firm. Exhaustion was already setting in. She took my hands and dragged me towards the bed. She climbed in and scooted over, making room for me.

I laid down next to her and pulled her body flush against mine. She gazed up at me, and I dipped my head to give her a tender kiss. "You're incredible, Maxine." I was truly in awe of my amazing mate.

"You're pretty incredible, too, Xander." She replied. She sighed as she wrapped her arm around my waist.

I drifted to sleep feeling completely content.

CHAPTER THIRTY-TWO

Maxine

Xander's wound was beginning to heal quickly. It was a great sign; he told me he even thought he heard Zeus. He could feel him somewhere deep inside. I was thrilled; I had been so scared that he was lost forever.

We had a few steamy moments since the doctor gave us the okay, but we had to take it easy. It was extremely difficult, and we were constantly forcing ourselves to stop before we got too carried away. I was worried about Xander overexerting himself.

I had been training again with the girls, while Xander did some physical therapy. He jogged on a treadmill and lifted weights with strict limitations from the doctors. He spent this time with Donovan, Heath, and Wiley.

I did some light yoga with him too, to help keep up his flexibility and balance. I enjoyed positioning his body for the yoga poses. It was fun to lead him in something physical.

Being away from each other was still incredibly hard. Anxiety gripped me like a vise at the thought of losing him.

He was getting his stitches out today, but he insisted that I go spend time with the girls instead of fussing over him at the hospital. My heart ached at the thought of not being there for him, but we seriously couldn't be together all the time. We had to force ourselves to be okay with being apart.

Donovan, Heath, and Wiley were leading their usual training class. I really wanted to train with the elite warriors, so I convinced the girls that this was how we should spend our time together. Of course, Wes was right there with me. Anytime I wasn't with Xander, Wesley was watching over me like a hawk.

Xander walked with me down to the training grounds before he would head to the hospital. We met up with our friends as Alpha Jackson approached us with my father.

"Hey, Dad!" I called cheerfully, but his serious demeanor sent a ripple of fear through me. "What's wrong?"

"Hi, Max." My dad pulled me in for a hug before continuing, "We have some news."

I glanced around; everyone's mood shifted in anticipation.

"We think we've found the location of Massimo Zanzara's coven." Alpha Jackson came straight out with it. "There is a large rogue camp about 3 hours north of here. It's located near an old, abandoned governor's mansion. That's where we think Massimo is hiding. There is an account in his name set up in a town not far from there."

I eyed Xander, his face was hard and serious. I slipped my hand into his and I felt how tense he was. I rubbed his arm in an attempt to comfort him. Donovan, Heath, Wiley, and Wes all had similar expressions.

"What do we do now?" I asked, knowing we had to act quickly before things changed or they attacked again.

"We have sent a team of scouts to determine their numbers. Once we have that information, we can begin to plan our attack." Alpha Jackson nodded to Xander. Panic began to creep in. Xander can't go into a fight against vampires, he doesn't have his wolf back yet. He couldn't even mindlink without Zeus. And he's still recovering from a silver bullet. I know he is not one to sit back while others jump into dangerous situations. He's going to want to lead the charge.

"Xander," I whispered to him, "You can't–"

He cut me off. "Let me know the minute you have the information from the scouts." He firmly stated to his father who nodded.

"Xander!" I pleaded, pulling him to the side. "Please! You need more time to heal."

"Maxine, we don't have time. I have to destroy those demons." He was so angry. Then he took in my worried face and his expression softened. He placed his hands on either side of my face. "I have to protect you, Maxine."

"And I need you alive." I replied, trying to hold back tears. The pain of almost losing him was still so fresh, I couldn't accept risking his life again. "Xander, you don't even have Zeus back yet."

He pulled me into his arms. "Just promise me that you won't go rushing into anything. Please." I pleaded with him.

"Okay." He replied softly and kissed me. "I promise."

"Alright, warriors, let's get started!" Donovan called out, it was time for the training session to begin.

My stomach twisted as I looked at Xander. "Are you sure you don't want me to go with you?" My separation anxiety spiked at the thought of being away from him.

He caressed my cheek and slipped his hand behind my neck with a smile. "I'll be fine, baby. Go, kick some elite warrior ass." He kissed me again, then turned me towards the training grounds and smacked me on the butt. I couldn't help the giggle that bubbled up as I made my way over to the group of warriors.

I called back to him over my shoulder, "Remember everything the doctor says to you, I want to know every detail!"

Xander laughed and saluted me. "Yes, ma'am!"

I watched him walk away towards the hospital. Blake and Calvin came trotting up to him. Xander threw his arm over Blake's shoulder, and they continued on. At least he's not alone.

"Come on, Max!" Ari called me. "Move it, lady!"

I jogged over to where the girls were spreading out for stretches and warmups. Wiley began leading everyone in stretches. Since Xander was injured, they had shifted training duties around. Donovan, Wiley, and Heath all lead the Epsilon warrior training sessions. Three of our top elite warriors were leading the Zeta training classes for the time being.

"Good Goddess, my man is so hot up there!" Jazzy declared as she winked at Wiley. He winked back, not missing a beat.

"So, Max, what is Xander's mate scent?" Ivy quietly asked me as we continued stretching.

I bent at the waist to touch the ground between my open legs, stretching. "To me, he smells like cedarwood and fresh spearmint." I said dreamily, missing his scent already. "What about Heath?"

Every wolf has a scent that all wolves can smell. But they also have a special scent that only their mates can detect. It's how we scent out our mates. It's intimate, but I didn't mind telling my closest friends.

"Heath smells like sandalwood and geraniums." Ivy told me as we grabbed our left ankles and pulled our chests down to our legs.

"Oh, Donovan's scent is cypress and lime, almost like a summer breeze." Ari cooed, thinking about her mate. Interesting, I'd know Donovan's cypress scent anywhere, but I wouldn't have guessed lime would be his mate scent.

"What about Wiley? Sage and...?" I asked Jazzy, because now I needed to know everyone's. We switched to our right legs.

"Sage and ginger. Warm and spicy with a hint of sweetness, just like my man." She laughed.

We stood up, ready to warm up. I glimpsed back towards the hospital; I was beginning to wish I had gone with Xander. It was going to be difficult to concentrate.

CHAPTER THIRTY-THREE

Xander

Leaving Maxine was a real struggle. We had been through so much already and I still wasn't able to mark her yet. The need to protect her was insane. I was thrilled to learn we had a solid lead on the vampire's location, though.

Whether I had my wolf or not, I was going to end those fuckers. I didn't want to live in fear that some demon was coming to try to kill my mate or even further down the line, our children.

Our children. An image of three children gathering flowers in a meadow flashed through my head. The dream I had while I was in a coma came rushing back to me. It was so real, more like a memory than a dream. Is this what our future holds? I smiled at the thought. Goddess, I hope so.

"What's with the goofy grin?" Blake came bounding over to me, followed by Calvin.

"Hey, troublemaker." I wrapped my arm around his shoulders. "How's it going?" I had grown really close with Blake while Wesley was away at school. We spent a lot of free time together; I taught him some fighting moves and ran with his wolf, Steel.

"Great. But seriously, what are you so happy about?" He pushed.

"I was just thinking about my mate." I replied honestly.

The two of them groaned. "Seriously? You guys are all ridiculous. So mushy and soft now." Blake teased.

"Obsessed." I clarified with a smirk. I couldn't deny it. I was definitely obsessed with my perfect mate. "You will be too, one day. Just you wait."

"Yeah, right." Calvin replied. "Blake isn't a one-woman kind of guy." He laughed.

"You be careful with that, Blake. I'm serious. It could end up hurting your mate one day. There are also a lot of shewolves out there that would do just about anything to get pregnant with an Alpha's pup." I told him seriously.

"Oh, sure, like you didn't have your fun with all the girls before your mate came along." Blake jabbed.

"Not like that." I answered seriously. "Yes, I dated girls, and we had our fun, but never slept with any of them." I wasn't ashamed to say that I waited for my mate.

"You mean, you never?" Calvin asked, shocked.

"Nope. Saved the best stuff for my gorgeous mate." I answered proudly.

"But you dated Valerie for so long?" Blake countered.

"Yeah, and she pressured me like crazy. I think she would have loved to trap me into being her chosen mate. But I was always firm in drawing the line." I informed them.

"Wow." Blake was genuinely surprised to hear this. We stopped outside the hospital.

"What are you doing here?" Calvin asked when he noticed where we were.

"Getting my stitches out." I smiled. I was excited to be getting this over with.

"Cool! Can I watch?" Blake eagerly asked.

I laughed. "Sure. You can come, too, Calvin. If you want."

"Awesome!" He high-fived Blake. I just shook my head, laughing as we went inside.

"That was so gross!" Calvin declared as we left the hospital. "But like, really cool, too." He quickly added.

"Do you think you'll have a scar?" Blake asked, curiously.

"Most likely. It was a silver bullet." I answered. Silver was a weakness for werewolves' healing; it tended to leave a scar. Especially if you didn't have your wolf. I sighed. I was really hoping that Zeus would be back by now.

We walked towards the woods. I wanted to go for a short jog outside today, instead of on the treadmill.

"I'm going to go for a run. Do you want to come?" I wouldn't mind the company, and I hadn't seen Blake as much lately with all the crazy stuff that's been going on.

"Yeah, sure." "Definitely."

I noticed Calvin moved to pull his shirt off, and Blake nudged him. I could tell he mindlinked him, probably reminding him that I couldn't shift.

We ran along the path that wound through the northern woods. It was a beautiful day with a slight breeze blowing from the south.

We joked along the way. It was great to spend time with Blake and Calvin, the two of them together were very comical. Out of the blue, Blake shoved me aside, "Let's see what you got, Alpha!" He yelled over his shoulder as he sprinted away.

Calvin and I raced after him. I was feeling good, no pain. I was definitely starting to get my stamina back. I just wished I had my wolf.

I caught up with him as we came to a little clearing and slowed down. "Nice try!" I chuckled. "Gonna have to do better than that!"

"I was taking it easy on you. Didn't want to send you back to the hospital." Blake teased me.

All of a sudden, I noticed how quiet the woods were, and I got a strange feeling in the pit of my stomach. Blake and Calvin noticed it too and their demeanor changed instantly. They sniffed the air.

Blake let out a low warning growl. We all stood in a fighting stance as we surveyed the woods around us.

"What do you smell?" I whispered to them as we stood with our backs to each other in a small, protective circle. Without Zeus, my sense of smell wasn't what I needed it to be.

"Rogues." Calvin gritted through his teeth. Rogues had a distinct rotting, wet dog smell. Shit. I really needed to shift.

"Mindlink Dad." I told Blake as I heard growling coming from the woods in front of me. "Shift. Now." I ordered them. Blake shifted into his large, red wolf, and Calvin shifted into his tan wolf, Echo. They would be safer in wolf form.

Slowly ten rogues made their way out of the treeline, half were in wolf form, half in human form. Anger rose within me, thinking about everything these filthy rogues had put me and my mate through recently. I was fuming.

"We only need the big one. Kill the other two." A disgusting rogue with greasy, black hair said. The wolves jumped into action.

I caught the first wolf that jumped at me and snapped his neck like a twig. Steel and Echo were fighting off other wolves. They were both incredibly strong and skilled fighters.

I punched a wolf in the throat, and it slid across the ground. I turned and grabbed a wolf off of Echo, as he tore into another rogue. I threw the rogue at the one I had just punched. They both staggered to their feet.

Blake and Calvin had both killed a wolf and a human. We were down to five rogues left.

The rogue with the black hair took out a tranquilizer gun. Fuck. He aimed at me, and I quickly grabbed one of the remaining wolves and locked my arms around his neck. The dart went into his shoulder, and I took this opportunity to end him.

The black-haired rogue growled at me. Then, a wicked sneer crossed his dirty face, and he aimed at Blake. It was as if everything happened in slow motion. I couldn't get to him; another rogue jumped at me. "Blake!" I shouted.

Steel turned just in time to see the dart hit him in the shoulder. He growled and pulled the dart out with his teeth before he stumbled. The rogue wolf he had been fighting used this distraction to his advantage and sunk his teeth into Steel's neck.

I threw the rogue in front of me to the side and raced towards Blake. I punched the rogue wolf so hard in the head I heard a crack, and he let go. Blake's wolf collapsed on the ground, and he began shifting back to human form.

Fuck! There was so much blood. "Blake!" I yelled. I applied pressure to the gaping hole in his neck that was gushing blood. He had a look of panic in his eyes as they slowly closed. "Stay with me, Blake!" I shouted. The tranquilizer knocked him out.

The fighting around me had stopped, Calvin shifted back as he ran to my side. There were only three rogues left, and they were all standing there in human form.

"You're going to be okay." I was practically begging Blake, rather than comforting him. "Mindlink my dad again! Where the hell are they?" I directed Calvin.

I glanced back at the rogues to see the black-haired man point the tranquilizer at me and pull the trigger. The dart pierced my skin, and I roared out, "No!"

I pulled it out and threw it down. I turned back to Calvin; I had to tell him quickly before the tranq set in. "Apply pressure to his neck! Don't let him bleed out. Mindlink the hospital. Get someone here, quick!"

Calvin's hands replaced mine as I fell forward onto my hands and knees. The ground was spinning, and my vision became blurry. The rogues were stalking towards us.

I fought with all my strength and crawled away from my brother. I had to protect him. I swung my fist and hit the closest rogue between his legs, and he fell over.

I lifted my head and the black-haired rogue's fist crashed into my face, knocking me to the ground. I tried to get back up, but my arms and legs were so heavy.

I heard howling nearby. I pushed over onto my back. The black-haired rogue looked nervous and rushed as he glanced around the woods.

"What do we do with those two?" The other rogue asked him. My eyes started to close; I couldn't fight it anymore.

"Leave them, that one is as good as dead." He replied coldly. "We only need him."

I felt hands grab at my arms and lift me as I slipped out of consciousness.

CHAPTER THIRTY-FOUR

Maxine

Once we had finished warming up, we practiced some skill drills. We threw jabs, crosses, hooks, and uppercut punches in the air. Then, we cycled through side, roundhouse, push, and hook kicks, focusing on the techniques.

Next, we practiced different combos, applying all the different techniques together.

After about 30 minutes of drills, the guys instructed everyone to pair up for sparring. I stepped up to my brother and gave him a sly grin.

"What do you say, big brother? Care to get your ass kicked by your little sister?" I asked with my eyebrows raised.

He narrowed his eyes at me and scoffed. "Bring it on, little girl."

"You'll pay for that." I told him coolly.

We found an area to spar in and backed up, giving ourselves space to work with. I eyed him and he took his ready stance.

I waited for him to make the first move, reading his body language. He briefly glanced down at my left leg, and I knew he was going to make his move. Just as he did, I swung my right leg around and kicked him in the face.

Donovan stumbled back and readied himself again. This time I knew he was going to try to fake me out. He threw a jab towards my face, but instead of ducking, I stepped back. I misjudged Donovan's plan, and he kicked his leg out, swiping my feet out from underneath me.

I fell to the ground on my back and quickly kipped up back to my feet. Donovan swung a left and then a right at me, I ducked down and punched him twice in his left side. Then pushed back, creating distance between us again.

He moved forward and I push kicked him in the chest, sending him backwards. He recovered quickly, charged at me again. He threw two jabs and a hook at my head, which I had to block with my arms. Donovan used this opportunity to hammer me in the side.

I skittered away and refocused. I came at him hard with a cross, jab combo low on his body and then sent another roundhouse kick to his head. Then I ducked down and spun as I swept my leg into his, knocking him to the ground. I jumped to pin him down, but he tossed me to the side.

I rolled and scrambled back to my feet. A nervous, jittery feeling filled my chest. I shook my head, trying to redirect my attention. Donovan was back on his feet and coming at me with a hook. I moved out of the way, but he grabbed me in a grappling hold from behind. I felt anxious all of a sudden.

I bent over and twisted, throwing him to the ground. Panic and anger spiked within me, causing me to glance around. Something is wrong. Distracted by these overwhelming feelings, I didn't see it coming when Donovan kicked me squarely in the chest, blasting me to the ground.

"Shit!" Donovan was by my side in an instant as I gasped for air. "Are you okay, Max? I didn't mean to. I thought you were going to block me."

I clutched at my chest as I sat up, but not from the kick. Onyx was growling in my mind, hackles up.

I peered up at Donovan with fear in my eyes. "Something's wrong." I whispered.

"What is it?" Donovan's voice was full of concern as he checked me over.

"Not me." I huffed, as Onyx snarled in my head and my blood ran cold as I realized. "Xander!"

I scrambled to my feet and looked towards the hospital. Onyx howled and I took off at full speed.

"Max!" Donovan called after me and I heard a commotion as I tore out of the training grounds.

I could sense he wasn't at the hospital anymore; my heart was pulling me towards the northern woods. I can't mindlink him. My mind was racing, trying to get to my mate.

I paused at the border of the woods and took a deep breath and smelled his familiar scent, along with two others. Blake and Calvin! I quickly mindlinked them. *Blake! Calvin! Where are you?*

Max? We're in the northern woods, in a clearing. Rogues are attacking us! Blake's rushed voice filled my head.

There are ten of them. We need help! Calvin added.

I'm on my way! I replied quickly.

Just as I started to take off again, Donovan's hand caught my arm. "Max! What's going on?"

"Rogues!" I yelled out as I threw his arm off of me and ran, following Xander's scent. "Xander is with Blake and Calvin." I informed Donovan who raced beside me. Heath, Wes, Wiley, and the girls weren't far behind.

Donovan mindlinked someone. "Alpha Jackson and warriors are already on the way, but we're closer." He filled me in. I pushed harder, running as fast as I could.

We were getting closer; I could feel it.

Max! We need help now! Calvin's terrified voice filled my head. *Blake is bleeding out!*

I let out a massive howl, quickly joined by the others.

"Over here!" I heard Calvin shouting. We broke through the treeline to a small field filled with seven dead rogues, Calvin and Blake. Where's Xander?

I ran to Calvin's side. "Oh Goddess!" I gasped when I saw Blake. He was extremely pale and there was so much blood everywhere. I quickly checked his pulse, I couldn't feel anything.

"Calvin, keep the pressure on his neck." I instructed as I started chest compressions. They taught me this at the Academy.

I didn't even know what else was going on around me until Donovan came rushing up with two doctors. "It's okay, Max, let them take over." He told me. I stepped back as the doctors worked on Blake.

"Where's Xander?" I asked Donovan and Calvin. My heart was pounding.

"They took him. The rogues. They darted both of them and took Xander." Calvin's voice sounded so frail as he stared at his best friend, lying on the ground. I growled and I heard another growl behind me. I spun around to see Wes, furious and scared.

I turned to run but Donovan snatched me by the arm. "Heath and Wiley are tracking their scent. The girls are helping."

"I have to find him!" I shouted, trying to pull away. Tears filled my eyes. Donovan pulled me into his arms, and I sobbed.

Wes dropped to his knees by Blake's head. He looked completely broken as he let out a heartbreaking howl.

CHAPTER THIRTY-FIVE

Xander

I woke up feeling so heavy. My head was throbbing. I slowly opened my eyelids, they stung and felt dry. I was so disoriented. Where am I?

It took a minute for me to be able to actually feel my body. I was sitting up, with my head drooping on my chest. There was a hard floor beneath me. I slowly lifted my head with great effort. My vision was blurry. I tried to focus.

I moved to rub my eyes, but my hands were stuck. I pulled with my arms, but I quickly realized that I was chained to a pole.

I blinked over and over, until my vision cleared. I scanned the dim room. No, it was more like a shack. The floor was concrete, covered in dirt. There wasn't anything in the room with me. The walls were an army-green colored corrugated metal, with large rust spots.

I turned my head to look behind me and became dizzy. "Fuck." I breathed out. I rested my head back on the pole I was chained against. There was a single light bulb hanging from the shabby roof.

I struggled with the chains, trying to free any part of my body. But it just left me exhausted. I was so sluggish from the tranquilizer. I leaned back again, huffing.

I heard a door unlock from behind me and I strained to turn again and pulled on the chains, trying to give myself some room. It was no use, I felt so weak.

A door creaked open, and I heard someone take a few steps in before the door groaned closed again. It was silent for a moment, until the footsteps started to make their way around me.

That disgusting black-haired rogue appeared in front of me with an evil grin on his face. His teeth were yellowed with black spots near his gums. His clothes were filthy and torn. They were probably the only clothes he had.

He crouched down in front of me. "Have a nice nap?" He croaked out, he sounded as if he smoked five packs of cigarettes a day.

"What the hell do you want?" I gritted out, pulling forward on the chains as anger rose within me.

He cackled and scratched his neck as he tilted his head pensively.

"I want a nice big packhouse, full of pretty little shewolves that are ready to serve me whenever I want." He explained. "I want enough money to buy anything I want and throw lavish parties for the hell of it. I want the freedom to run around like I own the place, like all the rest of you Alphas do regularly." He sneered at me.

"You won't get any ransom for me. My pack will fucking kill you all." I spat at him.

"Oh, I don't care about your pack. I don't need their money." He replied coolly, "The vampires have more money than they know what to do with, and they plan on paying me handsomely for you."

Of course. The vampires. My mind raced back to what Maxine had told me while I was in a coma. I could only remember parts of it, but the Vampires wanted to stop our bond from being completed. There's no way I was going to let them keep me from my mate.

I was so pissed. I tried to lunge forward but the chains dug into my arms. I let out a frustrated yell.

The dirty rogue laughed at me. "Oh, Alpha, there's no use in any of that. Without your wolf, you're not going anywhere." He sneered at me. Damnit, how did he know about my wolf?

"I've been watching you, just waiting for the right time to make my move. It's too bad you had those two young wolves with you." He mocked, shaking his head. "Such a shame that we had to end one of them."

His words were like a dagger to my heart as images of Blake's bleeding body flashed through my head. I felt a rage build up inside of me and I thrashed against the chains. "I'm going to fucking kill you!" I yelled at the rogue.

The rogue slowly stood back up. "This has been fun. We'll talk again soon." He left me alone in the dingy shack. I heard the door bolt behind him.

I tried to think clearly and remember Blake's condition before I passed out. He had lost a lot of blood, and he was tranquilized, so his wolf wouldn't be able to heal him. He was going to die unless help arrived quickly.

But I remembered hearing howls before I passed out. He had mindlinked Dad when they first smelled the rogues. He could have gotten there in time. I was still hopeful that they were able to save his life. I needed him to be okay.

I tried to shift my weight. My body ached from sitting in the same position on this hard floor. I was parched; my throat was so dry. The grogginess of the tranq had worn off.

They left me alone in this tiny room for hours. I had only seen the black-haired rogue the one time, no one else came in. I couldn't stop thinking about Blake and Maxine. I was so worried about Blake, I prayed to the Moon Goddess over and over to let him be alright. I knew Maxine was probably losing her mind, I shouldn't have left her today.

I tried to formulate a plan. My only option was to strike when they came to move me. I wasn't sure how many rogues there were. Without Zeus, it would be a difficult fight, but I couldn't let them hand me over to the vampires.

I closed my eyes and focused really hard. Where are you, Zeus? I could feel him. Somewhere way down deep, I knew he was there. It was like he was stuck in an abyss; I needed to find a way to pull him back out.

A commotion outside made my adrenaline start pumping. I couldn't see anything, but I heard lots of shouting and the sound of people running. There was a familiar howl, followed by others. Chaos broke out around the shack. I could hear growling and scuffling. There was definitely a fight happening throughout this rogue camp.

Hope bubbled up in my chest. I struggled with the chains again, maybe if I twist my hands a different way I can break free. I needed to get out there and rip those rogues to shreds.

With a newfound energy, I rotated my wrist this way and that way. I used my other hand to hold the chain as I pulled hard. I could feel the chain cutting into my skin, but I was almost there. I twisted my wrist just slightly and felt my hand slip out.

I flexed my hand several times, it was achy and prickly from being in chains all day. My arms were still chained, but I was just attempting to free my other hand when I heard a powerful yell, followed by a low boom. The light above me sparked before it flickered off and back on. Then, something crashed through the door.

I heard groaning on the ground behind me. With one hand free, I could turn slightly further to see what was happening.

The door was lying flat on the ground with the black-haired rogue lying on top of it in pain. Standing in the doorway was the most astonishing woman, covered in blood and glowing all over.

"Maxine!" I heard Zeus growl out in my head.

CHAPTER THIRTY-SIX

Maxine

The doctors looked grim as they stopped pumping Blake's chest.

"No!" I shouted, tearing away from Donovan. I dropped to my knees and began chest compressions again. Frantically, I tried to think. I saved Xander once, I could save Blake, too.

I focused all my energy on not letting Blake die. "Come on, please!" I screamed to the Moon Goddess.

There were voices calling out to me, but I couldn't hear them. I was focused on Blake. "I have to save him!" I growled. I pushed my desperate emotions and energy towards Blake, but there was no surge of power. Nothing happened.

A gentle hand tried to pull me away, but I slipped out of their grasp and continued pushing on Blake's chest. I stared down at his face, so young and innocent. Tears were streaming down my cheeks and anger filled me. Why isn't this working?

I met Wes' haunted eyes, tears running down his face. He was completely shattered. "Wes." I sobbed out. "I can't... It's not working." Wesley slowly nodded his head as more tears escaped his devastated eyes.

"Max." A heartbroken voice called to me. Donovan's gentle arms pulled me away from Blake's lifeless body. I sobbed into his chest as he held me tightly.

Alpha Jackson fell to his knees beside his youngest son's bloody body. I didn't even know he was here. I glanced around; there were so many people here.

Alpha Jackson reached out and stroked his son's red hair. "My beautiful boy." He whispered as tears rolled down his cheeks. He turned to Wes and pulled him into a gripping hug. Wes sobbed into his father's shoulder.

After a minute, he pulled back and pressed his forehead to Wesley's forehead. Then he reached down and cradled his little boy in his arms. He silently carried Blake towards the hospital. We followed him without a word. Donovan kept an arm around my shoulder; I reached out and took Wes' hand in mine.

In the lobby of the hospital, we gathered together. The air was heavy with grief. Watching Luna Clarissa was the hardest. She fell apart when she saw her baby boy lying there. She screamed and cried, collapsing to her knees. Alpha Jackson sank down to the floor with her and held her close. It crushed my heart to watch them mourning their precious son.

Why couldn't I save him? I was furious with myself and the Moon Goddess. How could she let this happen? Why had I been able to save Xander, but not Blake?

Donovan had continued to mindlink with our friends who were tracking the rogues. He informed them of what had happened, and they decided to swap out with a tracker team. They came rushing into the hospital.

Heath ran over to Calvin and threw his arms around him. Calvin was a hollow shell right now. I knew he was beating himself up over the whole situation, but he did everything he could. The two of them had helped protect Xander against ten rogues and managed to kill seven of them.

Calvin stood there, looking like a ghost. There was an incredible sadness in his eyes as he just stared at his friend's lifeless body. When Heath hugged him, the wall finally broke, and he cried into his brother's arms. Ari moved in to comfort her brother, too.

I turned to Wiley and nodded my head towards the door. I wanted to give them space to grieve, but I also needed to find Xander.

We walked outside; Donovan, Ivy, and Jazzy followed us.

"They are definitely heading towards the rogue camp that Alpha Jackson mentioned. We put our best tracker team on it. They will let us know when they get to the camp." Wiley informed me.

"We heard back from the scouts Alpha Jackson sent; there are only about 60 rogues at the camp." Donovan added. "We should take a unit of our Epsilon warriors with us."

"What about the vampires?" Ivy asked. "Do we know how many of them there are? Maybe we should bring more warriors."

"The vampires haven't left the mansion. But based on surveillance, we are estimating about 50 vampires inside." Donovan concluded.

"We should contact the nearest pack for potential backup." Wiley added thoughtfully.

"But... that would be Dark Moon." I said hesitantly. Luke's pack. I'm not sure Luke and his father were going to jump at the chance of helping Xander after he punched him.

"They will help us." Donovan said confidently. "Alpha Phillip will help us." He nodded firmly at me.

"Okay, we need to go. Now." I didn't want to wait. I know that the vampires want to keep me and Xander from completing our bond. "They are going to kill him." I pleaded with Donovan.

"We're not going to let that happen." Donovan assured me. "I need to inform Alpha Jackson of our plan." He went back inside the hospital.

"Max?" My dad's worried voice called out as he ran up to me and wrapped me in a bear hug. "Oh Goddess, are you alright?"

I started crying all over again. "I couldn't save him, Dad!" I sobbed into his shirt.

"Shh... it's not your fault, sweetheart." He soothed as he stroked my hair and kissed my head.

Alpha Jackson had approved of our plan, but he insisted that we take four Epsilon warrior units with us. He needed to stay at the pack with Luna Clarissa. Heath, Ari, and their father stayed with Calvin. We had enough warriors with us. We couldn't leave the pack unprotected anyway.

My dad was leading one unit, Donovan would lead another, they put Wiley in charge of the third, and I insisted on leading the fourth. I needed to do everything possible to get to Xander quickly.

We raced down the forest lined highway in a caravan of SUVs and trucks packed full of warriors and supplies. We needed to be prepared for injuries.

The rogue camp was three hours north of our pack, but it felt like forever as we drove through endless forests and winding roads. My anxiety grew every minute I was away from Xander.

We had to hurry while we still had an advantage. Remembering what Selene told me, I know the vampires want Xander dead, just as much as they want me dead. We needed to strike while there was still daylight, before the vampires woke up. This would give us the greatest chance to defeat them.

We arrived at the site where our trackers and scouts had gathered. There was another unit with them. I jumped out of the SUV before it had even fully stopped.

I rushed over to my dad and Donovan who were meeting with the Dark Moon warriors. As I walked to the center of the group I saw Luke talking very seriously.

"Luke?" I was surprised to see him.

"Hey, Max." He gave me a sad smile. "I'm sorry to hear about everything that's happened. We're going to help you get your mate back." He informed me as he placed his hands on my shoulders. He was so sincere. I was sort of stunned as he continued talking with Donovan and my dad.

I shook my head. Now was not the time. I needed to focus on saving my mate. I listened carefully to what they were saying.

The rogue camp was about a 30-minute hike from here. The scouts informed us of the details of the camp. There appeared to be a heavily guarded shack in the middle of the camp. That had to be where they were keeping Xander.

There's still no movement from the vampire's mansion; there won't be until the sun goes down. It was getting closer to dusk, so we needed to move quickly.

We trekked through the woods. About half of the warriors shifted to wolf form. We wanted to be prepared for any kind of fight.

I raced ahead, unable to keep waiting. My unit followed close behind me. We slipped quickly and silently through the trees. When we reached the edge of their encampment, we spread out. We needed to hit them hard, all at once.

I could feel that undeniable pull, beckoning me towards that shack. I knew Xander was there. Goddess, let him be alright.

I waited impatiently for the other units to move into position. Once they mindlinked me that everyone was in position, my unit stealthily crept into the camp.

We were swift as we killed the rogues closest to the treeline. When the area was clear, my unit moved in further as the others rushed out of the woods.

It didn't take long before the rogues spotted us, and all hell broke loose. Rogues rushed forward to fight, but our warriors were skilled and deadly. These rogues, who lacked discipline and a real leader, were no match for our elite team.

I kept my focus on getting to the guarded shack, more rogues were moving to protect it. I broke past the fighting, making a beeline towards Xander. I could feel him, that magnetic pull tugging on my chest.

I raced towards the shack. A wolf jumped at me; I slid under him and got back to my feet. Another rogue in human form stepped into my path, halting me. I glanced around and I was surrounded by several rogues closing in. There were at least 10 of them and they all stared at me hungrily.

"Get out of my way!" I snarled at them as I roundhouse kicked the rogue in front of me in the face. Another fleabag rushed forward, and I slammed my palm upward into his nose. I heard it break as he stumbled backward.

I kicked backward, landing my foot in the center of a rogue's chest. I threw my elbow out and it collided with another face.

Filthy hands grabbed hold of my other arm, and I pulled my knee up hard into his groin. But several more rogues grabbed hold of me. I twisted and broke free of some while more held me in place. Anger rose inside of me. These mutts were not going to keep me from my mate.

I struggled against them as they tried to drag me away from the shack. I felt a fury inside of me like never before. The intensity was overwhelming. I closed my eyes and screamed as I threw my arms out. A surge of energy channeled through me with a thunderous sound.

When I opened my eyes, all of the rogues were lying on the ground about ten feet from me. I felt powerful and energized. I didn't waste another second as I ran toward the shack.

There was only one guard standing at the door now. He studied me with wide, scared eyes, as he hesitantly moved toward me. With speed, I grabbed him and threw his body backwards into the door, knocking it off its hinges.

I stepped into the doorway. Xander twisted against the chains that bound him to a pole in the middle of the shack. He peered up at me with glowing eyes.

CHAPTER THIRTY-SEVEN

Xander

Maxine rushed over to me; her entire body had a pure white light radiating off of it. "Xander!" She cried and kissed me. Goddess, how I missed those lips.

"Xander, your eyes are glowing!" Maxine exclaimed. I could feel Zeus howl in my head. He's back!

"Maxine, your whole body is glowing!" I replied in disbelief and amazement. Maxine examined her hands front and back, then frowned.

Then, she reached out and took hold of the chain still binding me. She yanked on the chains, and they snapped in her hands like they were nothing.

"Incredible." I whispered. She threw her arms around me and the tingles spread over my body, but more intensely than ever before.

"Come on, we have some vampires to kill." Maxine said with a hard edge to her voice.

She helped me up; my body ached from being chained up. I checked the cuts on my wrists; they were already healing. Goddess, it was good to have Zeus back!

The black-haired rogue was still on the ground, where Maxine had thrown him. He was attempting to crawl away in pain. I picked him up by the neck.

"I told you I was going to fucking kill you." I said in a deadly tone. His eyes bulged with fear. My grip on his throat tightened as I thought about what this piece of shit put us through.

He struggled against my hand, his feet kicking searching for leverage. These mutts had tried to kill my mate, and *this* bastard had taken me from her. His face turned a deep shade of red as he unsuccessfully gasped for air.

As I slowly choked the life out of him with a hand still caked in my brother's blood, I thought of Blake and how he used him to get to me, then left him for dead. I saw the terror in his beady eyes as I slowly squeezed harder until I crushed his windpipe and he was dead. I let him fall lifeless to the ground.

Maxine's touch gently pulled me back to my senses. She placed her hand on my cheek, and I reveled in the tingles, letting them calm me back to a rational state.

The camp outside of the shack was settling down. Dead rogues littered the ground. Our warriors were relatively unharmed. I noticed a few warriors that were unfamiliar to me.

Donovan ran up to us. "Xander!" He hugged me. "Glad you're alright, man."

We were quickly joined by Beta Charlie, Wiley, and... Luke? What the hell? Were those his warriors I saw. He was helping us?

"Woah! Max, do you know that you're glowing?" Luke asked in a state of shock.

"It's a long story." Maxine waved him off. He just kept staring at her like she was the most incredible thing he'd ever seen, and I couldn't help but growl. Maxine slipped her arms around me, and I took a deep, calming breath. Clearly, Luke was helping us, I couldn't claw his eyes out now.

"Okay, we need to move fast. The vampires are still asleep, so if we hurry, we can catch them off guard." Beta Charlie devised a plan. "We'll take half of the warriors around to the back, while the rest of you all go through the front. Stay in human form, it'll be quicker to kill them this way."

"I want extra men with Maxine." I declared. I saw the indignant glare she threw me, but before she could argue I added, "They are clearly going to target you, Maxine. You're glowing! I think they will easily figure out you're the one they're after."

"I don't think you have to worry about her too much." Wiley defended her. "You should have seen her out there. She knocked out a horde of rogues in one go. It was amazing." He was gaping at her in awe. My mate is truly astounding.

"We've got to move now, it's almost dusk!" Donovan interjected, pulling our focus back on the battle ahead.

We quickly gathered up our units and silently moved toward the mansion. I stayed with Maxine; there was no way I was letting her out of my sight.

We reached the front doors and waited for confirmation that Charlie and the others were in position. He had Luke and Donovan's teams with him, we had Wiley and Maxine's units with us.

Once everyone was ready, we gave the signal and busted through the doors. Luckily, vampires sleep like the dead, since technically they are dead. Nothing would wake them up until nightfall.

We crept through the house. We found several rooms filled with sleeping vampires. We sent men in to behead them before they awakened. We continued to move deeper into the house. We needed to find Massimo.

We came to a room that was some sort of grand chamber hall. Sleeping vampires lined the walls along an aisle that led to stairs with a sort of throne at the top. This must be where the demon was sleeping. Our men removed heads as we stalked towards the dais platform. There were definitely more vampires than we had originally thought.

We reached the dais and Maxine gasped. I darted my gaze to her, and she pointed towards the window. The sun had set.

All around us, vampires were slowly waking. It didn't take long for chaos to break out. Vampires were quick to attack, our warriors were fierce and strong, but we were outnumbered. I mindlinked the others for backup.

We rushed to the top of the platform as a large vampire rose up. He towered over the other vampires and appeared to be much more powerful. There were four other vampires with him.

He smiled an evil grin at Maxine. "Thank you for making this easier on me." His demonic voice was eerie, then he lunged forward. I threw a hard punch at his jaw, and he hissed at me before swiping a claw at my chest.

I ducked out of the way and kicked at another vampire that was coming for me. The other vampires had sprung into action and were fighting Maxine and Wiley too. I quickly surveyed the room; our warriors were struggling to fight off the vampires. Where the hell is our backup?

A female vampire dove for me, but I pivoted out of the way and caught her from behind. She hissed and clawed at me. I held her in a head lock and ripped her head off, tossing it to the side. Massimo screamed out, as his eyes burned me with fury and unfettered rage. He drew his claws out to the sides before he ran at me.

He swung his claws at me rapidly, over and over. I could barely dodge out of the way fast enough. I managed to land a punch to his face, but it didn't have much effect on his furious, wild state.

Another bloodsucker jumped at me from the side. I snatched him out of the air and threw him at Massimo. He stumbled back as another vampire knocked into my side. I fell to the ground but scrambled back up. He charged at me, and I elbowed him in the face and then grasped him by the throat. I tore his head off, slinging it to the side. Finally, more of our warriors entered the room and joined in the fight.

Massimo stalked towards me, his chest heaving in anger.

I hadn't realized I was backed into a corner. I push kicked Massimo in the chest, creating more space and punched him hard in the face. He swiped his claw at me and sliced into my chest. I roared out in pain and anger. I landed an uppercut to his jaw. He stumbled backward and fell down the steps.

Another leech came at me with his claws swinging. I managed to dodge and parry his arm away. I used this momentum to bash his head into the wall. While he was dazed, I decapitated him.

I turned just in time to see Massimo hit me with a side kick to my chest and I fell back against the wall. My head connected hard with the concrete wall, causing me to see stars. He came towards me with speed, his claws raised above his head, ready to strike. I had nowhere to go.

From somewhere behind Massimo, I heard Maxine scream out, "No!" The room filled with a warm white light that hit the vampires forcefully. It slammed Massimo into the wall and all of the vampires' skin sizzled.

Maxine was glowing so brightly, and it was burning the vampires. They writhed in pain on the ground. The warriors and I were quick to jump into action. We tore their heads from their bodies.

I stood over Massimo and growled viciously before I ripped his head off.

My head snapped back to Maxine. The light slowly faded back into her body and a wave of pure exhaustion washed over her.

"Xander." She whimpered as her legs gave out underneath her. I dashed to catch her before she hit the ground, her beautiful eyes closed.

"Maxine!" I yelled as she passed out in my arms.

CHAPTER THIRTY-EIGHT

Maxine

My heart raced and Onyx howled as we stared into our mate's glowing green eyes. Zeus. Thank the Goddess, he was back.

Losing your wolf was like losing a huge piece of your soul and I knew Xander would have been devastated if he lost Zeus.

When Xander pointed out that I was glowing, I looked at my hands and frowned. Why couldn't I save Blake? I needed to tell Xander what had happened, but first we had to get out of here.

I reached down and grabbed the chains that were binding my mate. I pulled them apart easily. I chucked the chain aside and flung my arms around Xander.

It had only been less than a day, but it felt like far too long since I had held him close. The mate tingles intensified stronger than before.

"Come on, we have some vampires to kill." I gritted out. Those demons were going to pay for everything they did to us, especially for what happened to Blake. They may not have been the ones to kill him, but they sent those rogues.

Xander grabbed the rogue I had thrown through the door. "I told you I was going to fucking kill you." I don't think I've ever heard Xander sound so menacing. This had to be the leader of the attack, the one who shot Blake. Xander torturously squeezed the life out of him, before he tossed him aside like the trash he was.

My heart ached for Xander, but a desperate need to protect him and kill all these bastards coursed through me like venom.

We gathered the teams to formulate a plan. We needed to move quickly, before the sun went down.

Xander, Wiley and I moved with our units efficiently through the mansion. We came to a large hall; it appeared to be some kind of throne room. Vampires were sleeping along the walls on silk-covered pedestals. These must be their higher-ranking vampires. The warriors that were still with us quickly got to work, killing the vampires inside the grand hall.

We continued toward the platform at the far end of the room. A few warriors trailed behind to protect us from the rear. At the top of the stone steps, Massimo and four other vampires slept. You could easily tell which vampire was Massimo, he was demonic and beastly.

Just as we reached the stairs, I noticed the sun disappearing into the horizon. I gasped and signaled Xander and Wiley.

The vampires woke to a room full of werewolves. Fighting broke out behind us, but our focus was on the waking vampires in front of us.

Massimo loomed over me; he was easily over seven feet tall. A truly demonic grin spread across his sharp face as he spoke to me. "Thank you for making this easier on me."

He hissed and came forward towards me, but Xander attacked before he reached me. Massimo's focus shifted to my mate.

Before I could do anything, another vampire came hissing at me. Wiley attacked a vampire to my right.

As the vampire dove towards me, I ducked and he went tumbling past me to the ground at the bottom of the stairs. As he struggled to get up, I kicked my leg up, contacting him under his chin. He fell to the floor, and I quickly climbed on his back to remove his head.

Wiley was fending off several vampires. I glanced at Xander. He had just killed a female vampire, and Massimo was in a frenzy. I wanted to help him, but Wiley needed backup. I ran over and slid, taking out one of the vampires' legs.

He came crashing down on top of me. He grabbed hold of me, his nails digging into my arms, but I rolled with him until I was on top of him. I punched him hard in the throat. He choked and sputtered, grasping his neck. I took the opportunity to decapitate him.

I quickly jumped on the back of a vampire about to attack Wiley from behind and ripped off his head.

Wiley was kicking ass now. With great speed, he was taking out vampires left and right. I needed to get to Xander, but another bloodsucker charged at me. My anger rose as I blocked his blows and kicked him hard in the stomach. He stumbled backwards. I felt a slicing pain in my chest and cried out.

I glanced down, but I wasn't bleeding. My heart raced as I spun around to see Xander with claw marks across his chest. No! I rushed towards him but the vampire I had just kicked grabbed me from behind.

I quickly bent my body forward and pulled him over my shoulder to the ground. I stepped on his chest and reached down to yank his head off.

I turned back toward Xander as he slammed back into the wall in the corner. He was dazed and Massimo was standing over him with his claws raised, poised to strike. Fear gripped my heart. I wouldn't be able to get to him in time.

A desperate fury filled me with rage as I screamed out, "No!" I felt a power surge out of my body with an explosive blast as the room shined with a bright, white light. Massimo was sent flying forward into the wall, as were the other vampires.

The room echoed with anguished hissing as vampires thrashed on the ground in pain. The bright light was burning their pale, cold flesh. I was frozen in place by an electricity that pulsed through my veins.

Xander got to his feet and stared at me with astonishment. Seeing that he was alright and that Massimo was dead finally allowed my body to relax and the light in the room dimmed. Crippling fatigue consumed me.

I could feel darkness taking over as I barely managed to call out, "Xander."

Like a bolt of lighting, he raced over to me in an instant. I collapsed in his arms. He called my name as my eyes closed.

I once again found myself on that familiar moonlit beach, but this time I didn't feel calm. I was full of emotions.

As Selene's orb made its way toward me, I focused on what had happened, not allowing this peaceful landscape to dull my thinking.

While I was happy that we had defeated the vampires and so thankful for Xander being okay, I was furious that I wasn't able to save Blake. Why would Selene allow this to happen? Why couldn't I use this power to save him?

Selene stepped down onto the beach in front of me, her hair and dress billowing around her. I could read her expression, she too was upset and without a word, she pulled me into her arms.

Hugging the Moon Goddess was like being wrapped in a blanket of literal love, peace, and comfort. I choked on my sorrow as I cried, and she rubbed my back.

"I'm so sorry, my sweet child." She said softly in my ear, "You have been through so much."

I pulled back. "Why?" I demanded with tears streaming down my cheeks. "Why couldn't I save him? He deserved to live."

She stroked my face. "It doesn't work that way, I'm afraid."

"Why?" I yelled, yanking away from her. "Why didn't you let me save him? He was only 16!"

"Maxine, the power of the Midnight Wolf can only be used to protect her own mate." Selene explained to me.

I shook my head, "No! I could have saved him. *You* should have let me save him!" I sobbed out and fell to the ground, picturing Blake's lifeless body.

The Moon Goddess placed her hands on my shoulders as she crouched next to me and once again pulled me into her embrace. "I am so sorry, Maxine. You did everything you could for him." Her voice was soothing but didn't ease the pain I felt in my heart.

She placed her hand under my chin and lifted my gaze to meet her silver eyes. "What you have done is incredible. I have only seen one other Midnight Wolf as strong as you, Maxine. You have protected your mate and eliminated the vampire coven."

She gave me a small smile and continued, "The immediate threat is gone, but be cautious. If others know what you are, they will come for you or your children."

"My children?" I echoed.

"You will be blessed with a little Midnight Wolf one day. You must keep your precious gift safe. Don't live in fear but use good sense to protect your blessings." She stood up and pulled me to my feet. "You must go back, Maxine. Your mate needs you."

She placed her hands on my face, kissed my forehead and her light shined brightly.

I opened my eyes as I heard a mournful howl.

CHAPTER THIRTY-NINE

Xander

Maxine was unconscious in my arms. But I could still feel the mate tingles. I scooped her up and stepped over the disgusting vampire corpses that covered the floor.

Wiley ran up to me. "Is she alright?" He asked me, staring at Maxine with a look of complete shock and awe on his face.

"I think so." I replied, hoping to see her electric blue eyes open soon.

"What was that?" Wiley asked incredulously. "I've never seen anything like that before."

"I don't know. She's amazing." I was completely amazed by this little wolf in my arms. She was more powerful than any Alpha I've ever seen.

"Shit, Xander, you're bleeding." Wiley pointed out as we walked out of the mansion into the night air. I glanced down at the claw marks on my chest. They were actually healing.

"I'm fine. I've got Zeus back and he's already healing me." I shrugged.

"That's great news." Wiley said as we approached the others. Donovan, Charlie, and Luke came running over.

"Max!" "What happened?" "Is she hurt?"

"She saved us all." Wiley blurted out, still bewildered by my beautiful mate.

"She should be alright." I added, "I think she just exhausted herself again. She passed out."

A medic came over to check her out, but I wouldn't let her go. He had to check her vitals in my arms. He confirmed that she was healthy.

We informed them that Massimo was dead. They had killed all the vampires on the other side of the mansion. Warriors were carrying rogue bodies inside the mansion. They also placed dry leaves and branches inside the front door.

Donovan made a makeshift torch from supplies in the rogue camp. He lit it from their campfire and carried it over to the mansion. He dropped the torch on the pile, and it burst into flames. We were burning the whole place down with all of the rogues and vampires inside.

Luke told us that he would have the camp dismantled. I thanked him for his help and assured him that if he ever needed anything, he could call on us.

I needed to get back home. I had to check on Blake.

As we made our way back to the rendezvous point, I noticed a strange silence hanging in the air. Why wasn't anyone informing me of what had happened after I was taken?

When we made it back to the vehicles, I turned to Donovan. "What is it? What are you not telling me?"

I looked into his eyes and knew it was really bad. He was so torn and sad as he struggled to find the words.

"Blake?" I whispered out, not wanting to hear the truth.

Donovan closed his eyes and lowered his head before he met my eyes again. "I'm so sorry, Xander."

It was like someone punched me in the heart. The wind was knocked out of my lungs, and a ringing filled my head. I dropped to my knees and Donovan was quick to help me with Maxine still in my arms.

This was all my fault. I should have protected him. We should have never been in those woods, just the three of us. I couldn't breathe as my heart shattered into a million pieces. I threw my head back in a heartbroken howl.

I felt a soft, delicate hand wipe the tears from my cheek. "Xander," She whispered to me. I peered down to see Maxine's devastated blue eyes full of tears staring up at me.

She pulled herself up and wrapped her arms around my neck. "I'm sorry." She sobbed.

Sitting in the back of an SUV with Maxine in my arms, we stared out the window silently. A numbing sadness had replaced my tears. There was a hollow ache in my chest and a twist of guilt in my stomach. I don't know how I am going to face my parents.

Maxine rubbed comforting circles on my hand, pulling me from my thoughts. I met her eyes, my chest tightened to see them so full of anguish.

"Maxine? Are you okay?" I quietly asked, wiping a tear from her cheek with my thumb.

"I'm so sorry, Xander. I couldn't save him." She softly cried. "I tried so hard, but I couldn't bring him back."

"Shh... Hey, it's not your fault." I pulled her closer to me as she sobbed. "I should have protected him."

"Selene said that I could only save my mate, but I tried everything I could." She cried harder, "I'm so sorry, Xander. I'm so sorry!"

I took her face in my hands, locking eyes with her. "This is not your fault, Maxine. Do you hear me? You did more than anyone could have asked of you. Okay?" I pleaded with her. I wrapped my arms around her and kissed the top of her head.

We stayed like that until we both must have fallen asleep, because the next thing I knew the car pulled to a stop outside the packhouse.

Maxine sat up, looking around. She turned to me and silently placed her hand on the side of my face. She leaned in and gave me a soft kiss before we climbed out of the SUV.

My dad came down the front steps of the packhouse, he rushed to me and gripped me in a desperate hug. I clung to him tightly. "I'm so sorry, Dad." I choked out.

He stared me in the eyes and cradled my face, "This is not your fault, son. Don't you think that for a single second. Your brother loved you so much." His voice cracked. "He wouldn't want you beating yourself up. There is nothing *anyone* could have done." He looked at Maxine reassuringly when he said that last part.

Tears sprang to her eyes again and my dad pulled her into his warm embrace. "Thank you for bringing my son back to me." Dad said sincerely, "Again. You are fierce, Maxine." He continued to hug her, and I made my way up the stairs to my mom.

She was so broken as I reached for her. She sobbed into my neck. "Thank the Goddess you're alright!" She cried out.

She pulled back and gave me a watery smile before turning towards Wesley.

The sadness in his face broke my heart all over again. There were no words to say as we clutched each other close, mourning the loss of our little brother.

We were holding a funeral for Blake tonight. The entire pack would join us in saying farewell to my brother. We had spent the day building a pyre. It was a tradition that family members built the pyre when able.

Dad, Wesley, and I chopped down the ash trees for the pyre. Ash trees were thought to connect the heavens and the earth, guiding our spirits and wolves back to the Moon Goddess. We constructed the platform in the open field near the ceremonial grounds.

My mother gathered bark, leaves, and branches from the birch trees to line the pyre. Birch trees symbolize renewals and purification, so that Blake's spirit and wolf can be reborn into another life.

When the time came, his body was placed on the pyre with lavender for serenity and baby's breath for love. The pack quietly gathered at the ceremonial grounds. Elder Mitchell was going to say a blessing before we released his spirit.

We stood at the front of the pack; my family and I. Wesley and I held onto our mother. Dad addressed the pack. "Our pack has suffered a great loss. We gather to mourn the passing of my youngest son, Blake. We will carry the pain of this loss with us forever. Blake was taken from us way too early, at only sixteen years old. His mother, Luna Clarissa, and I are extremely proud of the young man he had become. He died with honor, defending our pack. His death leaves us wounded, but we ask the Moon Goddess to take care of him and send his spirit back to us one day."

He nodded his head at Elder Mitchell who started the blessing.

"From the dawn of your birth to the sunset of your death,
We honor you.
From your missions completed to your duties left undone,
We honor you.

Selene, we ask you to embrace our fallen companion.

May you comfort this brave warrior and grant him peace.
May you allow his spirit to soar free and blissfully in your kingdom.
May you bless his soul and wolf so that they may be reborn.
May you protect his honorable heart and shield him from pain.
We ask you, Selene, to watch over Blake as he crosses the bridge from this life to the next.
And welcome him with glory as we keep his memory in our hearts forever."

The pack let out a mournful howl. My father, mother, brother, and I each picked up a torch and lit it with the symbolic eternal flame. We walked over to the pyre together and laid our torches on the bottom layer. We took several steps back.

The birch slowly caught fire and spread until the entire platform was engulfed in flames. Mom turned into dad's arms, sobbing. I placed my hand on Wesley's shoulder. Then, I felt a gentle touch on my arm. I opened my arms and Maxine slipped into them. She reached over and grasped Wesley's hand.

No one said anything, we just watched the flames grow higher, releasing Blake's spirit and wolf.

CHAPTER FORTY

Maxine

I stood with Xander and Wes, watching Blake's spirit be released back to the Moon Goddess. We looked on as the flames touched the sky. I closed my eyes and prayed to the Moon Goddess to take special care of Blake's soul and to give him a long, happy life in the next one.

We walked silently back to the packhouse. I continued to hold Wesley's hand as Xander and I walked with an arm around each other. When we reached the front steps, we each embraced Wes in a loving hug before he turned to go inside.

I found my sister and held her tightly as she wept. She was incredibly close with Blake. Calvin was with her. I hugged him too, knowing that the two of them had lost their best friend. I kissed Sabrina on the forehead and gave her another hug. Calvin wrapped his arm around her shoulder, and they went into the packhouse together.

Xander and I approached his mother and father. I held out my arms to Luna Clarissa, and she broke down in tears again and clung to me. I couldn't imagine the pain she's going through. Xander came over and touched his mother's arm, and she turned into his embrace. I gave Alpha Jackson a comforting hug as well, before he took Luna Clarissa inside the packhouse.

Donovan wrapped Xander up in a huge hug. I flung my arms around Ari, and she rubbed my back soothingly. When we pulled back, Donovan tucked me into his arms. He kissed the top of my head and rubbed my shoulder.

Heath, Ivy, Wiley, and Jazzy gave us comforting hugs, too, before we went upstairs ourselves.

We quietly entered the Alpha suite. Xander's parents had already retreated to their room. Hand in hand, we walked to Xander's room. Without a word, I helped him out of his suit jacket and untied his tie.

He sat on the bed and wrapped his arms around my waist, resting his head against my chest. I softly rubbed his back. I ran my fingers soothingly through his hair. He picked his head up and gave me a tender kiss.

Gently, I pulled his hands until he stood up. Holding his hands, I guided him into the bathroom. I started the shower and adjusted the water. I faced Xander, who was lost in thought, and began unbuttoning his shit before I slipped it off him too. Then, I turned to leave, but Xander lightly caught my arm.

"Stay with me?" He quietly asked. I nodded my head. I rotated and pulled my hair to the side, so Xander could unzip my dress. I let it slide to the floor. I discarded my undergarments as Xander removed his pants.

He took me by the hand. Without another word, he stepped into the shower, and I followed behind him. He stood under the stream of water with his arms outstretched on the tile wall in front of him. He hung his head low as the water beat down on him.

I wrapped my arms around him from behind and gently kissed his back. Xander slowly rotated to wrap me in his arms. We just stood there, holding each other as the water washed over us.

After a few minutes, I reached out to grab a loofah and pumped soap onto it. I delicately ran circles over Xander's chest and arms. We took turns affectionately washing each other.

We stepped out of the shower and wrapped ourselves in towels. I put on a pair of underwear and one of Xander's t-shirts, while he pulled on a pair of boxer briefs. In silence, we climbed into bed together. He gave me a sweet kiss. We held each other tightly, lying in the quiet darkness until sleep eventually found us.

The next few days were really difficult. The pack mourned our loss heavily. Everywhere you went, you could feel the sadness hanging in the air. Blake was truly loved by all.

We spent a lot of time with Xander's parents. They wanted us around and we wanted to support them in any way that we could. The time together seemed to ease their pain a little. I knew what it was like to lose someone you love, but I could only imagine the heartache they are feeling from losing their child.

We also visited Sabby and Calvin frequently. The three of them were as close as my friends and I. They were truly heartbroken and lost without him. The two of them relied heavily on each other for comfort, always together. I wished there was more we could do to help mend their sorrows.

Wesley was really quiet and withdrawn. He spent a lot of time alone. I was concerned about him. Xander and I tried to spend time with him, but he just refused. We needed to figure out a way to help him through his grief.

I was trying my best to be strong for Xander, I knew he needed me. He had been sharing stories with me about Blake. He spent a lot of time with him while Wes and I were at the Academy. They had grown very close. I enjoyed listening to him tell me sweet stories and we would laugh about the shenanigans they had gotten into. Blake was very mischievous. But sometimes, Xander would just get really quiet and sad. All I can do is hold him and try to comfort him. My heart was breaking for Xander and his family.

After a week had passed, we had to get back into the rhythm of our old routines. Training sessions had to continue, and meetings had to take place. We had to focus on what is still ahead of us. The pack wasn't going to run itself.

There was no way in hell that Xander was leaving my sight, so I went to his training sessions with the Epsilon warriors. Xander said it was great for the pack to have an elite warrior as their future Luna. I was still really nervous about becoming Luna. I started studying books on Luna duties during our down time.

Xander and I still hadn't marked or mated with each other, even though he had Zeus back. It just didn't feel like the right time. The importance was always there in the back of my head, but I didn't want to do it out of duty though. I wanted it to be special for us.

Donovan and Ari were fully moved into the Beta suite. They had begun renovating everything to their taste. Sabby and Dad moved into Dad's retirement home. I was currently living out of boxes in Xander's room.

With everything that had happened, Xander's parents hadn't done a whole lot of packing up. I wasn't in a rush to force them out, but it would be nice to have all my things and a sense of 'home' again. Right now, all I needed was Xander, though. The rest could wait.

Since I was now permanently attached to Xander's hip, I also joined him for his Alpha unit training. However, with me there, the numbers weren't even for sparring, so today I just sat back and watched my man spar against Wiley. I would be able to spar later during the warrior training class.

Wiley was incredibly fast and nimble, but Xander was quick too. Their fighting techniques were different. There were advantages on both sides. It was highly entertaining to watch. Especially because Xander was shirtless and glistening with sweat. I had to keep myself in check, so I didn't end up drooling in front of the guys.

Donovan and Heath were sparring too. It was really interesting to work with the Alpha team. They all had incredible skills and techniques that varied. I was learning a lot from them.

Wiley definitely liked using kickboxing moves, they played to his strengths of rapid strikes and agility. Heath tended to favor Jiu-jitsu. The grappling and submission holds were his skill of choice because he was so powerful and sturdy.

Donovan was more disciplined and focused on mentally beating his opponents. He used a lot of Taekwondo and Karate. Xander's skills were methodical and precise, he was very strong and fast. He combined techniques like Krav Maga and Aikido with Taekwondo. I really liked Muay Thai and Kickboxing. But because of my size, I really had to focus on reading my opponent and predicting their moves.

We were all learning from each other, and it was really rewarding. I had always wanted to train with them, and now I felt like I was part of their team. It was exhilarating.

After they finished sparring, it was time for the perimeter run. They run along the border of the entire pack daily just to confirm that all is well and that everything is functioning the way it should. They check in with patrols and verify that proper security measures are being taken. I was happy to join them. I love running and our packlands are beautiful. Any time spent outdoors is glorious and today was a beautiful day.

The run was intended to be continuous unless there was a need to stop and adjust something. So, as we ran, the Alpha unit mindlinked different Sentinel leaders checking in with the border patrols. They all had different roles in maintaining our security; Heath was watching for any unusual tracks, Wiley was searching for foreign scents, Donovan was checking for any unmanned stations, and Xander observed for suspicious behaviors and to see if anything looked unusual or out of place. I was just lending my skills in all areas, sort of as a backup for everyone.

The perimeter run usually took about an hour and a half if everything was as it should be. We were just finishing up our run, about to head back towards the packhouse when something felt off. I stopped walking and glanced around.

"Hey, what's up?" Xander asked as he turned to me. "You okay?"

"I don't know, something just feels off." I said hesitantly as I tried to smell the air for something unusual.

The guys were all surveying the area on high alert. Donovan's brows furrowed, "I don't–"

He was cut off by a woman screaming out in pain. Our attention immediately snapped towards the sound, and I took off running.

CHAPTER FORTY-ONE

Xander

Maxine bolted towards the screaming woman and my heart lurched. I tried my best to stay calm as I ran alongside Maxine. As an Alpha, I was prepared for anything, but as a mate, I was terrified. I couldn't let anything happen to her again and we could be running straight towards danger.

I immediately mindlinked the Sentinel leader that was stationed closest to the woman's location, including Maxine and the guys in the link. *Ethan, we're on our way. Is the border secure?*

There was another guttural yell from the woman as we got closer.

Yes, Alpha. He responded with panic in his voice. *It's my mate, she's in–*

"Labor!" Maxine announced as we reached the very pregnant woman, bent over in pain. Ethan was supporting her as she could barely stand from the discomfort. His eyes were wide in complete shock.

"My mate, she came to bring me lunch and she... I... I think she's having the baby!" Ethan quickly explained to us.

I recognized Ethan's mate; her name is Delia. She yelled out in pain and almost fell to her knees. Heath rushed in to support the other side of her body.

"Here, let's get her inside the patrol station." Donovan directed as her mate and Heath walked her carefully toward the small building. It was basically a tiny cabin, like a rest house for those on patrol for long shifts.

"I'll mindlink the hospital." Wiley volunteered. We were on the border, so I would take a while for anyone to get to us.

We burst through the doors, and they gently settled Delia down on the full-sized bed. She let out another cry as she panted.

"These contractions are really close together." Maxine pointed out. All the men stared at her expectantly, waiting for her to continue. "That means her labor might be pretty far along." She explained.

There was a collective look of 'oh shit' written on all of our faces. She's going to have the baby out here? Maxine ignored our reactions and turned to Delia.

"Delia." She focused on Maxine with fear in her eyes. "How long have you been having contractions?"

She thought as she let out a shuddered breath. "Since last night, I guess. I thought they were just Braxton Hicks; they weren't that bad at first. I thought going for a walk might help." She said before she groaned in pain again.

Maxine washed her hands at the small sink in the corner of the room. I just stared at her, not knowing what to do. "Okay." She said calmly, thinking this through. "Okay, at the Academy, my main focus was warrior training, but I also took quite a few medical training classes. Do you mind if I check to see how far along you are?" Maxine sounded confident and reassuring. I was really glad that she's here for this, otherwise, we'd all be freaking out.

Delia groaned out again, "No, please, go ahead!"

She was wearing a sundress, Maxine positioned her in a way so the entire room wasn't getting a full view. Maxine had a flash of surprise across her face, but she quickly recovered and composed herself.

The baby is crowning already. She mindlinked the Alpha unit. I glanced at Donovan whose wide eyes mirrored mine, looking terrified. I ran my hands through my hair, stressed out that I didn't know how to help.

"Alright, Delia," Maxine soothed her. "The baby is coming now. But everything is going to be alright. You can do this. Ethan, why don't you sit behind her for support." He nodded and hurried to slide onto the bed behind Delia so she could lean against his chest. That was excellent thinking, the mate bond should help ease some of her pain and anxiety.

Maxine turned toward us, "I need clean towels and blankets." She directed calmly. Heath and Donovan rushed off to search the closets. I was blown away, was Maxine really going to deliver this woman's baby?

Wiley rushed inside, "The doctors are on their way, they should be here in 10 minutes."

I don't think we have 10 minutes. Maxine mindlinked us. I felt useless, standing here like a petrified oaf. Wiley's eyebrows shot up, and his eyes were as big as saucers. This was a new experience for all of us.

"I also called in a backup Sentinel to fill in for Ethan." Wiley quietly informed me. I nodded in approval as we continued to watch the scene in front of us.

Delia cried out loudly, Maxine focused her attention back to her.

"Okay, Delia, breathe." Maxine stared her in the eyes and she breathed deeply with her. "Good. How is your body feeling? Do you feel the urge to push?"

She breathed deeply again and then grunted. "Yes, I think the baby is coming now!" She wailed.

"Ok, Delia, listen to me. When your next contraction comes, take a big breath in and go with the urge to push. Your body is ready. Okay?" Maxine guided her reassuringly. She nodded.

Heath and Donovan brought two stacks of towels, wash clothes, and a soft blanket. Maxine laid one of the clean towels down on the bed below Delia.

Seconds later, she took a deep breath in and began pushing. "That's it Delia, just like that!" Maxine called to her.

When the contraction ended, Delia's body relaxed a little and she heaved deep breaths. "Okay, great! You're doing great. Breathe, Delia, and get ready to push again on the next one."

She was panting and sweating. Then, she sucked in another large breath before she pushed again. "There you go, Delia, big push, big push!" Maxine positioned her hands down where she could help hold the baby as it emerged.

She reached back without looking and I quickly grabbed a washcloth of the stack and handed it to her. She used it to gently clear the baby's face before Delia pushed again and fully delivered the baby. Maxine caught the baby and lightly toweled off the delicate little body before placing the crying pup on Delia's chest. She was now lying back against Ethan, exhausted. Maxine draped the blanket around them. "Congratulations, it's a boy!"

Delia gazed at her son in awe as tears slipped down her face. Then, she laughed and glanced up at Ethan who just stared at the two of them with so much love in his eyes. "He's perfect!" She cooed.

"He is." Ethan agreed, "And you are so amazing, Delia." He kissed her sweetly before they resumed gazing at their little miracle.

Maxine watched them and then smiled at me.

Just then, the doctors rushed into the cabin. Maxine quickly informed them of all that had happened as they checked Delia and the baby over. We all said a quick congratulations to the new parents before exiting to give them more privacy.

Maxine washed her hands again. I stood in the doorway staring at her, completely astonished.

She came over to me as she dried her hands. "What?" She asked me.

"You are truly incredible, do you know that?" I said as I pulled her into my arms. "You just delivered a baby!"

"Actually, Delia delivered a baby, I just kept her calm." She said matter-of-factly as she pulled away.

I caught her and lifted her chin, so she met my eyes. "Maxine, seriously, that was astounding. I just stood here like a complete idiot and you jumped right into action. You're amazing."

She blushed a little. I kissed her before we walked outside to join the guys. They all gawked at Maxine like she was glowing again.

"Max, how did you do that?" Donovan asked incredulously. "That was insane!"

"Seriously, is there anything you can't do?!" Wiley called out. Maxine frowned slightly and sadness flashed through her eyes. I knew she was thinking about Blake. I squeezed her shoulder and kissed her temple.

"I think this calls for a celebration!" Heath quickly added. "The girls will definitely want to hear all about this."

We stayed outside of the cabin making plans, while the doctors finished taking care of the afterbirth and checking their vitals. They brought a stretcher in to get Delia back to the ambulance. They were going to double-check everything with her and the baby at the hospital. Werewolves heal fast, so she won't have to stay there long.

As they wheeled her out, Maxine smiled brightly and checked in with Delia. "Hey, Mama, how are you feeling?"

"Honestly, I'm in sort of a daze. Exhausted but so happy. Thank you so much, Luna! I don't know what we would have done without you." She gushed to Maxine, who looked surprised to hear someone call her Luna.

"Oh, please, call me Maxine or just Max." She said as she took Delia's hand.

"Well, Max, we'd like you to meet *our* little Max." Ethan beamed as he gently placed a little bundle in Maxine's arms.

She peered up at him completely shocked. "Max?" Delia and Ethan nodded at her with huge smiles.

Maxine stared down at the little pup that shared her name. "Hi, Max!" She whispered to him. Then, she gazed up at me with tears in her eyes and a beautiful smile.

I stepped up behind her, placed my arms around her waist, and kissed the top of her head before meeting my newest pack member sleeping in her arms. I touched his head gently and congratulated Ethan and Delia again.

CHAPTER FORTY-TWO

Maxine

I was still reeling from everything that happened earlier in the day. I had never experienced anything like that before. I was so thankful that I chose to take those extra medical classes at the Academy, it really came in handy in a crisis.

I was so completely shocked and honored that Delia and Ethan named their baby after me! My heart felt so full holding him. What a little miracle!

Of course, the guys were making a huge deal about it. They wanted to have a celebration. I was happy to celebrate the birth of that adorable little boy. I just wasn't crazy about all the focus being on me. I only did what needed to be done at the moment.

Tonight, we were going out to a restaurant in the city and then a nightclub afterwards. The restaurant was owned by our pack.

Our pack owned several different businesses that helped bring in funds. We owned two restaurants, a cafe, a few hotels, and a construction company. The hotels were a venture that started due to all of the Alpha summits and meeting at other packs, it was nice to have somewhere to stay that accommodated werewolves' specific needs.

The construction company formed organically, we were always improving our pack and adding houses for newly mated couples. We had wolves that were highly skilled in carpentry and construction, so we expanded our services and it took off. That's where most of our pack's income came from. We do a lot of projects for other packs and in the human cities as well.

The restaurant we were going to tonight is called Luna D'Argento, which means Silver Moon in Italian. It was a fine dining restaurant, so we were dressing up a bit for the occasion. Which meant the girls were all gathering at Ari and Donovan's place to get ready.

It was difficult being away from Xander, even just for short periods of time. We really haven't been apart much at all since everything happened. I could feel the anxiety creeping in as we parted, but I pushed those feelings down, I would be with him again soon.

It was weird, being in our old Beta suite that was now my brother's home. They did an excellent job redecorating the suite. Everything was black and white with pops of teal, the same color as Ari's eyes.

The girls gushed over me as soon as they heard about the baby. They asked me a million questions and were all highly impressed with my ability to remain calm in such an intense situation.

When we were ready, we made our way down to the main floor of the packhouse to meet the guys. I was wearing a black, off the shoulder bodycon dress with black pumps. I left my long, dark hair down in loose waves.

We had invited Sabrina and Calvin to come out with us, but they were having a movie night with some of their friends in the packhouse theater room. We did insist that Wes come out with us though, we were hoping it might help him a bit.

As we came down the stairs, we spotted the men already waiting by the entryway. My eyes instinctively landed on my mate. Goddess, did he look good! He wore grey slacks and a black dress shirt with the top buttons undone. His auburn hair was styled back with a couple of loose strands hanging down. He was leaning against the wall, eyes on me as I descended the stairs, and pushed off when I reached the bottom. He greeted me in the middle of the room.

"Hi, gorgeous." He said as he placed his hands on my hips and kissed me tenderly. "That dress is sinful." He whispered in my ear, sending a shiver down my spine.

"Mm, well, that's perfect because you look devilishly handsome." I told him with a gleam in my eye as I slid my hands up his chest. I grabbed his open collar and pulled him in for another kiss. He snaked his arms around me, and we got lost in the moment.

"Eherm." Donovan cleared his throat, pulling us from our love haze. He was standing with his arm around Ari, not looking at us. "We should probably get going, don't want to miss our reservation." He was definitely uncomfortable, probably not enjoying seeing his little sister making out with his best friend. Ha! Payback's a bitch.

Ari rubbed his arm and he smiled down at her, completely smitten and forgetting what he had just seen. Wiley held

Jazzy's hand and Ivy was wrapped up in Heath's arms as we walked out.

Wes really didn't want to be here but still managed to look sharp. I was happy he was coming with us. I pulled away from Xander and gave Wes a hug.

We were taking two SUVs with us. Heath drove one of the SUVs with Ivy in the passenger seat, and Wiley and Jazzy climbed into the back seat. Donovan was going to drive our SUV and Wes sat in the passenger seat. Xander and Ari sat in the back with me in the middle.

The entire drive Wes was pretty quiet, he was really anxious though. He kept shifting in his seat and checking the time. We tried to start conversations with him, but he would just give us short responses. Xander and I exchanged worried glances.

When we finally arrived, we pulled up to the valet and Xander took my hand, helping me out of the car. The restaurant was so cute and romantic. The sign out front was black with silver writing that was lit up. There was elegant fairy lighting along the outside patio.

A maître de greeted us as we walked in. "Good evening, Alpha. Luna." He gave a slight bow to Xander and me. I was thrown off again, being called Luna was something I was definitely not used to yet. "Ladies and gentlemen." He dipped his head to the rest of the group. "Please follow me, we have your table ready for you."

He led us to the back of the restaurant, in a private dining room. We all sat down and a waiter brought us a bottle of champagne and told us the specials.

We had a lovely meal; the food was absolutely divine. We all talked and laughed. Even Wes was to be enjoying himself, finally.

"I'd like to raise a toast." Xander declared. Everyone picked up their glasses. "To my truly unbelievable mate, Maxine. You never stop amazing me. Today, you blew me away not only with your knowledge of how to deliver a baby, but the incredible way you kept calm and in control of the situation. You stepped up like a leader, telling everyone what to do and helped bring a new pup into the world. You're absolutely brilliant. To Maxine!"

"To Maxine!" Everyone echoed and I blushed.

"You are going to be the best Luna in the history of all werewolves." Wiley added. "Seriously, no offense to Luna Clarissa, she's awesome. But damn, Max, you're already crushing it."

"I'm really proud of you, Max." Donovan said to me. "You're an amazing woman."

I was feeling shy with all of the attention focused on me, so I raised my glass again. "To our newest pack member, Max!"

"To Max!" Everyone echoed, we all drank and carried on.

"Alright, who's ready to hit the club?" Ari asked as she stood up, ready to go.

"Yes! Let's get moving." Ivy replied, "I can't wait to dance!"

We left the restaurant and our vehicles were already pulled up out front for us. It was a short drive to the club. This club was a werewolf-owned club, but I didn't know which pack owned it. It was called Howlers.

We pulled up to the valet and got out of our vehicles. Xander rolled up his sleeves and looked even sexier somehow. There was a line down the sidewalk of people waiting to get in. Xander held my hand as we approached the doorman, who bowed to us. "Alpha. Luna." He said as he let us all in.

Inside, the music was bumping loudly. The dance floor in the center of the club was packed. There was a bar to the right and stairs to the left that led to a lounge area. The entire club was done in a dark purple, sleek motif.

We maneuvered through the crowd over to the bar. Since it was a werewolf establishment, we could all drink. I noticed that Wes was super tense and on high alert. He quickly downed his entire glass of whiskey.

"Are you okay?" I asked him with concern. "You seem on edge."

"I don't know. I feel really anxious." He replied honestly. "Maybe shots will help me loosen up." He suggested and then ordered tequila shots for everyone. He slammed his back and then took a deep breath. "Woo!"

I couldn't help but laugh at his behavior, but he did seem to be a little more at ease. We took our drinks to the lounge area. I was just about to suggest that we go dancing when...

"Oh my Goddess, Xander?!" A beautiful, tall shewolf came bounding up to my mate and threw her arms around him. I couldn't help but let out a growl.

CHAPTER FORTY-THREE

Xander

We were having a great evening out when all of a sudden, Valerie grabbed hold of me. Maxine growled at her possessively. It was hard to hear over the loud music, but I thought it was really sexy.

Wiley was super annoyed by Valerie's presence, but Donovan and Heath watched Maxine with worry. Donovan glanced at me, then stepped closer to Maxine, just in case he needed to intervene.

I quickly put distance between myself and Valerie, clearing my throat. "Valerie. It's nice to see you." I said politely, moving closer to Maxine. "How have you been?" I asked as I slipped my arm around Maxine's waist. I felt her relax a little and melt into my touch.

Valerie watched me and then eyed Maxine before redirecting her attention to me. "I'm great! How have you been, Xander?"

"Actually, things have been really crazy." I replied. "I'd like you to meet my mate, Maxine." I said as I smiled sweetly at Maxine.

When I looked back at Valerie, she had shock written all over her face as her eyes darted back and forth between me and Maxine. Then she squealed. "Oh my Goddess! Your mate?! Congratulations, Xander!" I was taken back by how genuinely excited she seemed for me. "It's so nice to meet you." She said as she moved in to hug a baffled Maxine.

"Maxine, this is Valerie." I told her. "We dated for a while before you came back home." Maxine's eyes widened in shock for a split second and then she smiled politely at Valerie.

"It's nice to meet you." She said so genuinely, composed like a true Luna. "What pack are you from?"

"Oh, I'm from Dark Moon, this is our club." She said nonchalantly. Maxine's head snapped towards me.

"Dark Moon? That's Luke's pack." She said with confusion on her face.

"Oh, you know Luke? That's my brother." Valerie told her. "What a small world."

Maxine looked like she was having an information overload, I dated her ex-boyfriend's sister. Just then, a muscular man walked up behind Valerie and put his arm around her shoulders.

"Hey, baby, everything okay?" He asked, as he sized me up. I internally rolled my eyes; I could easily take this guy. But I had no interest in fighting over Valerie.

"Yes! This is Xander and his mate, Maxine." She told him and his demeanor changed upon hearing that I had a mate, his features softened and he grinned.

"Oh, Valerie has told me good things about your pack." He stated.

"Xander, this is my mate, Marcus." Valerie said excitedly. I reached out to shake his hand.

"Nice to meet you." I told him. "Wow, congratulations." I said to Valerie. She was so happy and different.

"He's the Gamma for the Winter Claw pack." She said proudly. "He's been helping me pack up my things, I'm leaving with him tomorrow."

The mate bond is an incredible thing. If you accept your Goddess-given mate, they are supposed to bring out the best in you. This Valerie standing in front of me was completely different. The Valerie I knew was title hungry, shallow, and spoiled rotten. She had wanted an Alpha mate to the point that she was ready to accept a chosen mate. It seems the Moon Goddess had other plans for her. I'm truly happy for her.

"Is Luke here?" Maxine asked Valerie.

"Yeah, he's around here somewhere." Valerie said as she searched the crowd. "Well, it was great to meet you, Maxine, and so nice to see you, Xander. Guys." She said and waved to them. They all nodded at her. "We're going to head out, we've got a long drive ahead of us tomorrow." She said as she took Marcus' hand. We said goodbye and they left.

Maxine turned to me with her eyebrows raised. "Wow, she's gorgeous!"

"She doesn't even compare to my stunning mate." I said as I bent down and locked my arms around her hips and lifted her. Holding her like this, she was actually taller than me. She held my face in her hands as she kissed me tenderly. I slowly slid her body down mine until she was back on the ground, enjoying the mate tingles as I gazed into her brilliant blue eyes.

"Alright, can we please go dance now?!" Jasmine whined, causing us to laugh.

"Yes! To the dance floor!" Arielle commanded. The girls all took off to go dance. I stood on the balcony of the lounge with the guys, watching them. I leaned forward, resting my elbows on the railing. Goddess, my mate is perfect. Watching her swirl her hips around in that tight fitted dress was making my wolf go crazy.

Suddenly, I became aware of all the unmated wolves around. Maxine isn't marked, and men were watching her hungrily. I noticed Heath was gripping the railing tightly. He wasn't happy about his unmarked mate dancing out there either. Our eyes met and I nodded my head.

We made our way through the crowd to the dance floor quickly. The rest of the guys followed us too. I growled at a wolf that was approaching my mate, and he instantly backed down to my Alpha aura. I grabbed hold of Maxine's hips and pressed the front of my body against her backside. The tingles spread all over.

She continued to dance, swaying her hips and rubbing against me. Good Goddess, she's so tempting. I moved her soft, dark hair to the side and kissed her bare shoulder. I trailed kisses along the top of her shoulder and up her neck. She moaned softly, but with the loud music, I was the only one that got to hear her sweet sounds. Her delicious bare skin, the seductive way she was dancing, this slinky dress, and her alluring moans were getting me worked up.

I spun her around in my arms, so she was facing me. *Maxine, the things you do to me.* I mindlinked her as I leaned in for a steamy kiss. We weren't dancing anymore, just lost in each other as the club thumped on around us.

"Get a room!" I heard Arielle tease us. Maxine pulled away blushing. The girls all giggled at her. I didn't let her get far though; I kept my hands around her waist.

"Wes, you okay?" Maxine frowned as she called out to him. That's when I noticed he was standing completely rigid with wide eyes.

"What is it, Wesley?" I asked him. He started taking deep breaths. Is he having a panic attack or something?

"Do you smell that? It's like peaches and... nutmeg." He closed his eyes and took another deep inhale and growled.

Maxine gasped excitedly. We all looked around as if we'd be able to identify the source for him.

Wesley walked in a trance-like state towards the bar. We all pushed through the crowd to follow him. He froze as we reached the edge of the crowd. "Mate."

There was a tiny shewolf with fire red hair trying to shove a very large, drunk man away from her. He was holding onto her and trying to move in to kiss her. The petite woman stopped struggling and snapped her attention to my brother.

Wesley let out a ferocious growl and the drunk wolf looked at him with annoyance. But he held onto the girl.

"Let her go." Wesley gritted through his teeth. His hands were closed in tight fists by his side. I placed my hand on his shoulder, and he shrugged it off.

"Fuck off." The drunken wolf said to Wesley before pulling the shewolf closer to his body.

Wesley snarled viciously and flew in, slamming the wolf back away from his mate and into the wall behind him. He quickly shielded the girl as the drunk came back swinging at him. I dashed forward to pull the redhead away from the fight. Maxine and Ivy rushed over to comfort her, placing their hands protectively on her shoulders. Heath instinctively shielded his mate and Luna.

Wesley ducked down to avoid a punch and came back up with an uppercut. The wolf stumbled back as another drunk wolf threw a punch from the side, landing it on Wesley's jaw.

I punched that guy in the gut. When he bent over in pain, I hit him in the face. My men were flanking me, ready to step in when Luke ran into the middle of the fight and shoved me hard backwards. "Woah, woah, woah! Everyone settle down."

The two drunks were not stopping though; they came towards us again. Luke had security bouncers with him though and they quickly grabbed the two creeps.

"What happened?" Luke demanded.

"That piece of garbage was groping my mate!" Wesley growled out. He was still fuming.

Luke looked around and spotted the redheaded girl who was still clearly shocked and upset. "Is that true? Are you alright?"

She nodded to Luke, but her hazel eyes were locked on Wesley.

Luke jerked his head toward the exit, indicating for the bouncers to remove the two drunks. They dragged them away as they protested.

Wesley watched them leave, still trembling with fury. The tiny shewolf pushed forward and touched his arm delicately. He stared down at her hand, no doubt in awe of feeling the mate tingles for the first time. His eyes met hers and she softly said, "Mate."

Wesley placed his hand on the side of her face, and she closed her eyes, leaning into it. The fear and anxiety were gone from her eyes when she peered up at him again.

"Hi." Wesley whispered. She smiled at him and placed a hand on his chest as he leaned in and kissed her.

I looked at Maxine, she was thrilled. She stepped closer to me and wrapped her arms around my waist. I was very happy for my brother.

"Jeez, he's a hot head, just like his brother." Luke joked, as he raised his brows at me. I couldn't help but laugh, thinking about how I acted the night of the pool party.

I reached out and shook Luke's hand. "Thanks for your help, man. Again."

"No worries. Let's get a round of drinks to celebrate, on the house." He said as he moved, indicating for us to follow him.

Wesley nodded to us and hung back to take a moment with his new mate.

Luke led us back to a private VIP room and ordered drinks for all of us. We were all laughing about the situation, when Wesley walked in holding his mate's hand. She was so tiny compared to him.

"Hey everyone, I'd like you to meet my mate, Lillian." Wesley beamed with pride and his mate waved shyly to us all. He went around and introduced us all to her. Maxine gave her a hug, as did Arielle.

"Lily is the youngest daughter of the Alpha from Blue River pack." Wesley informed us. "I'm going with her back to her pack tonight to meet her family. We'll spend a few days there before I bring her home." He explained.

I was really ecstatic for Wesley. He finally looked like himself again and happier than ever. I thanked the Moon Goddess for blessing him with his mate at just the right time.

CHAPTER FORTY-FOUR

Maxine

We had such a wonderful night out. I was over the moon for Wesley. The Goddess knew that he needed his mate now more than ever. And Lillian was so adorable. She was petite and absolutely beautiful. I couldn't wait for them to get back from her pack, I knew we were going to be great friends.

We stayed at the club pretty late, so by the time we got back to the packhouse, we were all exhausted. Back in Xander's room, I stepped out of my dress and threw on one of his shirts. I brushed my teeth before crawling into bed. He silently slipped in behind me and wrapped me up in his arms. He kissed me goodnight and we drifted off to sleep blissfully.

The next morning, I woke up still in Xander's arms. I took a deep breath in, enjoying his delicious scent. I was just about to doze off again, when Xander's voice called me back. "Maxine?"

"Hmm? Morning." I mumbled sleepily to him as I wiggled closer to him.

"I want to take you away on a trip for a couple of days." He whispered in my ear.

My eyes popped open, and I turned to look at him. "A trip?"

"Yes. I think we need a break from all the chaos and just spend some time together." He watched me hopefully. I grinned at him.

"Okay. That sounds amazing. When do you want to go?" I asked, feeling excited about the idea.

"Today." I laughed, but Xander was being serious. "I've already made the arrangements."

"Really? Where are we going?" Excitement fluttered through me. I propped myself up on my elbow.

Xander smiled at me and tucked my hair behind my ear. "We're going to stay at our Seaside Hotel."

"Oh, that sounds perfect! I can't wait." I was giddy. I leaned forward and kissed Xander. "Thank you!" I said before kissing him again.

He caught me the second time and held me close for a longer kiss. He ran his hand down my body and slid it back up underneath his shirt that I was wearing. He growled when his hand found the cheeky, lace panties I was wearing.

He pulled me on top of him, and I felt his morning wood pressed against me. Desire flooded through me as I straddled him and continued to kiss him deeply. I moaned as I ground my hips into his member. Xander growled again and grabbed my ass with both hands.

I kissed my way down to his neck and sucked on his sensitive spot where my mark would go. He pushed his hardened length against my now wet panties. His hand slid up my shirt to my breast when there was a knock on the door.

We both stopped what we were doing with disappointment. "Yes?" Xander called out gruffly.

"Xander, you better get moving if you want to make it to Seaside before dark." His mother replied through the door.

Xander glanced at the clock on his bedside table and cursed. "Shit. Okay, thanks!" We slept later than usual.

He kissed me before I climbed off of him. "I'm going to hop in the shower. Why don't you pack a bag for three days?"

"Okay." I replied. As he walked towards the bathroom, I slapped him on his ass. He growled at me playfully and I giggled.

I pulled a suitcase out of the closet and packed some casual beach attire, a few bathing suits, and a couple of nice outfits just in case. I was just about done when I remembered the lingerie that the girls had made me buy during our last shopping trip. I quickly pulled out a couple of provocative sets and stashed them in the bottom of my suitcase. Now all I needed was toiletries.

Just then Xander came out of the bathroom with a towel wrapped low around his waist. His hair was still damp and tousled. Oh Goddess, my mate is so damn sexy. I bit my bottom lip as he sauntered over to me.

He reached out and gently pulled my lip out of my teeth with his thumb. "I know what's on your mind and Goddess, you smell so fucking good right now, but we don't have time for all the things I want to do to you, baby." Xander said huskily to me. He kissed me quickly, then directed me toward the bathroom and smacked my ass in return. I growled playfully at him just as he had.

I took a quick shower and left my hair damp to dry naturally. I brushed my teeth and filled my toiletry bag so I could pack that too.

When I stepped out of the bathroom, Xander was dressed simply in a white fitted T-shirt, some casual, blue shorts, and white sneakers. He looked clean-cut and handsome, leaning against the dresser while he typed on his phone.

He eyed me up and down as I stepped past him in my little towel. He growled and reached for me as I rushed past him into the closet, giggling.

I dressed in a lavender tank top, white shorts, and white tennis shoes. I did a quick mental check of everything I needed to pack, closed my suitcase and stood it up on the floor.

"Ready!" I smiled at Xander excitedly. He grabbed my suitcase along with his and we left the Alpha suite. I was feeling so excited. It was so sweet that Xander planned all this without me knowing.

We grabbed some food to go from the kitchen on our way out. Xander's parents were waiting for us outside with Donovan and Ari. I was super excited when we greeted them, but for more than just our vacation. "Tell them!" I urged Xander.

His parents raised their brows and waited expectantly. "Wesley found his mate last night." Xander told them proudly.

Luna Clarissa gasped and clasped her hands together. "Oh, how wonderful! Who is she? Do we know her?"

"Her name is Lillian, the youngest daughter of the Alpha at Blue River." Xander informed them.

"Oh, we've met them at a summit! I remember her, she has gorgeous red hair, right?" Luna Clarissa gushed.

"Yes, that's her. She's stunning. I'm so happy for Wes!" I said beaming.

"And she's so tiny! They are adorable together." Ari jumped in.

"That's wonderful. Are they here?" Alpha Jackson asked.

"No, Wesley went back to Blue River to meet her parents and help her pack up. He should be home around the same time as us or maybe the next day." Xander replied.

Xander ran through some pack business with Alpha Jackson and Donovan, while Ari mindlinked me some inappropriate things. She was teasing me and being dirty about my time alone with Xander. If it wouldn't have raised a few eyebrows, I would have flicked her to cut it out.

With the car all packed, we said our goodbyes and hit the road. It was a long drive to the Seaside Hotel. Xander and I talked for hours about everything. Conversation was so natural and easy with him. He really is my best friend, and I feel like I'm more myself when I'm with him.

We laughed and joked, reminiscing about our childhood. We discussed training techniques, listed places we'd like to visit, and I even serenaded him with different songs that came on the radio. Xander talked about Blake and how much he missed him. I was excited about Wesley's new mate and decided we needed to have a lake day to get to know her better. Apparently, Xander's dad is ready for him to take over the pack now. Xander's anxious but excited to step up as Alpha. I told him about my Luna studies and how I was nervous to take on the role. Many Lunas train for years to prepare for the responsibility, while I had focused on warrior training. We also exchanged ideas and goals we have for the pack and ourselves.

We pulled up to the front of the Seaside Hotel around midafternoon. We didn't hit any traffic and made good time. When we stepped out of the car, the hotel porter came and took our bags. Xander took my hand as we entered the hotel lobby. A concierge greeted us and handed Xander a leather portfolio. He scanned over something inside, then nodded as he gave it back. "Very good." Xander said coolly.

"Excellent, Alpha." The concierge said as he bowed slightly to him. "Luna." He acknowledged as he dipped his head to me. Then, he handed Xander a black key card. Xander guided me over to the elevators. The hotel was luxurious and polished. The floors were white and gold marble. There was an elegant staircase that led to a classy lounge on the second floor. Large golden columns lined the grand foyer. A beautiful crystal chandelier hung above.

Once we were inside the elevator, Xander held the black card over the access reader, then he placed the card in his pocket. He leaned back against the shiny, golden wall and pulled me close to him. He gently nuzzled his nose with mine and then kissed my forehead as he wrapped his arms around me. "This place is beautiful." I told him as I hugged him back.

"You haven't seen the best part yet." He replied with a grin.

The doors opened to the private penthouse floor. There was a hallway leading to the suite doors. Xander used his black card again to open the double doors. I peeked inside and gasped.

CHAPTER FORTY-FIVE

Xander

Maxine's face was priceless when she saw the view from our suite. The exterior wall was floor to ceiling windows, giving the most exquisite view of the ocean. I loved the awe and excitement in her eyes as she gazed around.

"Xander, this is phenomenal." She said softly to me, stepping closer to the windows. There was a wrap-around balcony with a glass wall railing, so it didn't obstruct the view. Once you stepped out onto the balcony, you could see not only the ocean, but the cityscape to the left and the beautiful rocky cliffs to the right.

"It's breathtaking." She said. I walked up behind her and snaked my arms around her, kissing her neck.

"*You're* breathtaking." I told her. She turned her head and kissed me sweetly. "Come on, let me show you around." I pulled her hand towards the large living room space we had walked right through. The room was decorated in creams and gold colors. There was a large, cushy sofa with a matching armchair, a chocolate-colored coffee table, and piano. The floors were marble with a lush, gold area rug.

I showed her the full-sized kitchen, it was sleek and modern with marble countertops and a full bar. There was a large dining room as well. On the other side of the kitchen was a spare bedroom with access to the balcony, along with a separate sitting room with a desk overlooking the ocean. Then, I led her back through the living room to the bedroom on the other side. I opened the door for her to walk in.

"Oh, wow," she exclaimed. Two of the four walls were windows with blackout curtains that rolled up and down with the push of a button. A sliding glass door led out onto the wrap-around balcony. There was a large California king sized bed, a chaise lounger, and an armchair. The ensuite bathroom had a giant round tub, a huge walk-in shower, and a full vanity.

Maxine wandered around, admiring the amazing scenery. Then she flopped down on the bed with her arms outstretched to the sides. "This place is amazing!"

I laughed, she was so adorable. I crashed down on the bed next to her on my side, propped up so I could face her. "Do you want to go down to the beach?" I asked with a grin.

She sprang up. "Yes! Let me get changed!" She dashed over to her suitcase that was already waiting for her. Maxine pulled out a couple of dresses she brought with her, hung them up in the closet before grabbing her swimsuit and ran into the bathroom. I chuckled at her eagerness.

I changed into my swim trunks and flip flops. I sat on the bed waiting for Maxine. She came out wearing a little black bikini and a sheer black cover up that was open in the front. I groaned as she walked closer to me. When she was within reach, I placed my hands on her hips and pulled her to me.

"Are you sure we have to go down to the beach now?" I asked as I kissed the valley between her breasts. She giggled and wiggled herself free from my grasp.

"Yes, it was your idea. Let's go!" She demanded as she inched her way towards the door.

Once we were on the beach, we kicked our flip flops off and went for a stroll down the shore, hand in hand. The sun was sinking lower, and the sky was displaying vibrant colors. It was really beautiful. The ocean breeze made the weather perfect.

"Maxine, I'd like to have our mating ceremony soon." I told her thoughtfully. "I want to be fully mated to you, and I want the entire world to know that you're mine."

She beamed up at me. "And you're mine."

"Always, baby." I smiled back at her. She wrapped her arm around my waist, and I held her close as we moseyed down the sand with our feet just barely in the water.

"I'd like to do it after Wesley gets back home. If that's okay?" I asked her hopefully.

"I'd love that." She replied. We discussed some ideas about our ceremony. Then, Maxine got really quiet and pensive.

I stopped walking and gently pulled her to me. "Hey, you alright?"

"Yeah." She smiled at me hesitantly. "I was just thinking... Well, I was wondering... Do you want kids?"

I couldn't help the grin that spread across my face. Of course I wanted kids. Alphas instinctively wanted at least one heir to their pack. I thought of the dream I had when I was in a coma, and I debated whether or not I should tell her about it. It felt more like a memory than a dream, like a vision of what was yet to come. It had to be real.

She raised her eyebrows questioningly and bit her lip slightly waiting for my answer. She's so gorgeous and in this lighting, she almost seemed to glow. I placed my hand on her chin and gently tugged her lip loose from her teeth with my thumb. She had no idea how sexy she was when she did that.

"With you. I want as many kids with you as the Moon Goddess will gift us." I stared at her with my most loving, sincere eyes. Her beautiful smile made me melt and my heart beat faster.

I leaned down and kissed her tenderly. Affectionately resting my forehead against hers, my heart felt so full and happy.

I gazed into her eyes and tucked a loose strand of hair behind her ear. "I love you, Maxine."

I had been dying to say those words to her. So much had happened to us and I was bursting to tell her how much she meant to me, but I wanted the moment to be magical.

She stared back at me with those electric blue eyes, so full of emotions. "I love you, Xander."

She slid her hands up behind my head as I tightened my arms around her body and kissed her passionately. When we broke for air, I held her close to me, her head on my chest. We stood together just like that watching the sun sink lower in the sky.

Eventually, we had to head back to the hotel to get ready for our dinner reservations. I dressed in black slacks and a white dress shirt with my usual style of leaving it unbuttoned at the top. I really wasn't fond of ties. I had just slipped into my black suit jacket when Maxine strolled out of the bathroom looking divine.

She wore a deep burgundy dress that hugged her body and hips but hung loosely around her thighs. The straps of her dress curved just around her arms, leaving her back completely bare. Her hair was twisted up so her back and neck were fully exposed. She was stunning. My wolf howled inside my head. The urge to mark her was overwhelming.

I just stared at her and shook my head. "I didn't think it was possible for anyone to be this beautiful."

She blushed. I walked over, took her hand and kissed it. "Shall we?" She nodded with a smile and we left.

We had a romantic candlelit dinner at the pack's second restaurant Luna del Mar, a fine dining seafood restaurant. It is even better than our Italian restaurant. The place is right on the water, with a gorgeous view.

I enjoyed every minute with Maxine. Being near her was like being home. We talked and laughed all evening. Everything felt perfect. After the hardships we've been through, I just wanted this trip to be flawless and special for her. I love her so much, I would do anything for her.

After dinner, we decided to go back to our hotel room, it was getting late. I thought maybe Maxine would like to watch the waves with me on the balcony before bed.

Back in the room, Maxine said she wanted to change. She grabbed her things and slipped into the bathroom. While she was in there, I stripped out of my dress clothes and put on some black, silk pajama pants. I opened the sliding glass door in our room and stood on the balcony with my elbows resting on the glass railing.

It was a spectacular night. The beach stretched toward the city lights on the left, but the city was far enough away to not cause too much light pollution. We had a gorgeous black sky full of stars. The moon hung low over the cliffs to the right. It was peaceful with just the sounds of the waves crashing on the shore.

I felt tingles spread across my back as Maxine's hands danced across my skin. She stood next to me, watching the waves. She looped her arm through mine and held my hand, resting her head on my shoulder. She sighed, "It's absolutely beautiful out here."

"Not as beautiful as you." I stood upright and turned so she was in my arms. I hummed when I saw that she was wearing a little, black, silk robe. "I like this." I said softly as I ran my finger just inside the collar of her robe.

She raised her eyebrows at me with a smirk. "And I like these." She said as she slid her hand down to squeeze my ass. She had taken her hair down, so I let my hand glide up her shoulder into her hair as I moved in for a kiss.

I gently brushed her lip with my tongue, and she parted them for me. We deepened the kiss and my other hand snaked around her body. Her hands caressed my neck and the back of my head. I pressed her body between me and the railing. She moaned softly into my mouth. She's so irresistible.

I pulled back to gaze into her exquisite eyes. "I love you so much, Maxine." I told her as I stroked the side of her face.

"I love you too, Xander. More than anything." Her eyes sparkled in the night as she looked at me with so much affection.

My eyes wandered down and noticed that her robe had fallen open a little to reveal a sexy, little lace number. I groaned in appreciation. "Oh, baby, what are you doing to me?"

When I peered back up at her beautiful face, there was a mischievous glint in her eyes.

CHAPTER FORTY-SIX

Maxine

I picked out a lacy, black bralette with tiny, matching panties, and slipped my black, silk robe over it. I had never worn anything like this before. I let my hair down and took a deep breath in the mirror to calm my nerves before exiting the bathroom.

Xander was out on the balcony. He was only wearing some silky pants, and I was admiring the view of his muscular, bare back and his fine ass. I couldn't fight the need to touch him as I approached.

This view is stunning. The night was dark, but the moon made the waves glow as they crashed down onto the sand. There was a slight breeze that kept the air cool. You could see a million stars twinkling in the sky.

Xander held me in his embrace, and everything felt so right. I love this man more than I knew was even possible. The Moon Goddess made him just for me and he was absolutely perfect.

Xander seemed to really like my little robe, I couldn't wait for him to see the rest of it. He kissed me passionately. Our kissing quickly turned heated, Xander's hard body pinned me up against the railing of the balcony. He peered down at me with so much love and desire in his eyes. His eyes drifted lower and he groaned as I realized my robe had slipped open, revealing my lacy top.

"Oh, baby, what are you doing to me?" He asked with hungry eyes.

Our eyes met once again and I grinned as all kinds of naughty thoughts ran through my mind. I slowly ran my hand down his body, starting with his collarbone to his strong pecs. Then, my fingertips trailed over every groove of his washboard abs. My eyes followed my hands, drinking in every inch of his flawless body.

I gazed back into his fervent, green eyes that were watching my every move. I untied the sash of my robe. I brought my hands up to the opening of my robe and little by little pulled it down my shoulders. I let the robe fall slowly to the ground, fully revealing my lingerie to Xander.

"What about this? Do you like this, too?" I asked innocently.

His eyes darkened and a low rumble came from his chest. Xander slowly shook his head, and his eyes roamed my body. "No, I don't like it." He said seriously, then he gripped my hips and pressed his hardened member against me. "I love it." He whispered in my ear in an extremely sexy, husky voice.

He kissed and nibbled at my neck, I tilted my head back, reveling in the shiver of pleasure it sent straight to my core. His hands explored my body, and I moaned as he massaged my breast.

He slid his other hand down around my ass, then trailed down my thigh, lifting my leg. I hooked my leg around his hip, drawing his body closer to me. Tingles spread everywhere.

"Xander," I sighed as he sucked on my marking spot. He lifted his head and caught my moan with his lips as they crashed into mine. He trailed his hands down, one arm snaked around my lower back and the other slid under my bottom as he lifted me up. I wrapped my legs around his waist and held his head as we continued kissing.

He carried me into the bedroom and gently lowered us down onto the bed. He propped himself up on his elbows above me. I gazed into his eyes that held so much love for me.

I reached up and stroked his face. He closed his eyes and turned into my hand, kissing my palm.

"Xander," I called to him, "I want you." His heated eyes darted back to mine. "I want all of you."

Xander studied me intensely, as if he was peering into my soul. "Are you sure?" He asked me.

"I don't want to wait anymore. I just want to be with you." I assured him, I had been ready for a long time now. "I love you, Xander."

"I love you, Maxine." He said as he leaned down to kiss me tenderly. I ran my hand through his hair and held him close to me.

With my legs still wrapped around Xander's waist, I pressed my hips upward against his erection. He growled into my mouth. He caressed my breast and moved his hips, so his member rubbed slowly against my wet panties.

He kissed down my neck as his fingers played with my nipple through the lace. He gently bit my sensitive marking spot and pleasure radiated through my body down to my core. I cried out in delight.

Xander's hand skimmed down my stomach to my hip. His fingertips danced across my lace panties, and he hummed. He sat up on his knees and slowly slid my panties down my legs while keeping his eyes locked with mine.

He held one of my legs and placed a trail of little kisses, gradually working his way up to my inner thigh. When he reached my middle, he didn't stop. He placed a delicate kiss on my lower lips before diving his tongue into my core. I gripped the sheets and moaned as Xander twirled his tongue around. He slid his tongue up and circled it around my clit.

He held onto my thighs, spreading me wider as he buried his tongue deep inside me again. His tongue snaked its way up and he sucked on my sensitive bud.

"Xander," I breathed out. The pleasure was building, and I was tingling all over.

He slid his fingers inside of me while his tongue swirled around my clit. He watched me with his smoldering green eyes as he sucked hard on my bud. The intensity pushed me over the edge, and I cried out loudly as my orgasm consumed me.

Wave after wave of ecstasy filled me. I felt pleasure all the way down to my toes. As I came down from the high,

Xander continued to move his fingers in and out of my core, causing little residual jolts of pleasure to shoot through me. Once my body finally relaxed, Xander came up and kissed me hungrily.

I threw my arms around him as he settled his hips between my legs. I skimmed my fingertips across his back and down his sides. I traced his defined muscle lines along his abdomen, following each dip and curve. I gradually found my way down to his drawstring and pulled the tie until it came loose.

I kissed down Xander's jaw to his neck as my hand slipped inside the front of his pajama bottoms. I lightly trailed my hand down his hard member. His skin was so soft and smooth as I wrapped my fingers around his cock. I licked up his neck as I stroked his hardness. He moaned softly in my ear.

I nibbled on his earlobe and danced my fingertips around the head of his cock. I pressed the palm of my hand to his smooth shaft and slid it up and down. I kissed my way back down his neck as I stroked his member. I picked up the pace, and he automatically started moving his hips.

I gently bit down on his marking spot, Xander growled and shivered. He pulled back to stare into my eyes. "I want you, Xander," I whispered to him as I slid his pants down his hips. He pulled them off the rest of the way and repositioned himself between my legs.

I could feel his rigid member at my core. He rubbed the tip against me, coating himself in my wetness. He held my gaze. "Are you ready?" He asked me in a low voice.

"Yes," I responded breathlessly.

He leaned down and kissed me tenderly. Our eyes were locked as he slowly pushed inside of me. It was a tight feeling, but it wasn't painful as I had expected, the mate tingles spread through me causing me to only feel pleasure. I gasped at the new sensation as he filled me. He groaned and stilled inside of me for a moment. Xander placed his forehead on my shoulder as he breathed out my name.

I was breathing heavily. I reached up and pulled his face to mine to kiss him ardently. When he was ready, he pulled his hips back, sliding his cock out ever so slowly before slipping back into me. The feeling literally took my breath away; I could feel every inch of him. The mate tingles were more intense than ever, igniting everywhere our skin touched and within me.

He paused inside of me. "I really do love this, baby, but I want to see all of you." Xander told me as he played with the edge of my bralette.

I propped myself up as he slid the lingerie up my body. I raised my arms; he pulled it off and tossed it to the side. His eyes roamed down my body. "Perfect." He growled before kissing me again.

As his tongue danced with mine, he moved his hips again, sliding in and out of my core. His hand massaged my breast and pinched my nipple. I tilted my head back, moaning and he watched me intently.

I gazed up at him, he's so handsome. My eyes trailed down his body, watching him move inside me. It was sexy as hell. I wrapped my legs around him tighter and he began to thrust into me quicker.

"Oh Goddess, Xander!" I gasped as pleasure was building inside of me again.

Xander shifted his body, so he was sitting up on his knees and lifted my hips up to his pelvis. His cock plunged deeper inside of me, hitting a spot that made me moan loudly. His hands gripped my waist as he drove into me over and over. His hand brushed up my body to my bouncing breast. He squeezed it and rubbed his thumb over my nipple.

He trailed his hand up and around the back of my neck, while he wrapped his other arm under my lower back. He lifted me off the bed, so we were both sitting up. I straddled his lap as he continued to move my hips up and down on him.

Our tongues danced together as he held my body against his. I rocked my hips with the movement of his thrusts. Xander groaned with pleasure. He kissed down my neck, and I threw my head back sighing in ecstasy.

Xander guided my hips as I rode him faster. The intensity was building inside of me as he caught my breast in his mouth and sucked on my nipple.

"Xander!" I cried out in pleasure.

"Yes, baby!" Xander's husky voice urged me. My moans filled the room as I reached the peak.

"Mark me," I commanded. Just as my body began to shake, Xander sank his teeth into my marking spot. Colors and stars filled my vision as the most extreme, orgasmic pleasure took over my body. The euphoria was intense as I cried out loud. Xander retracted his teeth and licked the fresh mark, still thrusting inside of me.

I wasted no time. Still trembling, I pulled his head to the side and plunged my teeth into his marking spot. He growled loudly as he climaxed. His arms held me firmly against him as he gradually slowed and stilled inside of me. I pulled my teeth out and licked his mark.

My wolf howled in delight. The mate bond was solidified as our souls intertwined. All at once, I could feel just how much Xander loved me. His emotions flooded through me with my own. I gazed into his eyes lovingly, in pure rapture. It was as if now I was finally complete. Our souls were forever one.

We stayed wrapped up in each other with our foreheads touching affectionately, lost in the moment. Breathing heavily and hearts racing wildly. There were no words needed, we could feel each other's emotions.

Xander reached his hand up and wiped a stray tear of joy from my cheek. He held my face tenderly in his hands and kissed me slowly.

After reveling in the bliss, we eventually cleaned up before laying down together. Exhaustion from being marked and mated took over us, we held each other close as we fell asleep peacefully.

CHAPTER FORTY-SEVEN

Xander

As the sun rose, light filled the room. We had fallen asleep with the curtains open after our incredible love making. Maxine and I were fully marked and mated; I was in heaven. I never thought I could feel so complete.

We had fallen asleep tangled up together and I woke up the same way. I gazed lovingly at the beautiful woman sleeping in my arms. I can't believe she's mine forever. Zeus howled happily in my head, wagging his tail like a puppy.

Both of my arms were wrapped around her torso. One of Maxine's hands rested on my chest and the other on my waist. She had one leg draped over my thigh.

Her silky hair was sprawled across her pillow. There was one strand laying on her face, I gently pushed it back. She stirred slightly in her sleep.

Looking down at our naked bodies, last night's pleasure flashed through my head and my cock twitched to life. A devious idea popped into my head.

I delicately trailed my fingers down Maxine's arm. She smiled in her sleep as the mate sparks were stronger than before. I grazed my fingertips up and down her back slowly. She arched her back a little but didn't wake. Then, I lovingly touched her fresh mark. She moaned and shivered. Goosebumps spread across her skin. My fingers ran down her back to her thigh that was draped over me and up the backside of her leg, gliding over her perfect ass. She sighed and wiggled a little. I was enjoying teasing her in her sleep.

I repeated the movement down her leg and back up, this time just barely brushing her lower lips before moving up her bottom, and all the way up her spine.

Maxine's eyes popped open, and I could smell her arousal.

"Morning, gorgeous," My voice came out deep and husky.

"Good morning to you, sexy," She replied with a gleam in her eyes.

I held her heated stare as I continued caressing her skin, gliding my hand back down her thigh. This time, I slid my palm slowly up the underside of her thigh and squeezed her ass. Then, I brushed my hand down her inner thigh and stroked along her slit.

She gave me a sexy little growl and kissed me. I ran my fingers along her skin a couple of times before dipping inside of her warm center. She was already so wet for me, I hummed in appreciation as I slipped my tongue inside her mouth.

She closed her eyes as I slid my finger back out and rubbed her responsive little bud. She pushed her hips forward and my fingers dove back inside of her. I moved my hand faster, gliding in and out of her as she moaned into my kiss.

I pushed my hips forward and my erection pressed against her smooth skin. She opened her hungry eyes and raised her brow at me. She gripped my back and pulled my body closer.

I slowly removed my fingers from her core. I repositioned myself to guide my hard cock into her tight walls. She gasped at the sensation and threw her head back in delight as she bit her bottom lip.

I growled, Goddess she's so sexy. I slowly moved in and out of her warm core and she grasped onto me tighter.

"Oh Maxine, you feel so fucking good," I whispered as I pushed inside of her more. She gave me a mischievous grin.

She firmly pressed my shoulder back as she pushed herself up, effectively rolling us over so she was on top of me. I growled, loving the incredible view of my naked mate sitting above me.

She placed her hands on my chest and slowly sank down on me. Her eyes never left mine as she sighed out in pleasure. She slowly raised her hips, sliding my cock almost all the way out of her slick core before lowering herself again. She bit her bottom lip.

Maxine rolled her hip while she moved herself up and down on me ever so slowly. Fuck, she's the sexiest thing I've ever seen.

She quickened her pace and her breast bounced slightly. I reached up and cupped both of them. I pinched and tugged on her nipples, and she sucked in air with a hiss.

I propped myself up on one of my elbows and brought my mouth to her breast. I licked her rosy bud, swirling my tongue around her peak. Then, I sucked her hardened nipple into my mouth.

Maxine pulled my head back and dipped down to catch my lips with her own. She kissed me fervently and rotated her hips as I pushed in and out of her. I slid down onto my back, taking her with me. At this new angle, my cock rubbed against her clit, and she cried out in pleasure.

She rocked her hips to meet mine as she slid along my shaft. I held onto her waist, increasing the intensity of each thrust.

Maxine pushed herself upright again and threw her head back with a moan as she rode my cock harder. "Oh, fuck, just like that, baby!" I encouraged her. I was getting close.

I slid one hand down her pelvis and rubbed her clit with my thumb. She moaned and called out, "Oh, Xander! Don't stop!"

I could feel her pleasure through the bond, along with my own and we were on the edge. I guided Maxine's hips with my other hand and thrust upwards harder as I circled her clit with my thumb. Our moans were filling the room as her eyes met mine and she came hard. Her body shook as I finished, too.

She slipped her hands up my body as she lowered her chest to mine. She nuzzled her face into my neck. We panted, trying to catch our breath and our heart rates began to come down.

I slowly slid out of her and cleaned up. I went to the bathroom and turned on the shower. I walked back into the bedroom and scooped Maxine's naked body up in my arms, she giggled as I carried her into the shower with me. I gently set her down.

I stood behind her and moved her hair to one side, kissing her shoulder and neck. I soaped up a loofah and washed circles across her back. I brought the shower pouf around to her front, caressing her perky breasts. She moaned as they were still sensitive.

Maxine leaned back against me. My member pressed against her ass, already stiff again with excitement. I set the loofah on the ledge and spun Maxine around to face me. Her eyes were on my hard cock, they slowly dragged up my body taking it in as water cascaded down me. The water washed over her too and I watched as the suds slid slowly down her perfect body.

I tilted her chin so that I could capture her lips. She snaked her arms around me, and I held her tight. I walked her backwards until she was pressed up against the wall. She gasped as her back touched the cold tiles.

I skimmed my hand down her body and lifted her thigh up around me. I kissed down her neck and collarbone. I sucked one of her breasts into my mouth as my hand groped the other one eagerly. Maxine's moan echoed throughout the bathroom.

I continued to kiss my way down her stomach. I got down on my knees in front of her and placed her leg over my shoulder. I stared up into her bright blue eyes as I ran my tongue up her entire slit. She raked her fingers through my hair and tilted her head back against the tile.

I plunged my tongue inside of her. I continued to pleasure her with my mouth, licking, sucking, and swirling over her clit with my tongue. When I could feel she was almost at her peak, I stood up. She whimpered before my lips crashed into hers.

I lifted her up against the wall and lowered her down onto my cock until I was entirely sheathed in her warmth. Without hesitation, I thrust myself inside her over and over.

Her clit was swollen and overly sensitive from her previous orgasm, she was already moaning out in pleasure. "Oh, Xander!" She sighed, "Oh, fuck!" I loved this naughty side of her.

"Mm, yeah, baby," I moaned in her ear. I increased my speed and pumped inside of her harder.

"Please, Xander!" She mumbled out, as she was on the edge.

"Please what?" I urged her, "Tell me what you want, Maxine." My voice was raspy and out of breath.

Maxine cried out, "Oh, faster, Xander! Please!" She was gripping my shoulders tightly.

I growled. My mate is so fucking sexy. I obeyed her wishes and slammed my cock into her faster. We were both on the edge now as I pounded into her. The bathroom filled with the sound of our skin slapping and the moans of our ecstasy as we climaxed together.

I held her there against the wall for a minute as we caught our breath. I pulled out of her and slid her slowly down the wall to her feet. I kissed her tenderly.

We cleaned ourselves properly and toweled off. We had exhausted ourselves again, so we climbed back into bed. This time, I remembered to hit the button to close the curtains. Maxine curled up next to me with her head on my chest and we drifted off to sleep.

That's how we spent the day, waking up, making love until we were ready to pass out again for an hour or two. We called for room service at some point since we were starving. Then, we explored each other's bodies all over again. I wish I could spend every day like this. It was heaven.

CHAPTER FORTY-EIGHT

Maxine

I woke up and stretched my tight muscles. Thank the Moon Goddess that werewolves have super-fast healing; I would be too sore to walk from all the sex otherwise. We literally spent the entire day making love yesterday. It was mind blowing. I wish we could stay here forever like this, just the two of us in our own little bubble.

I rolled over to seek the warmth of my mate but was disappointed to only find an empty bed. I frowned and glanced at the clock on the bedside table. It's 7:37 am. I reached over and pushed the button to slowly open the curtains. The room gradually filled with the early morning light, as the ocean came into view.

I scampered off to use the bathroom and brushed my teeth. I grabbed a silk robe and slipped it on, tying it closed. Then, I left the bedroom to find Xander.

I stepped into the main living room, he wasn't here or in the kitchen. I walked towards the balcony to see if he was somewhere out there. I stopped when I heard his deep voice. I followed the sound to the small sitting room on the other side of the suite.

I listened at the door to make sure he was alone before I entered. I couldn't smell anyone else and it sounded like he was on the phone, so I cracked the door open slightly. I peeked in to see Xander sitting in the desk chair, but it was turned around facing the balcony.

"That sounds perfect. And everything will be ready in time?" He asked whoever he was talking to on the phone. He was quiet as they responded to him.

I slipped into the room and silently approached him, not wanting to interrupt.

"Excellent, I can't wait." Xander felt my presence, causing him to swirl his chair around and give me a crooked grin that made me melt. "Thanks again, Mom. See you when we get back." Xander said into the phone before ending the call and setting the phone to the side on the desk.

I was a little surprised that he was talking to his mom, but I quickly forgot about it as I stared down at my shirtless mate.

"Good morning, beautiful." Xander greeted me as I leaned against his desk next to him.

"Good morning, handsome." I replied with a smile. "You're up early."

"I had a little business I had to take care of." He gently grabbed hold of my hips and slid me over in front of him with a devilish grin.

"Is everything alright?" I asked, not really concerned, seeing how he seemed to have other things on his mind that are definitely not pack related.

Xander positioned himself between my legs and leaned up to kiss me. "Everything is perfect." He whispers as he leaned back in the chair. He slowly tugged on the sash that was holding my robe closed. Once it was loose, Xander let the robe fall open, exposing my naked body to him.

A low rumble came from his chest as he snaked his arms around my waist, pulling me down until I was straddling his lap. He leaned me back in his arms as his head came forward and kissed my mark which sent an intense shiver of pleasure throughout my body, then he kissed my collarbone. He continued lower, taking my nipple into his mouth.

I ran my fingers nails across his back, while my other hand danced through his hair. He massaged my other breast in his hand and pinched my hardened peak. I let out a little gasp.

Xander's lips crashed into mine as his arms tightened around me, causing me to grind down on his hardened member. His hand descended to my ass, giving it a squeeze and then he slipped it under me, finding my core.

He hummed, "You're so wet for me, baby." I rose up just enough to allow him to wriggle out of his boxer briefs that he was wearing.

I slowly sank back down onto his thick cock. He slid right in and filled me. I moaned and threw my head back at the amazing feeling and Xander groaned, leaning his forehead against my chest.

He gazed up at me, "You're so perfect, Maxine." He captured my lips with his own, deepening the kiss as I moved up and down on him. He slid my robe the rest of the way off my arms, letting it fall to the floor.

I held onto the back of the chair for leverage as I built up my pace. Soon, we are both panting and moaning.

Xander quickly lifted me off of him, set me on my feet, and turned me around. He gently spread my legs apart as I leaned over the desk. He thrusted his shaft back into me quickly, causing me to cry out in ecstasy. He gripped my hips as he pounded into me rapidly. I leaned forward until I was fully bent over the desk, as he hit a new spot that sent pleasure radiating throughout my body.

"Oh, Xander!" I moaned.

"Yes, baby!" Xander panted as he continued to slam into me.

"I think... I can't..." I didn't even know what I was trying to say to him when I felt a tingling pleasure take over my body. "Oh, I'm gonna cum." I said breathlessly.

Xander growled and increased his pace, causing me to climax hard and tighten around his cock. He groaned as he found his release, too.

I just lay there with my chest on the desk, panting. Xander slumped forward on me, still holding himself up so he didn't completely crush me. We stayed like that as we caught our breath. Xander placed tiny kisses on my shoulder, then gently pulled out and grabbed some tissues to clean up.

"I love waking up like this." I told him with a wicked grin.

He hummed and kissed me, "Mm, a million times better than coffee."

I slipped into my robe as Xander pulled his underwear back on. He was built like a Greek God, chiseled to absolute perfection. He winked at me, catching me ogling him. I could feel my cheeks flush. Xander pulled me close to him and kissed me slowly. I draped my arms behind his head, and he slid his hands down to my lower back.

Our kiss began to turn heated again when I pulled back. "As much as I love doing nothing but you all day, I do want to go down to the water before we have to go back to the pack."

Xander chuckled and kissed the tip of my nose. "Alright, love. Let's get changed then."

I wore a red bikini with my sheer black caftan. Xander was wearing some black and grey swim trunks. We grabbed a couple of towels and strolled down to the beach.

The beach was relatively deserted; there were a few sunbathers further down. It's almost like our own private beach. We laid our towels out on the sand, and I dropped my caftan on the towel.

I stole Wiley's favorite line and said, "Last one in's a rotten egg!" As I took off towards the water. My feet were just about to hit the water when I felt two muscular arms wrap around me and lift me up.

I squealed as Xander ran with me into the ocean, spun and fell backwards, causing us both to crash under the water. When we came up, I gasped and splashed water at Xander. The water hit him right in the face and he froze. Then, he peered up at me with the most devilish look in his eyes and I knew I messed up.

I giggled as I turned to run. Xander came splashing after me and tackled me into a wave. We surfaced from the water laughing as we wrapped our arms around each other. We continued to play in the water for a while before laying out on the beach towels to dry off.

I lay on my stomach with my head resting on my folded arms. Xander was lying next to me on his stomach but propped up on his elbows.

I gazed up at his sun kissed shoulders, gorgeous eyes, and wet, messy hair. I couldn't help but sigh. How did I get so lucky?

"Thank you, Xander." He tilted his head questioningly. "This was just what we needed, the perfect getaway."

He grinned at me and my heart fluttered. "Anything for you." He slid his hand across my lower back as he leaned over and kissed my shoulder.

"I love you." I told him with sincerity.

His smile widened, "I know, I can feel just how much you love me now." He said as he lightly brushed the mark on his neck, which somehow sent a shiver down my spine. "I love you, Maxine."

CHAPTER FORTY-NINE

Xander

We decided to explore the little seaside town for the afternoon. We showered and got dressed. I wore some khaki shorts and a white shirt. Maxine looked amazing in her denim shorts and a green tank top.

We stopped into a little French bistro for lunch, and the food was delicious. There was lots to see, so we walked around the shops and boutiques, while admiring their art and architecture.

I was so happy just being near Maxine, like this was what I had been missing my whole life. I've always heard people talk about the mate bond like it was this unparalleled love. This was beyond what I could have imagined, though. I never thought I would feel like one person was my entire world, like I couldn't breathe without her.

Beyond that, I could feel her emotions. My happiness was amplified by Maxine's joy filling my soul. Every feeling was magnified by Maxine's emotions. Her love for me, her happiness, her desire; it just made what I'm feeling that much stronger. It's overwhelming at times, but I wouldn't trade it for anything.

I had a special surprise for her tonight, so after we spent most of the day out and about, we went back to the suite to get ready. I didn't tell her where we were going, so she was just getting dressed for dinner.

It didn't take me long to get ready. I dressed in a navy suit with a white dress shirt and styled my hair. I went to the kitchen to grab some water when my phone rang.

The name on the screen surprised me. I quickly answered it and moved to the spare sitting room to close the door.

"Alpha Luke, to what do I owe the pleasure?" I said calmly.

"Xander, please, after everything we've been through, just call me Luke." He replied.

I chuckled. "Okay, Luke, what can I do for you?" It's weird to think that we would be even remotely friendly towards each other after the pool party incident. But Luke had helped us so much since then, with the rogues and vampires, and then again with Wesley at his club.

"Actually, I've got some rather disturbing information for you." He said seriously.

"What is it?" I asked curiously.

"Well, as you know, we tore down the remains of the rogue camp. My team and I combed through everything, but there wasn't much to it. The rogues were just in it for the money from the vampires." He paused and my mind was racing with what he could possibly say next.

"I decided that we needed to check the mansion's remains before we had the land cleared. After the fire, there wasn't much left. However, we did find what appeared to be an office that had a fireproof safe inside. It took some time, but we finally figured out how to crack the safe open." His pausing was starting to irritate me now; I just wanted him to get to the point.

"Inside, we found valuables, gold, jewelry, gemstones. But we also found some files... I think you need to see them." He told me hesitantly.

"What kind of files?" I inquired impatiently.

Luke sighed. "Files on Maxine."

"What?!" I growled, feeling anxiety creep in. There are files on Maxine? How much did they know about her? Is she safe now?

"There's more..." Luke said clearly unsure how to continue.

"Tell me." I gritted out.

"It would appear that there is another coven of vampires that they were working with, I think they know about Maxine, too." I could hear the concern in his voice.

"Fuck!" I said under my breath as I began pacing the room. "I need to see everything that you have found. Can you meet us back at our pack? We will be back tomorrow evening."

"I'll be there the next morning." Luke firmly stated. It's clear that he realized the severity of the situation.

"I appreciate everything." I told him sincerely, "Thank you for your help."

"Any time, man." Luke said before ending the call.

Fear and anger flooded through me as I paced the small room. I needed to know everything about this other coven. Who are they? Where are they? How much do they know about Maxine?

She's not safe. We are already marked and mated, our bond is complete, but that didn't stop those bloodsuckers from murdering Maxine's mother. They must have learned that it didn't work, but what if they try to end the Midnight Wolves by killing Maxine before she has kids? Or what if they come after our children?

Zeus let out a fierce growl. I could feel myself losing control. I whirled around and slung the books sitting on the desk to the side, sending them flying across the room.

I stood there huffing with my hands in my hair, when I felt two gentle arms slip around my torso. The sparks spread and her scent filled the air, immediately calming my beast. I placed my hands on her arms and pulled her to my front, wrapping her in a tight embrace.

"What happened?" She asked quietly.

I met her eyes, and they were full of worry. Shit, I didn't want to ruin the night. I leaned down and kissed her pretty lips. She has such a soothing effect on me, the anxiety eased off.

"I'm sorry, love, I didn't mean to lose my temper." I told her, stroking her soft cheek.

"It's fine, Xander. Is everything okay?" She asked as she rubbed little circles on my back.

"There's been some news…" I replied hesitantly, "But we can deal with it when we get back to the pack." I really don't want to ruin this trip.

"Xander, wh–" She pushed, but I cut her off.

"I promise, I will tell you everything, Maxine." I held my hands on either side of her face, peering directly in her eyes. "It can wait." I told her reassuringly.

She was so torn, she clearly wanted to press further, but she decided against it. "Okay." She whispered with a tiny smile.

I kissed her forehead and pulled her in for a long embrace. I noticed the clock on the wall and pulled back.

"We have to get going or we're going to be late." I informed her as I sheepishly went to collect the books that I tossed across the room. I was embarrassed by my outburst.

I set the books back on the desk and turned to get my first real look at my mate tonight. My heart skipped a beat. She's the most gorgeous thing I have ever seen in my life. She was wearing a simple but elegant blue dress that hugged her body just right. It had the thinnest straps and a V-neck. The skirt was straight and fitted, coming down just below her knees. She wore matching high heels. Her dark hair was down in soft waves.

I realized I was just frozen there, staring at her beauty. I swallowed and met my mate's eyes. She had a knowing grin as she winked at me. "You look good too, handsome."

A wide grin spread across my face as I moved toward her. I rested my hands on her hips and kissed her tenderly. I took her hand and led her out of the suite.

Once we were in the elevator, I pressed the button for the lobby. Then, I faced Maxine, placed my hand on her hip, and slowly backed her up to the golden wall behind her. Her electric blue eyes stared up at me as I pressed my body against hers.

I slid my hand up into her hair and kissed her lips. I let my hand slowly trail down her neck, touching her sensitive mark, eliciting a sweet moan from my mate. My hand drifted further down, across her collarbone. My fingers followed the edge of her dress, down the top of her breast.

Her eyes were heated, and her breathing was uneven. I stopped at her cleavage and placed a delicate kiss on her neck. "Soon." I whispered as the elevator dinged, announcing our arrival.

I pulled away from her body and held out my arm for her. She quickly composed herself and slipped her hand in my arm as the doors opened to the lobby. As we walked across the hotel, everyone was watching us, but my eyes were only on Maxine.

CHAPTER FIFTY

Maxine

I could feel Xander's anxiety and anger building like it was my own. It confused me at first, not being used to the mate bond yet. When I found him, his eyes were glowing, letting me know that Zeus had taken control.

I knew that something was really wrong, but Xander insisted on waiting to tell me about it. I didn't want to upset him more or ruin the evening that he had planned. The worry lingered in the back of my mind.

Xander erased any thoughts on the matter once we were in the elevator. His simple touch could turn me on in an instant. I was practically trembling with anticipation. Then, the elevator ding brought me back to my senses and I had to compose myself.

Walking across the lobby with this gorgeous man made me feel like royalty. I couldn't help but notice how everyone was staring at us. I glanced back at my mate to find his eyes locked on me. I could feel how much he loves me, causing butterflies to flutter in my stomach.

The valet already had our SUV waiting out front. Xander opened the door for me and helped me in before making his way around to the driver's seat. He wouldn't tell me where we were going but I could feel how excited he was about this.

He reached over and held my hand as he drove us through the little seaside town. It didn't take long before he was pulling over in front of a small marina. I scanned the area outside the window, then turned back to him with my eyebrows raised. He just smiled at me as he climbed out of the vehicle.

He opened my door and helped me out, not letting go of my hand. He gave his keys to a valet. He led me down a path that opened up to the docks. My intrigue and excitement continued to grow.

We walked all the way down the docks to a very sleek yacht. It was like nothing I had ever seen before. It was black on the bottom and silver on the top. There were port holes along the sides that had intricate swirls carved into the boat. Long curved windows mimicked waves above the port holes. A line of gold separated the black from the silver. The upper decks were all curved and rounded, making the yacht shaped more like a torpedo.

I stared up at the yacht in awe, when I faced Xander he was smiling. "Is this yours?" I asked him in amazement.

He shook his head. "It's *ours*." He clarified. "You haven't seen the best part yet." He gently tugged my hand, leading me down the slip towards the front of the yacht.

He stood with his hands on my shoulders and turned me towards the words painted in gold on the bow of the boat. *Luna Maxine*. I gasped and looked up at his sweet smile.

"I had it named after my beautiful mate." He said as he wrapped his arms around me from behind.

"Xander." I didn't know what to say. I was so shocked. "It's incredible." I told him as I slid my arms around him.

He kissed the top of my head. "Well, we better get aboard before they set sail without us." He chuckled.

The yacht was absolutely massive. I couldn't believe this was ours. "Can we live here?" I asked him dreamily, "We could just sail the world."

Xander laughed. "You would miss the pack too much." He was right, I would miss our family and friends, and I really do love the woods around our packlands. "But I promise to take you away on it as often as possible." I beamed at him, loving the idea.

Xander showed me around. The main deck had a large pool at the stern and a spacious patio at the bow. Cushy seats lined the railings. In between there was an elegant dining room with a long table and smaller, more intimate tables beyond it. There was a full bar and kitchen. Behind the kitchen was a decent sized bedroom and bathroom that led out to the pool.

Outside the dining room on either side were staircases leading up to a lounge. The lounge was so luxurious. Another bar lined the back wall. Several navy armchairs and chaise loungers were arranged in a cozy setting. Next to it, there was a piano. In the middle of the lounge, there were two steps down into a sunken sitting room. The stairs led down to lush, silver couches that wrapped all the way around the circular seating area. There was soft, mood lighting under the couches, around the ceiling, and along the bar. Navy blue pillows were scattered around the area, very inviting.

The ceiling above the sitting room had a large deep blue cutout to it. Xander pushed a button and the dark blue panels separated, revealing the early signs of sunset in the sky through the glass ceiling.

Across from the bar, glass doors opened to the upper deck. Xander took my hand and guided me out onto the deck. The view was absolutely beautiful.

There was a small table set for two with candlelight. "I thought we could have dinner here tonight." Xander told me with a crooked grin.

"That sounds perfect." We stood at the railing of the upper deck when the horn on the yacht blew causing me to jump a little. Xander rubbed the small of my back and chuckled.

"We're about to set sail." He told me soothingly. Just then, the yacht slowly pulled away from the dock. Xander wrapped his arms around me, and we watched the incredible view as we pulled out of the marina.

The sun was sinking, and the sky was turning the most vibrant shades of reds, oranges, and purples. "It's so beautiful." I whispered before I kissed Xander.

"Come on. Let's eat." Xander suggested, as he pulled out a chair for me. Once he sat down across from me, we were immediately greeted by a waiter. He brought us water and a bottle of champagne.

The food was divine, and we had such a lovely, romantic evening. I really didn't want to go back yet.

"What's wrong, Maxine?" Xander asked with concern in his eyes. I forgot that he could feel my emotions.

"Nothing! Everything is perfect." I reassured him, "I just don't want to leave yet. I wish we could stay longer and explore the yacht more."

A wide smile spread across his handsome face. "Your wish is my command." I raised my brows and tilted my head to the side, questioningly. "I took the liberty of having our things at the hotel packed and brought onboard."

Now it was my turn to grin like a Cheshire cat. "We're staying here for the night?" I asked hopefully.

Xander nodded and I threw my arms around him happily.

After dinner, we got dressed in our swimsuits and hit the pool deck. Xander dove right in without hesitation. When he surfaced, my heart raced. Goddess, he is stunning.

I slowly stepped down into the water. The temperature was perfect. Xander's eyes were traveling down my body and back up again as I lowered myself into the water.

I swam circles around Xander, he never took his eyes off me, slowly turning in a circle with me. I rolled over so that I was floating on my back and gazed up at the incredible night sky. From out here on the ocean, you could see even more stars than back at the hotel. It was phenomenal.

Xander joined me and we just floated next to each other in silence, admiring this incredible moment. Eventually, I lifted my head and faced my mate. "Xander, this is truly amazing. Thank you."

He pivoted his body and pulled me into his strong arms. "Maxine, you are truly amazing. I wish I could give you the world."

"I don't need the world." I shook my head, "I just need you." I held his face in my hands and kissed him slowly. He swam us over the edge of the pool and pressed me against the side, deepening our kiss as I wrapped my legs around his waist. I could feel his erection poking at my bottom.

He smiled sheepishly at me. "You don't know what you do to me, baby." He kissed me again more fervently before pulling back. "Let's go rinse off," Xander suggested. I followed him in a happy daze.

We entered the back bathroom attached to the bedroom by the pool deck. Xander turned on the shower, and two shower heads began spraying. He gladly helped me out of my bathing suit before removing his own. We stepped into the warm stream of water.

Xander spun me around, so my back was to him, and he washed my hair. The feeling was delightful as he massaged my scalp. He rotated me back around to rinse my hair and began washing my body. I grabbed a pouf and washed his muscular body too.

Soon, the goal of getting clean was forgotten as we caressed each other. I slid my hands up and down his hard shaft, and Xander slipped his fingers inside of me. We built each other up and found our release at the same time.

We finished showering and dried ourselves off. I found my red, lacy night set and pulled it on. Xander was wearing a pair of navy, silk pajama bottoms. I eyed him hungrily and moved toward the bed.

"Actually, we're not sleeping here." Xander informed me. I must have given him a confused look because he laughed and continued, "This is just a spare bedroom. We have a much nicer room below deck."

CHAPTER FIFTY-ONE

Xander

I gently pulled Maxine's hand, guiding her out of the room. She stopped me, hesitantly. "Xander, I'm not exactly dressed." She said shyly, motioning to her sexy, little pajamas. She was wearing tiny, red lace shorts, they didn't even fully cover her cheeks. Her tight top was low cut with tiny straps, and it barely went past her ribs, leaving her abs exposed. It was red lace and practically see through.

My eyes roamed over her body, and I growled. "You look perfect." I said, pulling her towards the door.

"No, Xander, I don't want the crew to see me like this." She planted her feet firmly.

I shook my head with a smile. "Baby, the crew is done for the night. I have sent them all below deck. Our suite is on level 2; the rest of the staff is on level 3 or lower. Don't worry." I said as I kissed her forehead and continued out the door, tugging her along with me.

Instead of going below deck though, I pulled her upstairs to the lounge. Confusion spread across her face. "We can't forget dessert." I told her with a mischievous grin.

In the lounge, only the mood lighting was on, giving the room a soft glow. I had the staff set up the floor in the recessed lounge with cushions, blankets, and pillows. I led Maxine down to the seating area. "Get comfy, I'll be right back." I told her as I dashed over to the bar.

The crew had placed dessert and drinks out for us. I grabbed the tray and brought it over to where Maxine was now sprawled out, peering up at the stars through the moonroof. I could feel her contentment through the bond. As I sat down next to her, she propped herself up, so she was leaning back on her elbows.

"Ok, we've got chocolate covered strawberries and champagne." I told her and her eyes lit up.

"I love chocolate covered strawberries." Maxine exclaimed.

I smiled proudly. "I know."

She picked up a strawberry, bit into it, and groaned. "Oh, it's so good!"

I laughed and popped the bottle of champagne, pouring two flutes. I handed one to her. "Maxine, I love you more than I thought was even possible. Here's to a lifetime full of happiness."

She gave me a gorgeous smile and clinked her glass with mine. We both sipped the champagne and ate a few more strawberries. Then, I set the tray to the side and laid back with one arm tucked behind my head. Maxine curled up next to me, and I wrapped my other arm around her. We lay there in silence, watching the stars.

Maxine's hand was resting on my chest. She gently glided her fingertips across my skin. She ran her hand over my chest ever so delicately. Then she traced the lines across my abdomen. My chest rumbled in delight as she caressed my body. I trailed my fingers up and down her back.

She propped herself up on her elbow, leaning over me, she kissed me gently. My fingers traveled lower down her back til they found her perfect ass. I gave it a little squeeze. Her eyes flashed with a glint of playfulness as she bit down on my bottom lip and pulled it gently.

I growled at her and flipped us over, so she was lying back on the cushions, with my body pressed against her. She giggled as she wrapped her arms and legs around me.

I gazed down at her, admiring my beautiful mate. Her hair was sprawled across the pillows beneath her, and her eyes were twinkling. I dipped my head down to capture her lips tenderly.

I brushed her hair away from her shoulder and kissed my mark that rested on her slender neck. I felt her body shiver underneath me. I smirked into her neck and slowly licked across her mark, eliciting a moan from her gorgeous lips.

I could feel tingling and pleasure radiate through the mark on my own neck. I ran my tongue over the mark again and another moan slipped from her lips as she pressed her body upward into mine. I gently sucked on the mark, and I could feel her immense pleasure through the bond mixed with my own.

I gently bit down on her mark. Maxine cried out loud, and her body quaked with an orgasm. I almost came myself. This bond was intense now that we were fully mated.

I lifted my head to meet Maxine's eyes. I smiled at her playfully. Her eyes were wide, and her cheeks blushed. "Well, that is a nice development." I teased, "I can really have a lot of fun with this." I bounced my eyebrows at her.

She gasped at me as she pushed against my chest, "You're evil!"

I chuckled and kissed her lips, "Oh, baby, you have no idea."

She laughed and her eyes danced with mischief, "Just remember, the bond works both ways. And I am not above embarrassing you during training or an Alpha meeting..."

My jaw dropped at her threat. I laughed, "Straight to public embarrassment. Who's evil now?" I joked.

"I'm just saying, two can play that game, so think real hard before you tease." She narrowed her eyes at me in the cutest attempt to look intimidating.

I laughed heartily, "Okay, okay. Truce!" I declared and kissed the tip of her nose.

I sat up on my knees. "I actually have something I want to show you, if you're up for it." I prompted, getting a little anxious.

She could feel the change in my demeanor and turned serious. "Okay." She said, sitting up nervously.

I stood and took her hands in mine, pulling her up to her feet. I quickly pulled her body flush against mine and gave her a long slow kiss, helping to calm my nerves.

I led her over to the piano and sat down, motioning for her to sit next to me. She did without saying a word. I could feel her curiosity piqued.

I never played the piano before she left for the Academy. I started learning while she was away, on nights when I couldn't sleep. No one else really knew that I could play now. I was going to play for her at the hotel, but... we were a little distracted.

I took a centering breath and placed my hands above the keys.

My fingers pressed down on the right keys, as I played the sweet song that I picked out just for her. She stared at my hands with awe.

It took a few notes before she recognized the song and her eyes snapped to me. I had learned the song that was playing at her birthday when she scented me as her mate for the first time.

I glanced over at her. She was so shocked and touched.

She kept her eyes locked on me as I poured my heart into the song. I could feel the emotions coming from her through the bond. She was surprised, elated, and moved.

It was hard to focus on the song and not on my mate, but I wanted to play flawlessly for her. She deserved the world, so I concentrated on every note.

As I was getting close to the end, I peeked over at her again and I could see her eyes begin to glisten.

She smiled sweetly at me as a tear rolled down her cheek.

I finished the song and gazed back at my beautiful, emotional mate. She gently reached over to hold my face as she kissed me passionately.

CHAPTER FIFTY-TWO

Maxine

Speechless. I was utterly shocked and just speechless. Xander had completely blown me away.

Not only did I not know that he could play the piano, but he played what I now consider to be our song! Like, oh my Goddess, this man is astonishing, he never ceases to amaze me. His fingers danced across the keys with ease and every note was beautiful.

I've known Xander is an incredibly strong and intelligent Alpha, but he was also a talented, skilled musician? The Moon Goddess truly blessed me when she crafted him to perfection.

I was so moved; I felt a tear slip down my cheek. He made my stomach flutter with butterflies, and my heart skipped a beat. I was completely smitten with this man.

When he finished, I had no words. Nothing I could say could ever be enough to explain to him how much I love and appreciate him.

The only thing I could do was show him. I kissed him deeply, pouring all my heart and soul into the kiss. Hoping that he understood how I felt.

He slipped his arms around me, and I moved to stand in front of him. He pulled my body close to his. I ran my fingers through his hair as our tongues brushed against each other.

Passion quickly ignited. Xander stood and lifted me off the ground all in one swift motion. He set me down on the piano keys and a cacophony of notes rang out. I could feel him smirk against my lips as I giggled into his kiss.

He ran his fingers through my hair, swooping it back away from my face. He kissed down my neck to my mark. "Xander..." I breathed out, half moaning and half warning. I didn't want him to tease me; I needed him for real this time. He just smiled against my skin as his fingers trailed across my lace top. He caressed my nipple over the lace.

His hands skimmed down my sides to the hem of my bralette. He went to lift it up and I pulled back, still unsure about being so exposed out in the open when I know there are other people on this boat.

"What if someone sees?" I expressed my hesitation.

"Then, they would be directly disobeying their Alpha's orders." He explained with a raised brow and a knowing look on his face. None of the crew would be able to defy an Alpha order like that.

I nodded at him and raised my arms above my head as he peeled my top off and tossed it to the side.

He kissed me as his hands massaged my breasts. I sighed and arched my back, loving the feeling of the intense mate sparks on my sensitive skin.

I reached down between my legs and pulled the string, untying his pajama bottoms. I slipped my fingers into the waistband and slid them around to his sides. Then, I pushed his pants down his hips until they were loose enough to fall to the floor and there was nothing restricting his rigid member anymore.

I took him in both of my hands and lightly ran them up and down his shaft, causing a groan to escape his throat.

His tongue swirled with mine as one hand rolled my nipple and the other glided down my body, between my legs. Xander rubbed his fingers against my lips through my lacey bottoms. He hummed into my mouth, "Mm, always so ready for me."

With my legs wrapped around him, I pulled his body in closer to mine, carefully guiding his hardened length towards my wanting core. "Xander…" I whispered, "I need you."

His fingers slipped inside my panties and pulled them to the side as his cock found my eager lower lips. He slid himself inside me ever so slowly. I threw my head back, enjoying the feeling of being filled by him. He lowered his mouth to my breast as I leaned back on my elbows against the piano top. He slowly slid in and out of me.

The pace was torturously slow but incredibly delightful. I never wanted him to stop but I needed more at the same time. The feeling was overwhelming. "Xander…" I called out, "Please."

I could feel him smirk against my breast as he teased the other with his fingers. He left a trail of warm kisses up my chest and neck, until his lips crashed into mine. He wrapped his arm around my lower back, leveraging our lower bodies so that he was hitting even deeper inside me somehow. The sensation was magnificent, and I cried out.

Xander held my leg up with his other arm. He was stroking a spot that was causing my pleasure to intensify quickly. He moved his hips faster.

He tilted his hips slightly and I moaned loudly; my body trembled with ecstasy. Xander ran his thumb over my lips and then his hand slid down my neck and chest.

"Fuck, Maxine. You're so sexy, baby." He groaned as his pace picked up even more.

I could feel a tightening and humming throughout my body, we were both getting close.

Xander lifted my leg slightly higher above his hip and thrust into me harder. We were both moaning over the sound of the random piano notes that were being played by our grinding bodies.

I felt the consuming pleasure building until it burst into a powerful orgasm, and I could feel Xander climax with me, adding to its intensity.

We panted against each other and reveled in the lingering ecstasy.

"We have to get a piano for our suite!" I told Xander with a naughty grin. He let out a hearty laugh, then he leaned forward and kissed my forehead.

"Anything for my Luna." He said as he gave me a crooked grin.

As we cleaned up, we couldn't help but laugh because every time we moved, the piano keys tinkled and clanked. I became acutely aware of just how loud we had been and was slightly mortified that the crew may have heard us.

"Let's head down to our bedroom, love." Xander suggested to me. I nodded, excited to see more of the yacht but was also starting to feel a bit tired.

Without further warning, Xander scooped me up and threw me over his shoulder like a caveman. I squealed and wiggled in his arm. He turned toward the door, and I spotted my top laying on the floor.

"Wait! Xander, grab my top, please! I don't want the crew to find it tomorrow morning." I cried out, tapping his back insistently.

He chuckled at me and set me down to grab the lace material, then hoisted me back over his strong shoulder. Just for good measure, he smacked me playfully on the ass. "Hey!" I squeaked out. I did enjoy the view of my mate's spectacular ass as he carried me down below deck to our room.

Once we were on the 2nd level, he paused and I heard beeping as he punched in a code to our bedroom. He walked in, letting the door close behind him and set me down. He kissed my nose before spinning me around to take in the room.

The suite was in the bow of the ship and had the most phenomenal view. The walls were all windows, allowing us a peak at the night sky and the ocean waves as the yacht cut through the water. There were dark shades that could lower to block out the windows if we wanted.

Along the windows were plush, silver window seats with luxurious black and navy-blue pillows scattered artfully about. Across from the window, next to where I was standing was a large, lavish bed that was calling to me with its dark sheets and soft, silver blankets.

The room was once again lit with soft mood lighting that was recessed into the ceiling.

"Absolutely incredible." I smiled up at Xander. "This whole trip is more than I could have dreamed. Thank you." I placed my arms around his neck and kissed him.

We made love several times in the bed, up against the windows, on the window seats, and in the shower before we collapsed in each other's arms, completely spent. We fell asleep quickly in our own happy little world.

CHAPTER FIFTY-THREE

Xander

I woke to the heavenly view of my gorgeous mate asleep in my arms. Her beautiful, dark hair was draped all around us. Her lips were slightly parted as she dreamed. Maxine is everything I ever wanted and so much more.

I lay there watching her sleep, completely enamored by her beauty. My eyes trail over every detail of her face; the little smattering of freckles across the bridge of her cute nose, the way her dark lashes splayed over her soft cheek, and the delicious cherry tint to her oh-so-kissable lips.

After a while, Maxine stirred and stretched as her eyes fluttered open, focusing on me. A smile instantly spread across her luscious lips. "Hi." She said sleepily to me.

"Hi." I replied back with my own wide smile. "Did you sleep okay?"

"Oh, I slept so well." She replied as she stretched, "I always sleep so peacefully in your arms." She kissed me sweetly. "Did you sleep well? How long have you been awake?"

"I had the best night's sleep. I woke up a little while ago. I was just enjoying the view." I said with a grin before kissing her nose.

"Oh, speaking of views!" Maxine perked up and reached for the button to raise the shades on the windows. As the shades rose upwards, light slowly filled the room, revealing the beautiful water and horizon in front of us. You could see the shoreline off to the side, with beautiful rocky beaches and tall trees beyond that.

"Did I mention how amazing all of this is? You really are so wonderful, Xander!" She told me.

"Anything for you, Maxine." I caressed her cheek and kissed her tenderly.

Maxine scampered off to the bathroom and I mindlinked one of the crew to bring in our breakfast. When she came back, everything was set up for breakfast in bed with an incredible view.

"Ah-mazing!" Maxine exclaimed as she hurried back into bed with a huge smile on her face.

By the time we had finished our breakfast, we were close to docking back at the marina. We showered, dressed, and gathered our things. Maxine decided she wanted to sit out on the main deck and watch as we pulled into the marina. I gazed at her as her hair blew gently in the wind and her eyes danced with excitement as she observed her surroundings. She was really enjoying this trip, and I made a mental note to take her back here at least once a year.

I placed my hand on top of hers that was resting on the railing. "Are you ready to head back home?" I asked hesitantly.

She turned to me with her bright eyes, "Yes!"

Her eagerness surprised me. "Really?" I asked with a raised brow.

"Mhm. Honestly, I could stay here forever, it's so gorgeous and peaceful. But I'm also super excited to get back to the pack. I'm thrilled to have our mating ceremony. I have to show Ari my mark and tell her about our trip. I really need to check in with Sabby and your parents too; I'm worried about them. Oh, and I can't wait until Wes gets back with Lillian! I want to spend time with her and get to know her better."

I chuckled at her as she talked quickly and excitedly. "I'm glad you're happy to be going home." I told her as I leaned down and placed a kiss on her lips. I honestly was relieved she wasn't stressing out about all of those things.

With the mating ceremony comes our transitions into Alpha and Luna. She worries so much about everyone, I was afraid she would have felt guilty leaving them, but she deserved a break more than anyone. My mom had thought it was such a great idea when I brought it up to her. When I voiced my concerns, she waved it off and insisted we go. I still hadn't told Maxine about my conversation with Luke yet, but it was nothing that she needed to worry about now. Soon we would have all the information and could figure things out from there.

"I need to go make a phone call. I'll be right back." I told Maxine before kissing her. She just nodded to me as her eyes continued to scan the scenery, taking it all in. She was so content.

I went up a level to the lounge. I could see Maxine on the main deck from here. Mindlinking at this distance would cause me a great headache, so I would just call my dad instead. The phone rang twice before he answered.

"This is Alpha Jackson." His strong voice answered.

"Hey, Dad. How's it going?" I asked him casually.

His tone immediately changed. "Xander! How's your trip?" He sounded jovial.

"It's perfect, Dad. It was just what we needed after everything." I replied.

"Good, good. Everything here is just fine." He paused for a minute. "So, you marked Maxine. Congratulations, son."

"Thank you. How did you know?" I asked, confused.

He chuckled. "When a new Luna is marked, the pack feels the change of hierarchy. That's why it was traditionally done in the mating ceremony. But many opt for a more private setting nowadays. As of now, your mother and I are just Alpha and Luna by title only. The pack belongs to you and Maxine now. Congratulations, I'm really happy for you, Alexander." He sounded genuinely happy, relieved even.

I was taken back a little, not realizing I had become the official Alpha. I felt different but I just assumed it was from being fully bonded to Maxine. I'm not sure how Maxine is going to feel once she knows everyone could feel the moment our bond was complete. I imagine her cheeks will turn a new shade of red.

"Thank you, Dad. I hope we continue to make you and the pack proud." I said as I watched Maxine braid her hair to keep the wind from whipping it around.

"I have no doubt that you will be the best Alpha, Xander." My dad assured me. "So, when are you coming home?"

"Today. We are docking now and should be on the road within the hour." I informed him. "Dad, are Donovan and Charlie around? I have some information."

"Oh, yes. Just a minute." There was a pause as I assumed he mindlinked them. After a moment, Dad said, "Alright, they are here and you're on speaker."

I jumped straight to the point. "I received a call from Luke at Dark Moon. He said in cleaning up the mansion's remains, they found a safe. They were able to crack the safe open and found files on Maxine."

"Shit." I heard Donovan curse under his breath.

I continued, "There appears to be another coven involved that they may have been working with. We didn't go into great details, but Luke agreed to bring the documents to us tomorrow morning."

"Okay, we will prepare for the meeting." My dad replied quickly.

"Obviously, this needs to be dealt with quickly. Maxine will never be safe if there are vampires out there that know about the Midnight Wolf." I told them, my fury and fear rising all over again.

"Don't worry, Xander, we will do everything in our power to protect our Luna." Donovan promised, but I could hear the anger and anxiety in his voice as well.

"I haven't told her anything yet, but she knows that I received a call that set me off." I informed them as I looked out towards my mate whose eyes were now locked on mine, filled with concern. "She can feel my emotions through the bond, but I didn't want to worry her yet. She deserves to be happy."

We wrapped up the call, and I made my way back down to Maxine.

"Is everything okay?" She asked me cautiously.

I pulled her into my arms, buried my face into her neck, and inhaled her soothing scent. I let her smell of orange blossoms and cinnamon calm me. She rubbed her hands comfortingly over my back, helping to ease my emotions.

"Xander?" She whispered.

I stood fully, kissed her forehead, then placed my chin on the top of her head, keeping her close to my chest. "It'll be alright, love. I'll tell you about it when we get home. It can wait for now."

I could feel her warring with herself to ask more questions, but she didn't push. She just let me hold her, knowing I needed it.

A crew member informed us that we could debark. Just before we turned to go, he asked me in a more hushed voice, "Sir, would you like me to go ahead and have the piano retuned?"

Maxine's head whipped around, completely mortified. I suppressed a laugh and cleared my throat. "Yes, that would be great. Thank you." I winked at Maxine and she looked like she wanted to disappear.

I wrapped my arm around her shoulder to comfort her. *Relax, it doesn't matter what anyone heard. You are the Luna, hold your head up proudly.*

Maxine took a breath to collect herself. I could feel her straighten up and we began making our way back to reality. The crew would have our things loaded into the vehicle.

Before we hit the road, we grabbed some smoothies at a little shop next to the marina.

The ride back was much quieter than the ride out. I know Maxine was worried about me. So, I tried to ease her mind, giving her a few more hours of peace. I asked her questions about our trip and her plans for when we got home.

She relaxed a bit and fell into conversation with me. I rested my hand on her thigh as I drove towards our pack. About an hour and a half into the drive, she fell asleep. I tried to keep my mind clear so that my emotions didn't disrupt her much needed sleep. I think I may have worn her out last night.

As we arrived back at the pack, I sent out some mindlinks to let them know we're back as the Sentinels opened the gates for us.

Once we passed the border, a feeling of belonging and strength washed over me that was more intense than before. I was now the Alpha.

I pulled the SUV up to the front of the packhouse and turned to gently wake Maxine. "We're home, love." I lightly rubbed her shoulder as she stretched and blinked her eyes. She glanced around and a smile spread across her lips.

CHAPTER FIFTY-FOUR

Maxine

I thoroughly enjoyed my time away with my insanely sexy mate. I couldn't have asked for a more perfect getaway. I am thankful we were able to really enjoy ourselves and complete the bond privately.

I won't lie though; I am thrilled to be back. I love our pack, and I miss it so much whenever I'm away. I couldn't wait to see our friends and family. There was so much to do, and I was looking forward to it all.

After Xander woke me up, I leaned over and gave him a quick kiss before hopping out of the car. There was a small group of people waiting to greet us at the top of the front steps. Alpha Jackson and Luna Clarissa stood together smiling. My dad and Sabby were there, as well as Donovan and Ari.

I smiled up at them. Ari squealed and ran down the stairs to me. "Let me see it!" She grabbed my shoulders and inspected my neck on one side, then pushed my braid back off my other shoulder, revealing my new mark. She gasped when she saw it. "Oh my Goddess, it's so beautiful, but why does it look so different?" She stared at it closely with wide eyes.

"What? What do you mean it looks different?" I said placing my fingertips over the mark. I could feel a tingling spread through my body as I touched it. Xander was by my side in an instant. He took my hand away gently and examined the mark closely.

"I guess it is a little different." He said cautiously. My eyes searched his face, and I grew concerned.

Hey, hey. Relax. Xander's voice filled my head. *It probably has to do with you being a special wolf. We'll look into it. Your mark is perfect.* He stroked my cheek, and I felt a little better.

Donovan noticed our interaction and helped change the focus. "Congratulations, kiddo!" He said as he gave me a bear hug. "Or do I need to call you Luna now?"

"Oh, please, that would be so weird. And I'm not the Luna yet." I told him, smiling over at Luna Clarrissa.

She smiled sweetly back at me and said, "Actually, sweetheart, you are the Luna now."

"What?!" I asked in shock as my head snapped to Xander. "But we haven't had our ceremony yet."

"Apparently, the ceremony is just for show. It's the marking that solidifies the transition of the pack." He informed me with a small smile as he rubbed the back of his neck.

"Did you know?" I was surprised to hear this from him. Why didn't he tell me?

Xander shook his head, "I just found out this morning."

My dad interrupted with his own congratulations and hugs; the others joined in and welcomed us home.

I felt very overwhelmed. I'm the official Luna now. But that also means Xander is the official Alpha.

I turned to him, our eyes met. "Congratulations, Xander. You're going to be an incredible Alpha."

He kissed me, "And you're going to be the best Luna. Our pack is so lucky to have you."

We all moseyed inside to the dining hall for a late lunch. There weren't as many pack members here as usual, since it was so late. However, those that were in the dining hall stopped when they saw us and let out a howl and clapped their hands. I blushed, Xander smiled and nodded his head at the pack before we took our seats.

There were dishes of food on the table for us to take what we wanted. We filled our plates and started eating. Luna Clarrissa said, "I hope it is alright, but I've taken the liberty of getting things ready for your mating ceremony. Xander relayed to me what you had in mind, and I just jumped in so we could have it as soon as possible." She seemed hesitant, like she thought I was going to be upset about her planning our ceremony for us.

"That's very thoughtful of you." I said sincerely, "You always organize the best events. I can't wait to see what you've done."

She was relieved by my reaction. "Oh, you're going to love it! I've already invited all the Alphas and Lunas of our allied packs and ordered the groceries for the menu. The decorations should be here tomorrow, and we are readying the guest rooms." She added excitedly.

I was surprised at how much she had done already. "When is the ceremony?" I questioned curiously.

"Saturday. And it's a full moon, so it will be perfect!" She gushed as she reached across the table and squeezed my hand.

Saturday? "That's in three days..." I replied in disbelief. My mind raced with all kinds of things I needed to do before then.

"Relax." Luna Clarrissa pulled me back from my panic. "I've taken care of everything. We can talk later to go over the details and set your mind at ease." She gave me a loving smile.

Xander rubbed my back. I peeked up at him and he winked at me. "Don't stress, love."

So, tell me, how good is the sex? Ari mindlinked me and I swear my face must have turned bright red. I glared at her. *Oh, come on, don't be like that! Was it amazing?*

Yes. I replied quickly. *It was absolutely mind blowing. The pleasure was earth-shattering, like nothing I've ever felt before. Now behave!* I scolded her, shooting her another look.

Xander chuckled softly under his breath. My eyes darted to his face. He just smirked at me, clearly amused.

What? I linked him.

I don't know what she said, but clearly Arielle is being inappropriate and getting you all worked up. His voice called back with a little laugh.

I huffed a little and pushed them both out of my mind. There is a time and place for such conversations and in front of my mate's parents, not to mention my dad, brother, and sister is definitely not that place or time.

After we finished lunch, we retreated to the packhouse living room.

Xander announced to everyone, "Maxine and I are going up to the suite to get unpacked and settled." He directed his next words to the men. "We'll meet you in my office before dinner to discuss things." They all nodded at him. His mom looked really excited about something. She must have more planning to do for the ceremony, she really enjoys it.

As we reached the door to the Alpha suite, Xander turned to me, placed his hands on my hips and slowly backed me up against the wall. He lifted his hand to cup my face as he kissed me slowly. My hands clung to his shirt as he deepened the kiss. When I felt as if I had no more air left in my lungs, he broke the kiss, resting his forehead against mine.

He didn't say anything, but he stayed like that for a long time as if he was savoring the moment. Then, he pressed his lips to my forehead and pulled away, taking me with him.

He entered the code to the suite and I noticed it was different than before. I glanced up at him, about to ask why, when he pushed the door open and I gasped.

The entire suite had been remodeled. Everything had an earthy, natural feel to it. The walls were a jade color with one forest green accent wall. The furniture had all been replaced. There were hunter green couches with sage and cream-colored throw pillows. Two cushy, cream-colored armchairs with grassy green colored pillows sat near the fireplace. A sky-blue blanket had been draped expertly over the couch, adding a pop of color. The end tables and coffee table were dark mahogany. There was a tray on the coffee table that held river rocks. A distinctively twisted piece of driftwood sat on top of the mantle.

A large, beautiful picture of my favorite place hung over the couch. The gazebo sat on the right side of the frame, the surrounding forest matched the color scheme of the room perfectly, and you could see the beautiful waters of Plum Creek running through it. Above the mantel was a smaller picture of the gorgeous view from the lake house at Rock Lake. You could see the crystal blue waters, and the rocky shore surrounded by beautiful green trees. My gorgeous pack was decorating our home.

I peered up at Xander in shock. "How? How did you do all of this?"

"My mom. They officially moved out." He informed me with a smile. "Do you like it?"

"I love it! It's beautiful." It's exactly what I would have wanted done with the space, but somehow better.

I peeked into the kitchen. The cabinets had been stained a darker color, almost black. The walls were painted in the forest green color. The countertops were replaced with slate and there was a back splash of stones. The faucets and handles were all brushed nickel.

"Come see our new bedroom." He tugged on my hand, pulling me towards the largest bedroom. Although all the bedrooms up here were huge and had their own ensuite bathroom, the Alpha's room was very grand.

I was always afraid that moving into his parents' old room would feel weird, but this was an entirely new room. Nothing was the same in it at all. The walls had been repainted, the flooring has been refreshed. The furniture was all brand new and arranged in a completely different manner. It was as if we were in a brand-new house.

The walls were all jade, but the wall behind the bed was a forest-green. The bed frame was the same dark mahogany wood. The bedspread was sage with a mix of decorative pillows on it in hunter green, cream, and sky blue. The floors were dark hardwood, with plush, mossy-green area rugs under the bed and in the sitting room area. There was a cushy cream couch and two forest green armchairs with large emerald pillows. The drapes were the same mossy color as the rugs.

Above the bed was the most breathtaking portrait of Zeus and Onyx. They were sitting in the woods, looking majestic as they nuzzled each other lovingly. Onyx howled in my head, happy to see her handsome mate. I was in awe of the gorgeous picture.

"Where did this come from? How did you get this?" I was so surprised and curious.

Xander stood behind me, wrapping his arms around me and resting his chin on my shoulder as he peered up at the picture with me. "Believe it or not, your sister has quite the knack for photography. A newfound passion of hers, helping her deal with her grief."

I turned to him, completely shocked. "Sabby took all of these photos?"

He nodded at me with a proud grin on his face. How did I not know that she had taken up photography?

"They are stunning." I said in amazement. I walked over toward the sitting room to look at the picture hanging above the couch. "Is this the meadow out by the small pond near the eastern border?"

"It is." Xander said with a chuckle, "You really know the packlands well."

"I do. I love our pack. It's so beautiful here." I smiled at him, absolutely loving the way he had our home decorated.

"I saw this place in a dream I had when I was in a coma." Xander told me as he gazed at the picture dreamily. My attention snapped to him. "I think this will be one of our favorite places, too."

There was something hidden in his eyes as he admired the picture. It was a truly magnificent place, filled with pretty flowers of all different colors. It felt familiar to me, like it was meant to be a special place.

"They did a wonderful job. This is better than I could have ever dreamed of for our home. It's perfect." I told him happily.

After we thoroughly explored the newly remodeled Alpha suite, Xander insisted on taking me to my new Luna office. It had been redecorated as well in my style. There were two large, handsome portraits on the wall. One was of Zeus looking regal, standing on top of a rock at the edge of the water. His deep auburn fur stood out against the lush, green forest behind him. And the other was of Xander in a suit outdoors, staring off into the distance with a peaceful, content look on his face. They were both stunning. I was happy that I would be able to gaze up at them every day.

Xander let me take it all in and explore my new office before I felt his mood shift. My eyes darted over to him as he eyed me nervously.

"Xander? What's wrong?" My voice was laced with concern.

"I have some things I need to tell you." He said hesitantly, making me more worried.

CHAPTER FIFTY-FIVE

Xander

I let out a deep sigh. I knew this was going to upset Maxine. She has been through so much already. I just wanted her to be safe and live in peace.

I took her hand and led her over to her new, dark green sofa in her office. We sat down and I kept her hands in mine.

"I received a phone call from Luke while we were at the hotel." I paused and Maxine nodded, encouraging me to continue.

"He told me that they found a safe in the ruins of Massimo's mansion. They were able to open it. Inside, they found files... on you." Maxine's eyes widened and I could feel her heartbeat increase.

"I don't know all the details of what's in the files, but Luke is bringing them here tomorrow." I quickly added.

"Luke is coming here?" She whispered, so lost in her thoughts.

I nodded. "There's more." I said cautiously, "He thinks they have been working with another coven. They might know about your wolf, too."

I could feel the full-blown anxiety attack taking over her and I quickly pulled her into my lap, holding her tightly against my chest. "I won't let anything happen to you, Maxine. Everything will be alright. Luke will come, we will gather as much information as we can and formulate a plan. If we have to go hunting down 20 vampire covens, we will. I will do anything to keep you safe."

I tilted her head up so that I could catch her eyes. "Don't stress out. We will know more soon. As of right now, we can't be sure if there is anyone else who knows about your wolf." She slowly nodded her head, deep in thought.

"I love you, Maxine. I'm sorry I haven't been able to protect you from all of this, but I promise you I will put an end to all of this. We will live in peace." She caressed my face and kissed me tenderly.

"I love you, Xander." Her voice came out small and shaky. I tucked her into my arms safely, holding her there for a long time.

We made the rounds after Maxine managed to calm down. She held herself together extremely well considering the information she just received.

She gushed over the remodel to everyone and thanked my mom profusely. Mom was thrilled that she loved it. Maxine was so excited to talk to Sabrina about her photographs. She complimented her talent and insisted that she needed to show her more.

I talked with the guys about our options before we heard what information Luke has for us. It is clear that Maxine is so deeply loved by everyone and that they are all willing to go to whatever lengths necessary in order to ensure her safety. We went over pack business, while Maxine discussed the plans for our mating ceremony with mom.

We had dinner in the dining hall with everyone. It was great to have everyone together, only Wesley and his mate were missing. It was a nice distraction for Maxine. She was so happy talking with everyone. Every now and then, though, I noticed that she would get really quiet, and I could feel her worrying. I could only rub her back to try to comfort her.

After dinner, we said good night to everyone and headed home. Our home. I loved that we had a place of our own now. I had given my mom directions on how I thought Maxine would want the place decorated and she did a phenomenal job with it. Maxine really loved it.

Back in our suite, we got ready for bed. I preferred sleeping in very little clothes, so I just wore my boxer briefs. Maxine was wearing a little purple nightie. After she was done in the bathroom doing her nightly routine, I went in and brushed my teeth.

Maxine's arms snaked around me from behind. She didn't say anything, just rested her head against my back, holding me. I placed one hand on top of hers while I finished rinsing my mouth. When I was done, I turned around slowly to hold her in my arms and rested my chin on the top of her head.

She didn't move or say anything. Finally, I reached down and lifted her chin up to meet her eyes. There was so much worry in them.

"Hey..." I caressed her cheek. "It's going to be alright."

"Can we just stay in our little bubble for one more night? Pretend we are still at the beach or on the boat. Tomorrow we can deal with everything, but tonight, I just want to be ignorant and happy." She pleaded.

"As you wish." I said before I leaned forward and kissed her deeply. She brought her arms up behind my neck, savoring the moment. My hands roamed over her body.

I lifted her and she instantly wrapped her legs around me. I carried her out of the bathroom, over to our bed. I took my time and poured all my love into each touch. I wanted her to feel worshiped as we made love for hours, until we were both beyond exhausted. Maxine fell asleep quickly in my arms and I watched her for a little while, vowing to myself that I would do whatever it takes to protect her.

In the morning, I woke to an empty bed and the smell of bacon. I pulled on some sweatpants and moseyed my way out into the living room. Maxine was in the kitchen, cooking breakfast. She wore her little nightie with her hair tossed up in a messy bun. She had music playing softly and she was dancing around the kitchen as she cooked. I leaned against the wall, happily watching her. She was adorable and sexy all at the same time.

I could see pancakes, eggs, bacon, and fruit all ready to go. She was getting ready to bring it to the table when she turned around and saw me gawking at her. She froze and then a big smile spread across her face.

"Good morning, handsome." She picked up two platters and moved to give me a kiss before setting them on the table.

"Good morning, gorgeous." I replied, grabbing the other two platters and carrying them to the table, too. "This smells amazing, love."

Maxine went back into the kitchen and grabbed a pitcher of juice and a pot of coffee. Once everything was set on the table, I pulled her chair out for her to sit down before I took my seat.

"You seem to be in a good mood." I observed.

"Everything is going to be fine. I just feel it." She said with a beautiful smile. I reached over and squeezed her hand and gave her a genuine smile. Her mood was infectious; I felt more positive about the situation already. We had a lovely, peaceful breakfast together.

Once we finished, we showered together and got ready for Luke's arrival.

I received a mindlink that Luke had arrived at our gates. We walked out front to greet him as he pulled through the packlands. Both mine and Dad's Alpha units met us outside, along with my mom.

Two black SUVs pulled up and parked in front of the packhouse. Luke and his father climbed out of one SUV. Luke opened the back door for his mother to step out. More men piled out of the other SUV, I believed them to be Luke's and Alpha Phillip's Betas.

We greeted them with handshakes and Luke moved to hug Maxine. She smiled at him and eyed me cautiously as she hugged him. I was not happy with it at all, but I let it slide for all he has done for us.

Mom pulled Luke's mother into a hug, "Oh, Marlene, it's so good to see you! How have you been?"

"It's been far too long, Clarissa. I'm well. You look gorgeous!" She gushed as she pulled back, still holding her hands.

"Oh, and look at you, radiant as ever!" Mom replied before turning to Maxine. "You have to meet my lovely, new daughter, Maxine. Maxine, this is one of my oldest friends, Luna Marlene."

"It's a pleasure to meet you, Luna Marlene." Maxine politely replied, holding out her hand.

"The pleasure is certainly all mine!" Luna Marlene exclaimed as she pulled Maxine into an unexpected hug.

Mom excitedly pulled Luna Marlene away. "Come on, Marlene, I want to show you some of the ceremony plans."

The two of them walked off arm in arm, completely forgetting the rest of us.

Our fathers stood staring after their women, just shaking their heads in amusement.

"I know you are eager to see all that we have brought you, let's get down to business." Luke stated, more serious than normal.

I nodded to him and turned towards the packhouse. "This way. We will have refreshments brought to the conference room."

CHAPTER FIFTY-SIX

Maxine

My stomach was twisted in knots as we sat down in the conference room, but I tried to remain positive. Alpha Jackson, Dad, Xander and I all sat on one side of the table, across from Luke and his father. Donovan stood behind me with his arms crossed. Their Betas remained outside with the rest of our men, since we were going to discuss highly sensitive information.

Anxiety began to creep in and Xander reached over to hold my hand, running his thumb over my knuckles. His touch was calming.

"I'll get straight to it, I know you all must have a lot of questions." Luke said as he pulled out a stack of files from a briefcase. "There were many pictures in the file, pictures of Maxine and her wolf, along with you, Xander." Luke laid the photos out of the table in front of us.

There were so many pictures, from all over the packlands. These weren't just taken from the borders, there were photos of us on the training grounds, near the hospital, and there was even a photo of me shopping in the human town.

Fear spiked within me and my panicked eyes met Xander's furious ones.

These are from inside the pack. I mindlinked Xander.

They've been following you. He replied.

We have a traitor in our pack. He mindlinked our fathers and Donovan.

I could feel Xander's anger and it was suffocating. I was so overwhelmed, I didn't know what to say.

Luke slid another picture forward hesitantly. The picture was of me saving Xander after he had been shot. My hands were on his chest as I cried in agony, completely glowing and covered in blood.

My heart instantly ached as I stared down at the scene. This was the most terrifying moment of my life. Looking at this picture was like reliving the horror and anguish all over again. I clutched Xander's hand tighter. He rubbed gentle circles across my back with his other hand, but it wasn't helping. Not when neither one of us was calm. How the hell did they get this?

"They appear to have been keeping track of information about you as well. They have training schedules written down, names of your friends and family, lists of trips to the pack hospital." Luke continued, sliding papers across the table.

You could almost feel the air crackling with anger from everyone in the room. I could barely breathe as fear consumed me. Who was giving them this information? Are we not safe with our own pack members? I tried hard not to, but I began to tremble.

Xander pulled my chair closer to him and engulfed me in his strong embrace. I peered up at Luke, and I could see the concern in his eyes.

"We also found correspondence with a vampire leader named Mikhail Komarov. There is no mention of Max specifically, but he does ask him for help with 'ending the wolves,' as he worded it." Luke placed even more documents in front of us.

There are many different letters passed around the table. He must have created copies of the letters he sent to Mikhail, because we seemed to have both sides of the conversation.

"Is there anything else?" Xander asked gruffly.

"We believe this coven is located somewhere in northern Alaska. We've been able to recover a P.O. box address from the letters." Luke replied.

Alaska? That is so far from here. How will we ever find out more information about them?

Xander leaned back in his chair, pensively. "I have a very good friend from the Academy whose pack is in northern Alaska. I will reach out and see if he is up for a visit."

"Good. We need to see if we can find any financials for this Komarov. That is how we tracked Zanzara so quickly." Alpha Jackson spoke up.

Luke pulled out more documents and handed them to Alpha Jackson, "This is everything we were able to find on him so far. Perhaps you will have more luck with your contacts."

"Luke, Alpha Phillip, thank you for bringing all of this to us." Xander spoke, "You have already done so much for us, we cannot express to you our gratitude."

Luke nodded at Xander and then turned to me. "My wolf has always known that Maxine was special. We first thought it was because she was our mate." Xander tensed beside me, squeezing me just a little tighter. "I now know it is because she is a blessed wolf. I don't need to understand everything about her wolf, it's probably better that I don't know it all. But I do know that I will do everything I can to help you protect her. Whatever you need, just ask. I swear it, with Selene as my witness."

Luke's eye remained locked with mine while he spoke. His vow to help so selflessly overwhelmed me. My heart was pounding. This was all too much. I just wanted to live a happy life with my mate.

"Luke, your oath to protect Maxine is greatly appreciated. If I can make the arrangements, would you be willing to come to Alaska with us?" Xander surprised me with his offer. We're going closer to the vampires? And he wants to bring my ex-boyfriend?

"I would be honored to travel with you and help protect your Luna." Luke stated firmly.

I paced our suite, completely overwhelmed by everything that we just learned from Luke. Thoughts of staying positive and calm were long gone. Fear was consuming me. It was hard to breathe.

The vampires have already wreaked havoc on our world. It's not just about me; they will come after everyone I love. Last time, they shot Xander, killed Blake, and took my mate from me. I can't lose him. Or anyone else.

Strong arms wrap around me, pulling me from my dark thoughts. I inhaled a deep breath of Xander's soothing scent. Cedarwood and spearmint comforted me as I clung tightly to him.

"Everything will be alright, love." Xander spoke reassuringly. "We will make a plan; we will find these monsters and put an end to them."

"Xander, they had pictures from within our packlands." My voice came out shakier than I wanted.

"Whoever the traitor is will pay with their life." His voice was hard and cold. I pulled back to see his face. His anger was scary, but I wasn't afraid of him. I knew he would never hurt me.

He placed his hands on either side of my face. "For now, you need to relax. I made you a tea that will help you sleep. I need to meet with the guys to formulate a plan and I have to reach out to some contacts. But I am worried about you. I can feel how upset you are."

He pulled me toward the kitchen and placed a mug in my hands. "I have asked the girls to come over and stay with you while I am gone. They should be here any minute."

I nodded my head and slowly sipped the tea. The warm liquid was soothing, but my mate's arms were more comforting. I felt the slightest bit better already.

There was a knock at the door and Xander went to open it. Ari, Ivy, Jazzy, and Donovan walked inside.

Ari gave me a comforting hug, and the girls asked me how I was doing. I don't know how much they know about what was going on, but they were clearly worried about me. I shrugged a response and went to change into cozier clothes.

My friends were not their usual chatty selves, so I knew they at least understood the severity of the situation.

Xander made sure I drank all of the tea before ushering me into our bed. He pulled the comforter up around me and kissed me deeply.

The girls piled in around me and turned on a movie. I snuggled down into the bed, wedged between my best friends. I could already feel my eyes begin to droop as Xander and Donovan pulled the bedroom door closed behind them.

I finally gave in to the exhaustion that was sinking in and closed my eyes.

CHAPTER FIFTY-SEVEN

Xander

It was difficult to leave Maxine when she was so upset, but the faster we got to work, the quicker we could find this vampire to end him and his coven.

We gathered in the conference room with the rest of our Alpha units. I knew that there was a traitor within our pack, but I had no doubt in my mind that I could trust everyone in this room. These men are my family. Luke and his father didn't have to bring us the information, but they did. I could feel the sincerity in Luke's vow to protect Maxine. I am choosing to trust them.

As Luke pointed out, they didn't need to know all the details about the Midnight Wolves. But they all knew that Maxine is special and that her wolf is powerful. We filled the team in on the details about the vampires.

There was a collective growl of anger when they learned about the pack traitor.

"We must find this traitor as soon as possible without letting them know that we are on to them." I informed them. "We don't know if the traitor had any contact with this other coven or if they are still spying on Maxine. Either way, they have committed treason and the punishment is death."

No one argued.

I'm not sure how to find the traitor without revealing that we're on to them. If we start asking around, it could tip them off. I will have to do some digging into our surveillance footage and see if I can come up with anything. We will have to circle back to the traitor.

"Son, while you were upstairs, I reached out to some of my contacts about the vampires. They are doing their best to track down more information for us." Dad informed me.

"Good. I will reach out to my friend from the Academy. I am hoping that he may be willing to have us stay with him for a while, so we can investigate while we are closer to the vampires." I continued, "We will need to arrange for us to be gone for an extended period of time. I will want to take my men with me, that will leave you and your unit in charge of the pack." I told my father. "Sorry, it looks like it's going to be a little longer before you get to fully retire."

"We will do what we have to in order to protect our pack and Luna." Dad said without hesitation.

Everyone was researching, making arrangements, and contacting people, as I pulled out my phone to call my old friend.

The phone rang for a long time. I started to think no one would answer when I heard the line pick up.

"Hello?" A gruff voice answered.

"Asher? It's Xander." I waited for his response.

"Well, I'll be damned. Xander, it's been a while. How are you, man?" His voice sounded a bit more friendly.

"I won't lie; it's a bit complicated at the moment." I replied, "I found my mate."

"That's awesome, Xander. What's wrong, she won't put up with your crazy ass?" He chuckled.

"Actually, it's not anything like that. She's amazing and really special. You'd like her. But she's in danger." I informed him.

"Danger? What kind of danger?" He asked seriously.

I sighed. "Again, it's really complicated, but it involves vampires." I paused. There was silence on the other end for a while.

"Vampires. And you need my help?" He ventured.

"Actually, yes. We were hoping we could come visit you for a while." I continued hesitantly, "I know it's a lot to ask, and I wouldn't unless it were really important. But..." He cut me off.

"But the coven is in Alaska. I know of it." He stated.

"You know of the Alaskan vampire coven?" I asked curiously. I could feel the attention of the room turn to my conversation as well.

"They are quite dangerous. They have been a serious problem here for many generations." He didn't add more, but there was a hard edge to his voice. "When would you be coming?"

"We are about to have our mating ceremony. I need to get the pack settled and arrange a few things, but we were hoping at the beginning of next month." I replied hesitantly. It's not a lot of time for him to prepare.

"And how many would you be bringing?" He asked, all business.

"Ideally, I would bring my Alpha unit, three trackers, five of my best warriors, another Alpha and his Beta, and Maxine. So, 15 total." I began to worry that he wouldn't like this.

"Another Alpha? Who?" He questioned.

"Luke Vance, future Alpha of the Dark Moon pack. He has been helping us with the situation." I replied.

"Hmm, I don't know him." He mulled it over carefully. "Xander, I trust you, more than most. If you bring another Alpha, you are responsible for him and his Beta."

"That is fair. I trust him, Asher." I told him as I stared into Luke's eyes. He nodded at me firmly.

"Alright." He said after a moment longer. "I assume you will inform me of more when you get here. Let me know when you make the flight arrangements, so I know exactly when you are coming. In the meantime, I will gather the information we have on these vampires."

"Thank you, Asher. I owe you big time." I said with relief.

"Consider us even after you saved my ass in the Academy." He chuckled lightly. "Good luck, Xander. And congratulations on finding your mate."

"Thanks again, Asher. I'll talk to you soon." We ended the call, and I informed the room of what he told me.

We stayed a while longer, making arrangements and booking a private flight to Alaska. Once all of the travel plans had been ironed out, Dad said he would show our guests to their accommodations for the night. I thanked both Luke and Alpha Phillip again for their help before I went back up to our suite with the guys. They were eager to see their mates and I was longing to be with mine.

As we entered the bedroom, I saw my mate curled up with Arielle spooning her. They were both sound asleep. Jasmine and Ivy were on the other side of Maxine, snuggled together, barely able to keep their eyes open as they watched some chick flick. I glanced over at the clock; it was later than I thought.

Ivy switched off the TV, climbed out of the bed and into Heath's outstretched arms. Wiley tugged Jasmine over to him and she sleepily dragged herself out of bed. Donovan walked around to where Arielle slept peacefully. He peeled back the comforter and slipped his arms underneath his tiny mate. He lifted her and she just nuzzled right into his chest.

I escorted them all out and returned to my beautiful mate. I pulled off my clothes and got under the covers, where Ivy and Jasmine had been laying. It smelled like them, and I wrinkled my nose a little. It wasn't a bad smell, but it's not my mate.

Gently, I pulled Maxine towards me, placing her head on my chest. She didn't wake, but nestled in closer to my warmth, a smile pulling at her lips as sparks spread everywhere our skin touched. I breathed her scent in deeply, letting it wash over me. She has such a calming effect on me. It's addictive.

"I will keep you safe. I swear to the Moon Goddess." I whispered into her hair. I kissed the top of her head and settled in to sleep.

Today, I am determined to get Maxine's mind off of the vampire situation and help her get excited about our ceremony tomorrow. She deserved to be able to enjoy this special moment. Besides, there's nothing else to be done at this time.

I was about to sneak out of bed when a familiar voice filled my head.

Good morning, Alpha. I smiled. *Congratulations, by the way.*

Good morning, little brother. Thank you. How is life with your mate? I mindlinked back.

It is absolute perfection. I could hear how happy he truly was, and he deserved it. *We're on our way, we will be back home soon.*

That is fantastic news. Everyone is excited to see you both. I replied.

I need a favor. Wesley hesitated. *I need you to soften the blow and let Mom know that I've already marked Lily.*

You marked her before you introduced her to Mom? You've got guts, kid. I chuckled.

I know, I know. Please, just mention it to her before we get home? Wesley has always been a mama's boy; he's worried she's going to be mad at him.

Alright. I told him. *But you owe me*.

Of course! You're the best, Xander.

I'm not afraid of our mom, I have no problem telling her. But I couldn't let this opportunity pass without having my brother owe me. I chuckled to myself before turning to my beautiful mate who is going to be thrilled to have Wesley and his new mate back.

CHAPTER FIFTY-EIGHT

Maxine

I woke up to sparks up and down my arm where Xander gently caressed me. I smiled without opening my eyes.

"Good morning, mate." I sleepily sighed.

"Morning, love." I could hear the smile in his voice. "I love when you call me 'mate.'"

I ran my fingers across his chest, still snuggled into him with my eyes closed.

"I have a surprise for you, Maxine." Xander's deep voice said softly. "Wesley is coming home today."

My eyes opened immediately, and I gazed up at my smiling mate. "Really?"

"Yes, he will be here soon." Xander kissed the tip of my nose.

I sprang up in bed. "We have to get up! I want to have a nice welcome breakfast for Lillian. We have to get everyone together before they eat on their own. We should be waiting for them outside when they arrive." I gasped, "Oh my Goddess, where are they going to live now that we have the entire Alpha suite?"

I turned to Xander in a panic, but he just watched me with amusement.

"Relax, baby. Everything has already been taken care of, my mom had a house built for Wesley while he was away at the Academy, just in case he found his mate. I'm sure she had it readied for them while we were gone, too. It's what she loves to do."

He climbed out of bed and sauntered off towards the bathroom. "And I've already sent out a mindlink, letting everyone know they are on their way. The kitchen is getting breakfast ready, feel free to link them with any special instructions." He trailed off as I heard him start the shower.

I mindlinked our head chef and we discussed breakfast plans.

When I was finished, Xander strode out of the bathroom in just a towel around his waist, as he walked into the closet. My brain turned to mush as I just gawked at him, watching his muscles flex as he strolled by. Once he was out of sight, I shook my head, focusing back on what I needed to do. I entered the bathroom.

As I readied myself, I thought about the information we received yesterday and how much I let the fear and anxiety take over me. I need Xander to fill me in on what was discussed last night after I went back to the suite, but it can wait. I decided not to think about it for now. Today, we welcome home Wes and Lillian. And tomorrow is our mating ceremony. I need to focus on all the good right now.

After we were both ready for the day, we left our suite to help prepare for their arrival. I found Luna Clarissa in the dining hall, setting everything up for a breakfast feast. She hugged me, clearly excited to meet her son's new mate. I set to work helping her.

Xander came over and draped his arm over his mom's shoulders. "Wesley wants me to tell you something before he arrives."

"You think I don't know? He marked her." She said matter-of-factly.

"How did you know?" Xander asked, clearly confused.

She laughed and shook her head, "Honestly, you boys don't know anything about familial bonds? Don't you think I would feel it when I have a new daughter in my family?" She smiled at me with a wink.

"I didn't think about that." Xander answered plainly. "Can you pretend to be upset with him?" Xander asked with a mischievous smirk.

"Absolutely not!" Luna Clarissa replied. "I don't want Lillian to think badly of me! They will be welcomed home with nothing but love."

"Oh, well. I tried." Xander laughed. Luna Clarissa rolled her eyes at her son as she rushed off to adjust a table setting.

"You're so bad." I swatted at him playfully.

Hey, Sis. Wes' voice filled my head. *Or should I say Luna? Luna Sis?*

Wes! I can't wait to see you! I replied excitedly.

The wait is over. We just pulled through the gates.

I beamed up at Xander. Excitement filled me as I bounced on the balls of my feet and squealed. I reached up on my tiptoes to kiss Xander before taking off towards the front door. "They're here!" I called out to everyone.

A small crowd gathered outside with me. Xander and I stood together, next to his parents, and our friends were all there, too.

Wes' SUV pulled up in front of the packhouse and parked. It was a while before I saw his door open and he rushed around to open the passenger door. He reached in and took hold of a tiny hand, leading Lillian out of the car. He stood shielding her from our view for a moment, then turned to us.

Her long, red hair was flowing in the breeze. Her eyes darted around nervously, but she held her head up confidently. As her gaze landed on me, I gave her a warm smile.

Xander and I stepped forward, and he embraced his brother in a bear hug, patting him on the back. I pulled Lillian in for a gentle hug and welcomed her.

"There are so many people." She whispered to me.

"This is your new family." I assured her. I wrap my arm around her shoulders to walk her up the stairs. Wes never let go of her hand.

"Mom, Dad, it's so good to be home." Wes hugged his mother and father. Then he gently tugged Lillian away from me as he pulled her into his own arms. "This is my mate, Lily." I've honestly never seen Wes look so happy before.

"It's a pleasure to meet you." Alpha Jackson said as he took her tiny hand in his and covered it with his other.

"Oh my Goddess, you are so beautiful!" Luna Clarissa gushed as she threw her arms around Lillian. "I'm so happy you're here! It's good to finally meet you."

"It's nice to meet you, too." Lillian replied shyly.

"Lily, do you remember our friends from the club?" Wes asked as he guided her along to say hello to the others.

She smiled and nodded, but Wes reintroduced her to everyone in case she forgot any names. He's very thoughtful with her, definitely a different Wes than I have seen with girls before.

"Alright, Luna, lead the way." Wes said playfully. I turned towards his mom, but I realized he was talking to me. I glanced back at him and he winked.

I took the lead and showed Lillian through the packhouse, giving her a quick rundown, knowing that Wes will show her around more after breakfast. I directed everyone into the dining hall. Those inside all stood waiting for us.

Lillian inched closer to Wes as everyone stared at her.

"Silver Moon, we are delighted to have my brother, Wesley, home. Please join me in welcoming his new mate, Lillian." Xander addressed the room.

"Oh, please, just call me Lily." Her soft voice clarified.

Xander nodded at her. "To Wesley and Lily!"

Everyone in the hall replied, "To Wesley and Lily!" Then, there was a collective howl, followed by clapping.

We walked over to the largest table in the hall, where Alpha Jackson's unit and their mates stood waiting for us. Xander and Wes introduced them all to Lily before we sat down.

Some kitchen staff brought out platters of food and delivered them to all the tables in the hall. Everyone feasted and talked excitedly to Wes and Lily.

Lily relaxed quite a bit once we were all seated. She was still quiet but talked cheerfully as she got to know the pack. Everyone was laughing and smiling. I felt good to feel so happy again. I was determined not to let my situation ruin this joyous occasion.

"You all made it home just in time," Luna Clarissa informed Wes and Lily. "Xander and Maxine's mating ceremony is tomorrow." She beamed.

"Congratulations, Max." Wes told me. "It's about time, Xander!" He jabbed playfully at his brother.

"That is so exciting." Lily said to me. "You will make such a fine Luna."

CHAPTER FIFTY-NINE

Xander

After breakfast, we gathered in the large living room on the main floor. Mom and Dad hurried off to take care of some pack business, preparing for the arrival of our guests for the ceremony. They insisted that we could not help, and instead, needed to spend the day relaxing.

The group all sat cozied up with our mates around the room.

"I would love to see more of the packlands." Lily said to Wesley, tucked safely under his arm.

Maxine smiled excitedly at me from my lap. I winked at her, knowing exactly what she was thinking.

"We should spend the afternoon at the lake." I tossed the idea out there.

The girls all agreed enthusiastically. I knew none of the guys would say no to their mates. Lily smiled questioningly at us.

"It's one of our absolute favorite places." Ivy explained to her.

"I'm sure you'll love it too!" Arielle replied animatedly.

Wesley peered down at his mate, silently asking her if she was up for it. She gave him a huge grin and nodded her head.

"We're in!" Wesley exclaimed. "But first, we have to go see our new home."

Lily perked up at his words. "We may take a while..." Wesley informed as he smiled hungrily down at his mate. Her cheeks blushed. "We'll meet you out at the lake sometime after lunch." His eyes never left Lily's.

He stood and pulled her up with him.

Just then, Luke and his Beta, Ryan, came wandering down the stairs. Luke grinned when he saw Wesley.

"Wes! It's good to see you, man." They hugged each other. "It's nice to see you again, Lily."

The way Luke watched the two of them, you could see the longing in his eyes. There was a sadness behind his eyes, wishing he had his own mate. I'm just glad he is no longer chasing after mine.

"It's good to see you too, Luke." Wesley clapped him on the back. "But we were just heading out to see our new home. I'll catch up with you later." His hand found Lily's again.

"Have fun, you two!" Arielle giggled.

"Let us know if you need anything." Maxine called after them as they walked towards the entryway.

"Oh, we won't!" Wesley waved her off as he leaned down and whispered in Lily's ear causing her to giggle and squirm away from him.

Maxine peeked back at me as I watched my brother. My heart swelled for him, finding his mate had brought him back to life. "I've never seen him so happy," Maxine said.

"Mates have a way of doing that to you." I nuzzled her nose with mine. "He deserves all the happiness in the world."

"Ok, so we've got at least a few hours before they'll be leaving their house." Wiley stated with a knowing grin, "What's the plan?"

"Well, just because they won't be joining us at the lake until later, doesn't mean we have to wait that long." Jasmine replied.

"Yeah, I say we pack up stuff for the lake and lunch, and head that way now." Arielle agreed.

I turned to Luke, "We're heading out to the lake if you'd like to join us."

He smiled weakly at us, "Actually, we have some pack business to take care of, I was hoping you'd let us use an office or the conference room for the day."

"Sure, no problem." I lifted Maxine up and stood to lead them to an office they could use. "We'll leave in a half hour?" I confirmed with everyone.

After I made sure Luke had everything he needed, Maxine and I returned to our suite to change and grab stuff for the lake. She had linked the head chef to gather a basket and cooler for lunch. We stopped by and picked it up before heading out front where the others were loading up vehicles.

It didn't take long before we pulled up to the lake house. We were unloading the SUVs, and we were just about finished when Wiley called out, "Last one in's a rotten egg!"

It never fails to send all the guys sprawling towards the water, tossing their shirts to the side. The girls, like always, just laughed and shook their heads at us.

We all splashed around, while the girls were content on the shore. Ivy tossed a football out to us. Arielle brought the basket of food inside the lake house. Jasmine and Maxine laid out some beach towels.

The girls turned on their music and decided to sunbathe on their towels.

I wrestled with the guys in the water for a bit before we tossed the football around. It's good to just hang out with them and talk like normal. They asked me about our trip. Wiley and Heath nudged me for dirty details, but Donovan was extremely uncomfortable. I wasn't going to tell them about my sexy little mate anyway, that's their Luna. I firmly ended that conversation, flipping the tables on Wiley.

"You and Jasmine have been together forever, man. When are you going to finally have a pup?" I asked with a raised brow.

Wiley gave a wicked grin, "Hey, it's not for a lack of trying." He said as he bounced his eyebrows up and down. "I don't know what the Goddess has planned for us, but I'm enjoying not having to share her with anyone else for now. One day, she won't be able to give me all her attention, so I'm soaking it in while I can."

I was surprised by his honest answer, but it made sense. I felt the same way. The thought of a family with Maxine caused my heart to soar, remembering those little faces from my dream made me eager to meet them. But I am greedy with Maxine right now, consuming all her time and energy. I know that will all change someday. I'm excited for it, but also happy to wait and enjoy what we have now.

Giggles erupted from the girls over on the shore. Like a magnet, we all stopped and gazed at our lovely mates. Maxine's eyes met mine and her cheeks turned pink. It made me curious as to what they were talking about.

What's got you blushing, baby? I mindlinked her.

I heard her adorable giggle in my head, and it made my heart flutter. *Oh, just Ari being Ari, again.*

I gave her a wink before tossing the ball back to Heath.

Heath decided to swap the football out for a volleyball. We played a game of Keep It Up, and it lasted a really long time. We all laughed as we dove into the water to bat the ball back into the air. Finally, Donovan caught the ball and informed us that we should get lunch started. My stomach agreed with him.

We made our way back to the shore where the girls were still sunbathing. They were all lying with their eyes closed, bouncing a leg or nodding their head to the music.

We stood in front of them, peering down at the gorgeous view. They each cracked an eye open when we moved into their sunlight.

"Are you trying to tell us it's time for lunch?" Ivy asked, clearly amused by our behavior.

Wiley leaned forward and gave his head a massive shake. His wet, shaggy hair sent water spraying all over the girls who shrieked. Jasmine jumped up to shove Wiley away, but he grabbed her quickly, tossing her over his shoulder. She screamed and kicked her legs as Wiley ran towards the water.

"Wiley, don't you dare!" She yelled out just before he fell back into the water with her.

When she resurfaced, she was pissed. "Wiley James Summers, I'm going to murder you!" He just laughed as she lunged toward him. He dodged her over and over, until he finally stopped and caught her in his arms. He pulled her close to his chest.

"You looked hot, baby. I just wanted to cool you down." He teased with a pout and puppy dog eyes. Jasmine sighed and rolled her eyes before wrapping her arms around his neck and kissing him.

Donovan said to me, "Yeah, I think Jazzy's hands are too full with Wiley to be worrying about pups just yet."

The girls all exchanged glances and then burst out laughing. Clearly, they must have been talking about this earlier as well.

I reached down and took Maxine's hands in mine, pulling her up into my arms. Her warm, sun-kissed skin pressed against my cool, damp skin.

I love a Maxine in a tiny bikini. I linked her before smacking her ass, causing her to gasp.

Donovan turned away quickly toward the lake house, hoping to dodge anymore groping. Arielle took his hand and lifted it up, twirling herself underneath like a ballerina. He smiled dreamily down at her, forgetting his best friend and sister's PDA. She's the perfect buffer for us.

CHAPTER SIXTY

Maxine

We entered the lake house and set to work on lunch. The girls pulled out all the side dishes, plates, and utensils, while the guys got started on the grill. Chef Ian packed a delicious meal for us. We grilled ribs and chicken, and there were side salads, baked beans, potatoes, fresh fruit, and apple pie.

We sat outside at the large patio table, enjoying our meal in the beautiful summer air. We laughed and talked all the while.

We were just getting ready to clear the table when Wes' SUV pulled up. He jumped out and ran around to open Lily's door.

"Is there any food left?" He asked as they walked up the patio. "We're starving!"

The girls all stifled a giggle and the guys just smirked at Wes. Clearly, everyone knew what they had been up to for the past few hours.

I stepped forward. "Of course! Let me make you both a plate."

I fixed two plates of food for Wes and Lily and set them down at the table.

"Thank you, Luna." Lily said sweetly to me.

It caught me off guard. "Please, we're practically sisters now. Just call me Max."

"Okay. Thank you, Max." She smiled before she looked out at the water. "It really is so beautiful here."

"What's your home pack like?" I asked curiously. I've never been to the Blue River pack, I'm not even sure where it is located.

"It's simple but lovely. Much smaller than this one though. It's basically just woods, the best part of it is of course the Blue River that it's named after."

"Xander, can you make Lily a pack member as soon as possible?" Wes asked eagerly. "I want everyone to be able to mindlink with her." Alphas can mindlink with anyone from any pack, but others can only mindlink those within their own pack. Since Wes marked her, he can link with Lily and technically she's of Alpha blood so she can link others, but no one else would be able to mindlink her.

"Of course. I can do it tomorrow before the ceremony, if that's what you want." He said to Lily.

She smiled and quickly nodded her head. "Yes, please, Alpha."

"Just Xander." He gently corrected her. She nodded at him.

After they finished eating and everything was cleaned up, we went back down toward the shore.

We stood with our toes in the water, admiring the lake.

"Water Volleyball?" Heath asked.

We all agreed.

"I'll grab the net." Donovan offered. We have the perfect net, adjusted to fit one particular spot so it stands evenly in the water. We've used it for years.

He pulled the net out and the guys waded into the water to get it set up properly.

I realized we have an uneven number of couples, making coupled up teams unbalanced. I turned to the girls and cocked a brow. "Boys vs girls?"

"Yes!" Jazzy replied.

"Oh, it's going down!" Ari exclaimed.

The guys just chuckled, thinking they would easily beat us because they are so much taller. But I know that some of these girls are prepared to play dirty.

We got into our positions and Jazzy served the ball. We volleyed back and forth for a while before Wiley spiked the ball down on our side. One point for the guys.

Heath served the ball and this time I knew that the girls were going to do their best to distract their mates.

After a few hits back and forth, I heard Ivy. "Oh shoot! My top came untied!" Heath missed the ball as his head jerked towards his mate. That's a point for the girls.

I served the ball over the net and noticed Xander staring at my chest. I rolled my eyes at him, and he bounced his brows.

On Donovan's serve, I could see Ari making kissy faces at Donovan. He grinned at her but stayed focused and hit the ball over the net. She reached up and ran her fingers over her mate mark. He growled at her as his eyes darkened. Ari shivered as she brushed it again. Donovan's expression changed right before the ball came back and hit him on the top of his head before it splooshed into the water next to him. Another point for the girls.

We scored again when Jazzy told Ivy she loved her bathing suit and slid her finger slowly along the strap down towards her cleavage. Heath and Wiley, heads craned towards their mates, crashed straight into each other.

"Ya'll are wicked!" Wiley called out, clearly frustrated that we were getting the better of them. A cacophony of giggles erupted from the girls.

It was Lily's turn to serve, and she peered at Wes with her doe eyes. "I don't know if I can make it over the net." She said timidly.

"It's okay, gorgeous, just do the best you can." Wes told her encouragingly. The guys all inched closer toward the net.

"Okay, here goes." Lily said before she delivered a hard serve that went right over all their heads. Wes tried to hit it as he dove backward but he only managed to cause it to veer off to the side where no one could reach it.

He reappeared from the water and stared at Lily with shock and played hurt, touching his chest. "You hustled me, you little minx."

Lily giggled and Ari high-fived her.

These tactics continued on until we were whooping them. The boys huddled together to strategize. They moved back into position and before Xander went to serve the ball, they all disappeared under the water.

I glanced at the other girls, who mirrored my confused expression, when the guys popped up in front of us. They each quickly grabbed their mate and threw themselves backwards, bringing us with them.

When we resurfaced, there were lots of giggles and squeals. I wrapped my arms and legs around Xander, who kissed me slowly.

By the time we exited the water it was getting dark, so the guys started building a bonfire. I went inside with the girls to pull out more food for dinner. I had asked Chef Ian to pack hotdogs and s'more ingredients for this purpose. I knew how our lake days usually went and had a feeling we'd be here for a while.

We settle down around the cozy fire, roasting our hot dogs and s'mores. The lake simmered with moonlight and the fire let off a glow that danced across the trees surrounding us. "Can we stay here tonight?" I asked Xander, not wanting this day to end.

"Sure, there's plenty of room for whoever wants to stay." He announced to the others. The lake house was open for pack use, but it was originally built with an Alpha unit in mind so there were plenty of bedrooms for us all in the two-story cabin.

"We'll stay for a while, but we're going to spend our first night back in our new home." Wes said after talking with Lily.

We enjoyed the rest of the evening around the bonfire with our best friends, who were definitely more like family. Leaning back into Xander, I felt content as I realized that I didn't spend the entire day worrying about the vampires. What's more, I can't wait until tomorrow.

After hours together by the fire, it was getting late. Wes and Lily decided to go home. I gave Lily a huge hug and asked her to come get ready for the ceremony with us tomorrow. She seemed very excited about the invitation. The rest of us moseyed inside to claim a bedroom.

Xander and I took the upstairs bedroom that had the balcony, probably because he's the Alpha. I brushed my teeth and tossed on Xander's shirt, slipping off my bathing suit. I pulled my hair into a messy bun before stepping out onto the balcony while he finished getting ready for bed.

The stars out here are just as gorgeous as they were out in the middle of the ocean. The almost full moon hung high in the sky, reflecting beautifully on the lake. The thought crossed my mind that Sabby should take pictures out here on the next full moon. They would be so stunning.

Xander's arms slipped around me as he buried his face into my neck and pressed his front against my back.

"Look at our beautiful pack." I whispered to him. "I love it here."

"Mhm, I know you do, love." Xander mumbled into my neck. "You are always so at peace when we're here or at the creek."

Xander kissed my neck and slid his hands down my sides. He stilled when he realized that I had nothing on underneath his shirt. His chest rumbled. "Come on, we've got a big day tomorrow and I'm not done with you yet tonight." He pulled my hips back, pressing his hardened length against me. Then, he backed away towards the bed, pulling me along with him.

"Try not to keep the entire house up." He teased as he slipped his hand up my thigh under his shirt.

CHAPTER SIXTY-ONE

Xander

We slept in a little later than we probably should have, but I ended up keeping Maxine up pretty late last night. It was totally worth it though.

We gathered our things and helped clean up downstairs before packing up the vehicles.

We pretty much ate all the food we brought, so we would need to return to the packhouse for breakfast.

Donovan was a bit gruff this morning, but really only towards me. I'm not sure what's up with him.

Arielle caught my eye after he grumpily walked away from me for the third time and she giggled.

What's up with him today? I mindlinked her.

We could totally hear you guys last night. She informed me with a smirk.

Oh shit. I glanced over at him, worried.

Don't worry, I think I did a pretty good job of distracting him and blocking out your noises with our own. She replied proudly before skipping over to him and jumping up into his arms. He just smiled at her with his goofy, lovestruck grin. She's so good for him.

Once everything was loaded into the SUVs, we drove back to the packhouse for breakfast. The dining hall was buzzing with activity. Everyone was working hard to prepare for the guests that would be arriving today and following my mom's orders to get set up for the ceremony and reception.

We ate breakfast together before everyone went their separate ways. Maxine and I returned to our suite to shower and change.

I linked Wesley and my parents to meet us in my office.

It didn't take long before they all arrived. Maxine remained seated on the couch as I rose from behind my desk. I pulled out an old wooden box and placed it on the desk.

"Did you let your parents know? They will feel the connection to your old pack break." I asked Lily.

"Yes, they understand." She wasn't nervous at all.

"Okay. Are you ready?" She nodded firmly. I opened the box and pulled out the ceremonial pack blade. It is a sacred blade used for blood oaths. It is specially crafted to allow the oaths to be made before our wolves can heal us.

I held out my hand, and she placed her right hand in mine, palm up. She flinched slightly as I slid the blade across her skin and a line of red bubbled up. I quickly took the blade in my other hand and sliced my right palm as well. I grasped her hand, so our palms were touching, the blood mixing.

"Do you, Lillian Walters, freely and completely give up your allegiance to Blue River pack from this day forward?"

"I do."

"Do you accept me, Alexander Black, as your Alpha?

"I do."

"Do you swear loyalty and fidelity to Silver Moon pack?"

"I swear it."

"Do you swear to honor and protect this pack, its lands, and people as your one true home and family?"

"I swear it from the depths of my soul, with Selene as my witness."

"Silver Moon officially welcomes you." I reached out in my mind and opened the pack link to her. The feeling of a new member joining washed over me as the pack howls could be heard all around us, welcoming our newest pack member.

I released her hand and our palms instantly healed. Lily turned to Wesley as he rushed forward to scoop her up into his arms. She beamed at him as a tear welled in her eyes.

"This is officially my home now." She nuzzled close to Wesley.

"Congratulations!" My parents hugged each of them. "And welcome, again, Lily. We're so thrilled that you're here."

Maxine and I hugged them both as well. I sighed, relieved that it went well, it was my first time initiating a new member into our pack.

You're so sexy when you're in Alpha mode. Maxine linked me.

Oh, really? Is that so? I pulled her to my side.

Yes, Alpha. The way she said 'Alpha' was so seductive. My eyes darted to her, and she peered up at me with one brow cocked. Suddenly, my pants felt tighter.

Oh, Goddess, what are you doing to me?

"Xander, our guests will be arriving soon. We need the two of you out front to greet them with us in 30 minutes." Dad informed me.

"Got it." I replied quickly. "If you'll excuse us, Maxine and I have an important matter to discuss."

Everyone congratulated Wesley and Lily again as they exited my office. As soon as the door was closed, I locked it, turned to my naughty little mate and stalked towards her.

Her eyes widened. "Xander, we have to greet guests in 30 minutes."

"That is plenty of time." I replied as I tugged her toward me and spun her around.

"But I will reek of you, everyone will know." She protested as I unzipped her dress.

"Good. And I will smell of you. Everyone will know who we belong to." I pushed the dress down her body as my lips found that special spot on her neck. I sucked on her mark, eliciting a delicious moan.

I draped her dress over a chair before I shrugged out of my jacket and placed it over the other chair. I unhooked Maxine's bra and let it fall down her arms. I quickly pushed her panties down her legs. Then I smacked her ass. "Go sit over there." I directed her firmly towards my desk.

"Yes, Alpha." She answered as she sat on the edge of my desk. I groaned as my cock pressed uncomfortably against my zipper.

I followed her over. She reached for my belt and undid my pants. She freed my hard cock, stroking it with her delicate hands and a sigh of pleasure slipped from my lips.

"Spread your legs." I demanded.

"Yes, Alpha." Maxine replied in a whisper. Every time she said those two words, it turned me on more.

I trailed my fingers down her face, along her slender neck. Her breath hitched as they skimmed over her chest, grazing her nipple. My fingers fluttered across her abs to her warmth waiting for me. I growled as I touched her wet center.

I grabbed under her knees and tugged her forward, lining myself up. I quickly pushed inside of her core, and she gasped loudly.

"Does that feel good?"

"Yes, Alpha." She moaned, making me lose what little control I had.

I thrusted into her again and again. She gripped me tightly, her nails digging into my skin as I pounded into her mercilessly. Soon, we were both moaning loudly as we were on the brink of ecstasy.

"Come for me, baby." I commanded.

"Yes, Alpha!" Maxine cried out in pleasure. One more hard thrust caused her to climax, and I quickly followed.

As we began to clean up, Maxine smacked me on the ass and said, "Nice hustle, Alpha!"

I laughed at my saucy mate. I helped Maxine back into her dress and I straightened my clothes before we walked out front to join my parents.

Mom's face fell as she sniffed and stared at me with shock, "Alexander!" She admonished me. Dad stifled a laugh. Maxine's cheeks turned a new shade of red.

"What? They're coming to my mating ceremony. I think they'll understand." I shrugged as I took Maxine's hand in mine and kissed it gently.

Mom clearly wanted to say more, but a car pulled up, and the first Alpha and Luna stepped out. Here we go.

I had to give credit to Maxine, she blushed with my parents, but if all the Alphas and Lunas knowing what we just did bothered her, she didn't let it show. She held her head high, smiled, and greeted our guests like a true Luna.

Their reactions were different, some pretended not to smell anything, they were usually those I didn't know as well. Others gave me a knowing grin, but everyone showed nothing but respect towards Maxine. No one seemed offended by our scents, as I had suspected. Most of them have been newly mated before, and those who haven't found their mate yet, long to be with them.

A lot of Alphas arrived with their sons and daughters. I was happy to introduce Maxine to so many of my Alpha friends from the Academy, Alpha Summits, and beyond. I was surprised by how many guests she already knew.

After we greeted each group of guests, some of our packhouse staff gave them an itinerary, showed them around the packhouse, and led them to their accommodations. Lunch will be provided in the dining hall for everyone. Our pack members are eating lunch at home today, so the hall won't be overcrowded.

Once all our guests arrived, I turned to my sweet mate, happy to be done with the formalities for now. I was about to wrap her up in a bear hug, when Arielle came bounding over, grabbing her arms and spinning her away from me.

CHAPTER SIXTY-TWO

Maxine

Meeting all the Alphas and Lunas was exhausting! But I was happy to do it now, rather than after the ceremony. I know I will just want to enjoy the evening with my mate.

It didn't escape me how the young Alphas smirked at Xander, clearly smelling our earlier escapades. I was just thankful that no one said anything or seemed upset by it.

I let out a sigh of relief after we finished greeting all our guests. But my relaxation was quickly interrupted by the effervescent Ari, as she swooped in and stole me away.

"Come on, Max! It's time to pamper our lovely Luna!" She sang out as she tugged me inside the packhouse.

I peeked back over my shoulder at Xander standing there with his hands in his pockets, looking like a damn model. I sighed as I resigned myself to my cheery friend.

As we entered my suite, I could hear the rest of the girls already making themselves at home.

Jazzy and Sabby shuffled around the kitchen, where they had a spread of food laid out for us to snack on. I greeted them and walked further in towards my bedroom to find Ivy playing with Lily's hair in the mirror.

"It's just such a beautiful color. And you have so much of it! It's absolutely gorgeous." Ivy said as she twisted it up on Lily's head and then let it down again.

I ran my fingers through Lily's hair too. It really is so unique. "Stunning." I smiled at her in the mirror.

The rest of the girls made their way into the room with trays of food and drinks, setting them down in our sitting area. I surveyed the room, realizing they had things strewn about everywhere. Makeup cases, hair curlers, flat irons, dress bags, shoes, and accessories littered my bedroom.

I laughed. "I see you've all made yourselves at home."

Lily watched me hesitantly, not sure if I was going to be upset about it. I just winked at her.

"Why on earth is there no music, yet?!" I questioned.

"I got it!" Sabby yelled as she ran over to get the music hooked up.

"Oh my Goddess!" Ivy sniffed me. "Did you really greet all the Alphas and Lunas smelling like sex?!" She gawked at me with wide eyes as she laughed.

Ari smiled at me proudly; I'm sure she must have smelled it when she first pulled me from Xander.

The other girls all gave me a sniff and burst out in a fit of giggles.

"Talk about marking your territory!" Jazzy laughed. "Men are so possessive."

"Don't worry, he smelled like me, too. All the shewolves know he's mine." I claimed confidently. I am not ashamed about loving my mate.

"Damn straight!" Ari cheered and we all laughed some more.

I hurried into my closet to change into the undergarments for my gown and slipped on a silk robe to relax in. All the girls similarly changed so we wouldn't have to pull any clothes off over our hair and makeup.

Ivy began working on Lily's hair after they decided what would work best with her gown. Ari got to work on Jazzy's makeup.

I was thrilled to see that Sabrina brought more of her photos with her like I had asked. We sprawled out on my bed with the photos spread across the comforter. I picked up photo after photo and was constantly amazed at her pure talent.

"Sabby, these are amazing." I said with the utmost sincerity. "Seriously, I'm not just saying that because you're my sister. This is your calling. People would pay good money for these."

I held up a stack of pictures of some kids playing at the playground. There was pure joy on the children's faces. The pictures were crisp and focused on the kids, with the perfect level of contrast in the background to make them pop. As I flipped through the stack, each picture was compelling and told a story. I couldn't help but smile looking at them.

I set them down and reached for another stack. This set was full of black and white candid shots of a young couple lying in a hammock. They were so relaxed and completely lost in each other. Sabrina captured their intimacy beautifully.

"Seriously, couples would love to have you take pictures of them like this!" I encouraged her.

"Yes! Please, take some pictures of Heath and me. Timber and Aspen, too!" Ivy chimed in as she admired the photo of Zeus and Onyx above my bed. "I would love to have some for our suite. We'll definitely pay you for it."

Everyone jumped in asking for the same. Sabby smiled from ear to ear as they all complimented her.

I shuffled through more photos of scenery. There are so many gorgeous photos of our packlands. Some are in black and white, but most of them are in full color, showcasing the true beauty of the nature scenes.

"Oh, this reminds me! You have to go out to the lake house on the next full moon and take pictures from the upstairs balcony. It is a stunning sight, and no one will be able to capture it like you." I informed her excitedly. "I am officially commissioning you as Luna." I said with an overdramatically proper voice.

She giggled. "Ok, I can do that!"

"Oh, Goddess! Speaking of the lake house, those walls are too thin!" Jazzy said as she raised a brow at me. "But it's good to know that the Alpha knows how to please his Luna." She teased.

I could feel my cheeks flame. They could hear us?

"Seriously, girl, we were probably the farthest from your room and we could hear everything!" Ari added.

"What?! Oh my Goddess!" I covered my face with my hands, completely mortified that my brother heard me having sex with his best friend.

"Is that all you two do when you're alone now?" Ivy laughed.

"Don't act like you're any different!" Sabby defended me. "I don't know how many times Calvin has told me that he walked in on you and Heath in compromising situations! You've scarred that boy."

The whole room erupted in laughter and teasing. Ivy didn't try to deny it; she just laughed with us.

"What can I say? I love my mate!" She shrugged her shoulders as she finished Lily's hair.

We took our time rotating through doing each other's hair and makeup. After a few hours, everyone was done and ready for our dresses.

I was a little nervous, because I hadn't even tried my dress on yet. Luna Clarissa had it made for me based on what Xander, Ari, and Sabby had told her. I was sure it was beautiful, but I was just worried about the fit.

When the girls were all dressed, they each looked absolutely stunning. Their poor mates would never know what hit them.

I finally stepped into my dress, and I should have known it would fit perfectly. I couldn't believe how stunning it was as I checked it over in the mirror. The white lace gown had a low open back and capped sleeves, with a scalloped V-neck and tight bodice. From the hips, the material fell into a loose mermaid skirt down to the floor. My hair was in a low bun, with little wisps of hair framing my face. I made sure to ask Sabby to put our mom's hair comb that Dad gave me just above the bun.

I turned to see Sabby with tears in her eyes. "You look just like Mom." She whispered. I hugged her tightly, then leaned back to wipe her eyes.

"You have to stop or you're going to ruin everyone's makeup." I gently scolded her as I noticed the room watching us with misty eyes.

Ivy sighed dramatically, "Alright ladies, let's move! The sooner we get this started, the sooner Heath can take this dress off of me!"

We all laughed, and Jazzy hollered, "Yes!"

We descended the stairs to the main floor where my dad, Calvin, and all the mates were waiting. Well, all the mates, except for my own. I knew he was already at the ceremonial grounds.

Each girl rushed toward their mate and there was lots of purring and growling. I couldn't help but laugh to myself as the ladies fussed over their handsome mates and the guys drooled over them in return.

As I approached Dad, I could see him bat a pesky tear away from his cheek.

"My beautiful daughter." He said as he squeezed me tightly. "You look so much like your mother. I wish she were here with us. I know she would be so proud of the woman you have become."

"She is with us." I reminded him as I gently placed my hand over his heart. He laid his large hand over mine.

"I couldn't be happier for you, Luna." He said with a smile before kissing my cheek and hugging me again.

When he released me, Donovan was next to us, pulling me into his embrace.

"There has never been a more beautiful Luna." He peered down at me. "I'm so proud of you, kiddo. You deserve all the happiness in the world." He placed his hands on either side of my face and kissed my forehead.

The couples all walked outside, headed towards the ceremonial grounds. Calvin escorted Sabrina, and I couldn't help but wonder if he might be her mate.

It was just Dad and me left inside. Butterflies fluttered in my stomach, as I was both nervous and excited.

CHAPTER SIXTY-THREE

Xander

I watched Maxine get pulled away, wishing I could spend every minute with her. I knew she needed time to relax with her friends, though.

"Xander, please clean yourself up before lunch." Mom pleaded.

"Absolutely not." I shook my head, appalled at the idea of washing my mate's delicious scent off of my body.

"Alexander!" She huffed, crossing her arms.

"Darling, do you think we ordered enough alcohol for the reception tonight? With so many Alphas, I'm just not sure." Dad's obvious attempt to distract her worked.

"Oh! We better go check to make sure. That would be a disaster." She dashed towards the kitchen.

"Thank you!" I mouthed to Dad as he chuckled, following his wife.

I found Donovan in his office, taking care of the Sentinel patrol and warrior training schedules. We had to change them up and rotate people around regularly so that outsiders couldn't learn our security measures. Donovan is particularly good at handling this, he has the brain for it.

"How's it coming? Everything looking good?" I sat down in one of the chairs in front of his desk. I heard him sniff and he tensed up for a moment. Shit, I was not doing myself any favors with him lately.

He cleared his throat and continued typing, not looking up. "Yes, I've gone ahead and planned out the new rotations for the next eight weeks. I will send them to my dad to release them when needed while we are in Alaska."

"Perfect. Thank you, Donovan." I ran my fingers through my hair as I glanced around his office. There was a picture of him with his sisters on the bookshelf, next to one of him and Arielle.

I sighed. "Will you guys be alright being away from your mates for so long?" I couldn't imagine leaving Maxine for what could end up being a month or more. I felt bad asking that of my men.

Donovan sighed and leaned back in his chair as he followed my line of sight to the picture of his mate. "I'm not going to lie, it's going to be really difficult." He leaned forward, resting his elbows on his desk as he answered me. "But we will do whatever we have to in order to protect our Luna."

I could see the fire in his eyes, clearly upset about the situation that his sister was in again.

"Do you think the others will feel the same even though they aren't related to Maxine?" I was starting to second guess my decision.

"Hell yes, we will!" Wiley declared as he walked into the room with Heath and Wesley. "Sorry, the girls are all getting ready together, so we came to find you. But seriously, dude, we'd do anything to keep her safe. And you, too."

Wiley plopped down on the couch, along with Heath. Wesley sat in the chair next to mine.

"I want to come with you." His hazel eyes pierced mine intensely.

"Wes, you just found your mate." Donovan interjected.

"Max has always been like a sister to me and one of my best friends." He told Donovan and then looked back at me. "And you are my brother; I can't let anything happen to either of you." There is so much anguish in his voice. I had to swallow a lump in my throat.

I reached over and squeezed his shoulder. "What about Lily?"

"I talked to her about it this morning. She wasn't thrilled with the idea, but she wants to stay here and get to know the pack. She's got some ideas about a pack library. Mom is going to help her get it running." He informed me with pride.

I looked at Donovan thoughtfully.

Having another Alpha to protect Max wouldn't be a terrible idea. He linked me with a shrug.

"Alright. But I told Asher 15 guests, so we'll have to bump one of the warriors." I told Donovan, "I don't want to take advantage of his hospitality."

Donovan nodded at me and pulled out the files on the warriors we had chosen to go with us. "How about we leave Derek here?" He suggested as he slid the open file towards me. "He's probably the least experienced out of the bunch and his mate is pregnant."

I scanned the file. "Perfect. I'm sure he'll be relieved to stay behind, even if he would never admit it."

"I'll let him know today." Donovan confirmed and then checked his phone. "We should head down to the dining hall, people will be gathering for lunch soon."

We stood at the entrance to the dining hall, once again greeting all the Alphas and Lunas. I enjoyed lunch with the guys and a few of our friends from the Academy. It was nice to reminisce about our training days.

Luke and Ryan joined us too. Luke shook my hand when I greeted him. I could see him inhale and hurt flashed briefly through his eyes. He clearly still holds feelings for Maxine, but she is mine. I hope I am doing the right thing by bringing him with us to Alaska.

They sat with Wesley and a couple of Alphas from their class, talking about their own days at the Academy.

After lunch, I invited some of the guys to play pool with us in the rec room. It was great spending time with my old friends and cracking jokes. I couldn't think of a better way to pass the time and relax until the ceremony. I was eager to see my Maxine.

As it got closer to time, I checked in with my parents to be sure everything was set. Once they confirmed that we were good to go, I went up to the Beta suite to get ready.

The guys gathered in Donovan's home to raise a toast. Heath said a quick blessing for Maxine and me. I hugged each of them before leaving them to wait for their mates, while I went ahead to the ceremonial grounds.

Mom really outdid herself this time. Maxine was going to love it.

The ceremonial grounds lie at the edge of Clover Lake, which is much smaller than Rock Lake, but across the lake from the grounds are rocky cliffs lined with a forest of trees at the top. Mom chose to set up the small platform for the ceremony here, with the beautiful cliffs and lake as the backdrop.

The platform was perfectly framed by two large oak trees. Hanging down from the branches were long garlands of white flowers and white lights. It was magical.

The guests and our entire pack were gathered already, some still mingling before they took their seats. My parents stood on the platform with Elder Mitchell. Next to them, there was a small pedestal with some ceremonial items on it. On the other side, there was an intricate brazier that held the symbolic pack flame. The pack flame was meant to represent the soul of the pack, always burning as long as the pack thrived.

I released a deep sigh as I ran my fingers through my hair and straightened my jacket. I walked down the center aisle toward the platform. Heads turned toward me, and they all quieted down, quickly taking their seats.

When I reached the platform, I shook the Elder's hand and embraced Mom in a hug.

"This is incredible, Mom! Thank you." I said sincerely to her.

"Anything for my boy." She said as she placed a loving hand on my cheek. "You are so handsome. I am so happy for you, Alexander."

I kissed her cheek and turned to wrap my dad in a bear hug.

"I'm so proud of you, son." He said as he pulled back to smooth out my suit. "I know you'll take great care of the pack. They are lucky to have you as their Alpha."

"Thank you, Dad. I will do my best to be worthy of the title."

I spotted my Alpha unit, Wesley, and their mates entering the grounds and taking their seats in the front. The ceremony would begin soon. I took another deep breath and waited for my Luna to arrive.

After a few minutes, Beta Charlie appeared with the most breathtaking woman on his arm. Zeus was standing so alert in my mind. Maxine looked like she could be the Moon Goddess herself, she's so heavenly. It was almost as if she was gliding towards me.

Dad leaned forward to whisper in my ear, "Breathe, son." I sucked in a quick breath, my heart was beating wildly.

Charlie walked Maxine down the center aisle, and all eyes were on my beautiful mate. But she stared only at me. Her electric blue eyes pierced my soul, I never want to look away from them.

When they reached the front of the aisle, Charlie took her hands and whispered something so only she could hear. She smiled sweetly at him, and he kissed her cheek before sitting down next to Sabrina.

Maxine turned back to me, my eyes instantly locked in again as if I were in her trance. She made her way elegantly up the platform. As she stopped in front of me, she placed her small hands in mine.

You look perfect, love. I linked her.

So do you, Alpha. She replied, causing me to grin at her.

Elder Mitchell's voice rang out next to us. "Thank you all for joining Silver Moon today on such a momentous occasion. Today, we not only solidify a most sacred bond gifted by the Moon Goddess herself, but we also start a new chapter in our pack's history as we officially welcome our new Alpha and Luna."

As I gazed into this remarkable woman's eyes a feeling washed over me. I knew without a doubt that no matter what we have to face, we will do it with love, and nothing can take that away from us. I would move mountains to keep her safe, and I won't let anything come between us ever again. I love her from the depths of my soul, and I could feel her love for me. It was more than I could have ever hoped for.

CHAPTER SIXTY-FOUR

Maxine

I love you. Xander mindlinked me.

Warmth spread through my chest, I could feel his love and happiness seeping through the bond. *I love you.* I replied with a smile.

He looked divine in his simple but dashing black suit, like the Goddess prepared him herself. I silently thanked her for the perfection that stood in front of me. He's my whole world.

Elder Mitchell's voice continued.

"Long ago the Moon Goddess created werewolves as her own children. She has blessed wolves for centuries with the gift of the mate bond. It is fated by Selene for us to find our soulmate, our other halves. It is a sacred miracle when two hearts become one under the full moon. This union is truly blessed."

Xander rubbed circles with his thumbs over the back of my hands. His intense, emerald eyes held me captive.

Elder Mitchell touched Xander's shoulder and nodded at him.

"Maxine Cooper, I have always loved you." Xander said with a gleam in his eyes, "When we were children, I longed to be near you. As we grew up, I would always seek to protect you. I realize now that my soul knew you were mine long before my wolf did. We have already been through trying times and we will most likely face more, but I know that we will persevere together.

My Love,
I choose you.
We will walk side by side,
Through sunshine and storms,
Health and sickness,
Good times and bad.
We will meet life head on together.
Under this full moon,
I promise to love and honor you
Forever and always.
I choose you
In this life and the next,
Until the end of time."

Xander reached up and wiped a tear from my cheek.

"Alexander Black, there has never been a love like ours. Not only can I feel it in the depths of my being, but the Moon Goddess herself told me. I am so truly blessed that she honored me by choosing you as my mate. I will cherish you forever, for you are a gift. I promise to always hold you dear and to never let anything come between us.

My Love,
I choose you.

We will walk side by side,
Through sunshine and storms,
Health and sickness,
Good times and bad.
We will meet life head on together.
Under this full moon,
I promise to love and honor you
Forever and always.
I choose you
In this life and the next,
Until the end of time."

Elder Mitchell enclosed our joined hands within his own two hands as he began the blessing.

"By destiny you are aligned,
Your love is eternal and true.
You will face challenges together,
And find strength in your union.
By the sun, the moon, and the stars
Your love is blessed.
May you always be as happy together
As you are today.

Now you will feel no more rain
For each of you will be shelter for the other.
You will feel no more cold
For each of you will be warmth for the other.
You will feel no more loneliness
For you are one soul in two bodies
And will always be together in spirit."

He released our hands and stepped back, as everyone erupted in applause.

We have already marked and mated each other, but I could still feel a surge of energy rush through me. Xander gently slipped his hand up to my neck as he leaned in to kiss me, snaking his other arm around my waist, pulling me to him.

I smiled up at him before turning toward the crowd and smiling at them as well.

Elder Mitchell raised his hand for everyone to quiet down. Xander took my hands in his again.

"This blessed union signifies the beginning of a new chapter for Silver Moon. For when a young Alpha finds his fated mate, his pack thrives. A true Luna strengthens and grounds her mate, helping him achieve his full potential."

Xander squeezed my hand as he beamed proudly at me.

"Silver Moon has flourished under the guidance and leadership of Alpha Jackson and Luna Clarissa. We thank you both for your years of service and sacrifice. May Selene bless you with happiness and peace as you enjoy your well-earned retirement."

The pack gave a standing ovation for their beloved leaders.

Alpha Jackson approached Elder Mitchell and shook his hand before he picked up the same old, wooden box from Xander's office. Elder Mitchell opened the box, and Alpha Jackson took out the ceremonial pack blade.

He stepped in front of Xander with a look of admiration on his face. Alpha Jackson held his right hand, palm up. He sliced across Xander's hand carefully, and the blood slowly pooled in his hand.

"Do you, Alexander Black, accept the title of Alpha for the Silver Moon pack?"

"I do."

"Do you swear to always do what is in the best interest of the pack and its people, no matter the price?"

"I do."

"Do you swear to lead with honor, courage, and compassion?"

Xander rotated his hand so that the blood dripped into the pack flame as he vowed, "I swear it from the depths of my soul, with Selene as my witness."

The flames turned silver.

"I, Alpha Jackson Black, hereby declare you, Alexander Black, as the one true Alpha of Silver Moon pack. May Selene bless you and Silver Moon."

The silver flames rose higher, and I felt an energy shift as Xander was named Alpha. The pack cheered loudly.

Alpha Jackson handed the ceremonial blade to Luna Clarissa. She approached me with an encouraging smile as she took my hand and made a matching cut. She held my hand, letting the blood pool.

"Do you, Maxine Black, accept the title of Luna for the Silver Moon pack?"

"I do." I beamed when she said my new name.

"Do you swear to always do what is in the best interest of the pack and its people, no matter the price?"

"I do."

"Do you swear to lead with honor, courage, and compassion?"

I rotated my hand so that the pool of blood would fall into the pack flame. "I swear it from the depths of my soul, with Selene as my witness."

The flames turned silver again, but there were extra sparks that rose up as well.

"I, Luna Clarissa Black, hereby declare you, Maxine Black, as the one true Luna of Silver Moon pack. May Selene bless you and Silver Moon."

The flames lifted higher and crackled with silver sparks, as another energy shift passed through me. I could see the questions on their faces, they didn't know what to make of the silver sparks. It was unlike anything I'd ever seen.

Xander moved to stand in front of me, we grasped hands so that our cuts were touching.

Elder Mitchell stepped forward, placing his hand on top of mine and Xander's to recite the blessing.

"May Selene bless this pack wherein we dwell,
Enrich every hearth and home, every tree and stone,
Protect every heart that beats within its borders,
Endow every hand that helps it grow,
Strengthen every wolf underneath its moon.
May Selene bless our new Alpha and Luna."

As Elder Mitchell released our hands, our palms instantly healed. I felt stronger somehow. Xander took my hand in his as we turned to face our pack and guests.

Xander let out an Alpha howl, and I responded with our pack as we howled at the full moon.

I gazed up at the most incredible man, so unbelievably happy. He slid his arms around me, pulling me close to him as the crowd cheered. I wasn't sure what our future will hold, but I felt like together, there's nothing that we couldn't overcome.

COMING SOON

THE MIDNIGHT WOLF
WILD MOON

CHAPTER ONE

Xander

"Harder, Xander!" Maxine called out.

I smirked as I pushed harder, panting.

"That's it, baby! Don't stop!" Maxine encouraged me enthusiastically.

"Yes, Xander, faster!" My mate yelled as sweat dripped down my body. I was getting close.

Somehow, I increased my pace even further. As I finished, I collapsed, completely exhausted. I could hear Maxine's voice crying out my name.

Maxine slapped my ass. "Good hustle, baby! That's a new record for you!"

"Thanks." I panted out as I rolled over onto my back to look up at her beautiful face.

After a moment, Donovan and Wesley crossed the finish line. I knew I was getting faster because they used to be right on my heels. Wesley bent over with his hands resting on his knees. Donovan held his arms above his head as he tried to catch his breath.

Wiley came bolting across the line. "Damn, I really thought I could catch up to you all in the sprint!"

Heath and our top warriors selected to travel with us, Malik, Aaron, Daniel, and Oscar, dashed across the finish line of the obstacle course. Maxine wrote times down on her clipboard.

"Wow! Everyone's time improved on this run!" Maxine informed us cheerfully. "Nice work, guys!" She handed out water bottles to everyone.

"Did I beat your time?" I asked with a smile, knowing it was not likely. Since Maxine and I completed our bond, I have been feeling stronger and faster than ever. However, it had the same effect on Maxine and let me tell you, she is fast!

"Close! But not yet." She said sweetly as she gave me a quick peck on the lips.

"Let me see." Donovan took the clipboard and studied the times seriously, then nodded in approval. "A big improvement. All the extra training is paying off."

In preparation for our upcoming trip, we've increased our training significantly. The last couple of weeks have been a blur of workouts, runs, sparring sessions, and what we had just finished, the obstacle course. I've pushed my men harder than ever, including our elite, Epsilon warriors that are coming with us.

I've tried to make sure that everyone has downtime each day to spend with their mates. I still feel bad that I'm taking them all away from their mates for so long. I don't know exactly how long we will be in Alaska, but I'm prepping the pack for us to be gone for two months. Hopefully, it won't take us that long to eliminate the vampires.

I took another drink of water before I stood and nodded my head for the guys to follow me on our cool down run around the training grounds.

When we finished, Maxine was typing our new stats into the document on her laptop. Wiley led us through our post workout stretches.

Maxine gathered her things as we wrapped up. We all walked back to the packhouse together, departing on our different floors. Maxine and I entered our Alpha suite on the top floor.

"I'm going to take this stuff to the office." Maxine turned down the hall towards our home office with her clipboard and laptop.

"Alright, I'm going to hop in the shower." I was still dripping sweat. I entered our bathroom and started the shower, then I took off my shorts and tossed them in the hamper.

I stepped under the water, letting it soothe my tired body. I grabbed my soap and lathered up. Once I was clean, I stood there a moment longer with my hands splayed out on the tiles in front of me. My head hung down with the water cascading over me, it felt good.

I smelled orange blossoms and cinnamon as tingles spread from my back around to my abdomen. My mate pressed her body against my back. I hummed at the comforting feeling of her skin on mine.

She kissed my back and caressed my abs. Her fingers danced across my muscles and ran slowly downward.